# WORDSWORTH IN BOGOTÁ

# SCOTT E. SUNDBY

Black Rose Writing | Texas

ISBN: 978-1-68513-550-8
PUBLISHED BY BLACK ROSE WRITING
www.blackrosewriting.com

Printed in the United States of America
Suggested Retail Price (SRP) $21.95

*Wordsworth in Bogotá* is printed in Garamond Premier Pro

*As a planet-friendly publisher, Black Rose Writing does its best to eliminate unnecessary waste to
reduce paper usage and energy costs, while never compromising the reading experience. As a result,
the final word count vs. page count may not meet common expectations.

# PRAISE FOR
## *WORDSWORTH IN BOGOTÁ*

"Sundby has crafted a captivating and amusing mystery packed with a unique blend of crime, adventure, and humor. I adored the narrative style right from the start, with a gentle undertone of the author's wit and tongue-in-cheek attitude subtly permeating the plot, letting you know you're safe with a confident storyteller. Sundby's playful approach to characters and plot made the novel a delightful read, celebrating resilience and the unexpected paths to understanding what truly matters in life ... [T]he plot moves at a great pace to allow the characters and their different influences to sink in, yet there's never a dull moment as you can always feel a new twist building up .... *Wordsworth in Bogotá* is a truly unique work of crime fiction that I would recommend to fans of accomplished writing and brilliant character work."
**–K.C. Finn,** *Readers' Favorite*, **5-Star Review**

"Scott E. Sundby excels at crafting a novel which defies pat categorization, at once operating as a story of literary and familial discovery, an account of illicit deals gone awry, and a probe of innocence and treachery .... Sundby's contrasts between the cultures and atmosphere of America versus South America are finely woven into the plot, lending a 'you are here' aura to unfolding events, while a host of characters fine-tune their relationships and interactions via the precision of literary and psychological undercurrents that run through the plot like a powerful river.... [Readers] seeking stories of suspense, intrigue, shifting relationships, and discovery will find *Wordsworth in Bogotá* ... hard to put down."
**–D. Donovan, Senior Reviewer,** *Midwest Book Review*

"*Wordsworth in Bogotá* thrusts readers into the heart of the Velasquez Cartel's quest to reclaim their cocaine empire after the seismic events of 9/11. At the center of this resurgence, Estaban, the quiet, bookish younger son, devises a cunning plan. His scheme, steeped in his passion for poetry and literature, becomes the unexpected vehicle for smuggling drugs into the United States....

*Wordsworth in Bogotá* brims with characters in flux, each striving to find their way as they become enmeshed in Estaban's intricate scheme. The novel

delves into themes of life, youth, faith, and the ethical dilemmas posed by fortune and power. It challenges readers to ponder what truly holds value in a world driven by ambition. This book is a remarkable piece of literature ... [as] Sundby skillfully weaves intrigue and conspiracy into the narrative. For those who enjoy a blend of philosophy and espionage, this book is an engaging and thought-provoking read."
–*Literary Titan*

"*Wordsworth in Bogotá* ... presents a fascinating narrative that intricately weaves together themes of ambition, identity, and the consequences of one's choices ... The narrative explores the conflict between what society expects and personal desires, highlighting the characters' struggles and insecurities... [The] writing is both engaging and introspective, with a blend of humor and poignancy. The dialogue is sharp and often laced with irony, adding depth to the interactions .... The portrayal of the characters' friendships and conflicts shows how complicated human connections can be. With its gripping plot and insightful exploration of human nature, *Wordsworth in Bogotá* ... shows strength of storytelling and the complicated aspects of life."
–Manik Chaturmutha, *Readers' Favorite,* 5-Star Review

"Building on the fervor that swept America in the wake of the 9/11 terror attacks, Sundby creates an engaging story of love and cocaine from the perspective of a Colombian drug lord.... Sundby creates remarkable depth by balancing humor and seriousness in equal measure .... The banter is entertaining and, in most parts, flows poetically, as can be expected from a narrative built around characters with a reverence for the spoken word. Sundby's deliberately slow pace in this chess game of wits adds to the excitement. It immerses readers as they discover a narrative whose romantic component is just as crucial as its adventure subplot. *Wordsworth in Bogotá* will thrill mystery and adventure enthusiasts thanks to Sundby's extraordinary storytelling abilities and captivating mini-mysteries within a perplexing larger narrative."
–Essien Asian, *Readers' Favorite,* 5-Star Review

# WORDSWORTH IN BOGOTÁ

# CHAPTER ONE

Months. That was all. To get his affairs in order, to say goodbye to everything he cherished. And, as had been made excruciatingly clear, the end would not be pretty. It was what he had feared most when he first noticed the signs something might be seriously wrong. It was what had awakened him in the middle of the night, wrapped in sweat-soaked sheets, his heart pounding as hard and loud as the bass drum in Hell's marching band.

Diego Velasquez had known that his business's financial situation had been slipping, but the accountant in an infuriating monotone had informed him that his empire was not only struggling, it was collapsing. Utterly. Cash reserves nearly exhausted, inventory losses escalating at an unsustainable pace, expenses skyrocketing with no end in sight. Like a callous physician nonchalantly informing a patient he had a terminal illness, the accountant had pronounced in the coldest bedside manner, "Señor Velasquez, you have five to six months left." Adding, as he snapped his briefcase shut, "At most." He had then abruptly stood up, turned his back on Diego, and walked out the door.

As his breathing slowed, Diego's panic was replaced by angry prickles of heat racing across his skin. The Diego of twenty years ago would have immediately known what to do. First, he would have had that self-righteous prick of an accountant shot before he'd even made it off the compound. How dare he sit there smugly stating that Diego's life was crumbling to pieces as if it were all simply a matter of mathematics. Then Diego would have gotten really angry. He would have called his subordinates before him, screaming, assigning blame, smashing objects, feeling the adrenaline rush of taking charge and the liberating release of giving full vent to his anger.

But not now. No longer under the intoxicating spell of youthful infallibility, he felt paralyzed. The anger he tasted was every bit as strong and bitter as that of his youth, but it was spiced with an emotion that he first began to detect several years ago—self-doubt. And so he brooded. Rather than summoning his subordinates, he looked out at the view of the city that stretched below his mountain fortress.

It was a view that when the compound had first been chiseled out of the mountainside, he had gazed upon in awe. Watching the valley floor majestically sweep out before him made him exultant, as if what lie before him was a paradise created only for him. He would peer down for hours on the valley, thinking with great satisfaction of how it was filled with thousands of lives grinding out their daily existence while he sat perched high above. And he had been certain those nameless people often looked up from their misery to admire the sun glimmering off the windows that encircled his living quarters, like subjects from long ago gazing at the king's gleaming castle nestled atop a promontory.

At this moment, though, the sweeping valley only made him feel small, seemed to actually mock him. Diego slowly rose from the desk with its glistening mahogany surface and rubbed his temples, the gray-tinged hair moving in unison with the circling of his massaging fingers.

A drug lord's life was never easy, but recently it had become brutal. Oh sure, Ronald Reagan's vaunted War on Drugs had been a royal pain in the ass when Diego was first establishing himself as a major player in the cocaine business. From the beginning, though, the War on Drugs really had been nothing more than another market force with which to deal. The price of doing business had gone up as everyone suddenly claimed how much harder their jobs had become. Pilots wanted more to drop their bundles of cocaine into the tropical waters off the Bahamas. Owners of the cigarette boats that skimmed across the turquoise waves at thundering speeds to pick up the bundles and bring them into the Keys demanded a higher cut. Customs agents, feigning fear for their jobs, demanded higher levies per kilo before agreeing to turn a blind eye. But at bottom, it had all boiled down to greed ... and, well, greed could be dealt with.

Cocaine was a commodity market, and, thankfully, the American public's appetite for his commodity was insatiable. If the cost of business went up, so did the price, making it possible to satisfy the greed of others. And if someone's greed truly got out of hand, that, too, could be dealt with through the marketplace. A comparatively modest payment could eliminate an outstretched hand attached to someone whining too loudly. Funny, too, how the well-publicized discovery of a whiner's corpse quickly dampened demand from others in the business chain.

In fact, the War on Drugs ultimately turned the golden spigot of money already flowing into Diego's coffers even wider. While American consumers came to accept that cocaine was something like oil for which they had no choice but to pay top price, Diego continued to pay the peasants who supplied the coca leaf the pittance that they had always received. The result was an even healthier profit margin than before. The War on Drugs simply turned out to be Adam Smith at work, and Diego found Adam Smith a very profitable business partner indeed.

But now ... *"Mierda!"* Diego whirled around and slammed his fist down on the desk's shimmering surface so hard his hand throbbed with pain. He faced an adversary who even Adam Smith could not seem to negotiate with. Two fucking planes smash into the twin towers of the World Trade Center, and everything changes.

When Diego first saw the film clips and watched the American government's hand-wringing, self-pitying response, he had felt an inner sense of glee. He had made his fortune off the American people, but he always despised what he saw as America's self-righteous attitude and sense of entitlement to dictate to the world what they should be doing. He found it darkly ironic that during the heralded War on Drugs, America, unable to control its own people's lust for cocaine, instead headed to South America to try and destroy the coca fields. Better to take away the livelihood of Latino farmers scratching furrows into the earth than crack down on rich American kids wearing Abercrombie and Fitch shirts worth more than a farmer would make in a month.

Fueled by this resentment, the attacks by some terrorist group Diego had never heard of filled him with the pleasure of witnessing an underdog gain the upper hand over a boorish bully. Now, though, he knew all too well the names Al-Qaeda and Bin Laden. They were in the process of destroying his life as surely as if they had directed the hijacked planes straight into his mountain-top compound.

After "9/11," as Americans referred to it with almost religious reverence, the US government had geared up a law enforcement effort at controlling its borders that made the patrols during the War on Drugs look like store security at a shopping mall. Diego had sighed with resignation when he initially realized America was reacting so dramatically to its newfound paranoia, but he was not particularly worried. He assumed the heightened security efforts simply meant higher payoffs throughout the smuggling chain. He and Adam Smith had handled such situations before.

But as reports started filtering back from his lieutenants in the field, he felt the first pangs of anxiety. A week after 9/11, Ramon, his employee in charge of bribing key American officials, told him that a customs agent in Miami said he would no longer accept the cartel's money. Diego had authorized Ramon to give the agent a raise in recognition of the changed circumstances, but Ramon reported back that the agent flatly refused.

Over the next few months, this story began to repeat itself. A small-town sheriff in Texas no longer accepting payoffs to allow Diego's light planes laden with cocaine to make nighttime landings on a secluded desert airstrip. A New York investment banker, the Rembrandt of money laundering, suddenly declining to handle Diego's accounts. A DEA agent in Mississippi, who each year earned three times his government salary in bribes, informing Ramon he no longer wanted any part of Diego's money.

What had filled Diego with dread was the gradual realization that these corrupt men no longer had a price. Their unexpected refusals to cooperate were not because of any new fear that they would be caught by law enforcement—damn it, most of them were high-ranking law enforcement agents themselves—but rather from some newly discovered sense of patriotism that completely eluded Diego.

Ramon told Diego how almost overnight, American flag decals appeared on the rear windows of cars across the United States, as if they were now standard equipment along with power brakes. Most distressing was that those individuals who before had laughed and smiled as they eagerly accepted Diego's money, now acted insulted that Ramon would even think they would accept a bribe. A Miami customs agent had almost punched Ramon when Ramon implied that more money would overcome the agent's newly found virtue. With nervousness still lingering in his voice, Ramon told Diego he was certain the agent was thinking of arresting him then and there. Fortunately, the agent ultimately came to his senses, remembering Ramon could point out to the agent's superiors how curious it was that a customs agent on a government salary could afford a condo with a hot tub and wet bar overlooking Biscayne Bay.

Diego had calmed himself in the face of these developments by repeating an optimistic refrain that, like all fads, this flag-waving patriotism would soon fade. Eventually, though, his reassuring mantra was no longer working, and he was forced to face the fact that his revenues were plummeting and the situation was only going to get worse.

This led Diego to resort to the techniques of low-level drug dealers, methods he had used when he was first playing the game, but which he had come to despise as the province of amateurs. Just last week, though, he ordered his underlings to search the barrios of Bogotá looking for "mules"— people so down on their luck that receiving five hundred dollars to swallow condoms containing cocaine and smuggle them into the United States seemed like winning the lottery. He had hired the mules less for the money they might bring in—maybe five thousand dollars for each swallower—than simply out of the desperate need to have a success that might squelch his growing sense of helplessness.

But even this effort failed miserably. A trembling bodyguard had timidly come into Diego's office yesterday and, with eyes transfixed on the rich design of the Persian carpet beneath his feet, told Diego all five mules had been caught by airport security. Diego felt as humiliated as if he was a mule himself, handcuffed to a metal toilet in a border patrol bathroom until nature forced him to give up the smuggled load in front of a uniformed guard's smirking eyes. Nor could Diego get out of his mind how the bodyguard's eyes eventually moved to Diego's eyes when Diego had said nothing, and how the bodyguard's confused look started to take on a predatory gleam as Diego sat there disabled by the news. After a few minutes, Diego found himself unable to do anything more than give an impatient wave of his hand, signaling the bodyguard to leave him alone.

Today's meeting with the accountant made his humiliation almost complete, although a few shards of self-dignity remained to be ripped off. He would, of course, have to call Carmen and break the news that the ninety-four-foot yacht, *Mas Es Mas*, would be permanently dry-docked. Finished were her lavish shopping sprees to New York and her impulse buys, like the purchase of the Jaguar, "because, *oh mi Diego*, its color goes so perfectly with my six-inch turquoise heels." Carmen had known full well that mentioning the stiletto heels would make him think of her incredible legs, and that he'd quickly be coughing up the delighted seller's asking price. In his gut, Diego knew that as soon as Carmen learned her open-ended American Express card was now a dead end, she would be gone as quickly as her Jag could accelerate from zero to a hundred.

Nor would Diego's wife be happy, although she would probably stick by him if for no other reason than to remind him daily of his fall from grace and how shoddily he had treated her. Then again, maybe Roberta had been secretly stashing away part of her fifty-thousand dollar monthly allowance so that she, too, would abandon the sinking ship that his life was becoming. He wasn't sure which scenario he preferred.

The hardest part would be telling Carlos. By the time Carlos was born, Diego had killed five competitors with his own hands, dumping their bodies into the Magdalena River and watching them float away like a child would drop a stick into a stream to see it ride the current. Yet, from the moment Diego held Carlos in the hospital, he felt a warmth and swelling pride he never imagined possible. The drug trade was a lonely and heartless affair in which you rarely trusted anyone, but as he cradled Carlos in his burly arms, Diego knew he no longer would be alone.

And how right he had been. Diego had felt one brief period of anxiety as Carlos grew into a young man, and he realized Carlos was reaching the age where he would inevitably begin to understand that his father was no ordinary businessman. His schoolmates' fathers did not have men driving up to their houses at two in the morning with their headlights darkened, entering the kitchen, and plopping down grocery sacks brimming with money as bundles of US hundred-dollar bills tumbled out and formed mountains of green atop the snow white of the Italian marble countertops. But, of course, while Carlos's classmates did not have fathers who carried out their business deals in the middle of the night, neither did they have fathers who owned estates or bought their sons expensive sports cars or took them on hunting trips for exotic game.

Finally, Diego decided to let Carlos be present for a late-night delivery, to hear the voices of his men full of bravado and feel the power and energy that infused Diego's world. To Diego's great relief, Carlos had sat in his bathrobe at the huge oak kitchen table mesmerized by the ritual, his eyes wide and mouth agape. And after that night, Carlos often wandered into the kitchen to observe Diego's "business meetings."

Carlos's time in school had shown promise as a future partner in the enterprise. Not in grades or academic honors—he was a miserable student— but in an ability to sense how to skirt the system without getting caught. By the age of thirteen, he ran a betting ring at his exclusive private school and had hired several older kids from the impoverished neighborhood surrounding the school to make sure his classmates didn't welch on their wagers.

More impressively to Diego, Carlos showed he knew just how far he could go in getting away with his escapades by relying on the goodwill the Velasquez name carried—a result of large donations to the school's annual fund—but without stepping over the line where the school was forced to take action no matter how fat the check Diego could write. Diego saw in Carlos an ideal mix of wiles and ruthlessness that made him the perfect heir to the empire Diego had labored so long and hard to build.

When Carlos turned sixteen, Diego began allowing him to carry out simple tasks for his business. Now, though, only eight years later and just as Carlos was taking over much of the day-to-day responsibility of supervising local distribution and collection, the empire was on the verge of vanishing like some ancient Mayan settlement reclaimed by the jungle. He suspected Carlos would react to the bleak news with blind anger, just as Diego would have at that age. Where that rage would take Carlos, however, Diego wasn't sure. He even worried that Carlos might turn the anger on him, accusing him of squandering everything by being weak and stupid—accusations that would hurt more than any of the innumerable knife gashes Diego had sustained in his rough-and-tumble youth when he had built his empire block by block, kilo by kilo.

Diego sighed and sat down heavily in his desk chair, the rich red leather creaking beneath his weight. He looked out the window and watched as dusk crept up the valley floor. Turning away from the window, he rested his elbows wearily on the desk in the growing darkness, holding his head between his hands as if it otherwise might explode.

Diego's eyes moved slowly to the family photo Roberta insisted he keep on his desk. The photo was from a decade earlier during one of the rare times the four of them had been together as a family on vacation. In the photo, Diego stood at the back, staring into the camera with his arm stiffly encircling Roberta. Carlos knelt before them, full of bravado, posing with a flexed bicep. And next to Carlos was Esteban, and as Diego's eyes focused on Esteban's smallish figure that was almost lost in Carlos's shadow, he could feel a sad smile tugging at the corners of his mouth.

Esteban had been born two years after Carlos, causing Diego's spirits to soar with the thought of a Velasquez dynasty. His birth coincided with the flourishing of Diego's ventures in the United States' cocaine market, and over Roberta's strong objections, he had insisted that the birth certificate read "Esteban Adam Smith Velasquez." As the years passed, Diego would occasionally wonder if he had tempted fate with such a brash move.

Whether it was Esteban's small size or something more intangible, Diego soon realized that Esteban and Carlos were not from the same mold. As a young boy, Esteban had shown no interest in roughhousing with the other boys, or learning to shoot birds with slingshots, or taunting the girls who came to the city park at the base of the mountain to play with their dolls.

And as he grew, Diego listened with bafflement as Esteban declined to go outside on a day God intended for soccer balls to be struck and hard tackles to be made by young men unleashing bellows of triumph. Diego and Carlos would come back into the house after these games, Carlos wearing his bruises like shiny medals with Diego's arm proudly draped around him, only to find Esteban curled up catlike in a chair, his head tucked deep inside a book thick with more pages than Diego had read in his lifetime.

When Esteban reached his teenage years, Diego's bewilderment turned to concern as Esteban's peers started to exhibit a clear machismo disdain toward him. Granted, no one dared to openly snicker and tease Esteban. Carlos had made sure of that early on. But Diego was fairly certain that Esteban was oblivious to his plight, and so Diego began attempting to help his youngest son assume his rightful place in the world.

These efforts failed abysmally. Like the bird hunting trip. Time after time, as Diego and Carlos pounced up from their blind with guns blazing at the birds flying overhead, invigorated by the dawn's cold and the rush of the hunt, Diego's side glance would find Esteban shivering and miserably curled up with his arms encircling his legs.

And much to Diego's irritation, Esteban's mother would encourage his behavior, calling him "my little scholar," oohing and aahing over his grades, telling him how proud she was when his teachers named him Student of the Month. Diego would challenge her that a parent's most sacred task was to prepare a child for the world, but Roberta would actually laugh at him and make snide remarks about Diego's lack of education. It was during this period Carmen became Diego's mistress, her noisy ardor in the bedroom making clear she understood that Diego's worldly savvy was the currency of real men.

As Esteban's high school graduation day approached, Diego had been greeted one evening by Roberta and Esteban's conspiratorial announcement that Esteban wished to study "literature" in the United States. Diego received this news with a mixture of displeasure and relief. He had been slightly insulted that they thought Diego would somehow be impressed that the university Esteban wished to attend was named Columbia, as if he somehow could be softened up by picking a school named after their country.

The thought had also flashed through his mind of how embarrassing it would be if his fellow drug lords should discover his son was going to the United States to study "literature." He hoped they might think it was a polite way of saying his son was going to be serving time in jail. Or perhaps he could tell them, with a knowing wink, that he was sending Esteban to the United States to study "Adam Smith and economics." At the same time, despite his lack of enthusiasm for the plan, Diego's relationship with Esteban had become so awkward and strained, he felt a guilty sense of relief Esteban would no longer be around the house.

Esteban had flourished at the university and was currently pursuing graduate studies. But now, of course, Esteban's little adventure up north would be over. With his empire collapsing, Diego could ill afford to spend his last cash on a Manhattan apartment or on books of poetry so Esteban could pursue his whims.

As luck would have it, Esteban was home for Christmas break. He had disembarked from the plane dressed in a black turtleneck atop black jeans, wearing his hair long and stringy, a gold stud in his ear. Upon seeing Esteban's appearance, Diego had instinctively glanced around the airport to see if he knew anyone.

Diego had said nothing as they walked out to the parking lot, but when Esteban saw him staring at the earring, Esteban said something about "an existentialist look." Diego had not responded, both because he had no idea what an existentialist was and because he took his son's look as simply another omen that life was slipping out of control. Adding insult to injury, Diego had been forced that morning to sit through a breakfast listening to Esteban talk excitedly to Roberta about his new passion for the Romantic poets, quoting lines by some poet named William Wordsworth while Roberta glowed with pride.

Well, they were both in for a shock. Their life of leisure and contemplation—"wandering lonely as a cloud," wasn't that what Esteban had said this morning while eating his grapefruit?—was about to implode in a very real way at the family council. No doubt as Carlos raged at the news, Esteban would silently get up and philosophically retreat to his room to contemplate just how lonely his cloud would be. And Roberta, oh Roberta. He already knew her glare in response to the news would carry every indictment ever lodged by a woman against a man.

# CHAPTER TWO

Esteban Adam Smith Velasquez wrestled the heavy oak chair back from the dining room table with a hip check levered against one of the chair's massive arms. His father had purchased the chairs from an antique dealer in Mexico City who had whispered in Diego's ear that "these very chairs once graced a palace owned by Napoleon," as if this were a secret to be shared only with the powerful and great, rather than a sales pitch, and most certainly a blatantly false one at that.

As a child, the chairs were so huge and Esteban so small that until he was eleven, he had always been forced to wait for Carlos to drag one of the chairs back from the table for him. Not surprisingly, therefore, Esteban hated any occasion in the formal dining room that required him to place his rear end in a seat supposedly once warmed by the posterior of one of Napoleon's sycophants. Fortunately, most of Esteban's meals growing up were spent not in the formal dining room but with his mother out on the patio. There they would sit beneath an arching canopy of bougainvillea that made even quick meals seem like a feast, surrounded by the flowers' perfumed scent, the rapid staccato of hummingbird wings, and a view that reached out to forever.

Perhaps, though, being away the past six months had made him irrationally nostalgic, for as Esteban now added a half-nelson around the chair's ornately carved back to budge the chair a few more inches, he experienced a twinge of fondness for these wooden goliaths.

Feeling beneath his fingers the intricate carving that sprawled across the chair's back, Esteban stepped back for a better look. The scene was of a

e woodcarver had clearly spent hour after hour lovingly
out in relief, causing Esteban to feel almost ashamed
given close attention to the carving before. His eyes
tip as he lightly traced the highly polished carving
lowing robes being chased across the urn's face by young
men, their muscles rippling out from the finely grained oak. The detail was
so impressive that Esteban wondered if the chairs might actually have been
carved for Napoleon.

Esteban's admiration of the carver's craft was interrupted by his father
entering the room. Esteban had been struck by his father's worn appearance
when his parents picked him up at the airport the night before, but he had
not thought much about it since. When away from home, Esteban's
memory always reverted to his father as the strapping figure of Esteban's
youth, so a little shock upon seeing him after a lengthy absence was to be
expected. And while Esteban had braced himself during the flight home
from New York for a snide comment or two about the earring that Esteban
now sported, he attributed his father's silence to not wanting to spark a fight
with his mother within minutes of Esteban's homecoming.

As his father entered the dining room, however, Esteban realized
something was wrong. Terribly wrong. The light of the afternoon sun
blazing through the windows spotlighted crevices digging across his father's
brow that Esteban was certain were newly etched. His father, whose linen
shirts were always crisp and whose hair was invariably slicked back in finest
Clark Gable style, was wearing a rumpled shirt with a tuft of hair standing
aloft on his forelock in open rebellion.

Most startling to Esteban, though, was how his father had quietly
slipped in across the dining room's threshold. This was not how Diego
Velasquez entered a room. He strode into a room exuding a confidence so
fierce, it often felt like he was challenging every man in the room to a fistfight
and extending an invitation of seduction to every woman in sight. And
while as a child, this had inspired in Esteban a state of fearful awe, Esteban
found the lack of such a presence far more chilling. Was his father about to
announce he was terminally ill? He looked over at Carlos for a clue, but
Carlos was oblivious to anything being amiss.

His father seated himself at his usual place at the head of the table, the two bodyguards who followed him everywhere took up their positions at the opposing entrances into the room. Esteban saw the bodyguards turn away from the room as they always did in following Diego's instructions not to listen. But then Esteban witnessed another event heightening his sense of unease—he could clearly see the bodyguards' heads were slightly cocked toward the center of the room so they could eavesdrop. Esteban had never seen any employee show the slightest disobedience of his father's orders, let alone in his presence. To do so was to ensure one's disappearance by the end of the day, never to be seen again. Yet as Esteban examined the bodyguards, there was no doubt they had positioned themselves so they might pick up snippets of the conversation.

Esteban's eyes were drawn back to his father as Diego cleared his throat. His father was staring at a spot in the middle of the gleaming teak table that was as long as a stretch limousine. In a voice that always reminded Esteban of hearing thunder rumbling on the horizon, his father began, "We need to talk."

Esteban's mother's eyes quickly rose up from their nun-like position of contemplating her folded hands. Roberta had perfected this posture of stoicism over the years as a way of weathering a parade of humiliations— from Diego's mistresses, who had come and gone as frequently as summer storms, to comments about her husband's occupation at high-society functions, comments strategically whispered behind her back just audibly enough to ensure Roberta heard.

But as Esteban watched his mother's eyes glance up at her husband, he knew she shared his sense that their lives were in trouble. He was also certain it was not Diego's words that caught his mother's attention as much his tone conveying the slightest hint of apology. Esteban was pretty certain his mother had never heard his father use a contrite tone, even when Diego had been courting her as the seemingly unattainable and beautiful daughter of one of the city's leading families.

His father's voice dropped an octave from its normal baritone, making it hard to hear him as he continued, "The world has turned against us." With this, he looked briefly around the table before returning his eyes to the table's shimmering surface.

Esteban glanced at Carlos and saw that his brother was just now beginning to realize this was not the usual family conference. About once a month, his father would call the family together because he wanted a chance to rant about some pet peeve, but then everything would return to normal. This was fine with Carlos, for whom normalcy meant the daytime pleasure of ordering other people around and nighttimes spent with an endless array of ravishing women.

Warily, as if the form of his question might affect the answer's outcome, Carlos asked, "What do you mean, Father?" Even at age twenty-four and with a physique that Achilles would have envied, Carlos always carefully addressed Diego as "father."

In response, Diego wearily looked at Carlos for what seemed several minutes, though Esteban knew it was only seconds. Esteban could see Carlos's growing discomfort as Diego studied his face, but he also noticed Carlos was afraid to look away. Finally, his father simply said, "Well, Carlos, the business is collapsing."

Carlos's face clouded over in a way Esteban had not seen since Carlos was a schoolboy puzzling over math problems that refused to yield up their solutions. Then, without warning, Carlos abruptly pushed back his chair and stood up, his face flushed and fists clenched. Shouting, he asked, "Who is it? Who the hell is it? Those fucking Escobars? We've fought them before and won, and we can do it again." Gesturing at the bodyguards, whose astonished faces had dropped all pretense of not listening, Carlos continued, "Give me Juan and Jorge, and we'll take five others and teach those motherfuckers to never, ever fuck with our territory again."

Carlos's anger seemed to have made Diego all the more weary. Diego softly muttered, "Sit down, Carlos, sit down," his hands barely moving in a gesture toward Carlos's chair. Carlos took his seat, but with a downward thrusting of his body that scraped the giant chair's legs back against the parquet floor and made clear he was ready to take charge and defend the family empire.

Once Carlos was seated, Diego continued, "You see, Carlos, this is the problem. There's no one to fight. We still have our producers, we still have our territories. The simple fact is we no longer can get the product where it needs to go." As Diego continued to tell his family of the changed economics of the cocaine industry, his voice grew a shade stronger, finding an odd momentary comfort in talking about a business he knew inside out, even if the news was unfailingly bleak.

When Diego finished the story, Esteban could tell that Carlos was ready to explode but did not know where to strike. With his muscles tensed and pupils dilated with anger, Carlos reminded him of the tiger his father once kept in a large cage at the back of the estate. Growing up, Esteban had spent hours watching the animal pad back and forth, back and forth, never doubting that as the tiger looked out through the bars he was thinking, "Give me one chance, kid, just one opening, and you're a goner." Far from feeling afraid, Esteban had felt sorry for the tiger, and he now felt that same sympathy for Carlos, thinking there was nothing worse than a man of action with nowhere to act.

Esteban looked from Carlos to where his mother sat sobbing. Her crying jarred Esteban from his reverie, and he instinctively began to rise to move to his mother. As he rose, he pushed back against the heavy chair. Esteban paused, feeling the distinct outline of the carving he had admired earlier pressing hard through his shirt.

"Father?"

Diego looked up, surprised that Esteban had spoken. These meetings were always conducted according to an unspoken code that he and his mother were to remain silent while Diego and Carlos conducted the family's business.

As if unsure how to proceed, Diego replied, "Yes, Esteban?"

Esteban felt the eyes of everyone on him, including the bodyguards. "Have I ever told you about Percy Shelley?"

Esteban heard the bodyguards snicker and saw his father's face take on an expression that seemed to say, "And I thought things could not get worse." Trying to cut him off before he could say anything more, Diego said, "Not now, Esteban, please not now."

Knocked off stride by the response, it took Esteban a moment to realize that they thought he was about to tell them about a lover. Esteban could not help but smile as he continued, "I have an idea of what we can do."

Carlos spat out, "Yeah, right, Esteban. Some asshole named Shelley is going to bail us out. Give me a fucking break. Have you not heard a thing that's been said? We're screwed, fucking screwed."

"Well, actually, it's a poet named John Keats, but Shelley was who first came to mind." Feeling a guilty joy at sensing, for once, that he had the upper hand, Esteban looked directly at Carlos and said, "I guess Shelley came to mind because I was reading 'Ode to a Nightingale' on the flight down."

Diego was looking intently at Esteban, as if debating whether he really wanted him to proceed, but finally said, "Okay, Esteban, what is your idea?"

In his peripheral vision, Esteban saw Carlos stir angrily in his chair. Sounding like the Vice-President of Marketing pitching the Board of Directors, Esteban began, "Well, here's what I am thinking ..."

# CHAPTER THREE

Moira O'Shaughnessy was gorgeous. Too gorgeous. About the time her reading tastes were shifting from *The Baby-Sitters Club* to *Pride and Prejudice*, Moira began to realize her looks were going to be a problem. Granted, nearly every boy at that age was a strutting bundle of hormones subject to the involuntary gravitational pull of a tight sweater, but Moira's arrival in a room had the effect of a hormone supercollider. Moira had iridescent red hair, a chest that made the Rockies look like foothills, and a bottom so perfect that the laws of geometry became understandable to even the densest of math students. One glance at Moira and the weeniest geek would rocket straight past puberty into a testosterone outbreak so severe, it would have been illegal at even the wildest Daytona spring break party.

But while most girls her age had spent hours trying to achieve a fraction of the effect Moira had on the male population of Calvin Coolidge High School, for Moira, it was a curse. Moira lived for one pleasure and one pleasure only—books. From the moment she had first gazed at *Goodnight Moon* while cuddled in her mother's lap, it was love at first sight. Head over heels in love with the world of words, Moira enjoyed nothing more than thinking and talking about books.

Her passion for books made her a perennial teacher's pet in elementary and middle school, but by the time she reached high school, her precociousness seemed of less interest to others than her emerging voluptuousness. Because she looked like a model destined to be a future Miss May of a *Sports Illustrated* swimsuit calendar, the female teachers assumed

Moira could not possibly be interested in *Hamlet*'s inner conflict. Meanwhile, her male teachers seemed unduly interested in having her read *Lolita*. Being taken seriously became a serious problem, and Moira retreated even deeper into a world populated by Darbys rather than guys wearing backward baseball caps. Still, she told herself, if she could only hang on until college, everything would be fine.

She envisioned the university as a sanctuary of learning where she would sit in class with fellow worshippers. Amid those ivy-covered walls, the only sighs of anticipation would be for the next great book on the syllabus. References to sex would not be the lewd adolescent jokes her high school classmates mistook for wit, but clever double entendres delivered with a puckish smile by a professor in a corduroy jacket and leather patches on the elbows.

If anything, though, college was worse. It hadn't helped that Moira had now fully blossomed into a young woman who triggered a chain of whiplash injuries every time she walked down the street. In large lecture classes, she could feel the guys stealing glances at her, not even pretending to be listening to the root causes of the Opium War. In smaller classes, she found professors staring at her breasts when they called on her even though her hand was raised high above her fiery-red bangs. Although she did not own any Pearl Jam, she had embraced the grunge look with its loose-fitting style, and she still owned a closetful of flannel shirts that would make a Maine lumberjack proud. Even now, long after grunge had given way to the next fad, she continued to dress as if she was attending a Nirvana concert every night.

By the time she entered grad school with a specialty in eighteenth-century English literature, Moira had shed her illusions. She loved literature as much as ever and still enjoyed dissecting a poem's similes and metaphors with the precision of a microbiologist. Moira was aware, however, that the perfection of her cold-shoulder look—a stare that could freeze the most egotistical male dead in his tracks at thirty yards—was now less of a way to deal with the singles scene and more of an attitude toward life. Moira's emotions had become like the slats of a venetian blind she learned to open and close with a quick mental tug, and lately, they remained tugged shut.

She had no real close friends, and at times this bothered her, especially when she realized this was largely of her own doing. There had been a few times she flirted with allowing a potential friendship to flourish. Ultimately, however, she always withdrew to her comfortable inner world where emotions developed neatly at the pace of iambic pentameter and her relationships could develop with the turn of a page or be put tidily on hold with the placing of a bookmark.

And so it was Moira found herself looking out the corner window of her favorite coffee shop, watching the small, wiry frame of Esteban Velasquez approaching through a schizophrenic January-mix that twitched back and forth between snow and sleet. She smiled at seeing Esteban. They had started graduate school together, and he was one of the few grad students who treated words with the sensuous awe they deserved. This shared feeling was as close to a friendship as Moira had at the moment.

Moira occasionally speculated to herself about Esteban's private life as they passionately shared a favorite passage, and the sight of him triggered her musings again. She guessed he might be gay, not so much because she stereotyped him for his love of literature, gentle manner, and dramatic hand gestures, but more because he did not act like a pheromone-crazed bee buzzing around her. With a touch of embarrassment, she wondered if she was now so jaundiced that she reflexively thought anyone not in hot pursuit of her must be unattracted to women. I guess, she confessed, Esteban couldn't be too much of a friend if after several years of shared classes and midnight espresso-fueled discourses on the merits of an obscure Romantic poet, she still had only the most cursory sense of his life story beyond the fact he came from Colombia.

Moira's musings ended upon hearing the café door open, followed by, "Moira, how are you? Thank you so much for coming." She always loved how Esteban said her name, making it sound like an exotic orchid, cooing "Moira" with a drawn-out 'o' breathlessly followed by a Spanish "i" and a rolled "r" before performing a crescendo into a soft "a" that sounded like it was gently landing on a goose down pillow. She stood up and gave Esteban a warm hug and kiss on the cheek, hoping he would sense the happiness she felt at seeing him.

"Did you have a wonderful trip back home, I hope?"

As Esteban replied, "It was good, good," nodding his head up and down vigorously, Moira noticed an Esquire-looking hulk staring at her over Esteban's shoulder. He was undeniably good-looking, straight off the cover of one of those men's "health magazines" with headlines that promised things like, "Eleven Ways to Drive Her Crazy with Your Electric Toothbrush."

Because she was pretty sure he must be with Esteban, she resisted giving the hulk her Kryptonite stare and simply averted her eyes back to Esteban. Esteban, however, sensing what had happened, quickly motioned to the hulk and said, "Ah Moira, let me introduce you to my brother, Carlos."

Carlos grinned ear to ear with a look that practically shouted, "And how lucky must you be that I am the brother of this guy?" And now she couldn't resist. She gave Carlos a withering look and was surprised that he actually seemed to stagger a step back. With concern, she glanced at Esteban but saw only the slightest smile dancing on his lips. Esteban broke the silence by asking, "Moira, might we join you for a moment?"

"Of course," and Moira slid a stack of books aside to make room for them. Esteban plopped down on the seat next to her with his usual energy, and Carlos, in a sulk, sat down heavily in the chair on the other side of the table. Moira thought how easily lust is turned into anger when not reciprocated.

"Moira, I've got a business proposition for you." Esteban watched Moira's bright-green eyes widen with surprise as he continued, "While I was home with my family over break, I was talking about how much I loved what I was studying, especially the Romantic poets, and they thought it'd be great to learn more about it." Esteban glanced at Carlos, whose glowering had only intensified as he sat in his chair not understanding a word of what was being said, and added, "Well, Madre and Padre thought it would be great. In fact, Padre thought it'd be inspiring to sponsor a conference in Bogotá on the Romantic poets. I was thinking we'd call the conference," he flashed his hands to the ceiling as if reading a movie marquee, "Wordsworth in Bogotá."

Esteban, who had rehearsed this opening spiel numerous times before approaching Moira, watched her face carefully. Moira was quiet for a moment before asking, "Esteban, what does your dad do, because that sounds awfully expensive."

Esteban's "He's in the import-export business" was immediately followed by a forced laugh accompanied by a resigned look. He then added, as if revealing a great personal burden, "And of course, since we're from Colombia, everyone assumes that means he's a drug dealer. But he's in pharmaceuticals, especially anti-depressants, and that is a truly international business, you know."

Esteban had known this was going to be the hardest part of the conversation. He genuinely liked Moira and relished their shared passion for literature. He had anticipated what she would ask and had tried to come up with answers that he could convince himself were not out-and-out lies. But now that he had uttered his lines out loud, he saw there was no moral tightrope to be walked. His fourth grade teacher, Sister Carmen, had been fond of having her students memorize various proverbs from around the world, and at the moment, "in for a penny, in for a pound" seemed quite appropriate, even if almost certainly not the context the good Sister had anticipated it coming in handy for.

Esteban looked directly into Moira's eyes and plunged on, "And so, well, Padre asked me how to do this, and I said I knew just the right person to help arrange it. You! And I explained that we'd, of course, have to pay you for your work and pay the professors who we invited to come speak and write papers. Do you think ten thousand dollars would make it worth your time? I know you're swamped with your dissertation."

Moira barely succeeded in not spurting cappuccino foam all over the tabletop. Almost every night, she went to bed mentally calculating her student debt and wondering how a specialty in eighteenth-century English literature would ever provide a way to pay it off. Faced with having to finish the dissertation by the end of the following year, ten thousand would let her have the summer to work on it without becoming a barista. Plus, she reasoned quickly to herself, quite apart from the money was the appeal of helping put together a literature conference, bringing Wordsworth to Bogotá.

"Wow, Esteban, that certainly sounds wonderful," she said, trying to keep her voice steady. "Would you like me to work on a list of possible invitees?"

Esteban again plunged into his rehearsed lines, "You know, I got really excited once I realized my parents were serious, and I pulled together a list of profs who I thought might be good." He motioned to Carlos as he rattled off something in Spanish, and Carlos, who was still brooding, morosely reached into a worn leather satchel on the chair next to him, took out a folder, and handed it to Esteban. Esteban flipped through some papers, pulled out a sheet, and pushed it across the table to Moira.

As Moira read down the list of names, Esteban could see her brow starting to furrow. She reached the end of the list and glanced up with a puzzled look. "I recognize only one of these names. What about someone like Casper Crenshaw? I mean, he's the rock star of Romantic poetry scholars these days."

Esteban hesitated a second and then said, "We didn't think we could get someone like Crenshaw and keep within budget. The names on the list are all people who've written on the Romantics and I think are rising stars. And part of the requirement is they write a fifty-page article that we'll bind into several published volumes for university libraries around the country. That's a *fucking* lot of work."

"True," Moira agreed, smiling. Although Esteban rarely swore, when he did, he launched the epithet as if it were on a verbal trampoline. "So how much am I to tell them we'll pay?"

"Fifteen thousand plus expenses, but we absolutely must have their manuscripts a month before the conference, and the conference will be a little over four months from today."

Moira stared hard at Esteban, and he squirmed ever so slightly in his chair. "Esteban, for an English prof, that is a helluva lot of money, and it isn't that *fucking* hard to write a fifty-page paper. Fifteen grand? That's probably a third of what some of these profs at the smaller colleges make in a year teaching five courses a semester and churning out articles so they can get tenure. I bet you I can even get Casper Crenshaw to do it for fifteen thousand." She paused, adding, "I know him a little," wincing as she recalled Casper's efforts to grope her at a wine-and-cheese reception the month before at a conference on Narrative and the Semicolon.

"I appreciate that, Moira, but let's go with this list. Do you think you can contact these people in person? We'll pay your expenses, including airfare for the ones farther out. But I really need you to wrap up everyone quickly, and you need to make it clear that the manuscript has to be fifty pages, minimum, on time—no extensions. No paper, no money." Then he added, "And if within the next week you can get all twelve of them to agree to do it, we'll bump your fee up another five thousand dollars."

Moira stared again at Esteban, this time not because of the offer of extra money, but because of his tone. This wasn't her Esteban, the bright, energetic friend who loved to hang out until 2 a.m. in a dingy apartment enveloped in a cloud of pot smoke, debating whether U2's lyrics counted as modern poetry. This was a conversation that had the feel of a Wall Street hedge fund broker striking a deal to buy North Sea oil futures. Esteban returned her stare, and she found herself saying "deal" as she extended her hand and they shook.

"Great!" Esteban's familiar smile once again creased his face. He said something to Carlos in Spanish, and as he handed Carlos the file to put back in the briefcase, a xeroxed sheet with photos of each professor fell out onto the table. Esteban glanced at Moira. Noticing that she had spied the paper, he smiled and said, "Have to start early on visas these days."

*Odd*, Moira thought, almost as odd as the fact that every photo on the paper looked as if the person pictured could be a finalist in an American Geeks contest. But as Esteban said goodbye and kissed her on the cheek, Moira had already started mapping in her mind how to get to twelve different colleges within a week. Five grand rode on it, and that was a lot of grande vanilla lattes by anyone's count.

Without thinking, she gave the brooding Carlos a smile as he turned to go out the door. The effect on Carlos was as if he had been jabbed with a syringe of anabolic steroids, and he strode out of the coffeehouse with a king-of-the-jungle look. There was no doubt about who he saw as his next prey.

"Men," Moira muttered.

# CHAPTER FOUR

The Fates had been bullheaded when it came to Percy Billings—he was to be an English professor, no ifs, ands, or buts. The Fates started by choosing for Percy's parents two high school English teachers whose idea of a honeymoon was a pilgrimage to Thomas Hardy's birthplace. Taking no chances, however, the Fates also bestowed upon Percy an innate ability to distinguish irony from sarcasm and to know when to use "that" instead of "which."

And to cut off any possibility that Percy might choose a life that did not rely entirely upon his 167 IQ, they chose DNA strands for him that were imbedded with the genetic code for physical attributes that deciphered into "nerd" instead of "film star." With only the slightest imagination, one could look at Percy's snapshots as a newborn and see him as he stood today at the front of the classroom—thick glasses necessitated by a severe astigmatism, a physique as wispy as a trembling aspen, and a voice that Mother Nature's tuning fork had placed only a half-note below soprano.

In ushering Percy toward his destiny, however, the Fates made one critical oversight—they forgot to tell Percy their plan. And as the dull winter light filtered in through the classroom windows, Professor Percy Billings, for the millionth time, thought of Fate as a four-letter word. It wasn't that Percy didn't enjoy books or words or ideas. He very much did. Rather, it was that his soul told him he was a man of action, not words.

And his soul had been telling him this from childhood. He had joined his elementary school compatriots in their worship of Michael Jordan and

Tom Brady, climbing into bed each night to dream of soaring dunks and perfectly arced touchdown passes. These dreams had slowly been extinguished after years of being picked last on the playground and by coaches subbing him into games because they were bound by rules that required them to play each child for a few minutes. By the end of junior high, his slumber no longer was marked by dreams of dashing from end zone to end zone. But that was okay because fantasies of being a sports hero had been replaced with a new dream of destiny—that of being a rock star.

He grew his hair so that it brushed against his shoulders, and he pleaded with his parents to replace his oboe lessons with electric guitar. They had compromised on the mandolin. With his bedroom door shut tight, he played air guitar to Lynyrd Skynyrd's "Free Bird," and when his eyes were closed, he had no trouble picturing a rainbow of brightly colored panties raining down on the stage of the shag carpet upon which he danced.

Percy had proceeded far enough in his lessons that he was able to do a Xerox-of-a-Xerox rendition of "Stairway to Heaven" on his mandolin, and he even thought of trying to form a garage band. His primary group of acquaintances, however, played Mozart, not Led Zeppelin, and the kids at the high school who were capable of ripping off a Black Sabbath riff would have been certain they were hallucinating if he had attempted to hang with them.

Percy eventually put aside his rock-star aspirations, but not quite in the same way as he abandoned his dreams of spiraling touchdown passes. He realized he might never play lead guitar in front of screaming groupies, but his inner-Mick Jagger still lived, and he vowed to keep the prancing figure of energy and passion alive no matter what the Fates had planned.

The Fates' next stop for Percy was, unsurprisingly, a topflight college. He breezed through his courses with the ease of Tiger Woods playing a nine-hole golf course. Recognizing Percy's talent, his professors squabbled with each other over the right to make Percy their protégé. But while Percy enjoyed the attention and the satisfaction of doing well in college, he soon wearied of erudite dinner discussions about the latest poetry tropes.

Restless and aware something was missing, he tried to challenge where the Fates wanted to take him. For a while, he tried lifting weights. Reading up on how to add muscle mass, he took to drinking foul-tasting protein shakes and going to the university fitness center each day. He tried to time his bouts with the dumbbells for when the gym was least crowded, as he had trouble with even the lightest weights and felt embarrassed when the football players were around. Wearing T-shirts with the sleeves ripped off, they would strut around like peacocks looking for a mate, screaming out grunts as they bench-pressed the equivalent of Percy's body mass three times over.

After six months of flexing in the mirror after his shower, Percy was forced to admit his biceps showed not the slightest inclination to expand. His trips to the gym became less frequent, and he eventually resigned himself to a physique where the only good news was that he still could be the hero who slipped through the narrow window if he was ever held hostage by a madman in a basement, preferably with a fellow hostage who looked like Ingrid Bergman since Percy was a big *Casablanca* fan.

After college, graduate school was the next station on the Destiny Line. The Fates arranged for him to study under the most brilliant Milton scholar of his time—a man who had completely transformed the world's understanding of the first three lines of the seventy-third stanza of *Paradise Regained*. But in what was viewed by many in the English department as a wild act of rebellion, Percy decided to study the Romantic movement instead.

A tight job market for purveyors of Wordsworth and Coleridge at the time of his graduation had made him feel fortunate to land at Arcadia College, a small liberal arts college hidden away in a valley of rural Virginia. Now, as he looked at his students slouching in their chairs, ineptly disguising that they were texting or revising their Facebook page instead of listening to his exposition about the influences of Rousseau on the Romantic movement, Percy remembered with a pang what he had hoped teaching would be like.

As a graduate student, Percy had eagerly anticipated gripping the sides of the lectern and delivering an impassioned reading of a Shakespeare love sonnet, drawing his students into the lines, leaving them breathless, panting for more. And he knew, he just knew, that every student would swoon upon seeing the poet's flame burning inside him. If he was destined to become a professor, and that was clearly the next station awaiting on the Destiny Line, reciting poetry to a college class of eager students just might be the rough equivalent of singing "I Can't Get No Satisfaction" to a packed arena of screaming groupies.

But as he gazed at their faces on this gray winter morning, he was greeted not by buoyant looks but by the vacant stares of frat boys coerced into attending by the college's attendance policy, and coeds whose eyes held no suggestion that he had kindled within their breasts dormant sixteenth-century notions of romance. Confronted with the indifferent looks, and never one to pass up the opportunity for overdramatization, he again thought of himself as a poor man's Oedipus, cursed from childhood by a fate he had resisted fiercely, but to no avail.

After an hour of lecturing and asking the occasional question knowing it would hang in the air unanswered as the students stared at their feet, Percy began to wrap up the class. As he glanced up from his notes to announce the assignment for the next class, he gave a start upon noticing a woman standing respectfully at the back of the classroom. Percy had never seen her before, and he suddenly realized he was staring at her. A number of students followed his gaze to the back of the room, and the male students did not quickly return their look to the front of the room.

Percy finally found his voice as he announced, "And so, we'll pick up with pages 121 to 146 next time. Have a good day." He fervently hoped the woman at the back of the room had not been present long enough to have seen how lifeless the class had been.

With Percy's announcement, the students slowly rose from their desks, packed away their laptops, and gathered their belongings. As they pulled on their overcoats to confront the January chill, several stole looks at Percy with questioning faces as to who this woman was wanting to speak to their professor.

Moira waited until the class had exited before approaching Percy and extending her hand. "Hello Professor Billings, I'm Moira O'Shaughnessy." She paused waiting for Percy to answer, who, upon taking her slender hand in his, had stammered a second before getting out, "Uh ... how nice to meet you. Please call me Percy. Can I help you?"

For Percy to stammer, even momentarily, was highly uncharacteristic. Percy might not exactly have been a smooth-talking ladies' man, but words were his currency and he rarely had an empty wallet. As Percy brought his attention back to Moira, he realized she was studying his face. Not a good omen, he thought. But before he could self-consciously dwell on his aesthetic shortcomings, Moira picked up the conversation.

"Okay, Percy it is, then. Well, listen, I'm a graduate student in English literature at Columbia, and I am part of a project that I was hoping you'd be interested in joining."

Happy to have a topic that allowed him to regain his composure, Percy quickly responded while fearing he sounded a bit too enthusiastic, "A project? Really? Well, yes, yes, I'd certainly love to hear about it."

He opened the classroom door into the hallway, gesturing for Moira to go ahead of him. "Let's go to my office where we can talk." And as she walked in front of him, Percy's unconscious took over. A few seconds later, Percy was startled to realize that he, Dr. Percy Billings, holder of the college's Distinguished Professor of Romantic Literature chair, was humming to himself a Paul McCartney song that had been popular when he was a teenager, and the distinguished professor found himself wondering, *What the hell?*

# CHAPTER FIVE

What the hell indeed. As they walked down the hallway, Percy made small talk with Moira, glancing at her through his peripheral vision and thinking that the clicks of her high heels on the yellowed linoleum hallway sounded like castanets with a Spanish rhythm. He smiled, wondering what Moira would do if he were to stomp his feet flamenco style and clap his hands in time with the snapping of her heels.

Percy was not immune to having such thoughts stray across his mind, but fortunately had long ago mastered the art of disguising such thoughts with a demeanor of somber rationality. Indeed, he had often survived tedious faculty meetings by focusing his eyes in a way that looked attentive while his imagination turned his colleagues' words into a surrealistic Salvador Dali painting. He wondered if everyone had such dual tracks. Maybe the only thing separating the sane from the insane was the ability to resist voicing out loud the wild musings that raced around the mind like shimmying roller derby skaters. But there was something about Moira as she walked next to him that made it harder than usual for him to maintain his well-practiced, dignified demeanor.

Percy was spared from any further urge to dance the fandango by Moira's interruption. After he unlocked the office door, she entered his office and immediately drifted over to a poster hanging on the wall. The poster was of a little girl with big brown eyes opened wide with a caption in red letters that said, "Every Time You Scream at a Driver, She Learns a Lesson." Moira turned back toward Percy, her head tilted questioningly.

"A friend in New York who works for the city's public works department sent it to me. The poster was part of an ad campaign to tamp down road rage. I keep it up there to remind me of what I didn't like about the city."

"So you don't miss New York?" Moira asked, making no effort to mask her incredulity.

"Parts of it, sure." Percy then pointed at a framed photograph on the opposite wall, "Which is why I keep that over there."

Moira walked across the fraying Persian rug that reached almost from wall to wall, its pattern made more intricate by patches that had faded with the randomness of where the sunlight had rested on it over the years. She bent in close to the photo and looked up, perplexed. "This is your tribute to New York City? Most people might choose a photo of Central Park newly dusted with snow at dawn, or at least a cheesy tourist shot of the Brooklyn Bridge lit up at night."

As Percy laughed, his glasses slipped halfway down his nose. Pushing the glasses back up, he walked over and stood next to Moira, keenly aware that their shoulders were within an inch of touching. Leaning in, he peered at a black-and-white photo of an old junker car being driven by a man with a scraggly white beard that disappeared out of sight beneath the driver's window. Neatly lined up on the car's hood were a dozen or so pairs of worn tennis shoes, and the top of the trunk was arranged with meticulous piles of items, such as books and shirts and pants.

"I took this photo myself. I would see this gentleman driving around my neighborhood every week or so, moving at a snail's pace so the items wouldn't blow off, and one morning I was able to catch him on film as he inched by."

"And this would show the beauty of the city ... how?"

"Oh, of a story on every street corner. I loved that you couldn't meander more than a block without witnessing five incidents begging to be written up as a short story. I mean, what was this guy about? Did he live in the car? Was he some mentally ill scion of a moneyed family with an obsessive-compulsive disorder? A poet who a century from now will have statues put up of him, but for now lives under an overpass because no one appreciates his art? A jilted lover who never overcame the heartbreak and drives endlessly around the streets looking for his lost love? I never came close to figuring him out, but he never failed to start me wondering every time he passed by." Musing out loud, Percy added, "I wonder if he still drives his route."

Moira turned slightly to look at Percy, surprised by the enthusiasm of his speaking manner and the way he had phrased his observations. She straightened up from the photo and asked, "So, does that mean you feel like an exile out here in bucolic wonderland?"

Percy paused, wondering whether to give Moira his fifteen-second stock reply that "it has its ups and downs, its pluses and minuses." Caught in indecision, he opted for a simple, "It's complicated."

But then, without further prompting, he continued, "I view it sort of like an arranged marriage. You see, this was the only teaching job I was offered when I entered the market, and I have to admit I felt like an exile after all my years in New York and Boston. But after a while, the beauty seeps into you, sort of like a long languid hot bath. I don't even need a photo to remind me of that." Percy motioned toward the large casement window which framed a view of the soft, undulating ridge of a mountain, beautiful even garbed in its winter brown. "And the people around here are friendly, and pretty soon, you know everyone. When friends visit, it's like a parlor trick when we walk down Main Street—odds are good I'll be able to greet almost every person by name. And so one day, I woke up and, like you sometimes hear about with arranged marriages, found out that while I might not have been passionately in love with Arcadia at first sight, I had slowly become content."

Percy was surprised how comfortable he felt in telling this to Moira. He was about to reveal that his real angst was whether he still wanted to teach and write about what others had written, but feeling that Moira must think he was rambling, he stopped. And although he didn't keep going, he felt a flutter, almost a giddiness, when he thought he saw interest in her eyes.

Percy broke the brief silence by going behind his desk and easing down into an old-fashioned, wooden swivel chair. Once seated, he looked at

Moira, who took a seat across from him and said, "So, tell me about this project."

"Sure. Well, it is a conference on the Romantic poets." She made sure she had a good view of Percy as she spoke. "It's to introduce scholarship on their poetry to a broader Latin America audience." Percy's eyebrow arched a little. "And so," Moira continued, "it will be held in Bogotá at the beginning of May, and we'd need a fifty-page paper by the end of March," which caused both of Percy's eyebrows to arch up like they had been yanked by strings.

"Bogotá? A fifty-page paper in under three months' time?" He gazed intently at Moira. "Surely you realize that is practically impossible. Why, I don't even speak Spanish fluently, let alone have the ability to write a mini-opus on Keats in it."

"Oh, the paper is in English. The conference organizers will provide translations." She then readied the punch line, "And they recognize it is a very short timeframe, which is why they'll not only cover all of your expenses, but they'll pay a stipend of fifteen thousand dollars if you can get the paper done in time."

Every professor she had talked to up to this point showed early signs of cardiac arrest upon hearing the sum that Esteban was offering, and she came to enjoy watching their reactions. It was like throwing a lit cherry bomb under an unsuspecting person sitting on a park bench and waiting for the explosion. Percy, however, simply continued to hold her gaze, leaned back in his chair, causing it to give an unoiled creak, and asked, "Why me?"

Moira hid her surprise that the fuse had fizzled out and found herself earnestly saying, "The organizers must have liked your monograph on Thomas Hardy as much as I did."

Now it was Moira's turn to be surprised as Percy looked chagrined rather than flattered, asking in a tone with a hint of despondency, "You liked my Hardy piece?"

"Well, yes. I pulled it from the stacks before coming to see you and read it on the plane." She paused, then went on tentatively, "I thought it wonderful satire. I laughed out loud at several points."

Moira jumped several inches in her chair as Percy half-stood up, slapped the top of his desk, sending papers flying in several directions, and practically shouted, "You got it!" And as Percy sat back down with a huge smile, he softly repeated, "You got it."

Percy had submitted the piece, *Thomas Hardy's Barking Dogs*, as an act of rebellion at feeling his life had fallen into a sinkhole. Tired of reading literary criticism, tired of teaching uninterested students, tired of sitting behind a desk while the sun lit up the countryside outside his office window, he set out to defiantly dump a full cup of black coffee onto the white carpet of all those literary scholars who took themselves so seriously.

He had written the manuscript in a caffeine-fueled forty-eight hours without sleep, allowing his cynicism to pour onto every page as he argued that by counting the number of times a dog barked in a scene, Hardy was secretly signaling to the reader how to react to the character. Percy had gone so far as to suggest that Hardy was deliberately supplying a type of Da Vinci Code for the reader through the symbolism of the barking dog.

He had half-hoped that the article, by making fun of what was held so dear, would get him drummed out of the academy, forcing him to make his way in the world other than as a professor. What he would have done as an alternative, he hadn't a clue, especially since rock star and professional athlete had long been abandoned, but he knew he desperately needed to get out.

Instead, *Barking Dogs* had won him a small measure of fame, including a nomination for best paper from the prestigious Scholars of Hardy Society. The paper probably would have even won if the esteemed Hardy scholar, Waring Carlington, had not written an impassioned rebuttal, contending that while Percy had been brilliant in uncovering the barking dog code, he had misunderstood the meaning of three barks in the barnyard scene of *Tess of the d'Urbervilles*. *Barking Dogs*, though, had secured Percy lifelong tenure, and now he sat looking at Moira as the only person who understood he had been trying to throw a Molotov cocktail rather than write a piece to be discussed over cocktails in a cherry-paneled faculty lounge.

And so it was that Percy found himself agreeing to write the article for the Bogotá conference, thinking, for the first time in a long time, that the

Fates may have a kinder side. And so it was that after Moira closed the door behind her, she walked a good twenty yards down the hallway before realizing she had not once thought about pulling out her Kryptonite stare. Indeed, she couldn't stop smiling at how the clicking of her heels on the yellowed linoleum sounded like castanets echoing off the walls.

# CHAPTER SIX

Prior to joining the Drug Enforcement Agency and eventually becoming the Northeast Regional Deputy Chief, Bronson McArthur Attles had been a military guy. And he looked it. Especially if one thinks of an army officer as spending every waking day for twenty years standing up in a jeep riding beneath a scorching desert sun. His tanned face was etched with lines so deep and rugged, it would have won a blue ribbon as a sixth grader's science fair project on the topography of the Sierra Madres. Many a cosmetic surgeon had eyed Attles's face with the zest of a mountaineer fantasizing about someday scaling Mount Everest. Attles, however, never would have allowed a syringe of Botox near him, let alone a scalpel, as he used his face and gravelly voice to good effect for intimidating those under his command.

This particular January day found Attles standing at the head of a conference room, his back so straight, shoulders so squared that they formed a protractor-perfect right angle with the carpeted floor. As much as the agents under Attles hated him—even despised him—for his despotic ways, they had to admit he had his benefits.

Ferociously enforcing the federal forfeiture laws that allowed agencies to "use" items seized from drug dealers, Attles had turned his unit into a cross between a high-tech showroom and a cover spread for *Architectural Digest*. Yellow and green lights from seized electronics blinked around the office like a mini Times Square. Agents talked on the latest smartphone while tapping away at the most recent Apple gizmo—drug dealers gave the market nod to Steve Jobs over Bill Gates—while other agents readied surveillance equipment well beyond any budget except the CIA and South American drug lords.

The agents at the table with Attles sat around a polished rosewood table so rich in its hue and grain that one felt slightly guilty resting one's elbows on it. The table came courtesy of a cocaine kingpin who had fled Cuba with the Mariel boatlift and taken his arrival in the promised land as a chance to build a wildly successful cocaine import business. That is, before a power-hungry lieutenant had betrayed him to the authorities. A lieutenant turned jefe who no doubt now sat around his own fifty-thousand-dollar teak table—at least until one of his underlings decided it was time to have a hand-hewn, two-hundred-year-old chestnut table of his own.

Attles glanced down at his notes, his crew cut of white hair so thick and cropped it looked like the bristles on a potato scrub brush. When he peered up, he simply said, "Fucking Esteban Velasquez is back in the city." At the mention of Esteban's name, the three agents around the table raised their heads like a synchronized swim team performing a rocket split. They all knew that Esteban was Attles's Moby Dick, the person who tormented Attles's dreams.

Last year, when Attles learned that the son of one of Colombia's most notorious drug lords was in the city, he had assigned around-the-clock surveillance. When that had uncovered no wrongdoing, he had one of the office's most talented agents, Callie Banks, enroll as a student and take an apartment down the hall from Esteban. Not only had Banks not turned up any wrongdoing, she eventually quit the agency and enrolled full-time as a graduate student, now avidly pursuing a doctorate degree in Medieval Chaucer Studies.

After a pause, Attles continued, "And this time, we're going to nail the motherfucker. And you know why? Because he's no goddamn Shakespeare scholar. You three are now the task force charged with figuring out where he is going, who he is talking with, and what the hell is going down." He gleefully rubbed his hands together so hard the agents half-expected smoke to appear. "Yes, oh yes, oh yes, we've got him this time. I don't want to hear any"—Attles raised his voice a pitch to mimic a whine—"'oh, I'm just studying poetry' smokescreen this time. And you three are going to nail him.

I want a report back in a week laying out a game plan. When can we all meet?"

"How about next Saturday?" volunteered Agent Mike Forreo.

"Saturday won't work," Attles said. "I've got a quadrathlon that day."

"A what?" Forreo asked without really thinking. Attles often brought up his triathlon feats in the office, complaining how race organizers kept sticking him in the "Masters" group even though he'd won it every time.

Attles looked at Mike, speaking slowly, as if Forreo had a mental disability. "A quad-rath-lon, as in four events instead of three."

"And the fourth event would be?" Mike asked.

"Skipping six miles."

Mike laughed out loud, amazed that Attles had finally told a joke four long, mirthless years after Mike joined the office. Then he realized Attles's eyes were boring into him with those yellow-green irises that made one feel like a pit viper was watching you. More than once, Mike had wondered if Attles wore colored contacts to make his eyes appear reptilian, envisioning Attles going into LensCrafters and asking for contacts in Amber Asshole.

"You think it's a fucking joke?" Attles asked. "Let's go, buddy ... you and me, right now, down to Central Park. We'll skip one lap around the park—six miles—and see who is laughing then. Mano a mano."

"Or canguro a canguro," Agent Michelle Esperanza muttered under her breath at the far end of the conference table. Attles snapped his head up. *Damn,* Esperanza thought, *it'd be just like him to get supersonic hearing implants.*

But Attles just gave her an odd smile as he said, "Agent?"

"Nada," Michelle replied, "just practicing my Spanish."

Attles gave her his two-beat stare, turned back to Mike, gave him a four-beat stare, and then said to all of them, "Listen, my friends, just so we're perfectly clear. If Esteban Velasquez is not in a federal penitentiary by the end of this investigation, when it comes to your career prospects, the *Titanic* will look like a bathtub accident. Now figure out another goddamn date and clear it with my secretary."

With that inspirational send-off, Attles left the room, and the newly formed task force of Agents Mike Forreo, Michelle Esperanza, and Carl

Chang felt their collective shoulders sag from the relief of his exit. In a second, however, they were sitting bolt upright again as they heard Attles's voice back at the doorway barking, "And, oh yeah, the assholes at HQ want some catchy name for the task force so when we catch the goddamn bastards it will sound good at the press conference. I'm pretty damn good with words but don't have the time, so you three bozos come up with something that isn't too shitty."

# CHAPTER SEVEN

Percy woke up the next morning wrapped inside his blankets like a five-layer burrito. He loved every creak and draft of his old Victorian farmhouse, but the mountains' evening chill that kept the home cool in the summertime went from refreshing to bracing once the leaves fell. By the time the winter solstice had shortened daytime to a mere blink of the solar eye, the bedroom was downright frigid when the alarm rang.

With tussled hair and eyes barely cracked, he shuffled his way to the coffeemaker, silently blessing the inventor who had figured out how to have freshly brewed coffee waiting for him in the morning. Forget curing polio, this was science deserving of a Nobel Prize. With a mug clutched in his fingers like a beggar's tin cup, he ruefully smiled and shook his head upon catching his image reflected in the window. Swallowed up inside a huge fishermen's sweater, he looked like a kid who had gotten into his dad's closet. But at least he was warm, and soon the coffee was working its black magic as he ambled over to his computer.

Turning on his email, he did his best to stifle the anticipation, the hope that he could feel involuntarily welling up in his chest. Ever since Moira had walked out of his office saying she'd email soon, he had barely kept one foot in the everyday world. The afternoon after Moira's departure, he had met with a student to go over her essay on *Wuthering Heights* and knew he had come across as even more of the absentminded professor than usual. He wished he could claim it was because he was thinking great thoughts, but it was because he was sneaking looks at his computer screen every twenty seconds—perhaps once he topped a half minute through sheer willpower—to see if Moira had emailed.

And the night had bordered on self-flagellation. Percy had tried to write a paragraph on the novel he exhumed every month or so when he was caught up in a moment of angst. Some people did shots of tequila when the black dog started its haunting howl outside their window. Some people wrote to drown out its bark. Percy did both.

In best Hemingway fashion, Percy would fling back a shot of cheap tequila, always having to consciously recreate the sequence—first the lime, then the salt ... or wait, was it first the salt, then the lime—and hope that his Muse would stumble in through the swinging doors of his imagination. Often the doors never swung, and Percy would stare at a blinking cursor, the contemporary equivalent of the wadded-up typing paper that once littered the study of the author suffering from writer's block.

Last night was worse than usual, though, because it wasn't simply some undefined anxiety causing him to gaze blankly out the window. Percy's soul, his id, sixth sense, whatever—after three shots of tequila it answered to "hey you"—had become convinced that a special connection had occurred with Moira. And for Percy to be smitten was a matter of some seriousness because Percy suffered from a severe case of the Sixteenth Century Romantic.

Percy was a devout believer in love at first sight, true love, timeless love, head-over-heels love, love for the ages, star-crossed love, a crazy little thing called love, and love eight days a week. That Percy harbored such views was occasionally a matter of embarrassment. He knew his view of love could be caricatured as nothing more than a gussied-up version of the adolescent mooning that gave rise to the societal blight of boy bands.

But Percy couldn't help it, and part of what drew him to poetry was the safe haven it provided knowing that others felt the same way. In fact, few news items incensed Percy more than a report of another scientific study suggesting love was merely an evolutionary adaptation.

Really? If true, then a first date was nothing more than Mother Nature in a white lab coat mixing up a test tube of hormones and pheromones to see if a chemical reaction occurred. And love was nothing more than a chromosomal Iron Man competition where the man's spermatozoa played a game of Capture the Egg to ensure his DNA stumbled on for another generation. According to these folks in their lab goggles, the man feeling his heart skip a beat as he looked at his beloved was delusional, the feeling of his spirit soaring nothing more than his endocrine levels spiking. Percy actually felt a twinge of sympathy for these scientists. Had they never read Browning? Shakespeare? Petrarch?

Being a Sixteenth-Century Romantic in search of one's soul mate, though, also meant that Percy tended to be reckless when it came to matters of the heart. Commitment problems? Not for Percy. There was no cautious testing of the emotional ice to see if it would support him. If Percy felt the slightest spark of his soul, his heart rushed out headlong, ignoring the cracking sounds, the fissures spreading out beneath him like lightning bolts in a thunderstorm gone mad, until the ice gave way and he went plunging into the dark, freezing waters with the realization that the person was not, in fact, 'The One.' But this had never kept Percy from letting his emotions madly dash out again the next time he thought someone might be his other half. Too much was at stake, and one never knew unless one tried. And he had become somewhat used to polar bear plunges of the heart, shivering miserably for a while but eventually resuming his search.

What Percy worried about with Moira was that he'd never felt such a connection before. And this, he knew, was the most dangerous part of the Sixteenth Century Romantic's credo—if one truly found one's soul mate, gave one's heart, there was no turning back. No solace in, "There's always another fish in the sea," or whatever the line was that friends comforted each other with when a relationship broke up as they threw back glasses of whiskey.

As much as he loved the books of poetry that made his bookshelves sag, he had also often thought the shelves should have a bright-yellow "DANGER AHEAD" flashing sign in front of them. True, the poetry that so drew Percy was full of odes to the exhilaration of love, but the volumes also overflowed with verses lamenting a love unreturned. These forlorn verses with their mournful laments had always struck Percy as a form of prophetic foreboding, albeit in rhyming couplets. And Percy understood well their warning—you may thirst for the exhilaration of true love, but if that love ends up unrequited, your fate will be a pitiful one of wandering the moors with a sheepdog as your only friend, writing sad poems that rhyme badly, and drinking homemade mead that gives you a headache.

So as Percy felt his heart dashing out onto the ice hoping to find Moira, it was with a sense of heightened peril. And it meant that every blink of a message popping up on his screen became an irrational roller coaster of hope and despair, the click, click, click of the roller coaster car going up as he opened the email ... and the plunge of a damn, damn, damn when it was someone other than Moira.

Percy wondered why scientists had gone through such elaborate experiments to prove Einstein's theory of relativity. They simply needed to ask someone falling in love to have proof of how every moment of uncertainty shot out to the ends of the universe and back, over and over, making every minute seem like an hour. And while such feelings might make for great lyrics in a Broadway musical, they felt like waterboarding when the chance for true love was in the offing.

Percy had begun to give in to a sense of resignation when an email address appeared in his inbox that had to be Moira's. Percy clicked the cursor and for the millionth time cursed his rural internet provider for being the cyber version of transatlantic mail transported via tramp steamer. Eventually, though, a message box popped up:

*Dear Percy, What a delight it was to talk yesterday. I am very glad, as I know the conference sponsors will be as well, that you will be presenting a paper. I am placing a packet in the mail this morning with details. I'm back in NYC and promise to be on the lookout for your William Butler Yeats in the '73 Chevy. Will tell him 'hi' for you. Best, M*

Percy realized he had been holding his breath since her message had appeared and exhaled slowly, a little light-headed from the lack of oxygen. He read the message again with the care of a cryptographer deciphering code. "Delight." Ah yes, delight was definitely a good word. Wouldn't one normally settle for a "how nice" or "it was a pleasure" if just writing a business letter? Surely, not every potential author who Moira contacted had received a "delight."

The next two lines, however, slightly depressed him. She was only "glad" he was attending? He pondered the likelihood that Moira had chosen such a bland word purposely. Perhaps these were the generic lines she had sent every conference participant. After all, Percy rationalized, she did need to convey some essential information, and he was charmed by the quaintness of her putting a "packet" in the mail.

And then he savored the last line and it's teasing tone. Flirtatious even? Maybe that was reading in too much, but certainly it was a gesture ... a flip of the hair and a light laugh that signified an interest in his world? And to sign it "M"? Oh, what he wouldn't give to see the emails she sent to the others and whether she had signed off as "M."

Percy's sense of well-being was warmed even more when a new email from Moira popped up with the subject line "P.S." He clicked the message immediately. After a maddening wait, the message materialized:

*And, oh, what do you think of inviting Casper Crenshaw? I know him slightly and believe he'd come if I asked. He strikes me as a rock star name that might generate interest in the conference. Can't figure out why he wasn't invited to start with. Thoughts? M*

*Thoughts?* Percy had a few. *How about damn, damn, damn, and quadruple damn.* Percy wasn't sure if an English professor could have an arch nemesis, but if so, Casper Crenshaw was Percy's.

Casper was everything Percy wasn't. He possessed striking good looks, wearing his hair with its luxurious, jet-black sheen pulled back in a ponytail, projecting a voice that hit every note like an Italian opera star, exuding a magnetism that left others swooning. Percy might have been able to forgive him these traits, except Crenshaw had used them not to become an actor or rock star but to pass himself off as a hip scholar who was the Neil deGrasse Tyson of Romantic Literature. Crenshaw's hit book, *The Dairymaid's Lament*, had landed him on *Oprah*, *The Daily Show*, and *Late Night*, flipping his ponytail around as he laughed heartily and peddled his favorite line that, "Poetry is far more erotic than pornography." Rumor had it that the *Playboy* channel had given him a six-figure sum for the rights to make a movie out of the book with Crenshaw narrating.

And what drove Percy mad was that he was certain Crenshaw actually could not care less about poetry. As Percy watched Crenshaw on television or heard him give a keynote address at a conference, he could just tell, feel it in the marrow of his bones, that Crenshaw loved his celebrity status far more than a beautifully crafted stanza. And as if that wasn't sufficient to provoke Percy's ire, Crenshaw somehow coupled his schtick with an air of superiority, implying he was the only one who could reveal the secrets of the poets. Did no one else see through this charade?

Yet, aware it would be dismissed as professional jealousy, Percy had never shared his thoughts. As he stared at the computer screen, he wondered if he should tell Moira what he really thought of Crenshaw.

Percy pushed back from the table and walked over to the window, still partly obscured by a thin sheen of ice from the night's frost. He blew on his coffee and felt the pleasing warmth of the mug on the palms of his hands as he looked out. The sun was starting to awaken the landscape, giving hints of the coming spring that sparked some ancient stirring of hope. Gazing at the foothills rolling up toward the mountains calmed him a bit, reminding him that nature has its own rhythm and mystery. Sometimes one simply has to trust.

*M, you make a good point. If Crenshaw is involved, you can be certain he will make sure others hear about it. I think you should do what you believe is best. Best, P*

# CHAPTER EIGHT

Fighting a wave of nausea, Special Agent Mike Forreo flashed back to a movie about a naval battle he had watched earlier that week. His head felt like the besieged submarine. Every closing of a door, each placing of a coffee cup on a saucer, was a depth-charge exploding next to his skull. His effort to focus was like a periscope slowly turning this way and that, vainly peering through a heavy fog that clung to the choppy sea.

After telling them to pick a time for the next meeting, Attles had gone ahead on his own and called it for 7 a.m. on Sunday, no doubt so that he could claim his frequent utterances of "Jesus Christ" were sanctified. Having straggled home at three the night before, Mike had to admit that Attles's loud, guttural growl as he entered the meeting room had him contemplating what eternal damnation must feel like.

Mike did his best to listen to Michelle and Carl as they reported on their task force activities, thankful they were going first, giving his head a chance to search for calmer seas. Mike listened as Michelle explained that a wiretap on all phones associated with Esteban Velasquez had turned up a series of conversations involving an upcoming meeting in Colombia. Mike was able to make a quarter turn of the periscope, just far enough to see Attles's face light up as he asked, "And do we know the kingpins who will be attending?"

Michelle did not meet Attles's gaze. "Not yet. So, it's kind of unclear, at this point, what is going on with the meeting, like I explained in the memo."

Attles's brow contracted inward as he barked, "Forget the memo," which they all understood meant he had not read it. "Jesus Christ, just tell me what the hell is going on."

"Well, the meeting is always talked about with code words, making it sound like it's a poetry conference."

"What the fuck?"

Carl, who had been monitoring electronic communications, chimed in, "Same thing, sir, with the email and text exchanges. All of them appear to be centered around a poetry conference." More meekly, he added, "And ... um ... that's why we suggested Operation Poetry Slam for the name of the task force."

Attles's face, which had been gathering itself into a storm mass of creases and wrinkles, suddenly relaxed. "Operation Poetry Slam, you say." Attles paused a moment, and Mike thought he had the look of someone judging the taste of a wine he had just sipped, although Mike was pretty sure Attles would never be caught within an arm's length of anything other than a bourbon straight up. "Hmm ... Operation Poetry Slam. That's goddamn good." Michelle, Mike, and Carl exchanged covert glances of surprise at the praise. Attles then continued, "So, it's like we slam the bastards in fucking poetic fashion."

Before the ensuing silence could become too obvious, Carl interjected a quick, "Yes, something like that."

Attles turned toward Mike. "Well, Forreo, you look even more like shit than usual. What in hell have you been doing?"

"I was on field duty this week. In fact, I was up until three last night hanging out at Esteban's."

"Hanging out?"

Mike couldn't tell if the incredulity in Attles's voice was that Attles couldn't fathom the idea of 'hanging out' or that the informality of the phrase rankled him the wrong way. "Excuse me, sir, undercover infiltration. I went to the bar where Esteban and his friends gather and managed to get myself invited with the group back to his apartment."

"And?"

"So we just basically talked."

Attles's voice was full of exasperation as he asked, "And do you care to tell us—excuse me, *share* with us—what *we* talked about into the wee hours of the night? I assume you were taping it all."

"The recorder malfunctioned." After he had returned to his apartment, Mike realized there was no way he was going to play a tape that would let Attles roast him like a pig on a spit at a luau. The recorder had "accidentally" dropped into the toilet bowl right after this revelation.

Mike was now tempted to pull the periscope down, plead illness, and leave, but whether out of a subconscious desire to poke a hornet's nest or from fatigue, he matter-of-factly continued, "But if you want to know specifics, we mainly discussed whether history would have been different if Cleopatra's nose had been shorter." Suddenly feeling more energetic, Mike plunged on, "So there was this guy Pascal, and he asked, you know, might the course of history have changed if Cleopatra hadn't been so beautiful that she'd been able to seduce all these Roman emperors? And turns out, there is a Roman coin that suggests that maybe Cleopatra wasn't so physically attractive after all, so you gotta also ask, 'Hey, what is beauty?'"

Mike had started to get caught up in the prior night's conversation again, encouraged by Carl and Michelle's interested looks. But then he saw that Attles's creviced face had turned so red it resembled a NASA photo of the surface of Mars. Mike did not need Mission Control to tell him to immediately abort. He had learned to think of Attles's shades of anger like paint chips, and it currently was at the danger level of Cherry Jubilee. "And, well, you get the idea. It was mainly just, you know, artsy-fartsy type talking. The good news, though, is I think they now trust me." This made Attles's face calm down a shade of red to Haute Pink. Time to play his trump card and bring Attles all the way back to his usual shade of Begonia.

"But here may be the key. I think I spotted Esteban's brother, Carlos, lurking in a back bedroom. He never came out and he clearly didn't want to be seen. But when I went back to use the bathroom, a bedroom door was closing, and I saw his reflection in a mirror of the bedroom before the door completely shut."

This piece of news made Attles practically glow Goldenrod. Attles had repeatedly touted Carlos as the heir to the Velasquez dynasty, and to hear he was in New York City was all the confirmation Attles needed that his instinct had been dead on—something was afoot.

Attles actually placed a hand on Mike's shoulder as he said, "Fucking good job, Forreo. We're going to slam those poets goddamn hard." It was the first "good job" Mike had ever heard from Attles. Rather than feeling great, though, Mike felt a strange pang of guilt. The nausea returned, and as his face turned a shade of Martini Olive, he ran for the bathroom.

# CHAPTER NINE

Yawning while doing a slow feline stretch, Esteban glanced around the apartment. The sun through the partially opened blinds cast a soft light into the living room, bouncing off the well-trod, hardwood floors that bore stains and spills dating back to the era of black-and-white television.

Bending down next to the sofa, he picked up a bright-red plastic cup with a leftover swig of cheap chardonnay and put it in the trash bag he clutched in his other hand. He slowly moved between the pieces of furniture doing the cleanup he now wished he had done before going to bed. In the corner, someone had set up empty beer bottles in a bowling pin arrangement so geometrically perfect, it would have made Spare Time Lanes two blocks over proud. Forty-five minutes later, the place was clean, the virtue of having an apartment not much larger than his bedroom back in Bogotá.

The apartment was one of the few times he had gone against his mother's wishes. Once it was decided he was coming to New York, she had immediately started condo shopping with a realtor on the Upper West Side, looking at stunning buildings offering services such as dog concierges and doormen turned out in freshly pressed uniforms that would have been fitting for a Prussian general.

But for Esteban, his time in New York was also his first shot at normalcy, free of all the baggage that came with being a Velasquez, and he'd insisted on finding "student housing." Granted, by grad student standards, the two-bedroom row house just outside the Village was not exactly squatting. Most of his classmates lived in tenements that would have been apt settings for a

Dickens' novel except for the laptops sitting on whatever seventh-hand piece of furniture acted as an ersatz desk. A studio apartment intended for one person often would be stuffed so full of students, fledgling actors, angst-filled poets, misunderstood balladeers, and down-on-their-luck friends needing a place to crash, it felt like being on a raft full of survivors tenaciously clinging to the sides. Esteban adored it.

Of course once his friends discovered his apartment didn't violate basic Human Rights' conventions, they often lobbied to end the evening at his place. And Esteban was happy to play host, especially since his monthly allowance at the time would have covered most of his friends' expenses for a year.

He studiously avoided, however, extravagances that would hint at just how much money was deposited into his account each month. True, you needed a corkscrew to open his bottles of wine rather than a twist of the wrist like the bottles his friends brought over, but the wineries were Australian, not Tuscan, and the clothes in his closet were from Goodwill, not Nieman Marcus (Esteban had soon learned the scavenger-hunt pleasures of joining his friends for an afternoon of scouring the Goodwill racks and finding a never-worn Ralph Lauren polo shirt).

So while he lived a very comfortable life compared to his grad student friends, who viewed macaroni and cheese eaten on a front stoop as Italian night alfresco, no one suspected that his family had Cayman Island holdings that would make a Goldman Sachs banker's balances look like a babysitter's savings account. Eventually, a group of friends gathered regularly every Saturday night at his place to drink, sing Beatles' songs off key, and have intensely serious discussions that would solve the world's problems if only they could remember their solutions the next day.

That, though, was before The Collapse, before Carlos came to live with him. In those hurried days before Esteban returned to New York, he and his father had talked for hours about the ins and outs of Esteban's plan. A psychoanalyst would have had a field day observing them. Once Esteban recovered from the shock that his father actually thought the idea would fly, Esteban at first assumed a somewhat righteous attitude. While not quite able to fully don the noble role of knight in shining armor since they were talking about smuggling kilos of cocaine, Esteban had stressed that his help was a one-time event to save his mother from the fallout.

Diego had remained silent through Esteban's admonishments, but then their talk had turned to hashing out the plan's details. And although Esteban was loath to admit it, he found himself slowly being impressed. He had, to be honest, never thought of his father as particularly intelligent. And while not quite the bonding experience of a father–son Boy Scouts' camping excursion, Esteban could see they were both surprised at the eagerness in their chatter as they brainstormed how to bring the plan to fruition. His father, it turned out, was Mozart when it came to orchestrating the movement of funds in perfect timing with the management of supply chains.

Despite Esteban's strong objections, Diego had insisted on Carlos going to New York. Esteban sensed his father's insistence was less because he thought Carlos could be of help in New York and more because Diego did not want Carlos's brooding presence back home. His father had a point, though. If Carlos stayed in Bogotá, he was liable to do something rash out of frustration or some misguided effort to save the family's fortune, and the plan critically depended on a veneer of legitimacy to have any hope.

So Carlos's fissionable, dark energy now resided in Esteban's tiny second bedroom, a Chernobyl waiting to happen, and he was at a loss with how to contain him. At first, he had tried including him in some gatherings with his friends, but between Carlos's macho brashness and his lack of English, it would have been as if Esteban attended a Monster Truck extravaganza and asked where one could find a cranberry scone and a spot of Earl Grey. Indeed, after watching Carlos painfully try to blend in with his group of friends, Esteban had an unfamiliar feeling when it came to Carlos—a sense of pity.

Carlos now pretty much kept to himself. He had mounted a chin-up bar in his bedroom's small doorframe, and he appeared to have taken a monastic vow to do fifty repetitions every time he bowed his head to enter or exit the room. During the daytime, when not bobbing up and down, he was sprawled on the couch with a protein shake of an unearthly fluorescent-green color, watching either a sporting event or a movie dubbed in Spanish.

Nights were what Carlos lived for, waiting impatiently for the sun to dip behind the skyline. Despite the chill that cut straight to one's bones as the winter wind rampaged between the high rises, he would leave for the clubs after dinner wearing an outfit so skintight, it would have enabled a medical student to practice her knowledge of human musculature right down to some rather spectacular pectoralis minors. And luckily for Carlos, his twelve-pack abs seemed to be the Rosetta Stone that transcended any language divide, as Esteban was constantly greeting someone new in the morning coming out of Carlos's room.

As frustrated as Esteban felt over what to do with Carlos, Moira, on the other hand, had proven to be every bit the brilliant academic consigliere he had hoped. He knew she had a keen mind, but what made her essential to the plan was her possession of a personality that was not easily bowed. He had repeatedly witnessed how Moira could firmly, and usually diplomatically, steer a situation to her advantage, whether it was a discussion of postmodern criticism or fending off an inebriated Casanova.

And it was this ability to make others walk a straight line he had been counting on. Getting the professors to agree to participate was always going to be the easy part. With the money they were offering to individuals driving cars with more rust than chrome, it was like asking a baby boomer sporting a gray ponytail if he minded recounting what it was like to have seen the Grateful Dead while Jerry Garcia was still alive.

The real challenge was to make sure they produced the manuscript by the deadline. Almost every professor he had ever met insisted the "creative process" could not be rushed. As brutal as they could be on students who failed to submit a paper on time, more than once he had overheard a professor tell a colleague how a looming deadline was only "a suggestion." And having walked hand-in-hand with Procrastination himself, Esteban was well aware how a cursor could stop midway in a sentence, as if suddenly bewitched by a paralyzing spell, and not be summoned back to animation until hours later after a "quick check" on social media had led through a series of byways, ending in an amazing article on how birds sleep with one eye open and half the brain awake and vigilant, while the other eye is closed with its half of the brain in deep REM sleep. And by then, it was time for one's own deep REM sleep, pushing off to the next day a resumption of the third sentence of the first paragraph of a paper examining the role of auditory imagery in *Romeo and Juliet*.

But Moira had reminded Esteban of his third-grade teacher, Sister Juanita, who wielded a wooden yardstick with the deftness of an Olympian fencer in encouraging her charges to toe the line. Moira had required each person to turn in at least ten pages a week, and whether it was a fear of displeasing Moira or the monetary incentive, Moira had ruthlessly driven Procrastination into exile. All but one professor had met their weekly goals. The one laggard was by far the most accomplished of the group, but Esteban had just authorized Moira to make a surprise visit to Percy Billings that week, and she no doubt would get him back on pace.

Esteban's only difficulty with Moira had been over what to do with Casper Crenshaw. Moira had suggested inviting him several times, and Esteban was unsure how to decipher her request. He had been touched by how Moira was trying to make the conference a success, even editing and sending suggestions to the authors as they submitted their weekly installment. And if one wanted to have a conference people talked about, Crenshaw would certainly be the type of celebrity academic one would invite as the keynote speaker.

Esteban also wondered, though, if Moira was in some way testing Esteban. Even someone of moderate intelligence would have questions about a conference being put together on such short notice with a list of very specific invitees and such generous honoraria. And Moira was anything but clueless. Quite to the contrary, she was the friend from one's childhood who would have deduced it was Professor Plum with the candlestick in the library before her competitors even had a second roll of the dice. Was she still raising Crenshaw because she suspected the conference might be about more than discourses on stanza structure, especially once she made it clear she could probably convince him to attend?

Crenshaw's flamboyant, narcissistic personality most definitely did not fit the profile of the low-key under-the-radar legitimacy they were striving for. Inviting Crenshaw would inject the constant anxiety of watching the obnoxious cousin at a wedding reception who with each successive drink got louder and louder, a sure sign he was on the verge of offering a spontaneous toast that would offend everyone from the bride's mother to the flower girl. But after Moira raised Crenshaw's name a third time, Esteban decided to at least sound open to the idea.

"You know, Moira, the more I think about it, you're right—we should invite him. But I looked at our budget, and unfortunately, it's simply maxed out, so I just don't see how we can make it happen. I'm sorry, Moira. I think it was a great idea in retrospect."

He knew that by signaling receptiveness to the idea he was running the risk Moira would figure out a way. He wasn't that surprised, therefore, when, a day later, Moira called back to say that Crenshaw felt "such a calling to spread poetry around the world" he would give a keynote address in return for nothing more than having his expenses paid. With grudging admiration and realizing his bluff had been called, Esteban agreed. Moira then added, "And, oh, he also said that because he's negotiating a British Broadcasting special, he wouldn't have time to write anything up. If we wanted to transcribe his remarks and publish them, however, that would be fine."

Was it just his imagination, or did Esteban accurately sense that Moira was sharing his eye roll? One of the ways a professor could establish Alpha status among his peers was to not have to write for a symposium when others did, the unsaid message being that one's thoughts were so valuable that just voicing them was manna for those hearing them. Esteban replied, "I suppose. We can't have ourselves interfering with his telly project, can we?"

After he got off the phone, he pulled out his running list of problems to brainstorm with his father the next time they talked. He wrote "egomaniac coming" right beneath "Carlos becoming restless," and then struck out "egomaniac," wrote "asshole," and sighed.

# CHAPTER TEN

Casper Crenshaw tapped off his phone and triumphantly leaned back in his chair as his eyes made their familiar orbit around his study. Modeled after Lord Byron's library with built-in bookcases of mahogany that glowed from the light cast by refurbished eighteenth-century lamps, the study was his pride and joy.

His gaze arrived first at the bound collection of the Brontë sisters' works perched at eye level in the bookcase directly across from his desk. He was always secretly amused when guests browsing his books would remark how impressed they were that he gave such prominent placement to early women writers. Little did they know that his interior designer had chosen the volumes for their striking robin's-egg-blue bindings, "the perfect color to be the centerpiece for all our other selections." The designer's other book choices led to a wide-ranging—and expensive—array of literature, all characterized by gorgeous bindings of various hues the designer had found by perusing vintage bookstores throughout New England. Forays that Casper had paid for handsomely by the hour.

The venture, though, had yielded unexpected dividends beyond the creation of a pleasing ocular experience. A columnist for *BIBLIO* magazine had heard of his growing collection, and after oohing and aahing as she surveyed the books arranged with premeditated haphazardness, wrote a piece about him, *The New Renaissance Collector: When Eclectic Meets Erudite.*

He had overheard one of his colleagues describe the accompanying photos as "library porn," but he took the comment in a flattering way. The shot of him casually leaning against one of the bookshelves clad in a Damson-plum colored shirt, sleeves rolled halfway up his forearms, shirt unbuttoned one hole shy of a GQ model, was now framed and proudly hung behind his desk. Most helpfully, the article opened the doors of Manhattan penthouses and Hampton summerhouses belonging to wealthy bibliophiles anxious to meet this handsome harbinger of a new Renaissance. These collectors would often ask for a chance to ogle his collection, and while Casper was not prone to being self-conscious, eventually he had randomly placed bookmarks in a number of the works to give the appearance that a volume had occasionally been pulled down and read.

The call from Moira Shaughnessy felt like a vindication. While she was but a grad student—indeed, precisely because she was a mere grad student— her cold shoulder at the recent conference had for a brief moment made him wonder if he might be slipping.

He had stared hard that night into the hotel mirror. There were a few silver streaks beginning to marble his hair, but his stylist had assured him just a week earlier that they gave him a "distinguished look." How had she put it? "If they weren't there, I'd recommend we put them in as enhancements." He did contemplate that at some future point he would have to abandon the ponytail when it went from whispering "hip" to shouting "damn it, I'm not old," but at forty-one, he surely had another decade before having to bring out the shears. And his morning and nightly moisturizing routine, undertaken with the solemnity and constancy of an Inca sacramental rite, had so far acted as the intended scarecrow in keeping the crow's feet away.

Gazing at his reflection that night, he had assured himself that his celebrity star power had never shone brighter. But hidden behind his self-assurances lurked an insecurity of just how quickly everything could slip away. And, indeed, in the still moments of a sleepless night, Casper involuntarily tiptoed toward a fleeting recognition that Fortuna, the goddess of luck, had caressed his life in a way few ever experienced.

Casper's teenage years—a time when he still went by his given first name of Larry—had been a rock-and-roll lyric celebrating the joys of youth brought to life, using his athletic build and good looks to play the role of James Dean on the small stage of his rural high school. An indifferent but naturally bright student, he had done well enough to gain entrance into the University of Wisconsin, where he floundered throughout his freshman classes until a coed in his English Lit class made a remark forever changing his life.

"You know," she observed, her fingertip caressing the photo next to the textbook's snippet of *Don Juan* that was the subject of the class discussion, "if you grew your hair longer, you'd look just like this photograph of Lord Byron."

Casper, whose mind had been mulling over which frat party to attend that night, stared hard at the photo and rather liked the dashing look peering up from the page. *And she's right*, he thought. Even if he was not Byron's doppelgänger, his hair had the right sheen and amount of curl that if grown down to his shoulders would make him look ready to embark on a nineteenth-century Grand Tour.

And so he had grown his locks and adopted what he saw as the rakish look and attitude of a Romantic poet. He read a biography of Byron, and then of Shelley and Coleridge in quick succession, and while their poetry did not greatly interest him, their lives did.

Disappointed to learn that absinthe was no longer available, he turned to Colombia Gold bud as a creative substitute and began to show up to class and free-associate on the poems under discussion. To his delighted surprise, he found his classmates, and even a few professors, started to treat him as though he was peering deep into the mysteries of the world. And upon his return from the winter holidays, he abandoned the name of Larry and started using his middle name of Casper, a family name dating back to a great-great-great-uncle who had been transported to Australia for murder. A tale he was quick to trot out whenever someone commented on never having met a Casper before.

He advanced through the curriculum of an English major with middling success, but then in his senior year, increasingly worried by what lie ahead,

Casper took a seminar from Professor Stanilus Sandiman. Sandiman had been a rising scholarly star with a specialty in Romantic poetry before three disastrous marriages, Scottish whiskey, and creeping ennui gradually transformed him into the washed-up professor who was the set piece of every academic parody ever written or filmed.

In his prime, Sandiman had been witty and charming with a devilish sense of humor, but disillusionment soured his wit into a toxic sarcasm that cleared out friends and colleagues with a Three Mile Island level of effectiveness. Showing up only to teach class, his English department colleagues disappeared with surprising athleticism into their offices if they heard his voice booming down the hall.

Casper had signed up for Sandiman's seminar, "Unfinished Business: Poetry as Procrastination," based on the class's reputation as an easy "A" so long as one put up with the teacher's withering comments from behind the podium and didn't report him to the department chair for behavior unbecoming a professor. But much to Casper's surprise, he found Sandiman's classroom soliloquies, what Sandiman called his "Glenfiddich lectures," to be insightful, especially if Casper himself preceded class with an aperitif of three long bong hits.

The lectures rarely delved deep into actual poetry but fell more generally into the category of life lessons, such as not letting youthful ambition dissuade you from accepting an offer to teach at what snobs might deem a "lesser college" with its campus suspended on a sunny promontory overlooking the Pacific Ocean. Otherwise, Sandiman intoned, with a sense of despair far more powerful than any poem Casper had ever read, one might find one's self in his late fifties staring out an ice-encrusted window into the descending gloom of a Wisconsin winter afternoon.

On the one paper that Sandiman managed to grade and return to the four students enrolled in the course, he had simply written on Casper's paper, "Never forget that Achilles did not have to die." Casper had no idea what the comment meant, especially since the paper had nothing to do with Achilles, but years later would repeat it to others with a mystic's assuredness when wanting to sound wise.

Perhaps Sandiman was simply flattered by Casper's unveiled admiration, or maybe he had some residual desire to leave a legacy before his cirrhosis-ridden liver gave way, but for the first time in years, he took an interest in a student. True, Sandiman was now largely *persona non gratis* in the halls of the academy after one too many a drunken rant at a conference, most infamously, dropping his trousers after one presenter's talk and mooning as he did a full orbit around the room shouting, "How about this for a post-modern bimodal critique?"

Sandiman, however, still knew his way around the palace's back corridors with the confidence of one who had once dined at the head table, and he became determined to smuggle Casper inside. Realizing Casper would never find his way into the inner rooms through a penetrating heuristic analysis of *Finnegans Wake*, he finagled, bullied, and blustered until Casper was finally admitted into the graduate program with Sandiman as his doctoral advisor.

Sandiman's last gift to Casper was a manuscript he handed him as he lay dying in a hospice bed, slightly delusional with morphine and too fatigued to talk. Typed on a brittle parchment that Casper later learned was called onion skin paper, it had been Sandiman's final effort, hammered out on a manual Remington typewriter at the height of his powers decades earlier, just before he plunged over the cliff into alcoholic apathy.

Sandiman never could explain to himself why, after arduously laboring to write the book, he had not undertaken the comparatively easy task of finding a publisher. He knew the slender manuscript was good, that it could have purchased a brief truce of credibility with his peers, but it sat in the middle of his dining room table for almost three years, like some religious artifact that had fallen into the hands of a non-believer who did not know what to do with it. Eventually Sandiman had slid the pages inside a manila envelope and placed it in the bottom drawer of his desk, where the paper had aged and yellowed over the years.

His final act before zipping his overnight bag and departing for the hospice ward, was to slowly shuffle to his study, raise the envelope out of the desk drawer that had served as the manuscript's crypt for three decades, and place it in the bag so he could give it to Casper.

Casper had taken the envelope home with him the night that Sandiman finally crossed the bar. He later felt a twinge of guilt for first wondering if the mysterious envelope might contain an insurance policy with him as the beneficiary. Upon seeing that the contents were nothing but an old manuscript, he had casually put it aside, where it languished on his desk for several weeks. Finally, Casper poured himself a Scotch in honor of Sandiman and began perusing the sheath of pages that he exhumed from the envelope. And while Casper might not have been a top-shelf scholar, with the crinkling turn of each page he realized that what he was reading was special.

Barely a hundred pages long, *The Dairymaid's Lament* was, at first glance, a clever scholar's look at how poets had utilized peasant girls as crucial but unappreciated foils to the main characters who commanded the verses' spotlight. What the paper really was about, however, and what vividly emerged from the shadows as one exquisitely crafted sentence followed another, was the excruciating heartbreak of unrequited love. By the time Casper turned the last page, he was, literally, breathless.

Some in Casper's situation might have wondered what Sandiman wished to be done with the manuscript, but Casper harbored no doubt what his mentor wanted. He retyped the manuscript on his computer, word for word, only correcting a stray typo here and there, and submitted it to his dissertation committee with a heartfelt dedication to his advisor.

While the committee members wondered among themselves how Casper, who until then had not made a ripple let alone a splash, could have written such a beautiful piece of literary exposition, they could not deny the dissertation was superb. The professors suppressed what doubts they had over the work's origins, in part from a begrudging homage to Sandiman, but far more so out of a lurking suspicion that Sandiman had almost certainly laid a posthumous trap to ensnare them if they crossed his prized student.

To enhance his chances of obtaining a teaching position, Casper then convinced a small, fledgling publisher, Flyspeck Press, to publish a limited run of two hundred copies of *The Dairymaid's Lament*. He knew that without an established reputation or major publisher, *The Dairymaid's Lament* was destined for the subterranean holdings of the few college libraries that would obtain the book. These underground stacks were a library's catacombs where books too obscure to claim a space in the main reading room were sent to rest undisturbed for eternity, other than, perhaps, by a stoned student who pressed the wrong elevator button and ended up wandering the stacks of Lower Level 6 in a daze. But all of this was fine with Casper. He still could say he was now published, and that fact, along with the curiosity value of having been Sandiman's protégé, might land him a few interviews.

Casper, however, did not realize that Fortuna had only just begun to show her affection and was about to set in motion a chain reaction of events. Christine Mastra, the graphic designer commissioned by Flyspeck Press to come up with a cover for Casper's book, had just returned from a honeymoon in Italy where, between servings of gelato and glasses of Chianti, she had become completely smitten with the painter Sandro Botticelli. For the book's cover, Mastra highlighted one of the figures in Botticelli's *The Daughters of Jethro*, a beautiful fresco from the Sistine Chapel that depicts a procession winding its way down a hill. The young woman brought to life by Botticelli's brush tip, and who now graced the book's cover, might go unnoticed as part of the train of people if not for a faraway look of weary longing that magnetically draws the viewer to her gaze.

And it was this poignant look of weariness on a face otherwise so beautiful and innocent that months later stared up at Talia Tyche from the Caraville College Library's new acquisitions desk. Talia, the reference librarian at Caraville, was just a few painful days removed from the final collapse of a long-term relationship. Upon seeing the book cover amid the pile of newly arrived books, she reflexively reached for the slender volume as if to find mutual solace with Botticelli's creation. Two hours later, Talia had finished *The Dairymaid's Lament* and was reverently placing it on the "Great New Reads" shelf that greeted all those entering the library.

Even this favor of Fortuna's, however, would not have been enough if Talia's placing of the book had not coincided with Caraville College's Reunion Weekend and the return of alumnae Theresa Jackson. After her graduation, Theresa had gained fame as a swimsuit supermodel, and her marriage to basketball superstar Rodney Baskitt had commandeered the tabloids' attention as if it were a Buckingham Palace wedding.

But while Theresa's curves busting out of a bikini may originally have been what put her in the spotlight, it was an IQ busting out of the Bell Curve that had made her a highly prized talk show guest, full of wit and insight. So when Theresa nostalgically paid a trip to the college library that had been her sanctuary while negotiating her transition to adulthood, it took only a slight push from Fortuna for Theresa's eyes to land on the cover of *The Dairymaid's Lament* as she pulled open the library's doors. Soon, the book was cradled in her long, slender fingers, and her eyes were eagerly devouring the first paragraph.

Theresa's later breathless social media posts to her legion of followers extolling "this beautiful meditation on love found and lost" soon had Flyspeck Press doing book printings in the thousands. The rise of *The Dairymaid's Lament* up the bestseller lists became meteoric once it was selected as an Oprah Book Club choice. Invited on the show to talk about his book, the pony-tailed Casper charmed Oprah and her television audience, and soon Casper—"the professor who makes poetry hip" as Oprah took to calling him—became an *Oprah* regular along with Dr. Phil. Even then Fortuna was not yet quite ready to take a well-earned rest, and within a year, Casper had secured a position in a prestigious university after a wealthy donor gave the funds to create a position that everyone understood was meant for Casper—at least if the university also wanted the new basketball arena the donor offered to build.

And Casper would have slept soundly knowing he was one of Fortuna's favorites if not for the knowledge that Fortuna enjoyed the gaming tables. And in the still moments of the night when sleep would not come and he wrestled the blankets, Casper needed to summon all of his effort to drown out the distant click-click-click of a ball spinning around a roulette wheel.

# CHAPTER ELEVEN

Having intercepted the text a day earlier from Esteban to his father setting up the phone call, Agent Michelle Esperanza had plenty of time to amble down to the surveillance room and drowsily push the button marked "Listen" at the appointed hour. She repeatedly twirled and untwirled a strand of hair around her index finger, a habit carried over from her childhood whenever she was bored. One would think the habit would at least have saved her the expense of curling her hair at a salon, except her unruly, thick locks were already so naturally curly and frizzy she never needed an umbrella except in a torrential downpour. Given that wiretap subjects who suspected they were being listened to rarely let anything of evidentiary value slip, Michelle assumed her curls were headed for a strenuous tonsorial workout as she settled in.

Having been raised in a household with grandparents who had fled Castro during the Revolution, a topic of aggrievement they raised so often it eventually became a hair-twirling moment, Michelle had no need for a translator when listening to Esteban and Diego. And although the DEA side of her brain might be bored as she listened, eavesdropping on Diego and Esteban still had a captivating effect. She found herself paying as much attention to how they talked to each other as she did to the details of what they were saying. It felt a bit like one of those French films —or were they Italian?—that she had watched in her Intro to Film Studies class back when she was an undergrad. She had discovered that the subtitles scrolling across the bottom of the screen mattered far less than the emotion one could feel jumping out from the intonations and the way the characters responded to each other.

She remembered one scene in particular where the actor and actress had looked at each other radiating such a sensuous heat that Michelle thought the screen was going to combust. She also recalled being amazed anyone was remotely surprised when the tabloids later reported they had been carrying on a clandestine love affair at the time of the filming. Spoken words, Michelle learned, often were only smoke signals for what was actually being said, which is why she always refused to rely on written transcripts if a recording was available, and preferred listening live if possible.

The first half hour of Esteban and Diego's conversation centered, as usual, on the details of an upcoming poetry symposium. Her hair did a continuous salsa dance around her finger as they discussed publication contracts, housing logistics, and arrangements with a local ceramic firm to make Grecian urn replicas as mementos for the speakers.

When she had first started listening to Esteban and Diego's discussions, Michelle would be on the edge of her seat, convinced code words were being used to describe a major narcotics transaction. But she had spent hours verifying that, indeed, an academic conference was to take place in Bogotá, bringing in a variety of American scholars to interact with Latin American academics on the topic of Romantic poetry.

After perusing the biographies of the speakers that Esteban had discussed with his father, and even calling a few on the pretense of being a graduate student interested in their work, Michelle had come to only two possible conclusions—either this was a genuine conference to discuss topics such as "Chiasmus Echoes," or this was the most brilliant long con in the history of humankind, beginning with a drug lord cultivating literary-inclined students years ago, nurturing them through the long slog of a doctorate program, and then having them enter a profession where their odds of getting a tenure-track teaching position were about the same as being drafted as a power forward in the NBA.

Throughout this first part of the conversation, Diego pretty much maintained a business-like tone, with a pinch of machismo thrown in here and there, while Esteban largely listened and replied in an evenhanded way that Michelle admired. Her hair-twirling came to an abrupt stop, therefore, when she heard Diego's voice downshift from alpha-male register to a tone just shy of deferential.

"So, I looked at the poem you keep talking about, 'Ode to a Grecian Urn'." Diego paused as if expecting a reply, and when one wasn't forthcoming, continued, "It is very hard to read."

Michelle pictured Esteban on the other end of the line coming out of a shocked silence as he said, "Yes, that's a hard one, especially if one doesn't speak English. Even with a good translation, there would be many archaic— old—words that would be difficult to understand today."

Diego gave a short, hard laugh. "I know what archaic means. But I meant hard as in, it makes you think about how quickly things slip away, change. I found myself envying the youth frozen in time painted on the vase." Michelle could hear the rustle of a page before Diego recited in a surprisingly wistful voice:

*"Hermosísima joven, nunca cesa tu canto debajo de esos árboles que no pierden sus hojas."*

The lines caught Michelle by surprise, and just as she was thinking to herself, *I'll have to look those up*, Esteban softly repeated the lines to himself in English, "Fair youth beneath the trees, thou canst not leave Thy song, nor ever can those trees be bare."

Shifting back to Spanish, Esteban asked his father, "But would you trade places with him despite his eternal youth? Since he's frozen in time, he can never kiss his love, even though he is so close to taking her into his arms."

"I don't know, and perhaps easier for you to ask since you are young. I ... I like the idea of being frozen forever in a moment when everything still seems possible." After another pause, Diego continued, "I had Rafael, the new bodyguard—I don't think you've met him yet—run down to the library and get me a book with a photo of the vase as I very much wanted to see it. I think, though, I need to see it in person. Maybe we could do that someday. I think it is in a museum in London."

Oh what Michelle would give to see Esteban's face. She had eavesdropped on enough conversations and so thoroughly researched the Velasquez family background that she was confident this was the first time Diego ever proposed a father–son outing, let alone to a museum rather than to a strip club. No doubt Esteban was wondering if his father had accidentally ingested some of the family's "export" product.

"I'd like that very much, Father. I've never seen it in person either."

Diego's voice cut back in, *"La belleza es verdad, la verdad es belleza."* ('beauty is truth, truth beauty' Michelle quickly translated in her head). Hearing the words through the resonance of Diego's deep voice, the lines almost sounded as if they were being played by a cello. "Maybe we should make those lines of the poem the theme of the conference. I could have the sign company make it a banner to hang behind the stage."

"Yes, Father, that would be nice. Actually, it would be perfect." Esteban then hurriedly added, "Hey, I have to run to class. I'll email you to set up our next call."

Michelle half-expected to hear an "I love you" from one of them, a sentiment she had never heard either say or even inch toward, but all that followed was Diego saying "Hasta luego" and then the line going dead. Michelle hoped Esteban was not driving to class. With the daze he must be in, good luck convincing a police officer that running a stoplight wasn't because he was on hallucinogens. She also realized that although she was running out of hidden real estate to place it, and being a federal law enforcement agent they had to be hidden, *La belleza es verdad, la verdad es belleza* would make a damn good tattoo.

# CHAPTER TWELVE

Blowing on her hands to dispel the early morning chill, Moira exited the airport serving the region around Arcadia. Flying from LaGuardia with its throngs of passengers to an airport that at peak time had two baggage carousels spinning with luggage, felt like switching from a station blasting out Guns N' Roses to hearing "Take Five" on the local jazz station.

The sleepy young woman at the counter had offered her a choice of a Ford Taurus or a Chevrolet Lumina, cars even her grandmother would balk at as too boring. Deciding to live it up, she chose the baby-blue Lumina over the Taurus's winter gray.

Within a few minutes, Moira was on the highway that gently wound its way through the foothills, leading to the valley where Arcadia would lay nestled like a cat enjoying a spot of afternoon sun. Glancing out the window, she was captivated by the way a band of sunshine could play off a field starting to don its springtime green, making it easy to believe that sprites and faeries were sleeping in the forest just beyond after a midnight rave.

An hour later, she stopped at a diner in one of the tiny towns that dotted the highway for a cup of coffee to fortify her for the last part of the drive. As she swung her legs out of the car and stretched, the cool freshness of the morning air that had migrated down the mountains during the night was so delicious, she wished she could have that feeling at will.

Perhaps that could be her brilliant idea—"artisan atmospheres"—if a teaching job did not materialize. Lord knows, the artisan booze industry was overly fermented with PhDs who had turned an expertise in a discipline like pre-Aztecan art or ancient Greek philosophy into distilleries with pithy names like Totonac Gin and Skeptical Spirits.

As the caffeine slowly traversed her circulatory system, Moira started imagining herself as the sommelier of her vapor distillery—perhaps *Memories by Proust* would be the name?—pulling miniature zeppelins filled with various "captured breaths of nature" from table to table.

"Oh, my dear sir and madam, I think you might like to start with an olfactory snifter of our First Dewfall straight from a secluded lake in the Rockies, captured just as the sun crests Longs Peak and the rays begin to warm the air. Please be sure to savor the hints of primrose and cinquefoil as their petals catch the morning's first light."

The next hour and a half was spent working her way through aromas that took her to various times in her past—freshly baked cookies, bed sheets newly out of the dryer, the smell of her father's coat as he came into the house after raking leaves. By the time she was finishing up Zummer Zephyr, comprised of a late-August bouquet of freshly mowed grass spiced by a steak just thrown on the grill, she realized she was about to enter Arcadia. She recalled from her first visit how this lone road into town swept around the hilltop of pasture straight ahead and then … and there it was. Arcadia appeared magically, as if it were a Brigadoon that would disappear back into the mists as soon as the traveler went farther on her way.

Arcadia had been through ups and downs in the centuries that followed its founding by Scotch-Irish settlers as a supply outpost for those who tilled the surrounding land. The establishment of its namesake college two hundred years ago, though, had proven to be the persevering heartbeat that over the years had kept the small town alive through depressions, recessions, wars, the Disco Era, and, most recently, the closing of several factories in the surrounding county.

Early black-and-white photos showed a village with dirt roads that had gradually added houses and businesses that today's real estate brochures gushed "exuded centuries-old charm." The type of charm that caused parents dropping their kids off at the start of the semester to excitedly think to themselves, "Perhaps I should trade my Dolce & Gabbana suit for overalls and open up a hardware store!" Sometimes one could practically see the thought bubble above their heads as they imagined themselves rocking back on two legs of a chair, debating a local whether one should saw the pin or tail of a dovetail joint first. These rustic imaginations presupposed, of course, that at some point the daydreaming corporate lawyer would learn what a dovetail joint was.

These escape fantasies experienced an uptick in volume once a former New York City day trader moved to Arcadia and used his Wall Street windfall to open up a trendy coffee store, Joltin' Joe. Soon, Joltin' Joe's biscotti and Frappuccinos were outpacing biscuits and gravy at the local diner as Arcadia's leading breakfast order. And now that a sushi restaurant had opened, making Arcadia a contender in the Spicy Tuna Rolls Per Capita Index (STRPC)—a measure that purveyors of the ubiquitous "Best Small Towns in America" lists seemed to heavily rely upon—parental fantasies reached a fever pitch.

Eventually, though, the realization would hit that one could consume only so many Rainbow Rolls before the next culinary option became a Chinese takeout on the edge of town serving a General Tso's Chicken that began plotting gastrointestinal uprisings with the first bite. And when that realization dawned, daydreams of being surrounded by wing nuts, U-bolts, and interlocking washers instead of spreadsheets would join shipwrecked fantasies from one's youth of living on a sailboat anchored in a turquoise Tahitian lagoon.

As Moira drove into Arcadia, spring was just beginning its shock and awe: dogwoods dropping petals of the purest white, clusters of magnolias blossoming cream and pink against leaves of deep green, azaleas exploding in purples so intense they seemed surreal. Moira pulled over in front of a little boutique housed in a historic building whose bricks glowed a vibrant red in the late-morning sun. A mannequin surrounded by straw purses and hats sported a sleeveless, white dress splashed with bright-yellow daisies in the store's display window. Moira could easily imagine it doing a little jig when she looked away.

But even if nature was tap dancing through the streets, hardly a person was to be seen. As Moira learned when she phoned the English department, the college was on spring break, which explained why the town, which appeared perpetually ready for a nap even at the height of the school year, had slipped into a deep slumber.

Fortunately, Moira had Percy's address from the contract he had signed to participate in the conference and a map she had obtained at the Visitor's Center during her first visit. She felt a twinge of guilt that she had let Esteban convince her the visit should be unannounced, and although it wasn't quite the same as a SWAT team launching a surprise predawn raid— well, okay, it was nothing at all like that—she worried Percy would be resentful. That said, she also felt, for reasons she deliberately was leaving unexplored, a voyeuristic curiosity to see Percy unannounced.

She pointed the Lumina toward a distant ridge the map identified as Hogback Mountain, turned onto Hawthorn Blossom, and set out toward the address Percy had written down. A left onto Highland Mary that took her past turnoffs for roads with names like Emmet's Inch and Eagle's Mile started her wondering, and by the time she had passed Mute Milton Lane, Road Not Taken Road, Lake Isle of Innisfree Circle, and Paradise Regained Turnpike, she knew her first question for Percy.

As Moira started up the gravel driveway next to a mailbox marked 41 Raven Way, she spotted Percy sitting in a rocking chair on the front porch, clad in jeans and a red-and-black-checkered flannel shirt. The house itself sat atop a small hillock with a panoramic view of the surrounding woods and pastures, framed by a backdrop of a mountain wearing a cloak of low-lying clouds.

Unlike the houses in town that looked like a *Southern Living* magazine cover, Percy's home proudly wore its years, maintained but not primped. Its white, clapboard siding basked in the morning rays beneath a green metal roof that had faded over the years to a soft laurel hue, a few patches of rust peeking through along the edges. Moira was reminded of a movie she had seen in her youth when a soldier-son, beaten down by the war, struggles back to his family and, in the final scene, gazes at his homestead as comforting sounds of home life—dishes clattering, children's voices—drift up to him through the open windows.

The sound of stones bouncing up into the car's undercarriage as the tires tried to gain a grip caused Percy to casually look up and then intensify his stare as he realized it wasn't a usual suspect, like the UPS driver, coming up the drive. When he saw Moira pop her head out of the car, his face lit up in a surprised smile.

"Ah, well, it's about time," he said, coming down the porch steps. "I was wondering what had happened to my pizza order. I called it in three weeks ago. Was it the extra cheese that took so long?"

"No, it was having to stop and read a poem every time I passed a road. Mute Milton Lane? Ancient Mariner Bypass? What the hell is that all about?" Percy gave an unguarded laugh that had Moira smiling. Forget eyes being the window to the soul. In her book, it was a person's willingness to laugh.

Percy settled in, leaning against the hood of the car, enjoying the residual warmth of the engine against his body. "It's actually a wonderful story. All these roads used to simply be called names like Route 162 or Highway 48, and they had no house numbers. If you were invited to someone's house, you'd get directions like, 'It's the house five oak trees past the Simpson's old barn—mind you, not their new barn with the pretty metal roof, but the old one—and if you get to where the Wilsons used to live before Thelma tragically passed after the rabid raccoon bite, you know you've gone too far.' But then the 911 emergency call network was extended out into the county, and it was thought that having an ambulance driver doing a scavenger hunt for a heart attack victim probably wasn't the greatest idea. Since the dispatcher would need a street name and house number, all the streets and roads suddenly needed to be named.

"They first turned the job over to a very literal-thinking fellow in the highway department, and soon, people were being told they were going to live on streets with names like Sewer Plant Place or County Dump Drive. Go figure, that didn't sit well with a lot of homeowners."

Moira laughed as she added, "Um ... yes, I can see where that wouldn't exactly do wonders for property values."

"Very true, and after a few raucous county commission meetings, they agreed to try again and turned the task over to a young woman who had just graduated from Arcadia and was working as a summer intern before starting law school. As you probably have surmised by this point, my dear

Watson"—he gave a knowing nod in Moira's direction—"this intern had been a literature major, and she brought considerable creativity to the task. Rather than going with no-brainers like Whispering Pines Lane, she went back through her poetry anthologies and scattered wonderful poem titles throughout the county.

"The commissioners expected some pushback but didn't get much, other than for a few names. I recall Howl Boulevard, Nevermore, Slouching Towards Bethlehem, and Paradise Lost being deep-sixed. And, oh yes, she had a soft spot for William Blake, and while you'll find a Tyger Tyger Lane a mile or so from here, Misers Land and Beggars Rags didn't sit well with the homeowners on those roads. But most people were quite happy, and today, a student could probably do a review for a poetry AP exam simply by driving around the county."

"Do you know what became of her? Your former student?"

"Unfortunately, last I heard, I think she ended up on Bleak House Highway. Did really well in law school and landed in some huge law firm's wealth management section. I'm probably projecting, but I can't help thinking that assisting rich people find loopholes in the Internal Revenue Code isn't particularly rewarding."

Moira, who had several half-filled law school applications sitting on a shelf in her apartment, kicked some of the gravel with the toe of her boot. "Well, I'm guessing she at least doesn't have insomnia from her student loans hanging over her like a guillotine."

Percy, who had been thinking how alive he felt standing in the sun leaning against the car and talking to Moira, suddenly felt like he had stepped on her toes right in the middle of a fox trot. "Oh, of course, and we never know, do we? What makes other people happy, I mean."

Moira, who had been enjoying the fox trot and had not taken any offense, took the lead. "Oh, it's true, isn't it," she said with a soothing smile. "I once got a ticket and had to take a remedial driver's safety class. The only one that I could get a spot in was called something like 'Traffic Safety Improv.' It was held in an abandoned Mexican restaurant, and the insane idea was that it'd be fun because it was taught by a comedian.

"At first, I felt so sorry for the guy trying to do a stand-up routine while teaching traffic rules to an audience that desperately—and I mean desperately—didn't want to be there. And, then, about an hour in, I realized he was really into it. I mean, like, really into it. He even wore a tux, as if he was onstage at Caesar's Palace. The occasional groan he'd elicit was for him a shot of adrenaline. I went from wanting to commit hari-kari out of sympathy to loving that he was able to feel like he was in Vegas, despite the sombreros hanging on the walls and lingering smell of salsa and stale beer. By the end, I remember thinking, 'Now, damn, that is real talent.'"

"And his best joke?"

"Oh God, let me think. I'm terrible at remembering jokes, and they all were truly groaners." Moira scrunched her forehead as she tried to recall the punchlines. "Okay, why did the stoplight turn red? No, wait ... yeah, that's it. Why did the stoplight turn red?"

Grinning, both at her story and because their dance steps were once again in sync, Percy played the straight man. "I don't know, why?"

"Well, if you had to change in front of everyone, you'd turn red too."

Shaking his head, Percy laughed and grandly swept his arm up toward the porch. "Come up to the house and tell me some more?"

# CHAPTER THIRTEEN

Percy eased into the rocking chair Moira had seen him sitting in when she pulled up. A stack of student papers was perched on a weathered end table next to him. Moving toward a porch swing across from the rocking chair, Moira warily eyed the chains hanging down from the porch ceiling.

"This safe?"

"What we call living dangerously out here, but pretty sure it will hold you."

Moira scooched backward onto the swing as if she was getting on a carnival ride, and after an abrupt backward movement of the swing when she finally sat down, she was soon gently swinging back and forth. She realized it had been years since she sat on a porch swing and had forgotten how soothing the metronome-like movement could be.

"So, to what do I owe this pleasure? Arcadia tends not to be a place people just randomly end up."

Blushing slightly with guilt, Moira pulled her scarf tighter, one hand slightly tugging on each end. "Esteban wanted me to check in with you."

"Well, I'm not sure if I should be honored or insulted that he thought it would take an in-person visit from you to motivate me. I'm pretty sure my paper doesn't justify a house call," adding, at seeing her growing discomfort, "not that I'm complaining."

Moira glanced up toward the top of the large oak that shaded the porch, its crown just starting to fill with leaves, then returned her look to Percy. "Yes, well, Esteban is being rather insistent, I guess because he's trying to pull this off in such a short time frame. He calls me pretty much every day for an update. And, you know, I didn't object when he said I should check up on you in person."

Not for the first time, Percy wished for the screenplay of the scene he found himself cast in. There was a scene in an old Woody Allen comedy where a subscript scrolled across the bottom to explain what the characters actually meant with their spoken words, and as he watched the bangs of Moira's hair sway gently back and forth in time with the swing, he wondered, *So why didn't you object? Because you didn't want to upset Esteban or because you wanted to see me?*

Ignoring the monologue in his head, Percy said, "Here's the thing. I've actually been hitting the page goals, pecking away at it between grading essays on"—he picked up the paper on the top of the stack next to his chair—"*If Ophelia Was a Spice Girl* ... hmm, not sure what that one is about. Anyway, I just didn't feel like I had a draft ready to share yet."

"And what are these musings you're keeping to yourself?"

"I'm exploring my newfound religiosity."

Moira gave the quizzical look she knew Percy was hoping for. "I hadn't pegged you as particularly religious ... or reborn."

Percy smiled. "Oh, I am the most religious atheist I know. I've become quite convinced that the Greeks and Romans had it right. Our lives are subject to deities who love to mess with us mortals for their amusement."

Nodding at the mountain peak they could see on the horizon silhouetted green against the crisp blue of the late-morning sky, Moira asked, "And they reside on Hogback Mountain?"

"Well, Bacchus, for sure. I've seen the empty wine bottles when I hike up there. Used to think it was high school students leaving them, but now accept that Bacchus is simply fond of sweet, cheap wines and isn't very environmentally conscious."

Giving a look of indulgence, Moira asked, "And the paper you're writing fits into your theological exploration ... how?"

"So I'm using Hercules as a figure in various poems and stories to explore my religious tenets."

"Hercules is your hero?" Moira's voice carried a hint and a half of incredulity.

"Absolutely, and not just because I share his physique." Percy rocked in his chair, enjoying the moment. "Seriously, though, I saw a sculpture of him back when I was a student doing my obligatory post-graduation backpacking trip through Europe. I sensed even then as a callow youth that the statue had special meaning, and lately, I've thought about it more and more. The Farnese Hercules ... have you seen it?"

Moira shook her head no. "I'm afraid my bank account after graduation meant the only sculptures I was going to see were the gnomes on the lawn of my parents' neighbor."

"Well, while not nearly as terrifying as a ceramic gnome at dusk, you must see it." Giving a hurried, "Be right back," he sprang up out of his chair as it rocked forward and quickly entered the house as the chair continued to rock in his wake.

Laconically swaying her legs back and forth to keep the porch swing moving, Moira's gaze wandered across the lawn where clusters of purple crocuses were proudly making their brief but triumphant annual appearance. It was one of those early spring days where the sun made all the difference in one's comfort. Occasionally a cloud would drift in front of the sun, and she'd feel a chill rapidly moving up her body until the sun popped out again with a warming glow.

"Here." Percy came bustling back, the wooden screen door giving a satisfying *whack* as it snapped shut like a mousetrap being tripped. He handed two photos to Moira. "I have these taped on the wall above my writing desk."

Pointing at the first photo, Percy said, "So at first glance, the sculpture is our classic image of Hercules, right? Over ten feet tall, washboard abs, looks like a model for a men's fitness magazine. But look at this one," and his finger moved over to the second photo, showing a close-up of the sculpture's face. "He's sometimes called the weary Hercules because of his expression."

Moira studied the photo. Hercules's head was tiredly tilted toward the ground, eyes downcast beneath a furrow running across the brow, and his body, although the envy of any bodybuilder, was exhaustedly leaning on a club as if it were a crutch. Moira's soft laughter filled the porch. "Oh God, I have so worn that expression myself—'I did what you asked, I have nothing left in the tank, but you're going to ask for more, aren't you?'"

Percy's eyes lit up. "You nailed it! Do you remember the labors of Hercules?"

"Only in a vague, comic book sort of way."

"So he was supposed to perform ten labors as a penance."

"For what?"

"Killing his wife and children—"

Moira interrupted, "And this is who you want to emulate?"

Excitedly, Percy exclaimed, "But he only killed them because Hera, Zeus's wife, hated Hercules and cast a spell to make him mad. She detested him from the start, you know, put a viper in his crib because he was Zeus's illegitimate son with a mortal. Anyway, so Hercules was supposed to do ten labors for atonement ... little things, you know, like killing the Hydra, slaying a three-headed giant, capturing human-eating horses. But after he finished the tenth labor, he was told that two of them hadn't counted because of an unexpected rule change, so he had two more to do."

"Well hell, no wonder he looks weary."

"True, but here's the beauty of weary Hercules. If you go to the rear side of the sculpture"—Percy pulled out a photo from his flannel shirt's front pocket as if he were performing a magic trick and handed it to Moira— "you'll see that in the hand hidden behind his back, he's holding the golden apples of the Hesperides that he had to steal as his eleventh labor."

"I might add," Moira noted, wagging her hand back and forth as if she'd just touched a hot stovetop, "that's also a rather impressive posterior he's sporting."

"There is that," Percy agreed, chuckling, "but out of insecurity, I prefer to focus on the apples. And this is Hercules's lesson for all of us—the gods are going to mess with you out of sport or spite, they're going to change the rules, you're going to get weary, Lord, you're going to get weary. But if you're clever and keep your wits, you may just complete the labor. Plus, you might get washboard abs in the process."

"And this is your theology?"

"You know the question that theologians always struggle to answer— Why do bad things happen to good people if there is a benevolent God? Well, I've never heard a great answer to it. It is always platitudes like, 'God doesn't give you more than you can handle,' or 'God has His purpose, we just can't see it.' Well, the Greeks and Romans had a great reply—it's because the gods are constantly meddling in the affairs of mortals, whether it be in love or war, helping their favorites and tormenting those who get on their wrong side."

"Or one could just not believe in deities?"

"Ah, but then you have to believe in pure chance and happenstance, and there is too much chaos in the world that seems orchestrated for that to be true, don't you think? I don't often pretend to know more than Einstein, but when he said, 'God does not play dice with the universe,' I think, in fact, the gods are often at the craps table, and we're the chips they're using to make the wagers. Now, it's not all bad for us. I like to think, for instance, of the gods throwing mortals together for their amusement to see if they click and fall in love ..."

"Sort of a divinities version of match.com? In my case, I think it has been Ares. He was the god of war, right?"

Percy grinned. "That he was," and plopped back down onto the rocking chair. "And now that you say it, I can think of quite a few couples where Ares appeared to play matchmaker."

Moira gave Percy a long, inquiring look as she swung and he rocked. "I can't quite tell how much you're just having fun and how much of this you believe," she said. Gesturing with a movement of her head toward some freshly tilled fields across the road, the upturned black soil looking startlingly rich and fertile, she asked, "If I wandered back into those pastures, I'm not going to find a sacrificial slab to Zeus, am I?"

"Of course not. Pure-white oxen are exceedingly hard to find." Noticing a shadow of exasperation falling across Moira's face, he stopped rocking. "Truth is, while I'm not ready to start living my life by soothsayers' reading of animal entrails, I don't see the Greek myths as just entertaining supernatural stories. In many ways, the stories accord more with my view of the human condition than most modern religions and philosophies ... a heady mix of mystery, intrigue, the sense there is some order to the world we can't quite grasp that sometimes brings us happiness, but just as often sorrow, and we should do our best to shape our destiny knowing full well Hermes or Athena or Cupid might decide to make jest with us."

"I'm guessing, then, you're not a fan of the Jefferson Bible," Moira observed.

Percy cocked his head inquisitively. "I haven't really thought about it. What are you thinking?"

"Do you know the essence of it?"

Percy turned his eyes up toward the sky as if the heavens were about to deliver the answer he was searching his memory for, and then returned his look to Moira. "Remind me?"

"In his retirement, Thomas Jefferson took several Bibles and cut out words and verses from the New Testament—and I mean, literally cut out, with a razor blade—that he then glued onto pages to make his own Bible. I always find it such a striking image to envision this storied man in his dotage, sitting by candlelight in Monticello, razor blade, glue pot, and magnifying glass in hand, spending his evenings trying to edit the Bible to fit his worldview. Shows a certain self-confidence, I think."

Percy slowly nodded in agreement. "That it does, and certainly wouldn't be nearly as vivid an image if he had done the cut-and-paste on a laptop, but why wouldn't I like the Jefferson Bible?"

"Because what he was omitting were the miracles and supernatural events. No turning of water into wine, Lazarus remains in his tomb ...."

"Ah, I see your point. For sure, Jefferson wouldn't have gone for gods constantly shape-shifting into swans and bulls because of amorous desires, and I'm guessing battling human-eating horses and Minotaurs also wouldn't make the cut ... so to speak." Percy paused and stared at the floor of the porch as the rocker slowed. "I wonder, though, if Jefferson's efforts to bend the Bible to his will wasn't a bit of a Herculean-type act itself? A weary Jefferson in his Monticello study, facing life's final act after some rather impressive labors of his own, and he takes—has the audacity to take—a text that his society views as sacred and inviolable, and says, 'I think I can do better.'"

Percy, who had been musing with the look of a mathematician trying to puzzle out a difficult theorem, returned his gaze to Moira. "Sorry, you clearly got me thinking."

"Oh, not at all." She smiled. "I'm just glad I can tell Esteban that you've been working on the paper." Glancing up at the sky, she said, "Looks like the sun god ... Helios? ... is saying it's lunchtime. And even if he isn't, my stomach is."

Percy looked a tad sheepish. "I fear my peanut butter sandwich did not earn the rave reviews I had hoped for from the Bon Appétit food critic. Want to go downtown and grab a bite?"

# CHAPTER FOURTEEN

Percy fought off disappointment as he drove into town with Moira following in her rental car. After Percy had suggested they take one car, Moira revealed she needed to head off to the airport after lunch as she had an evening flight back to New York.

After the surprise of seeing Moira pull up in the driveway had subsided, part of Percy hoped he'd discover that his feelings about Moira had been only a momentary attraction, dissipating once put to the test of seeing each other again in person. Life, in many ways, would be much easier if the emotional waters remained calm.

But the late morning spent on the porch had left Percy feeling a giddy joy, and he didn't want their time to end. His deflated mood upon hearing that Moira was headed back to the city had not been helped when he caught his reflection in the front picture window while walking to the car. Definitely not an image that would make any sculptor want to pick up a chisel.

Recriminations were also taking place in the car right behind. As Moira tailed Percy's aging Subaru Outback, dodging the occasional pothole in the poetically christened roads, she was chastising herself for having, as always, played it safe. She had no pressing need to retreat home that night and she was certain Esteban would have sprung for a hotel room in Arcadia.

Having studiously avoided anything that might pass as a romantic interest in recent years, she had wanted to make sure she had an excuse to leave. But while swinging on the front porch, she definitely felt something with Percy. Gravitational pull? Invisible connection? Force field? Her high school physics lessons might finally serve a purpose in describing something both real but intangible. If they lived in the same city, having to leave after lunch would be no big deal, simply a prelude to another time while she analyzed her feelings in the interim. With the conference not far away, however, built-in opportunities to see each other would soon vanish, and she might actually have to figure out if she wanted to reenter the world of relationships.

Her reverie was broken as Percy pulled into a parking spot on the largely deserted street. Above the spot hung a simply adorned sign with "Fifth Chance Saloon" painted in large block letters. Turning the steering wheel, Moira swung in behind Percy's car, put on the parking brake, and exited the car asking, "What happened to the first four chances?"

Percy smiled and tried to sound cheery. "No one knows. When the owner, Reggie, first moved here and opened the place up, he called it the Second Chance Saloon. Over the years, must be close to ten now, without any outward rhyme or reason, the sign would unexpectedly be painted over and the number ticked up a notch. If you asked him why, he'd just shake his head. Reggie puts the quiet"—Percy used his fingers to make air quotes— "in 'quiet type.' But for a cold beer and local food served well, can't beat it. He was ahead of the curve before the farm-to-table movement became all the rage."

The restaurant was one spacious room with a long, wooden bar extending almost the entire length of the far wall as one entered. The bar glowed a deep-chocolate color, oiled to a gleam. On the opposite wall stood a series of booths made from the same dusky wood.

A large man stood behind the bar, his mottled black-and-gray beard wildly cascading down his chest like a whitewater rapid before pooling atop an ample belly. He greeted them with a slow nod as they entered, and Percy offered a return nod.

The room was darkening as the day slipped toward mid-afternoon. A couple was in the booth farthest back of the otherwise empty room. Percy and Moira slid into opposite sides of a booth close to the front window that offered some sunlight to dispel the dimness.

As Moira studied the menu, Percy stole a look across the booth. Her bright-green eyes flickered back and forth as she scanned the day's specials. What was it about someone that made them beautiful? He had never quite figured it out. He had read descriptions of psychology studies finding that factors like symmetrical features made one more likely to be seen as gorgeous or handsome, but he often was surprised by who others saw as attractive. In Moira's case, though, he knew from watching how others looked at her that, despite her best efforts to downplay her beauty by refusing to put on makeup and wearing outfits looking like she had just spent two weeks hiking the Appalachian Trail, others saw her beauty as well.

After they had given their orders to Reggie, who in jotting down their choices uttered a total of three words in addition to a few "huh-huhs," Percy broke the silence while they waited for their food. "So, if you could be anyone who is not famous, who would it be?" Moira looked at him quizzically, and Percy laughed softly. "Odd question. Out of the blue, I know. It was the icebreaker question asked at some event I was at a few years ago to welcome new faculty. I admit I rolled my eyes when I heard it, but then as I listened to everyone's answers, I realized it works as kind of a brilliant Rorschach inkblot test."

"So you'll be psychoanalyzing me based on my answer? Good to hear there is no pressure."

Percy smiled warmly in return. "Incredible pressure. I might even bring Reggie over for his input, although if you have a plane to catch, we might not have the time to listen to what would undoubtedly be a lengthy diagnosis."

Moira leaned back against the booth, drumming her fingers on the table as she thought. "Can I name two?"

"Ah, a rule bender. I already have the start of a diagnosis. But, yes, go ahead with two."

"Well, the first one would be a man I heard speak at the New York City library branch near where I live. He was older by this point"—Moira's voice took on an excited tone—"but he had grown up *in* the library. His father was the janitor for the library, and as part of the job's compensation, they were given a small apartment on the library's top floor looking out over the borough.

"So every night after the library closed down, he, as a kid, would have the entire library as *his* place. Can you even imagine?" Moira's eyes were wide and beaming. "He did everything there. Learned how to ride a bike by weaving in and out of the stacks." Moira gave a little giggle at the thought. "And, of course," and she seemed to Percy to be almost swooning as she continued, "he was surrounded by all those books ... the magic of a library all to yourself. I mean, seriously, can you begin to fathom playing hide-and-seek with your sister, hiding behind volumes of Shakespeare while watching her trying to sneak up through the periodicals? Forget Hogwarts. That was a magical childhood."

Moira glanced up to see Percy looking at her with a fondness he couldn't disguise. "Well," Percy said in an affected, learned tone, "I'd certainly say we've had a breakthrough in today's session. I believe we've identified that living amid the Dewey decimal system, literally, is a clear life goal. I'm not sure, though, that isn't a bit like telling a compulsive gambler they might enjoy living in a casino."

They paused as Reggie brought over their dishes and set them down on the table without a word. Moira looked admiringly at her fresh trout stuffed with goat cheese, while Percy began to painstakingly construct a barbeque brisket-and-slaw sandwich in a manner suggesting considerable prior construction experience.

"Anyway," Percy resumed before taking a bite, "can't wait to hear who your other choice is."

Moira's face took on a somber cast as she looked up toward the ceiling as if an angel might be camped out in the rafters. "A person named Scharlette Holdman. I spent the summer after my junior year of college working as an intern for her down in New Orleans."

"Well, you can't beat a summer of eating crawfish étouffée at the Gumbo Shop and listening to jazz on Bourbon Street afterward," Percy offered. Moira's eyebrows knitted together in a way that made Percy immediately regret his flippancy.

"I wish." Moira hesitated. "No, actually, I don't wish, even if the summer wasn't what one would exactly call fun. Scharlette may be the most amazing woman I've ever known. I had taken a class on criminal justice that spring, and we read about this woman who helped defend people where prosecutors were seeking the death penalty. I wrote her what I guess you'd call a fan letter, and next thing I knew, she'd invited me down to work with her that summer.

"She wasn't a lawyer, she was kind of this"—again she hesitated—"ordinary person who simply believed everyone had good in them, even murderers, and went out to prove it. She'd investigate a defendant's past and find the heartbreaking stories—the whippings by sadistic fathers, the sexual abuse by an uncle, the mental illness that went back generations—that helped you understand how someone ended up doing a terrible act. And she did this when practically no one else did, while she was a single mom living on like six hundred dollars a month, and for no other reason than she believed in the humanity of someone almost everyone else had given up on as evil."

Moira's eyes slowly returned from the ceiling to Percy, who had sufficient sense to remain quiet. "And she did it with humor. Can you believe it? Even in the darkest times that summer, she would find a way to make us smile. One time, a judge was going to let someone be executed even though he was intellectually impaired, could barely function his IQ was so low. The judge was okay letting him be executed because a state psychiatrist said he was competent enough to play *fucking* tic-tac-toe."

Moira paused, seemingly a bit taken aback by her own outburst, and then unexpectedly laughed. "But Scharlette remembered as a little girl seeing a chicken play tic-tac-toe at a county fair, and so she went out and found a tic-tac-toe-playing chicken to show the judge that such a skill might not be the best psychological tool for determining if someone understood what was going on. Sometimes I think my memories of Scharlette's faith in humanity is what keeps me from retreating into a convent when I'm ready to give up on people."

In a quiet voice, Percy asked, "Did you think about continuing on with her?"

Moira absentmindedly ran a finger around the top of her water glass. "I did, but I wasn't sure I could handle it. I mean, she was brilliant, worked with brilliant lawyers, but still lost a lot of clients ... people she'd grown close to, fought for, only to have her last moments with them"—Moira looked up as if uncertain Percy could understand—"to be telling them she loved them as they started their walk to the electric chair."

Moira audibly took a deep breath. "I went back to college after that summer, and I've never really figured out if it was cowardice on my part or that I was being realistic about what I could do, but I applied to grad school and now"—she paused, spread her hands out palms up, and looked around—"here I am eating lunch in the Fifth Chance Saloon."

Unsure whether to speak, Percy eventually said, "Trying to untangle the past always reminds me of an Oscar Wilde quote, something like, 'The truth is rarely pure, and certainly never simple.' Probably never more true than when we try to figure ourselves out."

Percy and Moira sat enveloped in silence for a moment before Moira asked behind a weak smile, "And the non-famous person who you'd like to be?"

Percy sat up straight and replied, "Scot Halpin."

"You have the non-famous part down," Moira said, shaking her head in amusement. "Never heard of him."

"Well, first, I have to set the scene. San Francisco, 1973. Free love, flowers in your hair, drugs galore, and the rock band The Who comes to town." As a quick afterthought, Percy looked at Moira intently and asked, "You know who The Who are, right?"

Moira thought about trying a 'Who's on First' routine, but simply said, "Won't Get Fooled Again, Pinball Wizard. Should I go on?"

"You got it. Sorry, didn't mean to doubt your rock 'n' roll cred. Anyway, The Who is playing a concert and their drummer, Keith Moon ..." Percy cocked his head at Moira.

"Still with you. I spent a fair share of time with my dad's music collection."

"Great, so Keith Moon at some point takes some horse tranquilizer washed down with brandy ..." This time, it was Moira's turn to give a skeptical look. "It's true! Listen, it's no wonder he'd overdose a few years later."

Moira watched as Percy's hands started moving in time with the rising eagerness of his voice. "And he ends up passing out on stage during ... oh my, and there you go. It was actually during your song, 'Won't Get Fooled Again.' And so The Who are without a drummer. And Peter Townshend." Percy started to pause, but Moira gave him a 'don't even think about asking if I know who Peter Townshend is, one of the greatest guitarists ever' look.

Percy quickly continued, "So Townshend asks the crowd, 'Are there any drummers out there?' Enter Scot Halpin, who had arrived super early to be near the stage, a nineteen-year-old kid from middle-of-nowhere Iowa, newly arrived in San Francisco. And Halpin's buddy starts yelling, 'He can do it, he can do it!' Next thing Halpin knows, famous concert promoter Bill Graham has come over and is asking him, 'Can you play?'"

Percy's eyes lit up with enthusiasm, as if perhaps he'd had a side of horse tranquilizer with his brisket sandwich. "And Halpin, despite not being a professional drummer and not even touching a drum kit for a year, says 'Yes.' Next thing he knows, he's behind the drums playing songs like 'Magic Bus' and 'My Generation'"—Percy began banging away with imaginary drumsticks—"while Townshend does windmills on the guitar, and Roger Daltrey prances around the stage looking like some blond-curled, fifteenth-century knight."

Percy shook his head in wonderment. "Now it's my turn to ask, can you imagine? Halpin is on stage playing with the goddamn Who." Seemingly exhausted, as if he himself had just pounded out a two-hour drum set, Percy slouched back against the booth. "By the way, there is great black-and-white footage of all this out there."

"So," Moira asked, her voice expressing uncertainty of where to go with her question, "your dream is to be a drummer in a rock group?"

Percy laughed. "Maybe when I was nineteen." A shadow of seriousness moved across Percy's face as he averted his eyes to the back of his hands. "No. My fear," he said, looking up with a tentative motion, "is that I wouldn't have said 'yes' if that moment had come my way." His face brightened as he added, "Not that everything is about Hercules, but that kid's courage to seize the moment and not worry about making a fool of himself was to me Herculean. The gods gave him his chance. He might fail, but he said, 'Damn it, I'll give it a go' and try to steal the golden apples."

"You know, Percy," Moira said in a tender tone, "some might say the gods have already favored you—a tenured faculty position, recognized scholar despite being relatively young. Jesus, what I wouldn't give for that. Perhaps you're not the kid waiting to be invited up on stage but already part of the band?"

Percy gave her a pained look. "I sound unbelievably ungrateful, don't I? And Lord knows, the gods love to punish ingratitude. But truth is, it's always felt more like a trap than a bestowed favor."

"But you love literature, don't you?"

"Oh I do, I do. I'd join you in that library apartment in a heartbeat, surrounded by volumes of Austen and Shakespeare and Dickens as our bunkmates. But it's different to teach and write about literature than to read a book and savor it. And I know I'm sounding incredibly churlish and unappreciative, but ... ugh, this will sound like I'm nine years old in pajamas with rocket ships on them, but"—Moira could see him weigh whether to continue on—"I feel like I'm an astronomer who wants to be the astronaut. They both love the planets, but one wants to venture to the stars, not just gaze."

"So you want to be a novelist or a poet, just not a critic?" Moira's eyes crinkled with a smile. "I'm assuming you don't literally want to become an astronaut."

Percy gave a barely perceptible sigh of sadness. "Ah, I'm even more of a mess than that. I have my half-written novel, like every English prof, and somewhere are stashed my poems from my youthful existentialist stage when I smoked filterless cigarettes and donned a perpetual look of deep contemplation. Truth is, though, I don't really know. I like to think that if it were the eighteenth century, I'd go down to the wharves and try to sign on to a ship going out on a scientific exploration to help collect samples from unknown lands. But," he said, smiling wanly, "my tendency to get seasick might nix that. The optimist in me says I'll know the opportunity when it comes along. The pessimist says I'll just keep doing what everyone tells me

I'm good at, that I won't grab the drumsticks if they're held out to me since I know no one else sees me as the drummer."

Moira started to sympathetically reach for Percy's hand when her eyes caught the time on her watch, and she sat up with a start. "Holy shit! I can't believe how long we've been here. I need to jet or I'll miss my plane. Sorry to be in a rush all of a sudden." She stood up and started quickly gathering up her coat and belongings, then paused and looked at Percy. "Hey listen, I have no doubt you've got a gig coming your way."

"Thanks," Percy said trying to sound upbeat as they walked out to her car. The sun was in its late-afternoon descent, and the lengthening shadows lent a distinct chill to the air.

Moira opened the car door and tossed her purse and coat on the passenger seat. She turned and, with a sarcastic effort at donning a schoolmarm's attitude, wagged her finger at Percy. "Do get me that paper by the deadline, or I may have to refer you to the principal."

Percy gave a half-hearted smile. "Yes, ma'am."

As Moira drove away, he started self-analyzing everything he had said and wondered how he could have sounded so foolish. *And damn,* he thought to himself, *why can't Cupid simply send a handwritten note. Those arrows actually hurt.*

# CHAPTER FIFTEEN

Agent Michelle Esperanza liked working Sunday mornings. The building was largely deserted except for the security personnel at the front desk who had drawn the short straw. From their hungover looks, a few had decided to deal with their bad scheduling karma by coming straight to work after their night out. Spotlighted by the unforgiving fluorescent lights that lit up the cavernous entryway with its massive walls of faux green granite, their sunken eyes suggested *Saturday Night Fever* had morphed into Sunday Morning Anguish.

Michelle, however, had her Sunday morning routine down, starting with a stop at the hole-in-the-wall Cuban coffee stand a block from the office. And it literally was a hole in the wall. You shouted your order through a tiny window punched out of a cinderblock wall shedding lime-green paint, and, moments later, a burly hand would thrust your order out.

She always ordered a *colada*, a sweet Cuban espresso so strong that one was handed small plastic thimbles along with the larger Styrofoam cup that contained the brew. The idea was that one should share the *colada* and its Code Red level of caffeine with one's friends by pouring it into the thimbles, the caffeine equivalent of doing shots of tequila from a bottle with one's compadres. Michelle, though, preferred drinking straight from the bottle, tossing the thimbles into the nearest trash can and downing the Styrofoam cup's contents straightaway. Soon she'd be able to tackle a two-week backlog of paperwork by the lunch hour.

Best of all, on Sunday mornings she could crank up her music as she worked without worries of disturbing anyone in adjoining offices. Michelle looked up from the papers splayed out in front of her, ready to chime in with her favorite song in the world as Bob Marley began singing "Three Little Birds." With a voice pure and true that had earned her second place in her high school talent contest—and let's face it, who realistically could compete with Marty 'Fastfingers' finger-snapping rendition of Lynyrd Skynyrd's "Free Bird"—Michelle began sweetly singing and thinking every little thing really was going to be all right.

"You know," a voice sounding like an exploding oil tanker interrupted, "Bob Marley was dead less than a year after that song dropped as a single."

Michelle let out a mangled "all right" as she spun around in her office chair to see Bronson Attles leaning against her office's doorframe, his head tilted down vulture-like.

Michelle tried to get out a question, "What ...," but Attles cut her off.

"Yeah, whenever I hear that song, I think, 'Well, Bob Marley, those three little birds by your doorstep weren't very smart, were they? Didn't tell you about the mole between your toes that was going to kill you.' Maybe if they had shouted 'melanoma' at him instead of 'don't worry about a thing,' Marley would still be alive today."

Michelle just stared at Attles, who gave a little shrug, lifted his head, and disappeared down the hallway. Then, before she could begin to recover, he reappeared in the doorway to add, "And don't forget the task force meeting tomorrow at zero seven hundred hours."

Michelle angrily snapped off the music and turned to look out her window just as a pigeon staged a Jackson Pollack exhibition with its droppings. Her therapist was right, she thought. She needed to get into a different line of work.

# CHAPTER SIXTEEN

Moira creased the brown wrapping paper along the side of the box, her tongue unconsciously stuck out in concentration as she taped it down with precise symmetry. Three sides down, one to go. Moira paused to take a sip of her tea and smiled as her eyes wandered to the baseball trading card secured by a red thumbtack to the corkboard above her desk.

The player's photo was faded from the card's travels over the years. Its place of honor, through a succession of dorm rooms and apartments, had sometimes led to a placement that caught a few hours of the afternoon sun. That the greens and yellows were not as vivid as they once had been, and the cardboard edges slightly frayed, did not bother Moira. The card did not reside between a Maya Angelou quote and a treasured photo of her family because she collected baseball cards to trade like a stockbroker. Nor was it because she was a rabid baseball fan. She wouldn't need the fingers on one hand to tally the number of current baseball players she could name.

No, it was because the card brought her back to her father. Closing her eyes, she was standing in her dad's study, enshrouded in fragrant pipe smoke. Mike Gallego's baseball card sat precariously perched in a stand at the edge of an old dining room table, full of scratches and random coffee cup stains, that served as his desk. As chaotic as the scattering of books and papers could become, what her dad referred to as "his archaeological dig," the baseball card always kept vigil.

She grew up thinking Mike Gallego must be a baseball legend, like Babe Ruth, Willie Mays, or Mickey Mantle, names she knew from books and movies. Then one afternoon on the school playground following a wicked game of dodgeball, her fourth-grade classmates were talking about their favorite players, and she volunteered that Mike Gallego was her dad's favorite player. Given the confused looks her comment provoked, Moira quickly realized most people, even Manny Juarez, who could name every member of the 1927 Yankees, did not have the foggiest idea who Mike Gallego was.

When she asked her dad that night why his favorite player was someone who none of her classmates had heard of, his laugh had echoed off the study's walls as it so often did. With her dad, a question that delighted him was almost always responded to with laughter, and he was delighted a lot. Sometimes people who did not know him well were taken aback, even affronted, thinking he was laughing at them rather than relishing their comment or question. But once you knew him, you knew that his *basso profundo* laugh reflexively booming out was the highest honor he could bestow, his equivalent to pinning a French Legion of Honor medal onto the person's chest.

"Ah, Moira," he began with gusto, "let me tell you about Mike Gallego. You've heard of the players who hit the big home runs?"

Moira nodded her head tentatively, sensing a setup.

"Well, that's not Mike Gallego."

Moira smiled.

"Perhaps you've heard of pitchers who can throw one-hundred-mile-an-hour fastballs and rack up strikeouts like your older brother racks up parking tickets?"

Moira, always a quick study of where her dad's thinking was leading, chimed in, "Not Mike Gallego."

Her dad grinned. "The speedster who steals bases like you eat M&Ms?"

Moira happily volunteered in reply, "Not Mike Gallego!"

Her dad responded with an equally ebullient, "Correct you are!"

"So who, then, you ask, is this Mike Gallego," her dad said, picking up the stand holding the baseball card and rubbing his chin as if he were Sherlock Holmes pondering a perplexing clue. "Well, he played shortstop on the Oakland A's when they won three American League Championships and a World Series. He was surrounded by stupendous home run hitters, flame-throwing pitchers, and masterful base stealers. Though"—he took his eyes away from the card and stared at Moira in mock seriousness—"we've established he wasn't one of them."

He continued, "But here's the thing. Even with all those great players, the A's wouldn't have won those championships without him. He was the steady glove in the infield who was always in the right place at the right time. He was the player who sacrificed himself to advance the runner rather than swinging for the fences." He paused, realizing Moira had watched little baseball, and asked, "Do you know what 'advancing the runner' means?"

Moira gave a slight shake of her head. "No, not really."

"And why would you? Well, to score a run in baseball, a player must touch all the bases—get to first, then second, then third, and eventually to home, right?"

Moira semi-indignantly replied, "I *do* know that."

Her dad smiled. "Well, it is a lot harder, of course, to get someone who has gotten a hit all the way to home plate if that player is on first base rather than second or third. So sometimes the best play is for the next batter instead of swinging for the fences and the big hit, which would make the headlines, to instead hit or bunt the ball where they'll get thrown out but the player on first will advance to second. We colorfully call that a sacrifice bunt or fly because, well, they sacrifice themselves to advance the runner. Then the big guns who bat next can bring the runner home and get their photo splashed on the front page of the sports section. Advancing the runner, doing all the little but essential things that enabled the great players to be great? Now *that* was Mike Gallego."

Suddenly, in a way that startled Moira slightly, he looked at her intently. "Does this make sense to you? We always celebrate the person who does the glorious act but too often forget those who make the glory possible by performing their role with pride and perfection." He paused. "Do you know who The Rolling Stones are?"

Moira again shook her head no, this time offering up an, "I'm ten years old" in her defense.

Her dad rumbled out a laugh. "Fair and true, so just the right age to begin your education." Humming cheerfully, he turned around and ran his finger up and down a CD holder, ultimately picking out three CDs that he placed on the desk. "Listen to these before you go to bed tonight—one Who, one Beatles, and one Stones should start you off.

"Now then, each of these bands will have members who everybody goes gaga over. For The Rolling Stones, it's this guy, Mick Jagger," he said, pointing at someone on the CD cover with lips that looked like an exotic tropical fruit, "and this one, Keith Richards. Jagger is the lead vocalist and Richards the rhythm guitarist. Huge stars both.

"Most people don't know this one, though," and her dad's finger moved over to another face on the cover. "He's their bass player, Bill Wyman. So while Richards plays these incredible soaring riffs on his guitar, and Jagger shakes his booty all around the stage as if he were a human bottle rocket, Wyman is basically the band's human metronome." Her dad started strumming what Moira surmised must be an imaginary bass guitar. "He plays a sequence of chords over and over throughout the song. It isn't glamorous, which is why the Beatles,"—he picked up the Beatles CD and started waving it as if he was a lawyer showing a damning document to the jury—"fought over which one had to be the bass player."

"And yet ..." Her dad paused, put down the Beatles CD and picked up his pipe from the ashtray, drawing several puffs before blowing out a jet stream of smoke toward the ceiling. "And yet, the bass player lays the foundation of the song, which the other band members build off of. What, Moira, is the most beautiful building you can think of?"

Moira, who had just done a social studies report on France and was smitten with all things French, eagerly replied, "Notre Dame."

Her dad nodded thoughtfully. "Yes, beautiful for sure." Taking her little hand in his free hand, he said, "I'd love to take you there some day." He released her hand and leaned back in his chair. "And is Notre Dame so wondrous, my dear, because of its foundation?"

Moira creased her forehead questioningly in reply.

Her dad chuckled at her expression. "Precisely. No one thinks of the bricklayers and stone masons who dug the trenches and laid the brick and stone that has allowed that magnificent cathedral to stand for almost a thousand years. Nearly a thousand years, Moira, think of it! But all of the gorgeous artwork and stained glass and spires ... and the gargoyles—oh my God, how could I almost have forgotten the gargoyles—are able to speak to us today only because someone figured out how to build a foundation that would last practically forever." He leaned in conspiratorially and half-whispered to Moira, "By the way, if you ever meet Mick Jagger, don't tell him I kind of compared him to a gargoyle, okay?" Moira giggled and nodded her head in agreement.

"I heard someone once say the bass player is the crust of the apple pie. You notice if it is burnt or too doughy, but if done right, it is the perfect base for the fruit and filling. Get it, the base?" he said, laughing so hard he began coughing. Calming himself down, he went on, "The Rolling Stones, in other words, would not have been great"—he set down his pipe and started miming someone using a rolling pin to roll a pie crust—"without a Bill Wyman as the crust."

"And, so," Moira asked with an uncertainty she often felt within the whirlwind of metaphors and flights of fancy her dad loved to sweep her up in, "Mike Gallego is also the crust?"

"Yes! Though we might have a deep culinary debate over what kind of pie the A's were. I guess given their garish yellow-and-green uniforms, probably lemon meringue or key lime," he said with a huge smile. "But here's the thing," his voice took on a conspiratorial tone, "and will you promise me this as a sacred oath?" Moira earnestly bobbed her red hair up and down.

"Never let anyone call the Mike Gallegos of the world mediocre or average, okay? I'm serious about this. He was"—her dad turned over the baseball card and looked at its back—"a .239 career hitter. Many would say that's, at best, average and probably mediocre for a professional baseball player. But Moira, you know now that isn't true, right? He always advanced the runner."

Her dad's voice was tinged with the slightest tone of pleading, a tone she rarely heard during his gregarious, rambling ruminations. Without quite understanding why at the time, Moira had reached out and held his hand and again bobbed her head up and down.

He had died her senior year of high school from an aneurysm. "From the kiss of an angel," one of her mom's friends had comfortingly said, and she thought her dad would have liked that and bestowed an honorary chuckle on the friend's effort at kindness. His passing also gave Moira new insight into his devotion to Mike Gallego.

A middle school civics teacher who also coached the girls' basketball team, she had seen him every night trying to figure out some new way to make the walking hormonal petri dishes, also known as thirteen-year-olds, care about the Federalist Papers, or worrying about how to best support one of his players struggling with a home full of screaming and demeaning insults.

Yet despite how hard he worked, Moira recognized early on that when someone learned what he did, his position as a junior high teacher did not command the same respect as her friends' parents whose jobs took place in oak-paneled courtrooms or operating rooms full of glistening stainless steel, instead of a classroom with asbestos lurking in the ceiling tiles and linoleum floors scuffed into submission by generations of tennis shoes.

This had bothered her but not him, which is why she sobbed so hard when over two hundred of his former students attended his funeral. They talked of how her dad's caring about them and wanting them to learn, even though they were back-talking egocentric teenagers, had helped them successfully serpentine across that perilous border between being a child and an adult. Some were now the lawyers and doctors she once wished he had become. Others had become schoolteachers, in part, they said, because of her dad. It was then that it fully dawned on her that her father had advanced many runners over his lifetime, including her.

Moira had gone to the funeral planning on placing the baseball card inside his casket. Wasn't it the Egyptians who placed treasured items inside the tomb to help the deceased navigate the afterlife? But after hearing her dad's former students, she knew he would be just fine, and she kept the card for herself as a reminder of the promise she had made.

And now, as she contemplated the card pinned slightly askew to the corkboard, she wondered how her dad would have reacted to Percy. They certainly shared the same devotion to laughter, but she was pretty sure her dad never felt the need to steal the golden apples. In some ways, that was his talent. And she smiled suddenly to herself as she realized exactly who her dad would have been in Percy's story about the teenager playing the drums for The Who. When Peter Townshend shouted out to the crowd asking if anyone could play the drums, her dad would have been the buddy jumping up and down, pointing at his friend and excitedly shouting, "He can! He can!"

Moira turned back to the package in front of her, took off a piece of scotch tape from the roll, and secured the last loose flap of the brown wrapping paper by running her finger back and forth across the piece of tape. Then, with a black sharpie, she wrote in handwriting that had earned her many a penmanship award at Clear Lake Elementary—*Professor Percy Billings, 41 Raven Way, Arcadia, Virginia 24531.*

# CHAPTER SEVENTEEN

Squinting blearily across the conference table at his fellow Operation Poetry Slam task force members, Agent Mike Forreo winced as the pungent sweetness of the first shot of Red Bull hit his tongue. For Mike, zero seven hundred hours, once translated into civilian speak, was nothing other than a taunting, gleeful 'fuck you' from morning people with their smug sense of superiority. *If I ever become a higher-up*, Mike thought, *I'll have meetings at* ... He tried to translate a 10:30 p.m. meeting into military time, but his synapses were still at least three Red Bull gulps away from being able to make the computation. Well, whatever the hell it was, he knew that he'd enjoy watching the morning people suffer.

The morning people. Sounded like the name of a cult, and it kind of was. Just saying it conjured up for Mike an image of a marauding band of people with smiles plastered on their faces as they casually threw a chipper, "Oh my, what a beautiful day" or "Good morning" around like a hand grenade. What if he were to report them to Homeland Security on official DEA stationery recommending that "The Morning People"—no, that sounded too much like a sci-fi race of mutants ... how about "People of the Morning Way," yeah, that sounded appropriately sinister—be put on the terrorist watch list? With that comforting thought, he gave a pained smile and closed his eyes to lessen the sensation that the bank of overhead lights was burning holes in his retinas.

Across the table, and already halfway through her second *colada*, Michelle stared glumly out the windows as the rising mid-March sun gradually silhouetted the city's skyline. A true believer of The Morning Way, for Michelle, this time of day was usually magical, tingling with possibility. But ever since yesterday's encounter with Attles, she couldn't listen to a song without a darker meaning barging its way in. And as someone who played music either on the stereo or in her head pretty much every waking moment, this was a real problem.

Just now, as the sun crested a nearby skyscraper, Joni Mitchell's glorious voice singing "Chelsea Morning" had started in her head as it so often did with the sun's awakening. She had made it through the beginning verses just fine, but once Joni began singing about the sun pouring in through the window like butterscotch, her train of thought spun out like a car hitting an unseen oil slick. She suddenly could hear Attles's voice in her head mocking the lines. "Melted butterscotch all over the apartment? You want to talk about a goddamn mess, try getting butterscotch off the ceiling, the drapes, the sofa. For months, your feet would stick every goddamned time you walked across the floor ... squish, squish, squish."

*Oh Lord,* she thought, *please don't let a Jimmy Buffett or Neil Diamond song play in my head.* If her imagination ever let Attles get ahold of "Margaritaville" or "Sweet Caroline," it would be a bloodbath of Homeric proportions.

Sitting a few feet down from Michelle, Carl repeatedly ran his fingers over a small series of parallel grooves in the rosewood tabletop that otherwise was as smooth and glistening as a sheet of Zamboni-smoothed ice. Aware that the table had been a prize of the DEA's raid on a Cocaine Cowboy's mansion down in Key West, he had speculated during earlier meetings that the grooves must be from the repeated rat-a-tat-tat of the kingpin's razor blade cutting cocaine to keep his cabal energized as they plotted their next shipment.

Over time, Carl had staked out the seat in front of the grooves as his own. He treated them as his rosary beads and relished the calming feeling of unconsciously rocking his fingers in and out of the grooves while he awaited Attles's arrival. Carl, too, had a song playing in his head, the same one that played every time he knew Attles was about to appear ... an old blues tune that his father liked to play on their record player when he was a kid, "Hellhound on My Trail."

But before Carl could get past the opening stanza, Attles burst into the room as if he were storming the beaches of Normandy to take out a machine-gun nest. He spoke as he moved briskly to the front of the room. "I want some fucking good news today, people. I am not my usual rosy self this morning. Already had to put three assholes to rest, and I don't want to add to the casualty list."

Attles abruptly turned his white-bristled head toward Mike. "Forreo, tell me you've finally done something useful."

Mike contemplated claiming amnesia based on a story he had heard that morning about people who unexpectedly can't remember anything, but feeling Attles's glare penetrating him decided it was too risky a tactic. "Still undercover, sir, and going to Esteban's whenever he has a gathering. But there are fewer and fewer because he says that planning the Bogotá conference is sucking up all his time."

"You've got to be shitting me. That's all you've got? Who the hell is attending these"—he paused to foreshadow the sarcasm he intended for the next word—"gatherings?"

Mike tried to remain even-keeled as the Red Bull kicked in. "I've checked out everyone I've been able to get a name for without sounding like a narc." This was true, and he'd felt like a shit for doing it because, well, it made him into a narc. He pulled out a folder and started glancing at names and notations. "And, well, they're all twenty or thirtysomethings. If they're drug dealers, they sure aren't flaunting it. Some of them bring bottles of liquor that I'm pretty sure even a Skid Row wino wouldn't touch. Bunch of grad students, some actors trying to live off bit parts with parents chipping in each month, a few bartenders and baristas ... a DEA agent."

Completely ignoring Mike's effort at humor, Attles planted both palms on the tabletop and leaned aggressively toward him. "So fucking forget Esteban and his literary dalliances." Attles looked around, his bushy eyebrows raised into little Arc de Triomphes as if expecting kudos for using a word like dalliance. Seeing none, he bore in on Mike, "What of our surveillance of Carlos? He's clearly the cartel's lieutenant here in the city."

Mike braced himself. "Nothing, really. We've had him under twenty-four-hour surveillance, and he basically is either working out at the gym or else fuc—"As crass as an exchange with Attles was, Mike found his strict Methodist upbringing, where a 'ding dang' meant his father was really angry, just wouldn't let him go there. "Or having a night out with the ladies. We've got surveillance on his phone and computer, and nothing of interest there, other than looking for new ways to make a kale protein shake or his addiction to daytime telenovelas."

"Well, how educatingly romantic is that," Attles replied in exasperation.

His head swiveled to Michelle, who avoided his stare by opening a folder in front of her and not waiting for Attles to ask a question. "We've thoroughly vetted everyone going to the conference," she began, "and nothing new there either. They're all legit professors, really quite vanilla, nondescript, certainly no red flags. One academic superstar, Casper Crenshaw, wrote a best-selling book, *The Dairymaid's Lament*."

Attles gave a loud snort. "Their superstar is named Casper? Wrote a book about ... what the hell did you say? Milk maids?" He gave another derisive snort. "Oh God, I bet he's one pretentious prick. Can you imagine getting stuck next to that asshole on an airplane?"

Michelle was no longer surprised to hear Attles make Olympic-sized leaps based on a random fact like a name, but in this instance, from what she had learned from the wiretaps and her investigation, Attles was not far off. She also thought how delightful it would be to have Crenshaw and Attles sit next to each other on a long transatlantic flight, preferably in the middle seats of the middle row, every international air traveler's version of the rack and screw. She'd happily pony up pay-per-view to see that pissing contest.

Carl got in a few last Hail Mary's on the table's grooves as he sensed Attles's Gatling-gun stare turning toward him. "Chang," he heard Attles growl, "your chance to be a goddamn hero."

Carl nervously cleared his throat and pulled out several packets of stapled papers. "We've looked into the arrangements for the conference and"—he hesitated—"they, too, all look above board." Hearing no explosion, he continued as he held up a packet, "The hotel and conference center are all booked and paid for through valid bank accounts." He put down that packet and held up another. "They've got a printing shop on contract to bind the papers into bound volumes to go to libraries once the conference concludes, and"—picking up a final packet, he continued—"they even have a ceramics studio firing commemorative, full-sized Grecian urns for the participants as mementos of their participation. Pretty cool design ..."

"So fucking glad you like them, Chang," Attles interrupted. "Maybe they'll have an extra one left over for Grandma Chang's ashes."

"They're not that kind of urn," Carl started to explain, but Attles erupted full of frustration.

"Okay, listen up, you pus—" Attles proudly caught himself mid-word, already formulating his defense to Human Resources that he had shown impressive restraint by stopping before he got to the second "s." Not that he worried about losing his job, but Jesus Christ, he did not want to have to go through another eight-hour session in a goddamn reeducation camp having some self-righteous know-it-all lecture him on politically correct etiquette, the p's and q's of being oh-so-sensitive to others' feelings of inadequacy. His last Maoist instructor had spoken in a soft Mr. Rogers' tone of compassion while telling him and the other collected miscreants that the future belonged to those who knew how to earn the trust and respect of a rainbow workforce of ethnicities, races, and sexual orientations. Well, not for him. His whole career had been built on intimidation, and there was no turning back this late in the game.

His oversized aura of intimidation, when coupled with an impressive string of successful busts, had made him largely untouchable. But his last few operations had failed to produce the splashy arrests that garnered headlines and made his superiors happy and tolerant. And although he hated it, he was also astute enough to sense the shifting line of acceptable workplace behavior now that every agent no longer looked like a G-man on the cover of a 1950s comic book. One could still carpet-bomb a meeting with F-bombs—in his case, it was expected—but his cursing vocabulary had shrunk considerably in recent years. Words that some delicate-natured pansy-ass might see as derogatory to their gender or race or religion ... well, that now got you a trip to the principal's office.

And so Attles had caught himself mid-word and performed what he viewed as a rather nifty pirouette. "Okay, listen up, you pus—pissants. We have three weeks to make a goddamn noose to hang these assholes. Forreo, are you at least minimally competent enough to get an invite to the Bogotá conference? What's been your cover?"

Not having expected the question, Mike gave a startled look. "Ah, well … um … basically an aspiring, starving poet doing odd jobs to make ends meet."

"A poet?" Attles started laughing. "You've gotta fucking be kidding me. They believe you're some goddamn poet?"

"So, I haven't actually had to show them any poems," Mike said, feeling his cheeks and neck reddening and praying the others wouldn't notice. He wasn't about to give Attles the satisfaction of knowing that having been inspired by the late-night sessions at Esteban's, he had clumsily begun trying to write some verses, despite never having taken a literature course in college. "I bought a book of self-published poems—basically a stapled packet of Xeroxed pages—from a guy on the street and figured I could claim them as my own if pushed." In Mike's opinion, the poems, collected behind a cover sheet with *Angst Misbehavin'* handwritten in block letters, were not half bad.

Attles gave a surprisingly enthusiastic nod at Mike's revelation. "So Forreo, for once, that's actually smart. I've seen those losers on the street, peddling their poems like some hot dog vendor selling a Coney dog, and wondered who in God's name ever bought them, other than someone in quick need of some paper to blow their nose. Now we know. So, that should be a perfect way to get an invite. You tell that bastard Esteban you want to further"—Attles searched the ceiling for the right words and slapped the table when they came to him—"your craft." Attles laughed again at the thought of Forreo as a poet, causing Mike to redden a further shade of crimson.

"Even if I can wheedle an invite, how do I explain where I'm getting the cash to attend?"

"Wheedle? Wheedle?" Attles gave a derisive bellow, "Well, Jesus Christ, listen to our poet here. And I don't know, Forreo, how you fucking explain it. This is why you get paid the big bucks, so figure it out."

Attles swung toward Esperanza and Chang. "And you two need to get financials and travel info on every egghead who is going to this conference so we can be ready to intercept them and crack them open once they step foot back on American soil. I have to tell you that every instinct I have, and they've never let me down, tells me Esteban is a stooge for his steroid-hyped older brother. And remember, we can't let the Colombian authorities pick up the scent of what we're planning. Those sons of bitches are on the Velasquez payroll as sure as I am paid by Uncle Fucking Sam. Report back this Thursday at zero seven hundred hours. Time is getting short."

And with that, he bustled out of the room with his shoulders proudly pulled back, as if he'd just single-handedly raised the flag at Iwo Jima and was about to be cast in bronze. The Operation Poetry Slam task force members looked at each other, pretty sure Attles was counting them as three more assholes put to rest.

# CHAPTER EIGHTEEN

Percy pushed back his desk chair and stretched as a back spasm sparked a momentary grimace. His crumpled clothes, tousled hair looking like weeds taking over a vacant lot, and bags under his eyes packed for a two-week trip, gave him the appearance of having just drained the last pint on a marathon pub crawl. In fact, he had spent every night for the past week at his keyboard, madly pounding out his manuscript for Moira. While normally Percy was the Houdini of procrastination, adept at slipping out of even the most iron-clad deadline right before an editor's eyes, Esteban had acted wisely in sending Moira to see him.

Percy had promised to get her the manuscript by this morning and was intent on honoring that promise. He had finally hit "send" after an all-nighter that brought back college memories of typing the last page of a term paper, praying to the cyber gods that the printer would not stage a last-minute Teamster strike, and then rushing off to class and placing it on the professor's podium just as she was gathering up her notes to leave.

He wandered from his study out onto the porch with coffee mug clutched tightly to his chest, blinking at the morning sun like a prisoner just released from the hole. He felt a temporary joy from finishing the article and the sun's warmth on his face, but he also knew he was about to enter the doldrums. It was highly predictable at this time of year. Having left spring break behind, and with the semester's end still just beyond the horizon, the weeks now seemed to stand still as he watched the students leave each class a little more glassy-eyed and slack-jawed than the one before.

The doldrums. He loved the phrase if not the feeling. One summer vacation, he had immersed himself in a series of books by Patrick O'Brian set during the Napoleonic Wars about British Naval Captain Jack Aubrey and his ship's physician, Stephen Maturin, as they sailed the seas fighting for the Union Jack. The books were as much a celebration of an improbable friendship between the swashbuckling Jack and the erudite Stephen as an exploration of seafaring life and naval warfare. By the time Percy closed the final book—the author had the audacity of bringing the series to an end by dying—so strong were his ties to Jack and Stephen that he felt the sadness of saying a final farewell to friends.

But even after bidding adieu, much of the nautical lore that came from sailing for so long with Jack and Stephen remained with him. O'Brian had an astounding ability to make one feel as if they were actually on board, whether in the ship's mess wolfing down Spotted Dog and drinking mead, or standing next to Jack at the rail, tensely scanning the horizon with a spyglass for the enemy's sail. And as Percy learned from his time at sea with Jack and Stephen, one of every sailor's most dreaded moments was when a ship became stuck in the doldrums near the equator, a very real and feared place because the northern and southern trade winds wrestled each other to a standstill. A literal standstill. In an age when a warship's only locomotion came from billowing winds filling the canvas, to get stuck in the doldrums meant stagnant days passing with excruciating slowness, food and water supplies dwindling, gums bleeding as scurvy set in.

Percy realized, of course, that he wasn't quite stranded in the same doldrums as a sailor aboard the HMS *Surprise*. Far from going hungry, all too frequently, Percy's doldrums led him to the pantry hunting for a snack. And if his gums bled, it was because he had neglected his flossing routine.

Once, when a colleague scoffed at his declaration that this time in the semester was just like the doldrums that the sailors of old had faced, he claimed in his defense that he was suffering from 'mental scurvy,' if not actual scurvy. The cure was still lime juice, only it involved mixing it in with tequila to make a margarita. His colleague, whose sense of humor was woefully deficient, clearly thought Percy was being overly dramatic, and ever since, Percy had sailed the doldrums without companionship, making him miss Jack and Stephen all the more.

Which was why Percy welcomed a diversion like the UPS truck bumping its way up through the potholes that dotted his driveway. He saw the driver give a slightly alarmed look as she pulled the hand brake and took in Percy's disheveled appearance as he stood on the porch, a hand on the railing as if to steady himself. She came up the walk carrying a package in plain, brown wrapping and extended her arm for maximum distance to hand it to Percy.

Feeling punchy from lack of sleep, Percy gave an overly spirited "thank you" and a small, chivalrous bow, to which the driver gave a hurried nod of acknowledgment before moving as quickly back to her truck as could be considered polite.

Percy turned the package over in his hands, trying to think of anything he had ordered recently. It was a long and slender package, about eighteen inches in length, with the address written by hand. It took a moment, but finally, the handwriting registered. He had seen it on a note attached to a letter he received about the Bogotá conference. It was Moira's.

Percy's spontaneous guffaw sent the neighbor's cat, that had been lounging on the porch in a spot of morning sun, scurrying off in an annoyed huff. With a lightness in his step, Percy moved over to the rocking chair and placed his mug of now-cold coffee down on the side table.

He looked at the package, aware he had an outsized smile stretched across his face. Percy thought this must have been the soaring feeling a knight felt upon receiving his lady's scarf as he headed to the jousting lists for his next tilt. Of course, his upward spiraling exhilaration also meant that if the package turned out simply to be some mundane item related to the conference, like a commemorative coffee mug or set of pens, he'd be irrationally crushed. Percy had learned long ago that Sir Isaac Newton's laws applied to romance as well as falling apples—for every action there was a possible equal and opposite reaction.

Percy slipped his finger into one end of the package, springing the stiff brown wrapping paper free from its tape, and then turned the package around and repeated the motion on the other end. He was unsure if his deliberativeness was an unconscious way of savoring the anticipation or a delay tactic inspired by trepidation. But either way, he resisted the Christmas morning impulse to madly rip the packaging off. He then took his finger and ran it the full length of the package, and the tape gave way like a zipper being unzipped.

Inside was an elongated box, and when Percy saw what was printed on it, he gave an appreciative chuckle. She really had listened. He opened one end of the box and a pair of drumsticks slid into his hand with a piece of paper wrapped around them, secured by a rubber band. Hefting them in his hands, he admired them. The drumsticks looked quite beautiful as the polished, white hickory glistened in the sun. He then slipped the paper out from beneath the rubber band and opened it. In a gently rolling cursive was written:

*My dear P, I am so sorry I had to leave in such a rush. I have no doubt your chance to play the drums will come, and when it does, that you'll seize the moment. The enclosed will make sure you have no excuses. You mentioned an Oscar Wilde quote when we were talking, and as I drove back to the airport, I was reminded of another of Wilde's lines that my dad liked to trot out. 'When the gods wish to punish us, they answer our prayers.' Writing that, I realize I sound like the prophetess of doom, and I don't mean to, but I hope you realize how lucky you already are. Yours, M (a.k.a. Cassandra)*

Percy smiled. The problem with quoting Wilde was there almost always was another Wilde quote waiting in the wings to reply. Who else had captured all the contradictions of the human condition in such perfect, bite-size aphorisms? The best country-western songwriters sometimes came close, and much to the surprise of his friends, he kept the local country station on his car radio right next to NPR, switching over with a quick push of the button whenever a news item got too depressing. Like Wilde, they had the knack of being able to shine the light of humor into life's gloomiest corners.

Just yesterday, he had grinned when a song started off with a spurned lover calling for either Jesus or whiskey, whichever worked best for his broken heart. And had laughed so hard he had to slow the car down when the next song began, "It was bad enough you left me, but you had to tell me why." *Nailed it*, Percy had thought. Religion, alcohol, love, and heartbreak—the building blocks of life and literature. And if one added in bass boats, pickups, and Mom, you had the staple of country-western songwriters everywhere, performing songs in roadside honkytonks, dreaming of a bus ticket to Nashville as they pulled beer-soaked one-dollar bills out of the tip jar at night's end, still hoping for the best payout of all— hearing the bartender, as she turned off the lights, softly singing one of their songs to herself.

Looking out at the surrounding meadows that still clung to the morning mist like a favorite blanket, Percy began to ache for bed as fatigue enveloped him. He rapped out a few beats with the drumsticks on his thigh, realized it hurt, and with a wince and a quick laugh, got out of the rocker.

He was still in the doldrums, no doubt, but Moira had heard his SOS, and the conference was less than a month away. Traces of a cool breeze hinting of a fair wind to follow lightly caressed his cheeks. Smiling, he decided it was time to leave the next watch to the ghosts of Jack and Stephen, and he went inside to crawl into bed.

# CHAPTER NINETEEN

When Agent Mike Forreo first started hanging out with Esteban and his friends as his undercover assignment, he was petrified that he would soon be exposed as a fraud. His nervousness would spike as the discussions inevitably turned to books and movies he had never heard of and sometimes couldn't even pronounce.

To say Mike was a lackadaisical student growing up in rural Iowa would be a bit too laudatory. On a typical winter day at Herbert Hoover High, he would find himself tuning out the teacher as the ancient radiators churned out daydream-inducing heat. Instead of learning the Pythagorean Theorem, he would gaze out at the woodlands through frost-fringed windows, his imagination wandering with a fly rod in search of the bend in Elk Creek where the brook trout were feasting on the insect *du jour*. On beautiful school days during the spring or fall, he often would roam those woodlands with gun or rod in hand, an artfully forged parental excuse in his back pocket ready to turn in the next day to Principal Hesterman's office.

His parents would not have liked that he was breaking a rule, but otherwise cared far more that he be able to recite scripture than Shakespeare. Growing up, his mom was so worried about the influence of literature on his morals that she would read the books he brought home for class before he did, then staple together the pages she thought too racy for his spiritual development. This naturally led Mike to immediately go to the stapled "no trespass" pages and with a butter knife and a flashlight peek into the garden of words his mom had declared forbidden. Usually, they were the only pages he would read.

His parents' entire life revolved around Reverend Graver and the little Methodist church at the corner of State and Myers Roads, and they had done their damned best to make it the center of his universe as well. He sang in the choir, went to Sunday School, and attended summer Bible camps where every activity from canoeing to making lanyard key chains started with earnest prayers for God's guidance. And although he never dared confess it to his parents, while God apparently personally oversaw the making of pencil holders out of uncooked macaroni noodles, He somehow forgot to secure Mike as a true believer, leaving Mike to head off to Iowa State with extremely good manners but uncertain compass points.

At his parents' strong urging, as in, "We will not pay your tuition otherwise," he had majored in accounting and studiously avoided subjects in the liberal arts—subjects that Reverend Graver had warned were "Satan's ticket to the soup line." But then, the summer after his junior year, he spent hour after excruciating hour balancing accounts receivables against accounts payable as an intern with a Des Moines accounting firm. Mike concluded such an existence was easily a match for any of Satan's ways of tormenting a soul that Reverend Graver had described from the pulpit in lurid detail (these harrowing descriptions always followed a graphic recitation of the type of sin that might land one at Hell's gates—renditions of lasciviousness that caused Mike to glance around the pews, wondering if anyone else thought Reverend Graver had a secret sideline writing adult romance novels).

Knowing he desperately needed to ditch the accountant's green eyeshade, Mike decided to attend a campus job fair. On a glorious fall day with the leaves celebrating their last moments of colorful glory beneath a stunning cobalt sky, he stood in the courtyard outside the student union feeling a little dizzy as he took in the vast array of tables. Behind every table stood a smiling person acting like a merchant at a Turkish bazaar, assuring the potential buyer that if only they would come over to their table, they would find the most fulfilling of futures at the most handsome of salaries. Of all the tables, however, it was the Drug Enforcement Agency booth that

SCOTT E. SUNDBY 115

caught his eye, or, perhaps more accurately, the curvaceous brunette behind the DEA table with an array of brochures and literature spread out in front of her as if she was a blackjack dealer.

He had drifted over and struck up a conversation with Special Agent Marissa Barrett as he casually perused a "Careers in Drug Enforcement" brochure with photos of buff young men and women. The brochure looked for all the world like a promo for a Club Med resort, if not for the fact the young Adonises and Aphrodites were wielding battlefield weaponry and wearing sleek bulletproof vests, apparently preparing to raid a crack house instead of getting in line for an all-you-can-eat midnight buffet. The conversation with Agent Barrett led to a series of interviews, and he eventually found himself going through field training and ending up on Attles's team—an assignment that sometimes made him long for the quiet boredom of a ledger sheet.

It was understandable, therefore, that Mike initially felt clueless as he tried to work his way into Esteban's circle of friends. He certainly could not pass himself off as a grad student (ironically, his mom, as Grand Inquisitor screening all the books assigned to him in his high school English classes, would have been in a far better position to do so). He soon gathered, however, that many of Esteban's friends were also not members of the clerisy but self-styled artists, poets, and musicians—some with unmistakable talent, but many simply consuming copious amounts of drugs hoping to discover their muse. Someone once told him that a third of all baristas in New York City were aspiring writers, a figure he later learned was wildly off. It was more like two-thirds.

So it was that Mike landed on the storyline that he was fresh to the Big Apple from the cornfields of Iowa to pursue his dream of becoming a poet— a narrative he embellished slightly with each telling and had earned him the sobriquet of Jude the Obscure, a nickname that meant nothing to him but which he was fine with because he could tell it was meant fondly. In the name of law enforcement and maintaining his cover, Mike soon fully embraced what he perceived to be the bohemian lifestyle of an aspiring poet. But while that existence had done wonders for his mental well-being, it was now beginning to take a physical toll.

Not only had he started smoking, he rolled his own. With a new appreciation for the old men in Havana in their Panama hats who rolled cigars, he now understood that hand-rolling a cigarette was its own sensual ritual.

It started with the pulling of Turkish tobacco in lush, dark strings from a tin that felt like opening a prince's jewel box, the tobacco's deep fragrance providing its own pleasure as it wafted up to the nostrils. One then had to carefully layer the tobacco onto the rolling paper, a little patch of paper with its own magical quality—fragile, thin, waiting to be filled. If you took your time, kept your fingers unrushed, the returned pleasure would be all the greater. Then, once the paper was practically bursting with its rich, musky treasure, it was time to bring it up to the mouth and lovingly run one's lips up and down the paper's length before gently twisting the ends, lest the paper accidentally rip and spill its contents out prematurely. By the time the ritual reached its climax and you held the delicate cylinder between your fingers, one definitely felt like leaning back and savoring a cigarette.

Mike's appearance had also changed. He dressed entirely in black, grew his hair until it brushed his shoulders, and sprouted a hispid beard that looked like a lawn after a long drought. He even sported a small diamond stud in his earlobe. While Attles had reluctantly accepted Mike's explanation that the long hair and facial scruff was a necessary part of his undercover persona, the earring was an accoutrement that Mike double- and triple-checked to make sure he had removed whenever he was likely to see Attles. He could too easily imagine the biting comments it would elicit.

The turtlenecks and skinny jeans he had first purchased when starting the assignment, however, grew increasingly snug as his exercise regime was replaced with wine, song, and 2 a.m. carne asada burrito runs. Stepping out of the shower that morning, he was alarmed to see that the love handles, whose unexpected arrival a month ago had startled him, now appeared to have become love seats. He had already replaced the bathroom lighting with low-watt bulbs but realized the mirror itself might have to come down. Sucking in his gut as he frowned at his reflection, Mike thought, *Thank heavens for smoking. Can you imagine the weight gain if I wasn't inhaling the equivalent of a Superfund coal plant each day?*

So it was that Mike found himself later that afternoon knocking on Esteban's door, unlit hand-rolled cigarette lightly dangling between his lips, looking like a French Resistance fighter gone to seed after spending his post-war days and nights in cafés recounting his exploits. Esteban cracked the door and, upon seeing Mike, swung it open with a warm greeting, "Ah, Jude the Obscure, my favorite troubadour. Come on in." Esteban deftly stepped aside to form a passageway for Mike. "To what do I owe the pleasure of seeing you before nightfall? Many of us, you know, had speculated you might be a vampire, given your fondness for the midnight hours and voracious appetite for dark-red wines. I guess that theory is now thoroughly debunked."

Mike gave an uncomfortable chuckle as he sat down on the sofa, feeling the spring beneath the cushion trying to tunnel upward to freedom. Shifting his posterior to get more comfortable and taking the unlit cigarette out of his mouth, he nervously cleared his throat. "I had a favor to ask, to be honest. And well, honestly, I feel kind of awkward asking."

Smiling as he sat down in a chair across from the sofa, Esteban interjected, "I have no doubt of your honesty, Miguel. What is the favor?"

"Well, you know that I'm still trying to find my way in my poetry and don't have a formal education in it, but I'd really like to get to know the great poets better. And, well, I've heard you talk so enthusiastically about the conference you're organizing in Bogotá, and I thought, you know, wouldn't that be a really cool way to learn about the Romantic poets."

Esteban looked at him sympathetically as he spoke. "That is a real interesting thought, Miguel, but you know, a community college course would probably be a much easier starting point, and much, much cheaper. These are going to be academics talking about some pretty advanced and nuanced topics when it comes to the Romantics."

Mike had anticipated this response and went into his rehearsed spiel. "I'm sure that's true, and Lord knows, most of it will go way over my head." Mike made a quick gesture with his hand, simulating an object skimming just above his scalp. Looking around in a conspiratorial fashion, he went on, "It may just be, though, that I'm thinking part of my education as a poet is to get exposed to a foreign country. You know, I've lived most of my life looking out over the cornfields of Iowa. And, well, this is kind of crazy, but I have an uncle who thinks my coming to New York and trying to write poetry is the greatest idea in the world. He keeps saying he wished he had done it when he was my age instead of becoming the Rockefeller of pork belly futures. So you see, I'm betting he'd happily pay for the trip if I said it was to further my poetry. And man oh man, I just think it'd be really different and exotic and cool to attend, so I thought, 'Hey, no harm in asking Esteban.'" Mike had leaned forward as he earnestly made his case and now plopped back into the sofa, exhausted by the effort.

"Miguel, after hearing you present your case, I'm thinking perhaps you should become a lawyer instead of a poet." Esteban's lustrous, brown eyes sparkled mischievously. "But I think you are right. God put rich uncles on earth to help their impoverished nephews live out their dreams, and I would be the last person to defy the divine order. There also is something quite wonderful in thinking how years from now, when you are accepting the Pulitzer Prize for your latest volume of poems, you'll need to mention pork bellies in your acceptance speech, and perhaps, our little conference in Bogotá as well. So, yes, of course we'd love to have you attend if your uncle is willing to be the Medici to your Michelangelo." Mike had no idea what the last comment meant but understood he had succeeded in wheedling an invitation.

Esteban rose from his chair in a quick motion as Mike struggled to pull himself up from the sagging sofa cushions. Once both were on their feet, Esteban gently put his hand on Mike's forearm. "Miguel, I unfortunately have much to do before dinner, but I love your excitement and that you want to be a part of what we're doing. Let's talk soon, and I'll get you the details so your rich tío can get the plane tickets and hotel reservations."

"Really can't thank you enough," Mike said as he opened the door and stepped into the hallway.

Esteban smiled. "Of course, and, oh, I know you're not feeling ready for prime time yet, but I would love for you to recite some of your work one of these nights. Just let me know, and I'll tap the bong to quiet everyone down."

Mike laughed uneasily as he turned to go and said, "Sure, sounds good."

Exiting the apartment building and stepping onto the front stoop, Mike with some difficulty pulled a neon-green Bic lighter out of his front pocket and, after three tries, struck a flame and lit the cigarette he still held in his hand.

As he took the first long drag and weathered the violent hacking that followed, Mike felt a now-familiar pang of conscience. As he had become more and more enmeshed within Esteban's group and listened to their stories and desires, he reveled in realizing that Reverend Graver's fire-and-brimstone bellowing had faded to the background buzz of an annoying mosquito. But as the libertine lifestyle gradually liberated his soul, Mike's impostor complex had transformed from a fear of being unveiled as someone who knew nothing about literature into guilt over being an actual impostor helping hurt people he liked. He had become very fond of Esteban.

Looking down from his window, Esteban watched Mike wander down the sidewalk, causing oncoming pedestrians to take a wide berth each time a draw off his cigarette triggered a coughing fit. Feeling a presence at his shoulder, Esteban glanced backward and saw that Carlos had emerged from hiding in his room and joined him at the window. Carlos's eyes had a predatory gleam and every muscle in his body was tensed as if ready to pounce. Esteban shook his head with concern, thinking, *Miguel, Miguel, be careful.*

# CHAPTER TWENTY

Diego's fingers rested on the bottom of the page, the contrast of the page's milk-white background giving his skin the hue of a rich café au lait. It had taken four tries, going line by line, and numerous consultations of the dictionary that lay open to his left, but he had finally circled the walls of Xanadu where Kubla Khan had his stately pleasure dome decreed. The thought crossed his mind of renaming his compound Xanadu, but he then remembered that one of his hated Medellin rivals had named his complex Xanadu. *Hah*, Diego thought with a touch of sinful pride, *that prick Pablo probably named it after that terrible Hollywood movie Xanadu with a roller-skating goddess, I bet he didn't even know about the poem.*

At Esteban's direction, Diego had brought Professor Maria Angeles on as a consultant from the local university. They had circled each other warily at first. Maria was unavoidably aware of Diego's reputation and agreed to journey up the mountain to the compound only after reassurances from a mutual friend of Esteban's.

For his part, Diego bore an inveterate distrust of anyone bearing the title of teacher, a chariness bred from having felt looked down upon from practically the first day he had been forced to sit behind a school desk. Decades later, his cheeks still burned when he recalled his second-grade teacher, Señora Fernandez, making fun of him in front of the entire class because of his atrocious spelling.

But much to his surprise, he found Maria full of zest and entertaining knowledge. She had charmed him into reading 'Ode to a Grecian Urn,' meeting his protestation that he had no interest in poetry with a gentle rebuff of, "Diego, you are a human being. *Of course* you have an interest in poetry." He smiled at recalling Esteban's palpable shock when he learned Diego had read the poem, reacting as if he just discovered Diego was leading a secret double life as a concert pianist. *La belleza es verdad, la verdad es belleza*—beauty is truth, truth beauty. He still wasn't entirely sure what it meant, but he found it soothing and sometimes repeated it like a mystical incantation to calm himself when the bleakness of his situation started to wrap its hands around his throat.

The newly mounted bookshelf behind his desk was just shy of being half-filled with a jigsaw of books leaning on each other, and he secretly delighted in realizing he would soon need bookends to keep the volumes upright.

And this particular poet he was reading now, Samuel Coleridge, Diego wished he knew him as a person. When Maria explained that Coleridge had dreamt the poem 'Kubla Khan' after taking opium and was madly writing the lines down from the dream, only to be interrupted by a "man on business from the nearby town of Porlock" so that the rest of the poem was forever lost, Diego felt an inexplicable kinship to the poet's loss. When Maria told him a well-respected literature professor would tell his students that if anyone in the history of literature deserved to be hanged, drawn, and quartered, it was "the man on business from Porlock," Diego had nodded vigorously in agreement, leaving unspoken that he would have known exactly how to make it happen.

Diego took off his newly acquired pair of tortoiseshell reading glasses and set them gently aside. Part of him wanted to keep reading, but he knew he needed to think through his conversation with Esteban tomorrow. Most of the pieces were now in place, and he experienced the familiar mix of anticipation and anxiety of launching a plan and watching it unfold.

He knew well how events took on a life of their own once the greatest intangible of all—human nature—came into play. He recently heard a news report of physicists who were building a supercollider at enormous expense to explore what happened when different types of atomic particles collided at incredibly high speeds, and he thought, *Aha, welcome to my world.* You definitely deserve a Nobel Prize if you can figure out what will happen when you throw together an assortment of individuals with hundreds of thousands of dollars at stake, each motivated by their own high-speed amalgam of greed, ambition, ruthlessness, and fear. That had always been part of the adrenaline rush for Diego—to problem-solve on the fly as particles flew off in unexpected directions—and he had been a master of it. Now? He was taking a lot more naps.

Luckily, though, Esteban was providing the missing energy, and they were in about as good a shape as one could be before the whistle blew to start the game. A few key puzzle pieces remained to be snapped into place, the most perplexing being largely a personal one—what to do with Carlos.

Restless and marginalized, Carlos was a cruise missile fueled by fury looking for a target to lock onto. Usually, this would be an ideal weapon to have in one's arsenal when going to war, but what lie ahead would be won by Cold War intrigue, not battlefield incineration. Unless handled properly, Carlos's pent-up frustration and rage could trigger an inadvertent launch and unleash disaster.

Diego sighed and rocked his chair forward to the desk, placing his elbows on either side of the open volume. His eyes returned to the pages and he distractedly began leafing through it, relishing the smooth coolness of the paper between his thumb and fingertips. When he came to *La Balada del Viejo Marinero*, he paused as he recalled Maria telling him she thought he would find the poem powerful, but to prepare himself for needing plenty of time to get through it. Well, unless a thunderbolt struck him with how to handle Carlos, it was going to be a late night anyway.

He slipped his glasses on and began reading, "It is an ancient mariner ..."

# CHAPTER TWENTY-ONE

The urgent rap of knuckles on her office door awakened Michelle as she dozed at her desk. The messenger informed her the call between Diego and Esteban that she had been expecting was taking place, and Michelle hustled down the hall, half-running, half-skipping, her nylon-clad feet *swish-swish-swishing* on the carpet as she tried to get her shoes on. Putting on high heels while moving should be an Olympic event, Michelle mused, the professional woman's equivalent of a double layout dismount on the parallel bars.

Not one normally to fall asleep at work, Michelle nodded off only because she had suffered through a sleepless night, her insomnia triggered by a soreness radiating from a half-finished tattoo on her right bum. She had drawn out the tattoo design—*La belleza es verdad, la verdad es belleza*—in a stylish, cursive script and presented it to her tattoo artist, *the* Lou of Lou's Tattoos, and shown him where she wanted it placed. He had made it as far as *La belleza es* before the electricity suddenly went out in the shop, the casualty of a thunderstorm knocking out a transformer on the power pole outside.

To be honest, even before the power outage, she was already a little peeved with Lou, who had been her tattooist since she celebrated her eighteenth birthday with a silhouette of Mary Poppins with uplifted umbrella rising into the sky. Having presented Lou with what she felt was a perfect canvas after years of arduous Buns of Steel workouts, he complained how "some dimples" had made the first part of *belleza* look a bit like *pella*, a Spanish word her abuela used to describe cooking lard.

Some dimples? The electricity going out? Shit, the way her luck was going, maybe she'd skip the rest of the tattoo and just have Lou put in a question mark after *La belleza es*. Any future viewer would be on a by-invitation-only basis anyway, and if they were going to be waylaid by the question of the meaning of beauty while looking at her ass, it probably wasn't going to be a great night anyway.

She finally got her second shoe on halfway down the corridor, picked up speed, and swung herself into the chair behind the listening center just as she heard Esteban's voice say in Spanish, "Ten days and counting. I think we're in good shape on this end. All the transportation and hotels are booked and ready. I feel like I could be a travel agent after all this."

"Very good to hear," Diego said.

"And Father, as it turns out, we will have an extra attendee from the States, a young poet. He was very insistent on coming, and I felt that I simply couldn't say no. He is very likeable and I am certain will be no trouble." Recognizing that Esteban was talking about Mike, Michelle leaned forward.

There was a pause on the line. "Yes, of course, I completely trust your judgment. We will need to make sure he feels welcomed, though. Perhaps we should have someone assigned as a host to show him around? Enrique?"

"Enrique is a great idea." She heard what sounded like a pen crossing out an item on paper and realized Esteban was working his way down a checklist. "On a less favorable note, I don't think the libraries are likely to purchase the conference proceedings—"

Diego interrupted, "But we were counting on them to subsidize the cost. We went first class on the bindings, paper, all of that, thinking we'd make money. They're finished and ready to go."

"I know, I know." Esteban gave a weary sigh. "I talked to the librarian here, and she said university libraries are in a huge budget crunch when it comes to acquisitions because everything is going digital. She said twenty years from now, a librarian may be as much in the business of deciding which books to get rid of as which ones to obtain. I thought she was going to cry when she told me that ... said it'd be like having to choose between one's children."

*"Mierda,"* Diego uttered softly. Michelle was unsure if the epithet referred to the plight of librarians or to the conference's lost revenue. A few moments of silence ensued before Diego interjected, "I guess we'll have them take the books back to their colleges and write it off as a charitable contribution, but we never would have spent the money if I'd known that."

"I know, and I'm sorry. I just didn't know."

"It's okay, we'll make it work. That's why I have a world-class accountant." The phone line was quiet for a few moments as Esteban had apparently checked off the last item on his list. "Hey listen," Diego resumed, "I read *'La Balada del Viejo Marinero'* last night."

The stop-the-presses response by Esteban to these revelations by his father had abated in recent weeks as Diego regularly brought up his latest session with a literature professor named Maria Angeles. Michelle had thoroughly vetted Professor Angeles, and from all indications, she was indeed a profesora and not a narco. The conference had engaged her as a consultant, and she was even bringing her students to hear the presentations.

Diego's voice brought Michelle back to the conversation. "I have been thinking a lot about the albatross."

At the same time she was translating Diego and Esteban's conversation in her head, Michelle was trying to remind herself of the Cliff Notes' version of 'The Rime of the Ancient Mariner', not the easiest of multi-tasks. She vaguely remembered the poem from her high school AP English class. Let's see ... an ancient sailor shoots an albatross following his ship. Shit, she couldn't remember why, but she recollected it didn't go well for the seafarer, recalling a black-and-white etching in the textbook of a man with a huge bird hanging from his neck.

"And," Diego continued, "I was thinking how maybe, in the end, the albatross was a good thing because it led the ancient mariner to look at things in a new way. I guess walking around with a 15-kilo bird hanging from your neck would do that." Diego laughed, causing Michelle to realize she'd never heard him laugh before. "And I thought how you'd said how that one professor, *el carbon arrogante*"—'arrogant asshole' Michelle translated in her head and knew from prior conversations that he must be talking about

Casper Crenshaw—"was an albatross around your neck, and I began to think how, like the ancient mariner came to view his albatross, *el carbon* might actually be a good thing."

Michelle, who was pretty sure she had either heard or reviewed every conversation between them, ruminated, "I don't remember Esteban ever saying something about an albatross." Michelle also noted that Esteban, who usually kept up a rat-a-tat-tat pace in his conversations unless taken by surprise, was three … four … five seconds before responding.

"Ah, and now you know where my reference came from! You make a good point. Perhaps I've been too resentful that he bullied his way in. And the more I think about it, the more I think you're right. I should be more gracious, for sure, in giving him credit. Maybe then the albatross will fall off my neck too. Perhaps a special way of honoring him would be in order. Thanks for that. Can't wait to see you."

"Me too, son."

Michelle gave a slightly audible "hmm" in response to hearing the line click dead. She was accustomed to taking away subtexts from Diego and Esteban's exchanges. It was why she always put in for wiretap duty. Usually, though, it was because it felt like she was tuning in to a miniseries about a father-son relationship with plenty of unexpected twists.

At the start of the task force, Michelle would have prepared herself for a Mount Vesuvius eruption of cursing by Diego at some of Esteban's revelations today. And while Diego was still far from starring as a father lovingly guiding his kids through their youthful foibles with corny witticisms, he had not turned out to be the Darth Vader figure she expected.

Still, today's session felt different. Too much like a *Sesame Street* script with Oscar the Grouch and Big Bird acting out a lesson about how to get along. Was she being played? Michelle squirmed in her chair as *La belleza* shot out needles of pain, turned off the recorder, abruptly stood up, and took off in desperate need of ice.

# CHAPTER TWENTY-TWO

Bronson Attles sat at his desk in an office so spartan, it made a monk's cell feel as decadent as the penthouse suite at Trump Tower. He was in a foul mood, which, given his normal state of mind, was saying a lot. A whole lot.

He had started off the morning being told by his superiors in no uncertain terms that Operation Poetry Slam better produce results, or he could anticipate finishing his DEA career in the Sioux Falls, South Dakota office overseeing Operation Giddyup, an investigation of a drug ring that used the cattle stockyards to smuggle in cocaine. To describe it as a drug ring, though, was like referring to one's mint-green Vespa as "my Harley." Hell, a University of Florida fraternity snorted more cocaine on a Friday night than the Sioux Falls' drug ring imported each month.

Attles might lead the life of an ascetic, but he would be damned if he was going to reside anywhere that constructed their palaces out of corn. He needed the throngs of the city, the bustle of a large, urban office, the adrenaline rush of making a major drug bust every bit as much as a junkie jonesing for his next bindle of smack. Truth was, he had nothing else to keep him moving.

It wasn't meant to be that way. As a young man with shoulder-length hair that glowed black with the luster of an obsidian carving, he had loved every moment of college—the nightly ritualistic passing of a bong full of glowing Colombian redbud around the dorm room, the celebration with a number of coeds of the arrival on campus of something called The Pill.

Attles was a business major planning on taking over his parents' dry cleaning business, even spending one summer interning at *The Clothesline*, the trade magazine for dry cleaners, writing articles like, "Stop Wasting Steam—and Money," "Causes and Solutions for Fabric Rings," and his most literary effort, "A Tale of Two Cleaners."

The future looked as crisp and bright as a freshly pressed Oxford dress shirt, but then he made one terribly stupid mistake. Thinking he was being fiscally smart, he financed college through a Reserve Officer Training Corps Scholarship without realizing the Vietnam War was about to get very real. And real it got, bloody real.

A newly minted lieutenant upon graduation, he was sent as an infantry officer to the jungles of Vietnam. Scared and naive, within two months, he had blundered his squad into the middle of a nighttime ambush. He was the only one to emerge from the firefight alive. Six of his grunts were dead, another, Francisco "Paco" Garcia, unaccounted for. Rushed to a field hospital, the emergency surgery left a scar wending like the Amazon the entire length of his abdomen. He slipped in and out of consciousness for three weeks before the doctors were confident he'd survive.

When he was finally debriefed, he told the military investigators what had happened—the unforeseeable ambush, and his futile, repeated efforts to save the others amid the confusion and chaos of the midnight blackness. He was rewarded with a Purple Heart and a medical discharge. He then prayed every day that Paco never emerged from the dense, humid canopy of the Vietnamese jungle to contradict him.

People deal with intense guilt in different ways. Some take vows and enter a monastery, others view the world through the prism of a whiskey bottle, a few devote themselves to redemption through tireless good works.

Attles became a world-class asshole. As a decorated vet, he was offered a position at the Drug Enforcement Agency and became renowned for his over-the-top relentlessness in driving the agents unfortunate enough to be assigned to him. Like an actor, he would don the persona of the in-your-face-take-no-prisoners-broker-no-excuses leader every morning as he approached the office. For reasons he did not comprehend, nor really cared to, making others fear and despise him silenced the guilt and turmoil.

At first, being an unbearable asshole was a full-time job, but with the passage of time, he no longer needed to consciously work at it. Like the aging Shakespearean thespian who eventually becomes King Lear as he rants and rages around the nursing home's hallways, Attles, over time, became his role. It made life and people's reactions to him predictable, and that was good, even if it meant no friends or family. And although it took a few years, at some point his chest no longer twinged with a panicked tightness every time his phone rang, wondering if the voice on the other end would begin, "This is Paco ..."

Now all of that was under dire threat, and as he descended the stairs to the task force meeting—forget the goddamn elevator and the lazy losers who took it—he knew he needed to fight like hell. It also meant that when Attles stormed into the conference room, Mike, Michelle, and Carl could sense, even if they didn't know why, that they were in even greater peril than usual. Without a change of course, they were ground zero for a Category Five hurricane about to make land.

"Forreo, my budding William Shakespeare," Attles said with a sarcastic tone so astringent Mike wished he was wearing a Hazmat suit. "Unless you want to be reassigned to some hellhole like ... oh, I don't fucking know ... Shithole Falls, South Dakota, you better tell me that your pitiful, fat ass succeeded."

Mike cleared his throat. Even with good news to deliver, Attles's fury was so strong, he couldn't bring himself to look him in the eyes. "Yes, well, I convinced Esteban to invite me to the conference. The travel information is being processed by the front office. I should be in Bogotá in a little over a week."

Quiet filled the room, not a state of affairs one often experienced in Attles's presence. Mike thought, *Don't let your guard down. It's just the eye of the storm passing over*, and braced himself by putting his hand beneath the table and grabbing ahold of the leg.

"So, you wheedled an invitation after all," Attles said finally, his voice expressing evident surprise. Then almost to himself, he enthused, "That is damn good news, goddamn good news. We need someone in the hornet's nest ready to screw the other hornets to death." Mike was pretty sure Attles didn't have his entomological facts of life quite right, but all Mike cared about was he had survived his latest near-death experience.

Everyone sensed the projected landfall moving as Attles's stare pivoted in Carl's direction. "Chang, Chang, Chang," Attles began, shaking his head as if in sympathetic sorrow. "How does Shithole Falls sound to you?"

"Not very good, sir," Carl replied, a slight tremor detectable in his voice as he had expected Michelle to go next.

"Well, then, here is the greatest news in the world, Chang. All you have to do is deliver the goods I expect, and you'll get a gold star and continue living your life of ease and luxury. Otherwise, Grandma Chang better learn how one treats frostbite after going ice fishing."

Carl thought about informing Attles that Grandma Chang had passed away years ago, but in his usual measured way, he simply offered up a benign, "Yes, sir." He opened the manila folder in front of him, surreptitiously running his fingers a few times in the table grooves beneath the folder to calm himself.

"So, I had the forensic accountants run financials on all the conference participants. And well, between student loan repayments—some stretching back a decade or more—and salaries that don't break six figures, almost everyone is just barely making it. Moreover," he said, turning to a page in his folder, "there were no unusual deposits or expenses that raised alarm bells for our analysts about money laundering." He then added in an uncharacteristic attempt at humor while keeping his eyes riveted on the paper in front of him. "They simply should be buying knock-off Birkenstocks because they can't really afford the real ones."

Carl looked up and gave a bashful glance around. Mike and Michelle responded with tepid smiles, while Attles glared at him with an uncomprehending stare.

Before Attles could snuff out his secret dream of being a stand-up comic with a brutal putdown, Carl continued, "However, there are two professors doing significantly better. One," he shuffled the papers until he found the page he was looking for, "is a Professor Wanda Wollings, who made over one hundred fifty grand last year. But most of it was from a direct marketing business she runs out of her garage selling blue-green algae nutritional supplements and coffee enema kits. From what we can tell, it is a bit of a pyramid scheme where she collects most of her money from sales from people who she recruited, but nothing narcotics related. The second—"

Attles interrupted, "Coffee enemas? What the fuck is this world coming to? Does it matter if it's decaf? Instant?" And he gave a guttural laugh that was a bit frightening in its intensity. Mike, Michelle, and Carl exchanged quick glances, unsure how to respond. "Oh, never the fuck mind if you assholes have no sense of humor," and he laughed again. He definitely seemed a bit off kilter this morning, as if his fury had unbalanced him more than usual. Always difficult to read, in this meeting, he was as indecipherable as a Pink Floyd song.

"The second professor," Carl resumed as he worked hard to keep his focus, "is who Michelle mentioned last meeting." He nodded in Michelle's direction as he turned to a different page, double-checking he had the name right before proceeding, "Casper Crenshaw." Attles rolled his eyes but kept silent.

"So Crenshaw, it turns out, likes to live beyond his means despite a comfortable income between his teaching, royalties, and appearance fees. Easily cleared three hundred thousand dollars per annum each of the last five years," which drew a low whistle from Mike. "But he has a fondness for nice things—a Caribbean vacation home, travels only first class, has a weakness for fine wines, dines out almost every night at nice restaurants, collects paintings and books, three timepieces over ten thousand dollars each—"

"Timepieces?" Attles interrupted incredulously. "Do you mean goddamn watches?" he asked, holding up a forearm that sported a cheap, plastic, digital watch that looked like it might have been the prize at the bottom of a box of kid's cereal. And a disappointing prize at that.

Carl nodded and continued straight ahead, "Yes, watches, and he has all his clothes hand-tailored in Milan. Plus, he made a disastrous investment in"—Carl brought his face closer to the page as he read—"an Exclusive Collector's Ten-Year Anniversary Edition of *The Dairymaid's Lament*. Apparently expected to sell ten thousand signed copies at seventy-five dollars a pop but has had sales of less than five hundred."

Carl looked up as he continued his report. "During our agent's interview with the editor at the original publishing company, the editor said they didn't think a coffee table version of the book would sell when Crenshaw brought the idea to them. So Crenshaw, in a huff, went to a vanity publisher, paid out a ton of his own money for illustrations by a famous London artist, hand-stitched leather bindings, the works. Since sales have been a complete bust, he's apparently lost one of those finely tailored Italian shirts off his back."

Michelle gave an appreciative laugh, though Carl thought it might be to keep him from feeling bad. "In sum," Carl concluded, "Crenshaw has a big-time need for some quick money. He is, in the words of the report"—he flipped to the last page—"vulnerable to extortion."

Uttering a "Yes, yes, yes," Attles began pacing back and forth at the front of the room so energetically, Mike wondered if he might spontaneously combust. "Goddammit, I knew it," Attles practically shouted as he finally stopped pacing. "Crenshaw must be the fucking link to all of this. Hope for his sake"—he gave a slightly maniacal laugh—"Oprah does interviews with people in jail cells." In what appeared to be meant as praise, Attles added, "Tell Grandma Chang not to invest in that ice fishing hut quite yet."

"Esperanza." Attles's tone ticked down to a Category Four as he turned toward her. "Are you going to give us another goddamned *Father Knows Best* plot summary of how Diego is getting in touch with his inner self, or did you finally find out something useful?"

Michelle shifted uneasily in her chair, but for once, it was not from the discomfort of being under Attles's death-beam stare, but simply because her right bum still hurt like hell. In fact, Michelle was feeling kind of good because she finally had something to offer Operation Poetry Slam.

Smiling, she asked in a chipper voice as if hosting a book club with a glass of headache-inducing box wine in hand, "So does anyone remember 'The Rime of the Ancient Mariner' from their English classes?"

Mike, who had relaxed slightly, quickly braced again and looked at Michelle with eyes widened in alarm. *What the hell is she thinking deliberately stirring a hornet's nest, and these hornets weren't even fornicating.*

The low voice rumbling from the front of the room was surprisingly expressive in its inflection:

*He went like one that hath been stunned,*
*And is of sense forlorn:*
*A sadder and a wiser man,*
*He rose the morrow morn.*

Mike had been reading about parallel universes in a sci-fi novel and was pretty sure he had somehow just stumbled down a wormhole. But before he could get too far down the space tunnel, Attles spoke again, "English 101, Professor Skamser," he remarked casually as if giving a passerby the time of the next bus. "We had to memorize the final stanza of 'The Rime of the Ancient Mariner' for the final exam."

Michelle gave a stunned nod, gathered herself back together as best she could, and still somewhat flustered, said, "Yes, well, I want to talk about the albatross." She then reported on Diego and Esteban's conversation, first letting Mike know that his arrival had been discussed, along with some of the other conference details that were mentioned.

Her excitement was evident as she explained that there was something about the albatross discussion that seemed different, came across as coded. She handed out an English translation of that part of the transcript, and they all took a minute to read how Diego referred to Crenshaw—*el carbon arrogante*—as the albatross that Esteban needed to lose from around his neck.

"And," Michelle explained with a touch of pride as if she had just solved a difficult calculus equation, "if you listened to the conversation, how they interacted ... well, I feel certain they were talking about something other than Crenshaw simply being the proverbial pain in Esteban's neck." Her voice picked up speed as she concluded, "And now that we've heard Carl's report on Crenshaw, I think Mike focuses on Crenshaw as the possible conduit."

They all looked apprehensively to the front of the room. With a startling thunderclap of his hands that made them jump, Attles declared,

"Goddammit, Esperanza, you, for once, are right. Crenshaw is the goddamn albatross, and we've got to kill it." Michelle who had reread 'The Rime of the Ancient Mariner' after listening to Diego and Esteban's conversation, almost pointed out that it was killing the albatross that led to a string of truly terrible misfortunes for the ancient mariner. But given that Attles's fury had downgraded to a tropical storm, she let it slide.

Indeed, Attles seemed cheery in the way a Doberman Pinscher not growling qualifies as cuddly. "Okay, we'll finalize plans this week, get communications up and fully operational. We've got the Miami airport as our chokepoint as they return from the conference, and we'll have Forreo on the ground at the conference with Chang and Esperanza at the Bogotá airport." With that, Attles abruptly started to exit the room, and just as Mike was thinking that for the first time in his memory Attles had gone two full sentences without an expletive, he heard a parting, "By the way, Forreo, you look like goddamn shit."

# CHAPTER TWENTY-THREE

With but a week to go before boarding a plane, the wind had freshened considerably in Percy's sails, perhaps not quite to gale strength, but certainly to a strong breeze. Morale was improved all around. The students could now spy the end of the school year on the horizon. True, reading assignments and term papers that had been put off now loomed Kraken-like just off the shoals. But that was why God, on the eighth day, had created caffeine and Adderall.

Percy had achieved heroic status with his students by canceling the last week of class, his announcement eliciting a cheer so joyful, it left him slightly disquieted. His department chair had angrily blustered into his office later that afternoon at the news he was headed to a conference in Bogotá. Percy had calmed him by assuring him the conference was picking up the tab and not the English department, whose budget already was overstretched by the purchase of a cappuccino machine for the faculty lounge.

With that information, the chair's venomous scowl had instantaneously transformed into an envious glint, a look that actually alarmed Percy more. An administrator's envy could easily translate into a crushing committee load for the next semester, the professor's equivalent of being put on latrine duty. Percy wisely kept to himself the handsome stipend he was being paid.

Percy's travel itinerary had him spending a night's layover in Miami before heading to Colombia the following afternoon. Miami had received a lot of bad press lately, robberies and murders of foreign tourists tending to make the Miami Tourism Board's task of selling sun and sand a bit more challenging. A local humor columnist had proposed that the tourism board embrace the situation and try to make lemonade out of lemons, or being South Florida, perhaps, more accurately, margaritas out of limes, with promotional taglines like, "Free doughnuts at every lineup!" or "Come back, they weren't shooting at you!"

Percy, though, had a deep-seated love affair with Miami dating back to his childhood, and his emotional attachment wasn't about to be shaken by a few gangland-style killings. His grandparents had fulfilled their calling as retirees by moving to Miami, which meant that every Christmas holiday, the family station wagon was loaded up to make the southward sojourn from New England's bone-marrow cold to the land of bikinis and flip-flops.

As his father loaded the suitcases into the car, the falling snow collecting atop his knit cap like vanilla frosting on a cupcake, he would grumble that it was not part of the natural order to spend the winter holidays wearing sandals. Out of fairness, his father's remarkably pale skin meant once they crossed the Georgia-Florida state line, no amount of zinc oxide would keep him from burning to a red-hot crisp with all the spectacular fury of a NASA space capsule reentering the atmosphere.

Percy, on the other hand, always viewed the trip with mystical wonder. He would sit in the back seat, reading until the landscape gradually commanded his attention. Barren trees looking like an army of emaciated scarecrows eventually gave way to scrub pine as the sun strengthened from a watery yellow to a robust gold.

He loved the stops in Charleston and Savannah with their stately mansions and live oaks draped with moss lining the streets, making Percy feel as if he had stepped into an antebellum photograph. And then came the final stretch down Florida's coast on A1A. Billboards for surf shops and deep-sea excursions whispered to an adolescent Percy that if only his parents would move to a town with a name like Coconut Grove, he could live the life of a Beach Boys' ballad.

By the time the mileage signs to Miami ticked down to double digits, the sun would reflect off them with such marvelous brightness they often were difficult to read. Percy would rest his chin on his hands, gazing contentedly out the cranked-down window as the breeze licked at his hair, feeling the happiness of a dog in a pickup rolling down the highway with ears flapping in the wind.

And then, finally, Miami. It wasn't the beaches where the gaggles of snowbirds flocked that lured Percy, it was the lush tropical vegetation that held him in its trance. Limbs hanging heavy with sweet mangoes and plump papayas, plants and trees sporting delicious names like jacaranda, frangipani, bougainvillea, and cocoplum.

His favorite was the gumbo limbo, whose peeling bark revealed a trunk underneath of a polished red so deeply beautiful and magnetizing, you could not help but lay your hands on it, the cool, burnished feel offering up magical possibilities as if one were rubbing a genie's lamp. Even the palm trees, the cliché of every T-shirt, key chain, and shot glass sold at the tourist shops, offered untold delights if one looked beyond the royal palms that towered majestically into the sky.

Percy would often stroll with his grandmother as she pointed out from block to block the dizzying array of palm varieties – "And that is a Pygmy Date Palm over there next to the Marzari Palm ... and, oh look, up on the corner is a Dwarf Majesty Palm!" Each looked like the creation of a different artist's studio, many of the creators apparently dropping acid given the wondrous creativity of the different leaves and trunks. These strolls were always accompanied by a cacophony of bird calls that would emerge out of dense thatches of shrubbery as they walked by, each unseen singer hitting a different octave, playing a game of avian Marco Polo with each other.

If one never left the tourist haunts, one might think that civilization in the guise of glitzy condos and swanky nightclubs had conquered the mangroves and surrounding Everglades. But like most conquistadores, its ultimate fate was likely to be an unhappy one. Seemingly half the workforce in South Florida was in the landscape business, SWAT teams of flora warriors descending daily on neighborhoods in beat-up trucks pulling trailers full of machetes, pruning tools, and leaf blowers, the weapons of choice to keep the jungle at bay.

Mother Nature definitely had the edge, though, biding her time to reclaim her throne once the invasive species of humans was banished, whether by hurricane, climate change, or evolution. Percy had often thought during his visits that this must have been what it felt like to live in one of those Mayan or Inca cities discovered a millennia later entombed beneath the Amazon jungle. Even while they had been erecting their grand temples and palaces hewn from stone, they must have sensed the primordial throbbing of the jungle encircling it, waiting to uncoil its vines.

But while a developer might become depressed at the prospect of his buildings receding back into the mist, Percy never failed to find the primal undercurrent and sense of connecting to something timeless to be stirringly romantic, especially when the sultry moon filled the sky with a light as luminescent as the sun on a winter day back home. Which was why, many years later, Percy couldn't help but get his hopes up that an evening breeze fragranced by night-blooming jasmine might allow him to see if he and Moira were destined for each other.

Moira had voiced reservations about Miami when he first broached the idea, a hesitation he worried was more about him than the city's current reputation as the nation's murder capital. But as they talked and he gushed about how the region's tropical beauty had bewitched him growing up, she had agreed to schedule a layover in Miami as well.

Perhaps the clincher was his promise that he would show her a place he knew she would find as enchanting as Harry Potter felt upon first seeing Hogwarts, the place where his father had sought refuge from the sun almost every day, a place where his father never grumbled. When she had laughed and said, "Okay, okay, I'll see you there," Percy felt a full gust starting to fill the sails. He texted her the address, 265 Aragon Avenue, and then stared at it on his phone like he was seeing it for the first time. *Hell*, he thought, chuckling. *It actually sounds like the address you'd expect for the Three Broomsticks pub in Hogsmeade. Good thing, 'cause I'm going to need some magic.*

He swiveled back to his desk to start preparing class but soon found himself Googling a shard of a lyric he annoyingly couldn't get out of his head ... *"You have to believe we are magic"* ... but couldn't quite place. He watched as the search result came up and then slightly recoiled when Olivia Newton-John's syrupy voice started singing from a video, "You have to believe we are magic ... "

"Damn," Percy lamented. "An '80s roller skating pop diva is now my guiding star? I may be beyond saving."

# CHAPTER TWENTY-FOUR

Casper pulled the folding closet doors open until they were as wide as they would go. Crouching, he pushed his arm through a forest of hanging shirts and slacks toward the closet's back corner until his fingertips were rewarded with the cool, supple feel of the large black leather case.

He removed the case, took it into the bathroom, and placed it on the vanity's white, marble surface with the reverence of an archbishop placing the crown upon the head of a newly anointed king. The comparison was more apt than many would realize, as Casper had once worked out that, ounce for ounce, the substance inside the case was every bit as precious as gold. And although it made no sense since he was alone, he still instinctively gave a furtive glance over his shoulder before releasing the silver clasp that kept the case safely shut.

He gazed at the bronze vessel inside. He had discovered it while rummaging around an antique store in a small Tuscan village. As the elderly proprietor had slowly wended his way over to Casper through a maze of elaborately carved dressers, massive wooden cupboards, marble mantelpieces, and looming armoires, he prepared himself for hearing how the object he held had been brought back from the Second Crusade and later served as a temporary repository for Dante's ashes.

Casper's experience, based on considerable time spent in upscale shops, was that most antiquity dealers were the direct descendants of the fourteenth-century priests who promised salvation from the holy relics they sold like some Middle Ages eBay—a thorn from the Savior's crown, a splinter from the Holy Cross, a saint's femur. But unlike those buyers, Casper was prepared to ask some obvious questions. So just how many thorns did Jesus's crown have? How big was the Cross to have that many splinters? How many thighbones was Saint Mark born with?

To the old man's credit, he simply pointed at the vessel with its intricate etchings of prancing deer in a forest against the lusty, blood-orange backdrop of the tinned bronze and said, "*bellissimo*." Casper couldn't argue with that, and ended up forking over an amount of cash that probably meant Dante's ashes should have been thrown in as an add-on bonus. Indeed, if Casper had put it on display, he most certainly would have told his guests a story that would have had the vessel serving as Dante's temporary resting place, or perhaps even Michelangelo's. Casper, however, had a far more secretive purpose in mind.

His dealer, Francois—pusher was probably too strong a word—had advised him of the absolute necessity of having a proper, airtight place to safely store his treasure. And given what he was paying—cash, payable only in hundreds and fifties—it seemed only appropriate to have a beautiful reliquary for so valuable a commodity, one upon which he had developed a worrisome dependency.

Casper gingerly removed the lid that was designed to look like a minaret and gently placed it to the side. He stuck the index and middle fingers of his right hand into the jar, twirled them lightly around, brought them up to his nose, and applied the first swipes of a beautiful, viscous substance that glistened a rich ebony and smelled of an odd combination of licorice, seaweed, and musk.

This was mud harvested from a particular stretch of the Luangwa River just before it joined the Zambezi, a stretch that Francois had explained to Casper was unlike mud anywhere else in the world. "Not only," Francois enthused, "is Luangwa River mud off the charts in terms of its nutrients and moisturizing qualities, but"—and here he had lowered his voice to an awed whisper—"this small secluded stretch of the river, three hundred meters of an 800-kilometer river … think of it, Casper, as the proverbial needle in the haystack … is a hippo mating ground, which leads to a remarkably violent churning and enriching of the riverbed's already fecund mud."

When Casper had once questioned the astonishingly high price, Francois had sternly explained that between the dry season, the rainy season, and hippo mating season, his personal harvesters had a very limited window of time during which they were able to extract the priceless mud, a process they painstakingly did handful by precious handful at great risk of a hippo attack.

"If you don't think it is worth the money, Casper, I can get you some Lake Rotorua mud from New Zealand's North Island. It's fine, you'll be happy enough, although you'll smell a bit like old eggs. And, of course," he added, "you can always get some Dead Sea Mud off Amazon." And at this last thought, Francois derisively laughed as if someone sipping a Chateau Lafite Rothschild might just as likely ask for a mason jar of moonshine from the still his neighbor had built out of a 1978 Cadillac radiator.

Francois was the cosmetician to a short list of A+ celebrities whose identities he hinted at but never revealed out of respect for client confidentiality. Casper desperately wanted to be on that list. So he had quickly affirmed that of course he wanted the Luangwa mud. He had simply been idly curious why it was so costly. Casper was pretty sure from comments Francois had made that Luangwa mud was an unspoken bond he shared with George Clooney—a bond he was unwilling to give up despite the painful hit to his bank account.

As he completed the application of mud to his face, he thought of it as the type of ritual that warriors engaged in prior to battle, which seemed apropos since he increasingly felt as if he was in a contest where Moira was the prize. He had invited her to a "pre-game celebration" at his Antigua beach bungalow for a few days—and nights—on their way to Colombia, and to his astonishment, she had declined, explaining she already was meeting Percy Billings in Miami.

Casper's first reaction had been befuddlement, and he had immediately looked Percy up on the Internet to make sure he was thinking of the right person. He had been right, which only added to his incredulity. Percy had been introduced to him at a conference reception once, but after Casper realized Percy was at a no-name college in Nowhere, USA, he had quickly, and not very discreetly, scanned the room for someone with a more worthy *curriculum vitae* and then manufactured a flimsy excuse to slip away.

Casper studied the photo on Percy's faculty page to see if he was missing something. He was comforted to see that it appeared Percy bought his clothes from the clearance rack of a going-out-of-business store in a discount outlet mall. Percy's physical features placed him in the category that Casper and his friends jokingly referred to as "the forgettables." Casper was certain Percy and George Clooney had no secret bond.

Casper had asked Moira her plans with Percy while in Miami. He wrote down the address, failing to notice the immediate tone of regret that crept into Moira's voice after unthinkingly revealing the meeting place. A little more Internet sleuthing, and he had sussed out where they were rendezvousing and devised a plan.

After an hour of proper facial steeping, Casper smiled as he began meticulously removing the Luangwa mud mask with the moistened tip of a Kalymnos sponge. Like a photograph gradually developing in a darkroom, dab by dab, his handsome visage emerged in the mirror's reflection. Actually, handsome *and* determined visage, Casper revised. He found it almost unfathomable to believe that Moira's meeting with Percy could be anything other than a business matter, but if he was, in fact, vying with Percy for Moira's attentions, Professor Billings was about to be crushed.

Casper had once read a fascinating story about men in Cuba who instead of racing pigeons engaged in a sport they called *pluma loca*, or "crazy feather" competitions. Each of the *palomeros*, "the pigeon men," after painting their male pigeons' wings bright colors, would release them to compete with each other in seducing the same female pigeon.

To Casper's delight, the male pigeons were called *las palomas ladronas*—the thieving pigeons—since their goal was to steal the female's heart before the others could. The male birds would strut, show off their feathers, and fly with abandon, trying to woo the shared object of their ardor. The game ended when one of the male pigeons had successfully coaxed the female pigeon back to his cage and lured her inside, tripping the door and trapping her inside with the champion Casanova. This was known as a "capture," and unsurprisingly, not all male pigeons were created equal when it came to winning the prize. El Mas Tigre was the reigning champion with almost one hundred "captures" at the time of the article. Upon finishing the story, Casper had thought how if he ever was given a Spanish nickname, it should be El Mas Tigre, even if he wasn't quite sure what it meant.

Gazing into the mirror, Casper thought to himself, *Percy Billings, pluma loca on*, and smiled at the thought of Percy in his wrinkled, unpleated khakis and off-the-rack polo shirt. He did fervently wish that he could bring the vessel full of the wondrous Luangwa mud with him. Then he truly would be invincible. But he learned a very hard lesson last time he had flown, and he was not, in a million years, about to risk it. The TSA agents at the airport security checkpoint had confiscated both his Avocado Eye Cream and Tea Tree Toner, absurdly calling them "liquids" and cavalierly tossing them into a trash can as he protested with the impotent fervor of a New York Jets fan.

Oh, well, it was only two days until he left for Miami, and he and George Clooney surely could remain moisturized and wrinkle free for that long. With that comforting thought, Casper misted his body with rose water and slipped into bed, caressed by 2000-count, Egyptian Giza cotton sheets. Soon he was asleep and dreaming of executing a perfect double-barrel roll against a sapphire sky.

# CHAPTER TWENTY-FIVE

Moira believed that being places of worship, there was a bookstore and church out there in a shape, size, and denomination for everyone. The mega-bookstore and the mega-church both, for instance, offered convenient off-the-shelf selections pretty much around the clock. In the mega-bookstore, one can wander the generic, stain-resistant carpet of a cavernous space lit up with fluorescent lights as bright and personable as a prison visiting room. In the mega-church, one walks down mile-long rows to sit in a pew like an ear of corn in an endless field of cornstalks and seek contentment from Jesus-loves-me-but-He-can't-stand-you sermons.

Both mega versions admittedly have distinct downsides. In the first, you are strictly forbidden from taking merchandise into the restroom and are likely to deal with employees who would be just as content stocking pinto beans on a supermarket's shelves. In the latter, failing to put enough pieces of silver in the offering plate so the preacher can fly his Gulfstream to his mountain retreat can readily tip you into the "Jesus can't stand you" category. Neither, to put it mildly, was Moira's cup of tea.

More to her taste were the grand places steeped in history, awe-inspiring in their lineage and architecture. Bookstores like The Argosy or The Strand in New York City, or City Lights in San Francisco, were the spiritual siblings of the world's great cathedrals, mosques, and synagogues. A place that upon first entering had you pirouetting around and around, marveling at your surroundings. One immediately sensed the generations of worshippers who had wandered the aisles before you, the history that had accreted over the years like geological strata.

Having made a pilgrimage to the Canterbury Cathedral on a family trip her parents had saved a lifetime for, Moira had been struck by how the cathedral was as much, if not more, a repository of history as an active place of worship. The actual area for worship the day she visited was a cordoned area no larger than the roped-off shallow end at the neighborhood pool. A handful of congregants knelt, murmuring prayers, while throngs of visitors walked by, talking in hushed voices and excitedly pointing at the flying buttresses, the bronze plaques embedded in the floor stones, the stained-glass windows streaming color into the massive sanctuary. One could learn a basic outline of British history just from the remains of those who rested in the tombs along the apses, transepts, portals, and shrines lining the nave—Saint Thomas Becket, Henry IV, Edward the "Black Prince," Queen Joan of Navarre, the nobles and knights who had served them.

Like Canterbury Cathedral, magnificent and storied bookstores, such as the Argosy, seemed to Moira as much shrine and museum as bookstore. By the time Moira first visited, the Argosy had witnessed almost a half century of book lovers combing through its stacks. There were, of course, patrons popping in over the lunch hour to purchase a favorite author's book that they would crawl under the covers with that night like a welcoming lover. Many, however, pushed through the front door simply to bask in the atmosphere, ascend its stairs, and breathe in its history.

There was a level dedicated to first-edition books, and another to antique maps, prints, and historical artifacts. On the top floor, autographs of a Who's Who of American culture resided. Each ascending level added to the sense this was a place to gaze at and ponder the past, as if one were in the Smithsonian or British Museum. Moira once mused that just as the cathedral's walls housed the bones of many who called the building their spiritual home, she would not be surprised if someday the skeleton of a worker who had snuck off for a midday read was discovered behind a wall of remaindered books, a copy of the novel she had been reading cradled in her skeletal hands.

But as much as Moira loved these storied places of worship, she had a special tenderness for the place that existed for no reason other than to worship. This was the little, whitewashed church one stumbled upon off a country road after misreading the map, its timbers sawed, hewn, and planed by those who wanted a place to gather with their neighbors to give gratitude to God when the harvest was bountiful, to pray through tears when someone was gravely ill. Or the abandoned automotive repair shop turned into a makeshift church where a baker's dozen of parishioners gustily sang hymns behind a glass door that once swung open for $19.95 oil changes and free tire rotations.

And in Moira's case, it was the neighborhood bookshop, a place where one shared an immediate kinship with anyone inside, knowing they would only be there if also a fellow believer in the word. Whenever Moira was in an unfamiliar town or neighborhood, she made a pilgrimage to the local bookstore. These were the shops where piles of books rose from floor to ceiling like shaky towers of building blocks. Their shelves stuffed well beyond comfort, like the Thanksgiving diner who gave in to their temptation for a third slice of pumpkin pie.

From a financial perspective, the books that had not sold for literally decades no doubt could have safely been culled. That, however, would have felt like shunning a lifelong friend just because every time "Born to Run" played on the radio, he excitedly told the exact same story of how he had once flown three rows behind Bruce Springsteen between Newark and Los Angeles. One did not do that to friends, and what was a beloved book but a dear, dear friend with shared memories. Moira adored these lovable fire hazards of a shop, knowing that within a minute after the little bell rang signaling the door had been opened, the owner would emerge from the back like the village pastor wondering which of her flock had wandered in.

So it was that Percy had chosen wisely and Moira was smiling wide as she approached the address he had given her. It was a beautiful South Florida evening with a light breeze, almost making her wish she had brought a sweater, the lights of the storefronts lining the street having just flickered on as the sunset's orange, yellow, and red pastels faded into the dark.

The cause of her smile was a historic low-slung building whose design and appearance reflected Miami's early Mediterranean-inspired architecture. Beneath the outdoor lamps, the walls glowed white, topped by red terracotta roof tiles that peeked out like curious onlookers wondering who was about to enter. An open courtyard with an arched entryway separated two wings, with each wing sporting three large, arched windows facing the street. Each window, in turn, was separated by a Corinthian pillar, adding to the sense that the building must have a second cousin residing on a Grecian island.

It was these windows that Moira could not take her eyes off of as she crossed the street. Each window had sixteen panes, and in each pane's welcoming light a book was illuminated as if a model caught midstride walking down the runway. Moira felt a pang of envy for whoever got to choose which book took a turn on the runway.

This was Books & Books, the place where Percy's father had sought daily refuge from heatstroke and a respite from the tundra refugees who wore socks with their sandals and gingerly covered up their Day-Glo sunburns with newly purchased guayabera shirts, looking as at home as a penguin waddling through downtown Los Angeles. The store was an easy, six-block stroll from where his grandparents had lived and emanated charm from the moment one entered the courtyard, which was where Percy was nervously waiting at a corner table. At the last minute, he had changed out of his shorts after deciding that "spindly" was the word most likely to pop into one's head upon seeing his legs. He had opted instead for a pair of khakis partnered with a blue polo shirt, a decision he was now seriously second-guessing as making him look like a sales clerk selling televisions in a big-box electronics store. His self-critique was thankfully interrupted by Moira entering through the archway into the open-air courtyard, her face tilted up toward the stars starting to appear overhead.

Moira heard Percy before she spotted him.

"Welcome to my family's chapel."

Whether it was because Cupid was taking pity on Percy, or the Fates decided to make amends for Percy's spindly legs, or Percy simply was saying what first popped into his head, his greeting was pitch perfect, and he was rewarded with the sight of Moira turning toward him with a look of undisguised joy on her face.

"Percy!" Moira quickly came over to Percy and gave him an embrace and a European peck on each cheek. Motioning with one hand around the courtyard, she grabbed his arm with her other hand and said in an awed tone, "This is wonderful. I can't wait to enter ..." She paused, and in a voice of soft reverence said, "the chapel," and then gave a light laugh.

Percy loved the sensation of her hand resting on his arm, but eventually took her elbow and guided them toward the door to enter the wing to their right. Pulling the door open, they crossed the threshold into a room that reminded Moira of a library that would be the ideal centerpiece for a whodunit set in an English manor from the 1920s.

Thirteen shelves of dark wood climbed each wall from floor to ceiling. There was even the wood ladder that rolled along the top to allow access to the upper shelves. With some difficulty, Moira resisted climbing the ladder, settling for going over and placing her hand longingly on one of the rungs and looking upward. She half-expected to look over to the corner and see an elderly man smoking a pipe in a leather upholstered chair, book in his lap, snifter of brandy on the end table, and an Irish Setter serenely curled at his slippered feet.

All of the deep-hued wood might have been oppressive rather than cozy—even the ceiling was made of dark, wood slats—except that hundreds of colorful dust jackets glimmered like Christmas tree lights from the shelves and atop tables in the middle of the room. This was the room of "new releases," where countless authors dreamed their books might someday make their debut, to be picked up, thumbed through, and then carried over to the cash register. These were also books that, like the seasonal tilling of a field, would soon be removed and replaced by the next batch of new releases in their shiny covers. If extremely fortunate, a book would find an afterlife in one of the adjacent rooms holding the books that had crossed the treacherous strand from "new" to "classic," or at least to "occasionally asked for."

Moira turned her attention to a section of shelves marked "staff picks," with books lined up above rows of index cards where each staff member had written a short ode to a book they were recommending. Moira always found these shelves a sure sign she was in a place of true believers, where the peril in asking about a book was not that the employee wouldn't know of it, but that, in response, one might be proselytized for half an hour about a "better" author.

She sighed contentedly, turned to Percy standing next to her, grabbed his arm, and said, "How did you ever guess this would be my type of gin joint?"

"Incredible powers of deduction, really. I had but a lone clue—that your dream would be to live in a place where one navigates to the bathroom in the middle of the night by using the Dewey Decimal System. But given your response, it appears that, amazingly, I put it together. Perhaps being a gumshoe is a side gambit I could pursue." Was it Percy's imagination, or did her grip on his arm seem to tighten slightly?

"You know, as a child, I decided I wanted to be an oologist," Moira said with a smile, turning her eyes back to the staff's picks.

"Oooh-kay. Even if I knew what an oologist was, which I must admit I don't, that seems at least slightly out of the blue. And I'll go ahead and admit I'm saying 'slightly out of the blue' instead of 'completely' only because I was raised to be a gentleman."

Moira laughed, her green eyes sparkling with mischief as she turned back to face Percy. "So David Bowie ... do you know him? I know you don't keep up with music much." Moira was definitely having a good time. "He called the Oxford Dictionary a really long poem about everything, and he was so right. Even the way some words simply sound when spoken make me happy, whatever the definition.

"And so when I was, I guess, in the fifth grade, I heard the word oology in a nature documentary—it is the study of birds' eggs, by the way—and thought, 'What a magical word, and how cool would it be to tell people you're going to be an oologist.' Which I did, by the way ... I mean, tell anyone who would listen that oology was my career choice. Even did a presentation on it to my class on career day. I still feel guilty that I brought in robin eggs from my backyard, but they were such a beautiful blue, and I didn't realize I couldn't just put them back in the nest afterward."

"I'm guessing there will be a reckoning in the afterlife for that pig-tailed ten-year-old," Percy chimed in, and then saw that Moira really did look remorseful and quickly changed gears. "So do I get to see your egg collection sometime?"

"Ah, I fear that I've left a string of brokenhearted words in my wake. I forget what eventually replaced oology, but by the time I got to college, I remember it was being a cicerone. I mean, hell, to have a calling that invokes Cicero and involves beer at the same time seemed pretty hard to beat as a university student. Anyway, all that is a digression," Moira shook her finger at Percy as if in warning, "an ever so slight a one, mind you"—then grinned and concluded—"to saying how I love seeing what other people choose as their favorite books and poems. The best books for me are a painting, a song, a story all at the same time, where you can tell the author savored every word they chose because the words not only tell a plot, they engage all the senses to create wonderment."

Percy was nodding earnestly, listening to her but also marveling at how just being in her presence, feeling her energy, hearing her voice triggered a sense of happiness. Talk about all of one's senses feeling alive and engaged. Even the colors of the book covers surrounding them seemed to pop with more vivid reds, vibrant greens, vivacious blues. Some deep chord of emotion was undeniably strummed when he was with Moira, and the more he was with her, the more deeply resonant it became.

Percy came out of his reverie and was about to say, "Should we move on to the next prayer station," but thought better of it. The danger with metaphors was that at some point they became more annoying than apt. "Don't keep beating a dead horse" might be a pretty brutal saying when you stopped to think about, but it also was a pretty good metaphor for the overuse of metaphor. He settled for a simple, "I think the oology books are in the next room. Should we go see?"

But the staff was setting up chairs and a podium for an event in the room immediately next to them, so they exited back across the courtyard and began working their way through the rooms in the other wing.

As they browsed through the shelves, Percy observed, "The crazy thing about this building is it doesn't sound that old when I say it was built in the

1920s. But when you realize that Miami was largely wilderness until the early 1900s when the railroad came down this way, it's one of the city's earliest ... like a building from the 1700s in Boston."

"I didn't know you were such a historian of the area."

"Mainly know it because my dad loved this place and would learn tidbits about the building. I think it was first used as doctors' offices. We're probably standing on the very spot of a thousand 'aaahhhs.'" Percy pantomimed having a tongue depressor stuck in his mouth accompanied by an "ahhhh" that came out louder than intended, attracting a few annoyed scowls he found well worth Moira's bemused look. He shook his head sadly. "Yup, pretty sure this room is where many a tonsil said a sweet and swollen goodbye to the world."

"That's pretty specific. Is there a plaque commemorating those tonsils?"

"Sadly not. They fall in the unknown soldier category. And now I've pretty much exhausted my pool of knowledge. Please don't ask me about the Everglades. Would have to go with 'lots of alligators' and hope that earned me a 'C' because I at least knew they weren't crocodiles."

And so they bantered easily back and forth as they leisurely moved past the shelves and tables, pointing out favorite books like a couple strolling through an arboretum on a lazy Sunday afternoon drawing each other's attention to a particular tree or plant. Percy forgot his spindly legs, and Moira further let down her guard as they continued to tease and laugh, learning tidbits about each other along the way as if picking up clues on a scavenger hunt. If anyone was watching, and they did draw a few envious glances as budding romances tend to do, they both seemed to enjoy the direction the clues were taking them.

They entered the corridor at the back of the courtyard that connected the two wings and now served as a small café. With books propped open in front of them, people sipped cappuccinos and nibbled at confections so delectable looking, they would have tempted Marie Antoinette to opt for the cake instead of the crown. On the wall above the tables were signed photos of authors who had done book signings at the store, signatures that Percy and Moira tried to read as they edged their way down the room without getting so close to a table that a diner reflexively raised a fork in defense of their tiramisu.

They were almost to the end of the hallway and debating if a photo was of Kurt Vonnegut when Percy heard a vaguely familiar voice he couldn't quite place. Giving in to a curiosity that he would later kick himself over with the ferocity of a karate sensei, Percy wandered to the doorway that opened up into the room where the chairs and podium were being set up earlier.

Peering around the corner, he was startled to be greeted almost immediately with a "Percy!" so enthusiastic that one would have guessed they were two best friends from high school who hadn't seen each other in years. An equally ebullient "Moira!" soon followed, and Percy turned to see Moira looking over his shoulder with eyes wide in surprise as if she'd just seen a ghost.

"Come in, come in, you're just in time." With a voice oozing gratitude, as if no sight could bring him greater joy, Casper Crenshaw continued, "How remarkably kind of you two to make the effort to come. It means so very much to me."

Only a third of the thirty or so chairs arranged in front of the podium were occupied, and every occupant turned to see where Casper's attention was focused, their expectant faces beaming happiness at seeing the author greeting two people who were so special to him.

Percy saw no escape, at least without greatly embarrassing Casper. Percy gave Moira a helpless glance, and like sleepwalkers in a trance, they moved over and mechanically sat down in the last row of folding chairs.

Watching them take their seats, Casper smiled to himself and thought, *Professor Billings, meet El Mas Tigre*. Then, with a flourish, he spread his arms out wide and began speaking, "Friends, I know it is almost impossible to believe, but it has been a decade since *The Dairymaid's Lament* debuted and opened the eyes of the masses to the beauty of poetry ..."

# CHAPTER TWENTY-SIX

For a half hour, Casper did spins, barrel rolls, and double loops, his ponytail bobbing up and down as he moved, looking frequently in Moira's direction to make sure she was watching. He had spent over an hour choosing his outfit for the evening, settling on what he thought of as "tropical casual chic"—a peach melange linen shirt strategically left untucked as if he had just jumped onto the dock from his yacht's deck, white slim-cut chinos that clung just so, cuffs hemmed precisely two inches above a pair of tasseled chocolate-brown loafers to reveal that he wore no socks, thus allowing his bare, tanned ankles to boldly declare his utter disdain of convention and what others thought.

Casper had sprung into action as soon as he learned the address from Moira and discovered she was meeting Percy at a bookstore. He had been slightly taken aback when he first phoned down to Books & Books and shared the good news that he would be spending a night in Miami on his way to an international literature conference where he was the featured speaker, and, as a result, would be available for a book signing of his Tenth Anniversary Collectors' Edition of *The Dairymaid's Lament*.

The "I'm sorry, who are you? What are you lamenting?" response was unexpected, but he felt better when he learned he wasn't talking to the owner, who was away on a camping trip in the Everglades.

Casper had proceeded to convince the assistant manager, Julia, that it was utterly unfathomable that the owner would not jump at the chance to have him speak. He could hear the background clatter of typing on a keyboard as they spoke, and apparently the search result—Oprah Book Club choice, winner of various awards—convinced Julia she had better book Casper despite the short notice and not being able to run it by the owner first.

As Julia learned upon the owner's return, it in fact had been quite fathomable he would not have wanted the book signing, given that Casper stood him up when the book had been first released a decade earlier. Books & Books had been one of the few to schedule a book signing in response to the publisher's repeated pleas "to give Casper a chance." Then, only a few weeks before Casper was due in Miami, Casper had instantaneously become a hot commodity as the book skyrocketed to the top of the *New York Times* Bestseller List fueled by Oprah's turbo boost.

On the morning of the day he was to do the book signing, Casper had called to explain how ill he felt and regrettably could not travel, only to be photographed that evening walking the red carpet at the Met Gala with a Slovenian supermodel on his arm. Fortunately for Casper, who had not remotely recalled the incident, the owner did not regain cell phone reception until after Casper made his appearance.

An appearance that had Percy growing more miserable by the minute. Casper Crenshaw was the professor who every college used in their promotional materials to lure eighteen-year-olds with the promise of hip instructors who 'got them.' *Hell,* Percy dejectedly thought, *I wouldn't be surprised if Casper's university featured him in a two-page centerfold lying on a bearskin rug under a heading, Come to Where the Professors Rock the Classroom.*

The more he heard Casper talk, the more it confirmed how little Casper cared about what he was saying. It was all about basking in his audience's adulation. But Percy had to dolefully admit the audience was responding, chuckling at Casper's jokes, craving his attention. As gloom enveloped him, Percy unconsciously tried to smooth out his crumpled pants, only to have the wrinkles mockingly spring back after each pass of his hand.

In his peripheral vision he could see Moira sitting next to him, a smile upon her face. By God, she was lovely. He was so focused on their conversation, he hadn't fully absorbed how splendid she looked this evening, which now only added to his funk. *Percy,* he thought to himself, *you are so out of your league it isn't funny.* And he started to hastily retreat to his customary hideout when a broken heart appeared to lie just around the bend, the ideal of courtly love.

As a gangly teenager, Percy found comfort upon learning that the very idea of a knight's chivalrous love was to bestow it upon someone unattainable, usually a married woman, because that way, the love would be kept pure even as he wrote verses of longing to his beloved. Intrinsic to courtly love was the very idea that you would suffer pain and despair by loving someone so virtuous that even as you strove to do valiant deeds to prove your love, you knew the love could never be consummated, true proof of one's devotion.

Percy strongly suspected that, in reality, many a rendezvous had occurred between chivalrous knight and his supposedly unattainable love in turrets atop castle walls as Venus acted the lookout. But now, as he sat feeling despair listening to Casper, he sought the emotional companionship of those who rode off to certain death in battle, knowing their noble love would be unrequited.

And Percy wasn't wrong, Moira did have a smile on her face. In reality, though, she was doing her best not to laugh. At first, Casper's self-aggrandizing prancing around a room brimming with glorious books had seemed almost blasphemous, like playing polka music at High Mass, and annoyed her. And having found *The Dairymaid's Lament* quite moving because its acute sense of lost love was so painfully and beautifully expressed, she wondered, not for the first time, how Casper ever could have written it. He was concededly witty, but there didn't seem to be a lot of "there, there" once you moved past the glibness. Someone once said that when it comes to emotions, everyone is a millionaire, and while the author of *The Dairymaid's Lament* came across as a tycoon on that score, the person at the front of the room seemed to barely have a solvent checking account in terms of genuine feelings.

Gradually, though, Moira's annoyance transformed into a feeling she was watching a parody of a nature documentary about male mating rituals. She knew the display of peach-and-white plumage was for her benefit, but when she noticed Casper's bare ankles, she found it hard to suppress a surprised giggle. She tried to catch Percy's eye to share her reaction through an incredulously raised eyebrow or a subtle "can you believe this?" shake of the head, but Percy for some reason was focused on running his hands up and down his pants' legs.

All of which led Cupid to be quite upset as he watched along with the Fates atop Mount Olympus.

Cupid: *"Don't be a fecking idiot, Percy. Stop the goddamn self-pity and courtly love shite. Show a little backbone, will you? I set it all up for you. This is stressing me out. Why the hell did I let Athena convince me to give up smoking."*

The Fates: *"You are such an adorable little cherub. It's not his fault, you know, it's just his nature. He was not meant to roll the dice if there is a chance at losing. He has a safe, comfortable road ahead. Let him take it. He has a dog in his future, we're thinking sheepdog. His worst fear is being where he's not wanted and feeling the sting of rejection. Plus, you know, he has rather spindly legs."*

Cupid: *"Damn it, Percy. I fecking swear if you don't pick up the drumsticks and seize the moment, you're dead to me. I'm going to shoot one more arrow into your skinny ass, and then I've had it."*

A sharp pain caused Percy to shift uncomfortably in his seat and turn his focus away from his rumpled pants to Moira. Moira, who had returned her attention to Casper's fanning of his feathers, sensed Percy looking at her and began to turn back toward him when Casper suddenly, and with dramatic effect, slapped the top of the podium and declared, "And that, my beloveds, is why poetry is far more erotic than pornography." And while the fawning audience members held out their newly purchased Anniversary Editions for his signature like sports fans wanting their favorite player's autograph, Casper breezed by them to where Percy and Moira sat.

"Moira, a thousand—no, make that a million—thanks for giving me the heads-up on this place. They were so grateful to get me in for a book reading, and I couldn't have made it happen without you."

Percy looked at Moira as if it had just been revealed that she had been on the grassy knoll when JFK had been shot. Caught by surprise, Moira stumbled forward. "But I didn't ..."

"So here's the thing," Casper hurriedly interrupted. "I'll be done here in five minutes. Just need to put my John Hancock to a few books, and then let me treat you to dinner. You, too, Percy, to show my gratitude. Lord knows, with tonight's royalties, we can eat like kings and queens." His triumphant laugh made Percy's melancholy complete.

Before Moira could respond, Percy chivalrously decided to nobly ride away. "Thanks, Casper. I'm not feeling great, and my flight is an early one tomorrow." Moira reached out an arm to halt him, but Percy could not bring himself to look her in the eyes and instead wandered toward the exit with a, "You two have a good time." The door closed behind him, and Percy found himself outside on the sidewalk, alone and morose, no steed to ride into battle, no sheepdog, not even a windmill to tilt at.

Cupid cursed and turned sharply upon hearing a laugh from behind him. Fortuna emerged from behind a pillar, smiling victoriously. *"Can't win them all, amoretto, or, well, at least you can't. My favorites on the other hand always do ..."* And with a flip of her hair, she headed off to the gaming tables.

# CHAPTER TWENTY-SEVEN

Moira was still steaming from the prior night as she wearily plopped down into seat 4A. Normally, upgrading to first class would have had her feeling like Cinderella putting on a flowing silk gown to attend the royal ball. She had never flown first class, always having made the trek back to the "economy section," as the airlines euphemistically labeled it, to sit amid Ebola-sounding coughs, failing antiperspirants, and the wails of babies and first-time fliers.

What was the name of that part of medieval London where waifs and scoundrels always ended up and buckets of foul liquids got sloshed out of upper-story windows? Cheapside, that was it. Well, airline coach seating was the new Cheapside, and she always felt like a peasant as she navigated the scrum to the rear of the plane, walking past the already-seated first-class passengers sipping their Beefeater gin and tonics. Perhaps the only surprise was that the airlines didn't supply the first-class passengers heads of rotting lettuce to throw at the economy passengers as they shuffled by, lugging overstuffed bags that Archimedes himself couldn't have fit into an overhead bin.

Still, she almost turned down the first-class seat when the gate attendant, with a huge smile, advised her that Mr. Crenshaw had used his frequent-flier miles to upgrade her, delivering the news as if Moira had just won the Clearinghouse Sweepstakes. She had been livid with Casper's manipulations the night before and had been tempted to tell him so.

Ultimately, however, she decided it was just easier to beg off dinner and avoid him for the rest of the trip. Casper, though, clearly wasn't giving up.

Fortunately for Moira, before she could turn down the upgrade, Señora Consuela Mendoza had recognized Moira from the previous evening and approached her to gush about Casper. When Moira learned Señora Mendoza was also flying first class, Moira was able to magnanimously offer to swap first-class seats and let the pearl-laden dowager sit next to her idol.

With that resolved, Moira decided if the world was going to mess with her, well, then, for once, she would sip a Malbec while cutting a slab of Wagyu beef with real cutlery instead of washing down pretzels with a half ration of Diet Pepsi back in coach. Plus, Moira had the enjoyable pre-boarding entertainment of watching Señora Mendoza rush up to Casper, latch her hands onto his arm like twin lamprey eels, and enthuse how she couldn't believe her incredible luck that she was seated next to "*the* Casper Crenshaw." A bewildered Casper hadn't got in a word edgewise.

The most uncomfortable moment was when Percy, looking miserable and sleep-deprived, shambled down the aisle only to do a double take that practically gave him whiplash upon seeing Moira. His eyes darted back and forth between her and Casper, who he had spotted two rows ahead, as if rapid eye movement could solve a confounding riddle. He got out a halfhearted "Moira," but she looked out the window rather than meet his eyes, and soon he had disappeared beyond the curtain demarcating the purgatory between first class and coach.

She felt a pang of remorse, but it was overshadowed by lingering anger. She finally had begun to emerge from hibernation, her time with Percy rekindling long dormant feelings. True, she had not fallen head over heels in love, but that wasn't her way. Someone once wrote, "We are all asleep until we fall in love," which was true enough, only in Moira's case, the awakening of romance first required several cups of strong coffee and perhaps a scone with clotted cream.

But now, just as Moira was about to finish that second cup, Percy had to act like an idiot in what appeared to be some act of self-flagellation based on assumptions about her and Casper. Well, if he didn't have confidence in her judgment and common sense, she was just fine crawling back into a nice, cozy cave full of books.

Meanwhile, Percy had finally found his seat and was stuffing his bag into the overhead bin when he heard a voice. "Sir? Sir?"

Percy turned to find a man in a Hawaiian shirt standing in the aisle. Having gotten Percy's attention, he continued, "My wife and I are on our honeymoon and we were so hoping that you might switch seats so I can sit next to her." The man's eyes were filled with enthusiasm and love, and Percy looked down to see the seated bride peering up at him with a pleading look.

Percy inwardly sighed. He had paid extra to get an aisle seat, and the man's assigned seat was in the middle between someone who appeared to be an aspiring Sumo wrestler and a grandmotherly type looking all too eager to talk. Percy so wanted to say no, but perhaps still feeling an obligation to the inner chivalrous knight who had kept him company through the night, he found himself agreeing—an agreement that spawned an effusion of "thank yous" and "you're so kind" from the newlyweds.

Percy nodded stoically, squeezed past the Sumo wrestler, wedged himself into his seat, and pulled out his book in an effort to hang a "Do Not Disturb" sign on the proverbial doorknob. It was at most thirty seconds before the woman, who had been staring out the window, turned to him and asked, "Is that a good book? I think my friend Edith read it, or perhaps it was Marjorie from my book club. Or maybe I heard a review of it on Fresh Air. Don't you just love Terry Gross ..." It was going to be a very long flight.

# CHAPTER TWENTY-EIGHT

Agent Forreo stretched and yawned as daylight blazed through the open window. Damn the sun was bright, but guess that was to be expected in the middle of the afternoon. Having arrived in Bogotá three days before the conference in order to, as he had sold it to Attles, "do reconnaissance," Mike immediately fell in love with the city and its pace of life.

At Esteban's insistence, Diego's assistant, Enrique, had picked him up at the airport and been his constant escort ever since. Mike reasoned to himself that to make his undercover role believable, it was necessary to willingly let Enrique serve as his guide. Given that Enrique was charismatic, fun-loving, and spoke impeccable English, putting himself in Enrique's care was proving to be anything but a hardship.

And so it was that Mike had spent the nights not eating dinner until ten—he could picture his parents back in Iowa already fast asleep for an hour as he was just unfurling his dinner napkin and ordering an *aguardiente*, a drink Enrique said meant "fiery water" and fully lived up to its name. He would then ride on the back of Enrique's motorcycle to an eclectic collection of bars and clubs with his arms encircled tightly around Enrique's waist as the motorcycle careened around corners with abandon, returning to his hotel room around two in the morning, light breakfast at nine, hearty lunch at one, and then ... oh my God, and then ...

Mike knew, of course, that he led a very sheltered life before coming to New York. Some of the discoveries of what he had been missing during what he now called his "killjoy period" were relatively mundane. There were, however, worldly delights he deeply regretted not knowing before, that made him feel like he was playing a desperate game of catch-up. These were the pleasures Reverend Graver and his parents had hidden from him for the sake of his soul, the ones that caused his cheeks to flush red upon first discovering them. And learning over the past few days that entire parts of the world openly embraced what had always been one of his most shameful secrets, upset him greatly.

What Mike had been taught to believe was only morally permissible to do in the dark of night with the lights out, shades drawn, beneath the covers without a sound, it turns out was splendid, in some ways more so, when openly reveled in and relished with the sun at its apex. Mike finally understood what was meant by the phrase "afternoon delight." He had discovered siestas.

His parents were strict disciples of the "early to bed, early to rise" school of philosophers, and truly, honestly believed, to the marrow of their bones, that to sleep during the day exposed a decaying spirit that would soon turn to the bottle, or, most likely, was already decaying due to a fondness for drink. True, he knew some people in the States who occasionally slipped away midafternoon to curl up on a sofa, but it usually was for a quick catnap done sneakily and not admitted to in polite company.

But here in Bogotá ... oh my, come early afternoon, shopkeepers locked their doors and drew the shades, teachers put down their chalk, judges gaveled courts into recess, street vendors stowed their carts, and people went home for two glorious hours. Not everyone slept, but if you wanted to close your eyes, no skulking about was necessary. Rather, one could do as Mike had done, peeling off his clothes, pulling back the covers, fluffing the pillow into a cradle for his head, contentedly sighing at the feel of the cool sheets on his skin, and closing his eyes. As a general proposition, Mike was politically apathetic, but Jesus, Mary, and Joseph, if a Siesta Political Party ever formed and ran a candidate with a platform calling for the siesta to be recognized as a Constitutional right, he was all in.

Later that night, Mike had explained to Enrique how his parents would have looked at siestas as a shockingly decadent ritual. "One of their favorite sayings when they'd roust me out of bed on dark winter mornings was, 'The early bird gets the worm.'"

Enrique had laughed warmly and flashed Mike a smile that would have charmed a Puritan. "Ah, but do your parents think the birds of the night starve? I think of us as nightingales—we sing all night long because we are so well rested and happy. Your padres also have forgotten, I think"—he gave Mike a roguish wink—"about the worm at the bottom of the tequila bottle. That worm definitely belongs to us night owls." And with that, he signaled the waiter and ordered each of them a shot of tequila.

They had both laughed heartily, but now, as Mike let the water from the showerhead cascade over his head to wake him up from the siesta, his mind went back to an incident he had tried to ignore. They were at their final stop of the night, La Revoltosa, and Enrique had waded through the sea of partiers over to the bar on the far side of the dance club to get them one last drink. Granted, Mike was deep into his cups by that point, and it was hard to see through the crowd of bodies pulsating to the music, but he was pretty certain he had seen Enrique talking to Carlos at the end of the bar. The man he thought was Carlos appeared to be angrily pointing at Mike as Enrique tried to calm him down. Enrique, who was a good head shorter than the person he was talking to, had both hands planted on the man's chest as if trying to hold him back.

Eventually, Enrique had returned to the table with their drinks, beads of sweat standing out on his brow like rain droplets. Mike asked, no doubt with a bit of a tequila slur, who Enrique had been talking to at the bar. Uncharacteristically subdued, Enrique lowered his head, locking his eyes on his drink. "Just a friend needing calming." He added as an apparent afterthought, "Troubles with a woman had him upset. You know how that goes."

As Mike replayed the incident in his mind, he tried to cut Enrique every break he could—the haze from the cigarette smoke had been as thick as a San Francisco fog, Mike was more than a little inebriated, and Enrique seemed like a nice guy who genuinely liked Mike. But as the shower poured over his head and washed the grogginess away, Mike, with a strong pang of disappointment, knew Enrique had lied.

But why? Was his cover blown? Carlos had certainly looked like he wanted to rip Mike's head off, and Carlos undoubtedly would have recognized him from his evenings at Esteban's playing the role of beatnik poet. Mike felt a slight shudder if Carlos had him targeted. As gentle as Esteban was, Carlos's brutal role as the Velasquez family enforcer was legion within the DEA.

Perhaps naively, Mike had clung to a sliver of hope that Esteban was not involved in the family's drug business and the conference was on the up-and-up, but that slice of hope, already wafer thin, was crumbling. Well, tonight there was a welcoming reception for the conference, and Esteban had gone out of his way to have Mike invited, so perhaps he'd know more afterward.

# CHAPTER TWENTY-NINE

Esteban closed his eyes as the driver wound down the mountain road that corkscrewed away from the Velasquez compound to the city center. The window was down, and the evening air, cool bordering on chilly, calmed him, gently playing across his face as he leaned back on the seat. He needed this: the comforting feel of traveling a route he had taken hundreds of times, the full moon illuminating the stands of trees flanking each side of the road like well-wishers, familiar turns and landmarks reassuring him as if softly singing a song from his childhood.

In the days following his arrival in Bogotá, Esteban had been gradually consumed with an unfamiliar nervousness. His arrival a week ago had been a homecoming celebration he was not used to. As always, his mother greeted him warmly, smothering him with hugs and kisses as he playfully protested, but there was a look of hopeful expectation he wasn't used to seeing in her eyes.

The "*soldados*," as Diego called the men who helped him carry out his various missions, also received him in an unfamiliar manner. Usually after an absence, they treated his arrival at the compound as if the postman was delivering the mail, an event to be expected but not worthy of acknowledging. This time, however, there was a respect, even a hint of deference, in their attitude.

The oddest moment, though, without any close contender, was when Diego, upon hearing Esteban enter the house, practically burst out from what he used to call his office but now referred to as his study. Diego strode over to Esteban and, for the first time he could recall in his adult life, gave him a hug. Granted, it was a tentative hug, not one of those all-encompassing embraces featured in sappy commercials of families celebrating the holidays, but first times are almost always awkward. Diego had then immediately ushered him into his study to "talk business."

Esteban, fearful his mother would feel hurt since she had always been the focus of his attention upon first arriving home, glanced worriedly over his shoulder at her. But again, to his surprise, she waved him on toward the study with a quick flip of her hand as if that was where he belonged. Esteban's stomach knotted as he realized he was being greeted as a type of savior, a role he'd never had before or wanted. Walking past the crucifix his mother had hung in the hallway outside Diego's office, he also was struck by the thought that savior gigs rarely end well.

As the car now made its way to the conference's opening reception at the university center, Esteban's mind travelled back to a meeting with his dissertation advisor soon after he started grad school. Professor Henrietta Williams Clarke was a very proper, prim, and accomplished scholar who, after emigrating from Jamaica to England as a teenager, had hurdled over every educational barrier put in her way to become one of the leading authorities on the Romantic poets. She had recently moved from Oxford to Columbia to assume a chaired position in the English department, and Esteban was one of her first graduate students.

He had been more than a little intimidated. Her brilliant mind constantly dazzled him with ideas that arced and burst over his head like Roman candles. And her manner, while not unfriendly, was politely formal, often leaving him wondering what she thought of him. Which was why he had been slightly alarmed when one afternoon arriving for their weekly tutorial, she arose from her usual station behind the desk, closed the door, and solemnly sat down in a chair next to Esteban.

"Esteban," she began in a voice rich with layered pronunciations as if a reggae singer was fronting the Royal Philharmonic. "I am in need of some assistance, and I think you may be the person who can supply it."

Bewildered, wondering how much she knew of his family, he had reflexively nodded his head. "Of course, Professor Clarke."

She sat silent for a long minute, staring at the bookshelf behind Esteban's head. Finally, she began, "As part of my new position here, I am under an obligation to put on a conference every year."

"That's great," Esteban had interjected with relief, only to be met with a look of incredulity.

"You do not understand, Esteban. Arranging one of these conferences," she paused, "is"—she paused again—"fraught with peril." She stood up and started pacing. "Have you ever been involved with the planning of a wedding?"

"Not really."

"Well, be grateful. You can plot seating arrangements with the battlefield brilliance of Alexander the Great, but you will invariably spawn alcohol-fueled feuds between family branches lasting for decades. Oh, and don't get me started on having seated the groom's sister, Lucinda, and the bride's brother, Michael, together," –her example struck Esteban as awfully specific –"not realizing it would lead to a drunken assignation in a coat closet that would have gone blessedly unnoticed if not for the mysterious stain on Aunt Millie's favorite cashmere coat that"—she made an air quotes gesture with her fingers as she said the next word—"*apparently* slipped off the hanger and ended up spread out on the closet floor as if a blanket."

Straightening her blazer as if she had been the one emerging from the coat closet and with a slight look of embarrassment, Professor Clarke sat back down and looked at Esteban. "That said, as you are about to discover, wedding receptions are a piece of cake compared to arranging a conference."

The conversation had been a turning point in their relationship. While they never reached a level of friendliness where they bantered over a pint, they would share laughs and eye rolls in her office at the latest departmental intrigue or academic folly. And after helping Professor Clarke plan a series of symposia, he quickly learned why she had been less than thrilled with what otherwise seemed like a coveted perk.

Professor Clarke had not exaggerated—the drama of an academic conference was primetime programming more appropriate for HBO than PBS. Under the civilized shell of a scholarly exchange of ideas lay a rumbling magma of egos, insecurities, and personality disorders. True, the verbal knives used to stab each other in the back were inserted with perfect noun-verb agreement, but the wounds were still keenly felt and schemes of vengeance instantly hatched. Sometimes the squabbles were over whether one was a disciple of Professor X or Professor Y's view of narrative technique. Disagreements of such vehemence and insignificance that Esteban was reminded of a bitter religious schism he once read about where followers of one sect during church services said "Amen," while the breakoff group with proud defiance said "Ahem."

The bloodiest battles, though, resulted from competition over the breadcrumbs of prestige sprinkled along the professorial career path—wrangling an invitation to present a paper at the Western Michigan Shakespeare Conference in Kalamazoo, building the political coalition necessary to be elected chair of the Medieval Chaucer Scholars' Club, being seated at the "in group" table at the Biennial Congress of Modern Poetry dinner. Someone once observed that when it came to the academy, "The fights are so vicious because the stakes are so small," and from what Esteban witnessed during his brief time in the academic underworld, a mob boss could pick up a helpful pointer or two from a thoroughly pissed off Shakespeare scholar.

Which is why as Esteban labored to put together the Bogotá conference, he offered a silent thanks to Professor Clarke for the lessons she had taught him. The conference needed to be legitimate enough to survive outside scrutiny but low-key enough to avoid unwanted attention. He had invited professors he hoped would largely go unnoticed and would be so grateful for the invite, especially with its lucrative stipend, that they would play nice with each other.

Esteban had spent considerable time looking through the faculty profiles at small colleges in the outer constellations of the university universe, paying keen attention not only to their areas of scholarly interest, but also to their profile photographs. As Moira noticed at their first meeting on that frigid January day when the Xerox sheet of the attendees with their photos had fallen onto the floor, he had assembled a roster of professors who looked like the adult version of every kid who ate their bologna sandwich alone in the high school cafeteria. With the exception, of course, of Casper

Crenshaw, the unwelcomed intruder whose colossal ego offered unexpected benefits in addition to the dreaded hazards.

And now, ready or not, it was coming to a head. If the plan failed, not only would it mean the collapse of the family's fortunes, but, in all likelihood, that he would never return to the United States unless in a prison jumpsuit.

And Lord knew what would happen with Carlos. They had arrived back home about the same time, although on different flights to divert suspicion. From the moment Carlos's feet touched the ground at the Bogotá airport, it was as if a lightning strike had struck a drought-stricken forest primed to burn. Anxious to beat his chest and reassert his dominance, Carlos had already skirmished with a rival cartel leader's son, exchanging shots between moving cars. Even more worrisome was Enrique's report that he had been forced to restrain Carlos from wanting to "make Mike disappear" when they ended up at the same nightclub. Fortunately, Enrique was Diego's longest-serving lieutenant, and Carlos knew that to cross him would bring down the full wrath of his father—the only man who Carlos feared. With his father's help, he had figured out a way to bring Carlos into the master plan, starting with this evening's reception, but whether Carlos would have the patience to follow the script remained to be seen.

Esteban continued working down his checklist of worries. How best to handle Mike. And Casper. The entry back into the US with the contraband. So many moving pieces, each one capable of quickly unraveling and collapsing the plan. Esteban felt his chest contracting again, the acid reflux beginning to bubble, a low rumble like distant thunder on the horizon beating behind his temples.

Esteban impulsively stuck his head out the window, and a reviving blast of cold air hit him like smelling salts waved beneath a woozy boxer's nose. "*Esta bien?*" the driver asked, his worried eyes glancing up at the rearview mirror. Esteban pulled his head back into the car, rolled up the window, smiled, and gave an affirming nod toward the driver as the Mercedes pulled up to the university building where the reception was taking place. He might last three seconds—max—in a knife fight in an alley, but as he watched the guests entering the front doors, the tension began to gradually ease as he thought about his father's words upon leaving the house, "Never underestimate home field advantage."

Rejuvenated, Esteban ascended the stairs leading to the reception hall two steps at a time and pulled open the doors' ornately carved handles. He paused a moment to watch his guests mingle in an area stretching out in front of the stage where the speakers would present the next day. He smiled as his eyes moved to the huge banner his father had commissioned that now stretched from one side of the stage to the other. Bright-crimson letters three-feet tall against a white background shouted, *La belleza es verdad, la verdad es belleza.* A smaller banner in English hung beneath, its royal-blue letters declaring, "Wordsworth in Bogotá," the name he and Moira had come up with when first planning the conference.

On the stage were two long tables. The table on the left had the now-all-too-expensive bound copies of the conference participants' papers standing upright. The books, which were for the conferees to take back with them to their colleges' libraries, stretched from one end of the table to the other like a precariously balanced row of dominoes.

The table to the right had the twelve Grecian urns in two staggered rows, an urn for each participant to take back as a conference memento. Usually, a conference attendee received a "swag bag" with items like a pen imprinted with the conference's name and a faux-leather portfolio embossed with the hosting college's logo. The urns definitely were in a class of their own and ensured the conference would not soon be forgotten.

Esteban took a deep breath and moved forward into the crowd, ready to play the perfect host.

# CHAPTER THIRTY

As Mike approached the conference center's doors, his thoughts wandered to his freshman roommate. Mike's mom had been visibly upset upon seeing Ned that first day of college as they moved Mike into a dorm room the size of a mini storage unit. Ned had greeted them from the lower bunk bed with a wide grin and bloodshot eyes, wearing ragged jeans and a tie-dyed Grateful Dead T-shirt emblazoned with a jig-dancing skeleton.

Mike later learned that his mom, convinced Ned was a Satan worshipper, had desperately tried to get campus housing to move him into a different room. Fortunately, she had failed. While Mike never gave up his pastel polo shirts, crew cut, or even smoked a joint, he had surprised himself with how much he enjoyed Ned's company that year. Mike had been stoner curious but never given in, and after Ned dropped out of college had largely forgotten about him until these past months when trying to develop his beatnik poet vibe.

He once asked Ned if it bothered him that he was always the person who looked as if he had just been on a five-day backwoods camping trip, and Ned explained, "Hey, man, people don't appreciate the virtues of being the lowest common denominator. Everyone likes knowing that no matter how crappy they look, you're always going to make them look turned out for a debutante ball. And never underestimate"—Ned exhaled a huge plume of smoke from his favorite bong—"the beauty of being underestimated. Hell, man," Ned said, letting out a hacking cough that sounded like an old car engine desperately trying to turn over on a sub-zero December morning, "I bet if you traced my lineage back to medieval times, it'd say 'low expectations' on my family crest." Ned moved his hand through the air as he read his imaginary family crest through the haze of pot smoke. "Humilis exspectatione," he said slowly. "That's low expectations spelled out in Latin, and to think I barely passed high school Latin."

Another bong hit, another cough where Mike could hear Ned's lungs rattling around like loose change, and Ned continued, "Anyway, low expectations are better than a handful of quaaludes at keeping you calm. Not being taken seriously has benefits you can't even begin to imagine." With that proclamation, Ned had laughed, plopped his head onto his pillow, and drifted off to the Dark Side of the Moon.

Channeling his memories of Ned, Mike muttered a mantra of 'low expectations' to himself as he pulled open the doors and nervously scanned the room. He felt every bit as out of place as he had feared and was grateful to spy Esteban over at one side of the room, laughing and conversing animatedly.

He was about to beeline over to Esteban and cling to him until he got his bearings, when the sight of Casper Crenshaw's bobbing ponytail caught his attention. Attles's chiding from their phone conversation earlier in the day popped into his head. "You have one simple goddamn mission, Forreo—find out if Albatross is their conduit, and, if so, how he's going to get the drugs out. That's it. Can you manage that without totally fucking it up?" *Hmm,* Mike thought, *sounds like pretty low expectations to me.* He relaxed a little and even laughed at himself a bit, thinking Ned would have been proud. Almost accidentally upending a passing server, he grabbed a flute of champagne from the server's tray and started working his way over to Casper.

As Mike moved closer, he could hear Casper, with his head intently tilted forward, telling a beautiful, young woman, "I hear through the grapevine that my Spanish-speaking friends call me El Mas Tigre. I believe they mean that fondly, but I don't speak Spanish, only Italian and French, so I can't be sure." Casper then gave what Mike guessed was supposed to be a carefree laugh.

Mike approached with his hand extended. "Professor Crenshaw, I had so hoped we'd have a chance to talk."

Taking in Mike's look—greased-back long hair, scraggly beard, Goodwill-chic turtleneck and jeans, Keds high-top sneakers—Casper looked at him with such astonishment that a few forehead creases snuck back from their Botox exile. "And you are ... you are, whom?"

"I'm Mike Forreo, poet-in-residence." He proudly pointed at the name tag pinned to his chest with the title Esteban had graciously given him for the conference.

Filling the awkward silence as Casper continued to stare at Mike, the young woman put out her hand and, in English spiced with a light accent, said, "Señor Forreo, I'm Lucia Calvo, one of Professor Angeles's students here at the university taking her seminar on British Literature." She gestured toward Casper and continued, "Professor Crenshaw—"

"Casper, please," Crenshaw interjected putting his hand on her forearm.

"Casper then. He was telling me about ..." She looked at Crenshaw in a searching way.

"The 'Barcarolle,'" Casper filled in, looking pleased.

"The 'Barcarolle' he is presenting tomorrow."

"The what?" Mike asked.

"Barcarolle," Casper repeated without any effort to disguise the tone of condescension. "It is the song the gondoliers sing as they ply the Venetian canals"—turning back to Lucia, his voice lowered as if telling a secret—"and it is that sense of yearning, romance, a nod to both past and future loves that I try to invoke whenever I'm giving an invited talk, which is why I call them my barcarolles."

"So you sing your talk?" Mike asked as he downed the last of the champagne in his glass and exchanged it for another as a server passed by.

"What? No, of course not. It is simply ... Oh, never mind."

Ned was spot-on about the pleasures of low expectations as he watched Casper struggle to not add "you idiot" and risk alienating Lucia, who appeared to be slowly inching away from Casper.

Lucia turned to Mike and asked, "Will you be reciting one of your poems tomorrow?"

"Um ... no. I'm just here to learn," Mike replied somewhat absentmindedly as his attention focused on Casper, who was scanning the room clearly eager to jettison Mike onto a passerby and regain Lucia's sole attention. But as Mike followed Casper's eyes, he saw Carlos leaning against a wall fifty feet away, for once trying to look inconspicuous. And, then, unmistakably, as Mike watched Casper's glance move across where Carlos was standing, Carlos gave a surreptitious but distinct nod to Casper and the slightest jerk of his thumb in a universal get-out-of-there gesture. Mike quickly returned his gaze to Casper and was astonished at how well Casper acted as if Carlos's signal had never happened. *Damn, got to give Crenshaw more credit than I figured,* Mike thought. *That is CIA-level cool under pressure.*

Casper's attention finally returned to the conversation, and to both his and Mike's surprise, Lucia had wandered off, leaving just the two of them. Casper abruptly announced he was off to get another drink, and Mike, amped up by a sense of success, gleefully called after him, "Good luck with your boc ... boc ... choy" a few decibels louder than he intended, garnering several curious looks.

His confidence bolstered, Mike looked around the room pondering his next move. Carlos's considerable bulk was still propped against the wall, and he was now definitely tracking Mike, uneasily reminding Mike of those nature films where the lion, lounging at the savannah's edge, watches the herd of gazelles, mulling over which one would be tastiest. But Mike also noticed that Carlos was casting protective looks toward the stage whenever someone wandered near it. Following Carlos's glance, Mike, for the first time, fully took in the impressive site of the urns arrayed on the table, their rich earth tones glowing beneath the stage's overhead lights.

Intrigued, Mike moved toward the stage in a way he hoped would not draw Carlos out from the shadows. With square-dancing dexterity, he would join a cluster of people, introduce himself as the poet-in-residence, politely listen for a minute or two, give a knowing chuckle when someone laughed, make his apologies, and then move on to the cluster next closest to the stage. Eventually, he managed to promenade and allemande all the way to the front of the stage.

After a furtive glance to make sure Carlos was nowhere near, he ascended the short set of wooden stairs that led to where the table of urns stood. The blinding brightness of the overhead lights as he stepped onto the stage surprised him, and he sensed more than saw the figure quietly emerging from the wings.

"*Cuidado, Miguel.*" He stopped at the sound of Esteban's voice. As his eyes adjusted to the glare of the spotlights, Mike turned toward Esteban, their eyes locking for a moment before Esteban's warm smile appeared. "Forgive me if I startled you. I didn't want to take a chance of one of these accidentally getting broken." Esteban tipped his head at the urns. "They're quite wonderful, aren't they? I saw you admiring them and thought I'd come over and see how you're doing."

"Yes, yes, they're quite ... cool, for sure. I almost feel drawn to them. Can I look at one closer?"

Putting his arm around Mike's shoulder, Esteban gently moved Mike back toward the stage's edge and down the stairs. "So tell me," Esteban said, "have you been having a good time since arriving in Bogotá? Enrique certainly has enjoyed showing you the sights." Esteban waved his hand as if holding a magician's wand, and as Mike's eyes followed Esteban's waggling fingers, he saw Enrique hastily making his way to them, a smile beaming across his face as if he'd just found a long-lost treasure he'd given up on ever seeing again.

"Ah, there you are, Mike. I was looking everywhere for you." And like a shadow, Enrique stayed with Mike the rest of the evening, other than when Mike slipped off to the restroom where in a stall he madly typed out a text to Michelle, who was heading up Operation Poetry Slam communications. "Tell Attles, Albatross definitely in league with Carlos." He paused, moving the cursor backward to make an edit. "Tell Attles, *asshole* Albatross definitely in league with Carlos." Then he added, "Tell him, KNOW how drugs coming in. Will debrief fully tomorrow," and he hit send. After a few seconds, he sent a second text just to Michelle. "Albatross may be total jerk, but my God, skin tone is amazing."

\* \* \* \* \* \*

Like a pole vaulter readying himself to clear the bar, Percy blew out three quick breaths as he stared at the doors leading into the reception hall. A lifelong member of The Society of Introverts, he dreaded these events. One would think that someone who made a living standing in front of a classroom would find it easy to mingle, especially in a crowd of fellow professors, but by the evening's end, he'd know more about the bartender's upcoming vacation plans than anything about the conference goers. When it came down to it, thirty years later, he was still the kid trying—and failing—to muster the courage to ask someone out onto the gym floor at a middle school dance.

And tonight, his anxiety was at Red Level Alert status knowing Moira would be there. Was he only taunting himself to think there was any hope of salvaging what had seemed so promising? He had engaged in repeated mental flagellation since leaving the bookstore—one of his specialties—reliving, in agonizing slow motion, each of his missteps. But far from finding a road to redemption, he had simply become increasingly frustrated with himself.

As he watched the steady trickle of guests enter the reception hall, he was on the verge of spinning on his heel and retreating to his hotel when he saw a young man, scruffy as a stray dog, dressed all in black, pause, mutter something to himself, and then pull the doors open with a trepidation that struck a familiar chord with Percy. *Well hell,* Percy thought, *if worse comes to worse, I'm pretty sure this down-on-his-luck Johnny Cash will have an interesting story to tell.* With a vow to not look for Moira, he entered the hall before he could change his mind.

The vow lasted as long as a hungover New Year's resolution. Within a few minutes, he had spotted Crenshaw and felt an embarrassing amount of relief that he wasn't talking to Moira. As he began walking between the knots of people keeping an eye out for Moira, he exchanged a mutual nod of recognition with a person here and there but was struck again that almost all the conference participants were not familiar names.

As he wandered, Percy heard snippets of awkward conversation and the tell-tale nervous laughter of people trying too hard. Given the number of people staring at their shoes, the thought crossed his mind that an unknowing observer might think this was a footwear convention. Realizing this might be the closest thing to a meeting of The Society of Introverts he'd ever find, Percy's anxiety lessened a notch.

One person, however, seemed to be having a good time, and Percy quickly surmised this must be Esteban. Moira had talked fondly about Esteban, but Percy had yet to meet him. From his solitary corner, he observed Esteban meandering through the crowd, shaking hands with a politician's gusto, radiating a warmth that could get a misanthrope chattering away like a late-night talk show guest. He watched as Esteban migrated to the far side of the hall, guest by guest, and then seemingly vanish.

Welcoming the diversion from thinking about Moira, Percy scanned the hall for the missing Esteban, even standing up on the tips of his toes to peer over the minglers' heads. A few minutes later, he finally spotted him up on the stage talking to the Johnny Cash figure he had seen entering the hall earlier. As he watched, Percy grew increasingly transfixed by the interaction up on the stage that appeared to be more than a simple "hello."

"Percy."

He spun around, spilling half of his drink onto the floor as he did so, barely avoiding soaking his shirt by raising the glass up and away as if he were making a drunken toast, but in the process, also just missing drenching the person who had said his name.

"Moira! I was hoping I'd see you, run into you"—he gave a little laugh looking at the ice cubes at their feet—"but not baptize you."

Moira did not smile as she spoke. "To be honest, I was going to try and avoid you, but that seemed less than grown up. So, anyway, hello. I hope you enjoy your time here. And now, I need to go take care of some conference items." Percy could practically reach out and break the icicles clinging to her words.

"Moira, give me a minute, please, to at least apologize."

"I don't want your apology. There's nothing to apologize for. I just realize we see each other differently than I thought, and that's fine. Simply the way it is."

"Let me explain, though?" Moira stared at him as if at a fork in the road, trying to decide which direction to go. Percy plunged on. "So I was thinking about this wonderful line that someone once wrote about the painter Frida, that her work was like a pretty ribbon wrapped around a bomb ..."

"Really, Percy?" Moira's face reddened with anger. "Goddammit, that is where you want to go ... a pretty ribbon? I've spent practically my entire fucking life with people making assumptions ..."

"N-n-o, n-n-o," Percy stuttered. "I don't mean pretty ribbon as in you're beautiful. Well, you are, but, oh shit. What I meant is, it is so easy to underestimate someone, and I did that with you, and I did make assumptions ... that someone like you would prefer someone like Casper over me, like almost any other person does, it seems. But that I actually did— and do—know that you are far more than the pretty ribbon. You are packed full of life, you see through people and things. Damn, I know I'm not making much sense, but I needed to let you know that I let my own insecurities blind me to the fact that you see through Casper, and that out of whatever moment of temporary insanity you seemed to think we ..."

Moira held up her hand, a sigh of exasperation replacing the anger that had flashed before. "Here's the thing, Percy." She looked away for a moment and then wearily turned back. "The only relationships I've ever seen work are those where each person trusts that the other will always give them the benefit of the doubt, think the best of them. I heard someone at her fiftieth wedding anniversary celebration say something quite beautiful when asked how they had made it so long. She was an artist, and she said that she always thinks of every person as an impressionist painting—if you're up too close, they're all swirls and messy brushstrokes, if you're back too far, they seem blurry and not worth looking at, but we all have a sweet spot where we come together as a wonderful painting. And when you find the person who is perfect for you, they always view you from that sweet spot. They instinctively know when to take a step forward or back to keep you in focus, letting you rest happy, knowing they are always seeing the whole of you in the best light possible. That made such complete sense to me."

"That ..."

"So, Percy, I'm not angry, I'm really not. But I've got a good life right now, and I've been in those relationships where you're always having to say, 'No, no, stand over there and you'll understand'"—she gestured with her hand as if trying to position someone—"'no, move a bit that way and now you'll see' ... and, well, it is exhausting and not what I want. I won't do it anymore."

Percy waited to make sure she had finished. "I get it, I honestly do. And I think we can still have that. I feel a ..." Percy searched for the word, then said, "kismet with you. I didn't trust that our ability to laugh together could conquer all, but it can."

Moira looked at Percy with a tenderness for the first time since the disastrous night at the bookstore. "I do believe you think that is true, and I did too—"

*As he pulled the bowstring back between his pudgy fingers, Cupid shook his curly locks out of his eyes and thought, Damn, I've been doing this too long. A couple of millennia, and I'm going soft on giving second chances. Percy isn't exactly a Cyrano when it comes to romantic wooing, but at least he didn't give up this time ...*

The sharp ting, ting, ting of a spoon hitting a glass tugged the crowd's attention to the stage where Esteban stood. As everyone turned to hear Esteban, Moira leaned in and whispered, "I'm sorry, Percy, but I just don't know, and right now in my life, I can't deal with that."

*Cupid watched aghast as Moira leaned in, and the gold-tipped arrow flew over her shoulder and struck a server passing behind her, causing the server to drop his tray of hors d'oeuvres. Cupid angrily looked up at the stage just in time to see Fortuna smiling as she removed her hand from Esteban's arm, holding the spoon. 'Damn,' Cupid muttered as he watched the server gather up the bacon-wrapped dates scattered about his feet. Not only was Percy on his own again, but one never quite knew how a wayward arrow would play out. Could the world handle another Bob Dylan?*

As Percy stood frozen, watching Moira melt back into the crowd assembling in front of the stage, bits and pieces of Esteban's welcoming remarks flitted in and out of his consciousness ... "first annual Wordsworth in Bogotá conference" ... "excited" ... "esteemed scholars" ... "enjoy our city" ... "the schedule for tomorrow begins" ... "finish in time to get everyone to the airport for their flights."

But he wasn't really listening. All he could think about was how he fervently wished he had developed a taste for whiskey, the only cure-all for a broken heart according to pretty much every country song ever written.

182 WORDSWORTH IN BOGOTÁ

# CHAPTER THIRTY-ONE

Bronson Attles used to despise Miami. He first visited when it was still primarily populated by silver-haired retirees who had collected their gold watches, loaded up their Oldsmobiles and Buicks, navigated the eight-cylinder behemoths onto Highway 1, pointed their cars' hood ornaments south as if lining up a long putt all the way to Miami, and then drove ten miles below the speed limit until reaching their new home in a senior citizens' community with a euphemistic name like Casa de Mañana. From what Attles could tell, they would then play a round of golf during the day, a hand of pinochle in the evening, and wait during the dark of night with quiet dread as the Grim Reaper came cold-calling with increasing insistence until funeral-going replaced bingo as the main social activity.

Even a therapist with a mail-order degree would have had no trouble diagnosing Attles's aversion to Miami as the manifestation of a deep denial triggered after his parents sold their dry cleaning business and moved to the Sunset Acres retirement home, a six-building complex plopped down where a grove of orange trees had once hung heavy with fruit. With each annual visit, he would notice his father's once-nimble gait becoming a slow-motion shuffle, his mother's posture bowing forward until she resembled a hastily scribbled question mark, forgetful moments each would try to gently cover up for the other.

And although he knew it wasn't their fault, anger would well up in him because they were no longer the vibrant people he knew growing up, greeting a customer with a cheery good morning, providing a welcomed reassurance that, "Absolutely, Mrs. McFadden, we can get that red wine stain out of your grandma's lace tablecloth. Just be sure to tell Mr. McFadden next time to forego that third glass of Chianti." The ensuing group laughter would reverberate all the way to the rear of the shop and back as plastic bags of suits and dresses zipped along the shop's overhead conveyor belt, swaying back and forth like a conga line of Holy Rollers. Not knowing where to direct his anger, Attles simply decided to hate all of South Florida.

But then he loved it. His parents were at rest back north beneath the shade of a century-old maple in his hometown's cemetery. The throngs of retirees had largely given way to a bustling immigrant population where one heard a symphony of dialects and languages. A duet of English and Spanish comprised the main melody, accompanied by a diverse chorus of Creole, Portuguese, German, French, Mandarin, and Russian. Even the Spanish overheard while strolling down the sidewalk could vary in pace and tone from samba to tango, depending on whether the person had emigrated from the islands dotting the Caribbean like green paint drops, or a city like Buenos Aires where a lullaby of "*shh*" is sung every time a word containing a double-L is spoken.

But it wasn't the cultural vibrancy that came with Miami growing into the northernmost capital of Latin America that flipped Attles's heart from dislike to like, or that the influx of young people was making the city's nightlife hotter than blacktop baked by the South Florida sun. It was that drug dealers had discovered the same smuggling allure that once appealed to Prohibition rumrunners—a shoreline dimpled with hundreds of inlets generously camouflaged by Mother Nature with heavy shrouds of mangroves and thick stands of cypress. If one was looking to make their name in the DEA, coming to Miami was the equivalent of a plastic surgeon opening an office in Beverly Hills.

And Attles had taken full advantage. The advent of the Reagan years was like a snort of meth for the DEA's budget, kicking the agency into frenetic overdrive in an effort to corral the Cocaine Cowboys who were riding roughshod over local law enforcement. Attles's career had plateaued up in D.C., and he eagerly seized the chance to ride at the head of the Federales sent in to restore order. And although his efforts to be portrayed in the media as a modern-day Wyatt Earp had never taken hold, even down to wearing a white Stetson during interviews, he had overseen so many big busts, a full-scale replica of the Empire State building could have been built out of the bricks of cocaine seized on his watch.

The payoff had been his promotion from head field agent to Northeast Regional Associate Deputy Chief, and now that he again needed a career bump, he saw it as more than fitting that the trail led back to Miami.

Usually investigations that terminated with arrests in Miami were passed on to the South Florida office for final execution, but he had made a special request to personally oversee the final stanza of Operation Poetry Slam. He had presented his request at a meeting in the DEA's headquarters in D.C. One of the mid-level bureaucrats sitting at the conference room table had smirked and referred to Attles's presentation as his "Captain Ahab moment." Attles knew his reputation among the younger DEA higher-ups was of a brutish, foul-mouthed agent from a bygone era who had survived mainly through intimidation. He resisted the temptation to tell the smirker exactly what he could do with his Moby Dick reference, not so much out of any admirable show of self-restraint, but ... well, because he basically agreed with it. Instead, he had simply turned his attention from the smirker back to the head honcho at the head of the table and asked, "So?"

\* \* \* \* \* \*

Attles sat on a raised dais, swiveling in his chair. He was in the command center hidden directly above the intake corral where international air travelers arriving in Miami were rounded up, herded, and sorted through customs. From his vantage point, he could look directly down through the command center's special floor panels at the travelers gathered below waiting to have their passports scrutinized, while also keeping an eye on the monitors that continually broadcast views from every gate of disembarking international passengers.

He watched now as a passenger who had aroused a customs agent's interest in the intake area was diverted to one of the rooms off the main processing area. There he would be questioned and have his belongings inspected, item by item, down to the contents of his toothpaste tube. If the agent's suspicion was sufficiently heightened, the passenger would hear the snap of a rubber glove being put on in anticipation of the upcoming cavity search.

During his earlier time in Miami, Attles had seen it all when it came to smuggling, from the imaginative to the boneheaded—ecstasy secreted inside a kid's Mr. Potato Head, soccer balls inflated with cocaine instead of air, hollowed-out avocados stuffed with Molly, chocolate bars with heroin fillings, a Mickey Mouse doll packing a gun in its cotton stuffing.

Then there were the cruel schemes. One married the region's dual obsessions with plastic surgery and illegal narcotics. A ring of surgeons—Los Cirujuanos ("the surgeons")—working for a Cali cartel inserted breast implants of liquid cocaine, each worth over one hundred thousand dollars, into destitute women desperate to support their families. After their arrival in Miami, gang members, unconcerned about hygiene or anesthesia, would remove the implants during hasty operations performed in cheap hotel rooms, leaving the women disfigured, ill, and sometimes dead. Los Cirujuanos had added calf implants and even buttock augmentation to their surgical smuggling repertoire before being busted.

Luckily, Operation Poetry Slam was in a better position than most intercept missions. They knew both the "who" and, thanks to Forreo's surprisingly good undercover work, the "how." Attles was no longer quite sure of the mastermind's identity ... Diego, Carlos, or Esteban ... but whoever it was had just made a pretty smart move. As Agent Esperanza had confirmed, the conference was coordinating and paying for all the return travel by the professors. And whoever was pulling the strings had spread the professors out on three different return flights—one going to Miami, one to Houston, one to Chicago. The effect would be to spread the DEA interception team thin and increase the odds that some of the couriers would make it through.

Enjoying the chess game, Attles made a countermove. Knowing that all three planes would travel a similar flight path until just outside Colombian airspace, he arranged for Agent Chang to be a passenger on the flight to Houston and for Esperanza to have a seat on the plane headed for Chicago.

Chang and Esperanza would then each have a panic attack precisely at the moment where the pilots would need to divert to Miami as the closest major US airport rather than proceeding to their destination. As a result, the planes originally bound for Houston and Chicago would now arrive in Miami at almost the same time that the wheels of the Miami flight with Agent Forreo on board would touch down on the tarmac.

Then the trap door would be sprung. The team had given each of the professors a codename, and one by one they'd take them down. Agent Esperanza kept giving the professors the benefit of the doubt, calling them "dupes" instead of "couriers." Attles was unconvinced. After seeing the titles of the talks they had to sit through for eight hours, Attles couldn't imagine anyone willingly putting themselves through that without a huge payoff. No matter. The one co-conspirator he was sure of—Casper Crenshaw, the Albatross—was on the Miami flight manifest and would be a firsthand witness to the inglorious end of their plot. An involuntary smile came to Attles's weathered visage as he imagined how itchy the low-thread cotton of a prison jumpsuit would feel on the Albatross's pampered skin.

Attles glanced at his watch. The so-called conference would just now be getting underway, which meant the hardest part lie ahead—the wait until evening. He might as well go back to his hotel and rest in anticipation of the long night ahead.

He exited the command center out into the parking lot. The thunder of a quick-moving storm blowing in off the Everglades drew his attention to a gathering mass of ink-black clouds. Another crescendo of thunder exploded, this time practically right above him, its reverberations setting off unhappy car alarms like a mob of angry protestors.

Attles closed his eyes and felt the freshness of the incoming cold front sweep over him as he waited for the next peal of thunder. He'd never admit it to anyone because it sounded so New Age, but he felt a special connection to thunder.

In his senior year of high school, his parents had insisted he join the orchestra to bolster the extracurricular section of his college applications.

Given that he possessed no musical skills whatsoever, that was going to be tricky. So his father had bartered with the orchestra director for a year-long, half-price discount on all dry cleaning in exchange for letting his son play the kettle drums. What Attles had thought at first would be boring drudgery soon became one of pure joy. He wielded the mallets like a manic samurai, the drums' plangent sound pleasurably resonating through the whole of his body as if he were a tuning fork.

Because Attles couldn't read music, the band director limited him to one brief spiel each song, pointing directly at him with the baton so he knew when to play, and then making a huge X in the air with the baton to stop a few seconds later. And all went fine until the school's Winter Recital.

The orchestra was playing the Hallelujah chorus in accompaniment to the school's choral group when a strange euphoria overtook Attles as he pummeled the drums with the mallets. His section was supposed to last only fifteen seconds, but as the choir's *Hallelujahs* encircled him like a magic spell, and the growing swell of the other instruments took his rapture higher and higher, he simply was powerless to stop.

He wasn't playing rhythmic notes. He knew none. He was just hitting the drum skins as if possessed ... *Hallelujah* ... his shoulders heaved up and down with his effort ... *Hallelujah* ... at points, his feet left the ground from the force of his blows ... *Haaalleeeeluuujah*. And on he went, engulfed by the thunder of the drums, the soaring voices, the blaring trumpets, the throaty pulsing of the strings. The director looked as if he was having a seizure, making X after X after X with his baton pointed at Attles, each more emphatic and larger than the one before. Still, Attles couldn't stop. *Haaalleeeeluuujah*. It was only once he realized all the other musicians had put down their instruments and the choir had gone silent that Attles, his arms so weary they felt like they might fall off, stopped and saw everyone staring at him.

That was the end of his musical career, and a mortified, teenage Attles vowed to never, ever allow himself to get so out of control again. But now as the thunder roared and brought back the sound and reverberations of the kettle drums, Attles, not for the first time, felt a twinge of longing for that euphoric sense of complete release.

The rain beginning to fall snapped Attles out of his reverie, gigantic drops splattering like water balloons on the ground. He glanced around to make sure no one had seen him staring up at the sky like some barefoot Druid worshipper, and then made a dash for his car, serpentining around the rapidly forming puddles.

# CHAPTER THIRTY-TWO

The placard saying *Rio de Vida Café* was propped next to the row of coffee urns where a line of supplicants with half-opened eyes had formed. Even with his limited Spanish and without the benefit of caffeine, Percy smiled as he read the placard and thought, *River of Life, okay, that's a pretty damn good name for a coffee company.* In the depths of his despondency the night before, Percy never would have predicted his good spirits this morning. He pulled the spigot forward and watched the black liquid promising new life stream into his Styrofoam cup, after which he would return for another cup of resurrection.

He hadn't slept upon returning to the hotel, unable to quiet his thoughts after seeing Moira. Nor did it help that his room overlooked a street brimming with bars where patrons were singing and laughing until three. Around five, he had finally thrown in the towel on falling asleep and figured he might as well get a head start on packing for the flight back after the conference.

As he pulled the suitcase from the closet, the rattle inside made him pause and sigh. He unzipped the Samsonite, knowing the drumsticks he had thrown in at the last minute while preparing to fly to Miami and meet Moira would peer accusingly back. Without thinking, he picked them up and walked to the window where Bogotá slept in the pre-dawn darkness, except for the sounds of a garbage truck making its rounds.

It is understandable that a person hopes that if they have a life-changing moment, it comes in dramatic fashion—perhaps atop an Icelandic outcropping gazing at the unearthly colors of the Northern Lights, or maybe as one emerges from a tent high in the Rockies just as the Perseids meteors plummet into the atmosphere in a kamikaze act of blazing celestial glory. An experience, in other words, suitable for the founding of a new religion, or writing the lyrics to a rock 'n' roll song whose meaning will be debated for the next half century, or for serving as a memoir's epiphany that will have readers paying for the author's future eating, praying, and loving.

In Percy's case, the burning bush was the clattering of battered and dented trash cans full of empty beer bottles, used condoms, and half-eaten bocadillos being unceremoniously emptied into a garbage truck. But no matter. The cacophony of banging metal trash cans and lids would change the arc of his life as the sounds got him thinking, *Damn it, Percy, there are your cymbals. Are you ever going to actually play the drums?* And to his surprise, rather than going down the well-trod path of self-recriminations over failing to seize the moment, he pulled out his computer, sat down, put the drumsticks next to the laptop, and started fervently typing. He finished a half hour later and looked up just as dawn was bringing life to the bright pastels of the buildings surrounding the hotel.

Sometimes, it turns out, you need a shove. Like when he was nine years old, standing paralyzed at the end of the dive platform at the city pool, looking ten feet down at the translucent blue of the water, too scared to jump, too embarrassed to climb back down. In that instance, the shove had been provided by an impatient Billy Cantor, two years older and far more athletic, standing at the top of the ladder, waiting his turn, yelling over and over, "Just jump, you idiot. It isn't going to kill you."

And Billy had turned out to be right, even if Percy almost lost his swimsuit as the force of entering the water yanked the trunks down to his ankles, forcing him to madly scramble to pull them back up before resurfacing. The shove this morning had been a long time coming, and Percy finally stepped off the high board as he pushed "send" on his email.

Now, sipping coffee and still flush with the early morning boldness of a few hours earlier, he looked around the auditorium and smiled for the first time in a long time at a conference. He found himself charmed by watching the nervous energy of some of the professors just beginning to make their way in the profession, excited to be presenting their ideas.

Percy had always envied professors who approached every new idea with the eternal eagerness of a black lab bounding after a tennis ball. In his current convivial mood, he hoped for them that their enthusiasm would never ebb. Most were from colleges where getting national, let alone global, attention would be difficult, and they must have relished explaining to their bewildered department heads that they were headed off to an international meeting with all expenses covered.

He, though, simply could no longer generate enthusiasm after numerous conferences. The papers seemed highly predictable, whether it be the obligatory "hip" paper looking at the hidden ties between the music of a rock star like Bruce Springsteen and the poems of the Romantics, or a post-colonial-Lacanian-structural-deconstruction critique enmeshed in a bramble of jargon—dense, impenetrable, and painful. True, the titles changed from conference to conference, and each panelist would claim an insight no one thought of before. Percy, though, was always reminded of prospectors in a mined-out river, buffeted by freezing water gushing around their legs, numb but hopeful fingers sifting for a last nugget that might have been missed.

Today's conference did have him intrigued, however, even if the presentations did not. From the moment Moira had floated the invitation during her first visit to Arcadia, something did not quite add up—the money offered to participate, who his fellow invitees were, the short time frame in which the papers had to be produced. And the onstage interaction last night between Esteban and the man in black, who he later learned was apparently the poet-in-residence, was ... well, odd to say the least. And this morning, somberly dressed men with incipient scowls were discreetly positioned around the auditorium. While he hated typecasting, they appeared straight from the set of *The Godfather*.

Scrunching down into his chair to get comfortable as Professor Angeles gave the conference's opening remarks, Percy had the distinct feeling he was in one of those do-it-yourself mystery parties.

\* \* \* \* \* \*

With a welcoming smile, Professor Maria Angeles stepped to the podium and convened the Wordsworth in Bogotá conference. She thanked the Velasquez family for their generosity in bringing such wonderful scholars to campus and providing the chance for her students and colleagues to eagerly immerse themselves in their scholarship. As she delivered her remarks, she glanced around the audience to ensure her students were living up to their end of the bargain. She had made the standard professor-student bartering agreement to avoid the embarrassment of an empty auditorium—if you attend the symposium, class will be canceled for the week. She was pleased to see her students, even if looking a bit bedraggled given that it was 8:30 in the morning, were present.

As she scanned the room, she was surprised and charmed to see Diego sitting off by himself with a notepad and the book of translated poems she had given him. Upon spotting him, her first impulse had been to ask him to stand and be acknowledged, but realizing he looked uneasy and clearly did not want to be recognized, she refrained from saying anything. But upon concluding her remarks and turning the microphone over to Esteban to introduce the first panel, she went over and slid into the seat next to Diego, gently placed her hand on his arm, and whispered with a smile, *"Bienvenidos mi estudiante favorito."* Diego had sheepishly looked down and, Maria could have sworn, blushed.

And so the conference began. Each panel had four participants with either Esteban or Maria moderating. Although most of the attendees, including many of Maria's students, spoke flawless English, since the symposium was billed as bringing the beauty of the Romantics to a Spanish-speaking culture, Esteban had arranged a translator for each professor's presentation. The professor and translator would proceed in tag-team fashion—the professor would speak for several paragraphs, pass the microphone to the translator who would provide the Spanish translation, return the microphone to the speaker, and on they would go in alternating fashion until the presentation concluded.

The format had the potential to be tedious, and the translator for the first presentation infused a palpable sense of dread that it was indeed going to be a very long day. His droning monotone made it sound like he was translating a store clerk who was taking inventory rather than a manuscript looking at Hollywood's use of Romantic poetry memes.

The audience relaxed a little once the second translator took over for the next speaker. She was more earnest and garnered a few appreciative nods here and there from the Spanish-speaking audience members. If one was like Percy, however, who had no command of Spanish beyond catching a random word here or there, the translator's turn with the microphone became an interlude to surreptitiously glance at one's phone and catch up on email and text messages.

As the next speaker prepared to give her remarks, the third and final translator rose from her chair, wearing a simple black dress with a string of faux pearls, and stood demurely next to the podium. The presenter read the initial paragraphs of her paper entitled, *Onomatopoeia Throwdown: Tennyson versus Browning*, and handed the mike to the translator.

Percy's eyes, which had begun a downward arc toward his phone with the passing of the microphone, immediately sprang back to the stage as the translator spoke. Listening to the expressive undulation of her melodic voice, he felt as if he were surfing a fast-moving wave, both exhilarating and dangerous at the same time, and her delivery was accompanied by facial expressions that vividly cycled through a range of emotions so quickly, it left the listener breathless. Her performance—there was no other word for it— was all done as she stood stock-still, eyes closed, with her hands piously clasped in front of her chest as if in a confessional. Even those who barely commanded enough Spanish to order a cerveza had their eyes riveted on her with mouths slightly agape.

The voice whispered in Percy's ear, "You should see her do Lady Macbeth." Startled, Percy turned to find that Esteban had slid into the seat next to him. As the translator passed the microphone back to the stunned presenter, who almost dropped it, Esteban, in a hushed tone, continued, "She's from Miami, a translator in the criminal courts by day, actress by night. She has apparently become a problem, though. When she translates for a Spanish-speaking defendant, no jury will convict no matter how outlandish his story. I mean, really, who could convict after hearing someone who sounds as if she is an oracle of the gods? As I understand it, the prosecutors are trying to get her banned."

Percy returned his attention to the stage. She really did sound as if she was channeling some primitive, deeper truth, even if he could not understand a word. Esteban leaned in and said, "I brought her in specially so she could do Professor Crenshaw's keynote address." Noticing Percy's involuntary grimace, Esteban softly laughed and added, "Think of her, I think the saying is, as the sugar that makes the medicine go down," a comment that caused Percy to cock his head to get a full look at Esteban's face to make sure he understood the remark's meaning. Esteban's wry smile made clear he had.

After another few moments of sitting in silence together listening to the translator, Esteban started to rise from his seat and whispered, "I didn't get a chance to shake your hand last night and wanted to say hello in person and thank you for coming. Let me know if I can help with anything."

Percy, whose gaze had been drawn back to the stage as the translator started another mesmerizing segment, turned to Esteban. "Well, in fact, I was curious ..." But Esteban had already disappeared, leaving Percy alone with his curiosity about oracles, men in black, Grecian urns, and spoonfuls of sugar.

* * * * * *

The rest of the morning slipped away listening to presentations. Percy was on the late-morning panel, and while he felt fortunate to not have the droning translator, he also had not been lucky enough to draw the oracle. He wondered if there was a method being used to determine which professor got which translator before realizing he was going down the road of paranoia over perceived slights that drove him crazy when his colleagues engaged in such speculation. *"Can you believe Marissa gets to teach in Classroom 132? That is the classroom I always teach in, and now I'm in that classroom on the third floor where the heater never works and the wooden floors squeak whenever you walk. How did she suddenly curry the Associate Dean's favor?"*

He did kick himself a little for being unable during his presentation to resist peering around the auditorium to see if Moira might be listening. With his early-morning decision to blaze a new path, he had sworn to accept that Moira was now a part of his past and to focus solely on what lie ahead.

He tried, therefore, to rationalize that his hope of spotting Moira listening to his talk was simply one of common courtesy. After all, it was their conversation on his porch that helped him conceptualize the role of Herculean-like figures in Romantic literature as his paper's theme. However, since even a brief picturing in his mind of her swaying on the porch swing that beautiful spring morning, her ginger hair bobbing back and forth, caused him to feel an unbidden sharp constriction in his chest, he had enough self-awareness to realize it was going to be a journey to acceptance. In any case, Moira's duties as conference coordinator apparently meant she was being kept busy in the wings, as he had not seen her at all that morning.

Following Percy's panel, lunch was served. Small talk was the main dish, followed by dollops of gossip for dessert. Everyone then assembled back in the auditorium for Casper's keynote address. Percy could tell from the anticipatory looks on many of the conferees' faces that they saw this as a moment to be savored. For them, to be Casper was to have made it.

He had thought about skipping the talk but decided, for reasons he couldn't quite put his finger on, that although it was unlikely anyone would notice his absence, let alone care, he would persevere through it. He felt lucky to see an empty seat next to the man in black, who today wore a black T-shirt with *Everything Hurts* written in vivid, white letters to go along with his black jeans and sandals. Perhaps the hour wouldn't be a complete waste, and Percy eased into the seat, giving a quick nod of greeting that the scruffy poet-in-residence reciprocated with a smile.

Up on the stage, Esteban provided an introduction that Percy now realized was more an act of duty than true belief, ladling praise by noting Casper's many accolades without ever expressing any personal admiration. Esteban concluded his remarks by saying, "And so, please welcome our inaugural keynote speaker, Professor Casper Crenshaw." Casper then jauntily emerged from the wings with his ponytail bobbing, waving to the auditorium as though he were Elton John taking the stage at the Hollywood Bowl.

Casper gave the exact same remarks as the ones at Books & Books a few nights before. The big difference, of course, was this time, he was alternating with a translator who was providing her most spellbinding performance yet, trilling r's like a nightingale in full song, sashaying s's until they sizzled, humming m's like the rapid beating of a hummingbird's wings, vowels teasingly drawn out until each word became an erotic dance of the seven veils. Percy could have sworn he saw some people unbuttoning the top button of their shirts and pulling on their collars as if it were a scorching, mid-July afternoon.

At one point, Percy forced himself to tear his eyes away from the translator to look at Casper and was surprised to see an undisguised look of jealousy. Casper, who thought of himself as the poetry gods' personal messenger, apparently believed there was room for only one oracle at a time. The irony, Percy mused, was that the translator had probably just sold dozens of Tenth Anniversary editions for Casper that otherwise would languish in a storeroom.

But if Casper's pride had been wounded, what happened next was certain to salve his ego. With the keynote's conclusion, a smiling Esteban ambled back onto the stage. Taking over the podium, he announced, "I am pleased to provide a bit of a surprise. In honor of Professor Crenshaw's contributions not just to this conference but to all of poetry, we have commissioned a special commemorative work of art."

The poet-in-residence, who had draped his legs over the back of the seat in front of him, started to excitedly struggle to sit up, causing Percy to track where his seatmate's look was now riveted. Being pushed in from the wings on a dolly by two of the men from *The Godfather* cast was an urn at least five feet tall and two feet in diameter that even from a distance created a stir with its grandeur.

Casper practically fainted upon seeing it and reflexively reached a hand out to touch the ceramic design, only to have Esteban quickly walk over and gently catch his arm, telling Casper in gentle tones, "The artist says we must let the glaze dry a little longer before it can be touched." Casper dazedly nodded in acquiescence as Esteban assured him, "We have a special shipping crate to make sure it reaches your home safely."

Like everyone in the audience, Percy was trying to hear what Esteban was saying to Casper away from the microphone, but his attention also was distracted by the poet-in-residence who had finally untangled his legs and was now madly texting as if he was a tabloid reporter with an exclusive scoop on a presidential sex scandal. Percy couldn't resist trying to spy what his seatmate was so agitatedly typing, but other than seeing a word he bafflingly thought might be "albatross," failed to discern what had him so animated.

Esteban returned to the podium and began speaking once again. "Amigos, please give another round of applause for Professor Crenshaw." Clapping filled the auditorium. "As you saw last night," Esteban resumed, causing the applause to taper off, "we also have commemorative urns for each of you as a sincere thank you. Mementos that will, I am confident, make you think of us often in the future. They're a bit smaller than Professor Crenshaw's"—this triggered a few titters of laughter—"but the good news is you'll be able to take them back with you on the plane as part of your luggage and, I hope, give them a place of honor in your home or office." And with this announcement, two more burly-looking characters wheeled out the table with the twelve urns that had been on display the evening before, prompting another rousing round of applause.

Percy did not envy the final panel. It was always challenging to address a midafternoon audience whose digestive juices were just wrapping up lunch, leaving a drowsy sea of faces valiantly fighting the urge to close one's eyes. When Percy had drawn the short straw and was forced to give a talk at this hour—or worse yet, teach—he swore he saw Hypnos, the Greek god of sleep, wandering the room wielding his trademark poppy stem. A few audience members invariably would succumb to Hypnos's touch, often giving a disconcerting snore before popping awake like a jack-in-the-box, hoping no one had noticed. The bemused smiles of those around them suggested otherwise.

Percy, therefore, counted it as an impressive victory that he had resisted Hypnos's entreaties by the time Esteban popped back on the stage to give his concluding remarks. Exuding a sense of satisfaction, Esteban warmly thanked everyone for making the first Wordsworth in Bogotá conference a success, and informed them that vans were waiting outside to whisk them to the airport.

Just as the bustle began of people getting out of their chairs, however, Esteban's voice came over the speakers again. "But if I might detain you for one minute more, there is a final note of gratitude I must express. As each of you who presented knows so well, none of this would have been possible without the tireless efforts of Moira O'Shaughnessy. She has been an impresario extraordinaire in making this conference happen, and I'd love for us to give a round of applause for her."

To enthusiastic handclapping, and even a few whoops of appreciation, Moira walked onto the stage and gave a little wave. But despite what should have been her moment of triumph, Percy noticed that the smile on Moira's face appeared forced, her expression far more worried than happy.

# CHAPTER THIRTY-THREE

Percy tipped his hat once again to Moira's logistical abilities. Waiting vans whisked the exhausted professors off to the bustling international terminal where three airport employees greeted them at the curb. The employees divvied them up according to whether they were going back through Miami, Houston, or Chicago, and then guided each group to the appropriate counter where they and their luggage were processed by smiling airline agents specifically designated to handle their group.

Waiting at each counter was a cart that carried a square, wooden crate for each traveler, tagged and ready for loading, inside of which lay an urn nestled in protective packaging of straw and bubble wrap. Another cart held the corrugated cardboard boxes of the bound conference papers destined for each professor's university library.

After checking in, they breezed through security and were at their gates with time to spare. Unlike the usual free-for-all of a busy international airport teeming with weary travelers at the breaking point, this had been an airline commercial with passengers doing the rhumba down the corridors to their waiting plane while employees broke into tap dance routines.

After passing through security, Percy spotted Moira in the gate area for the Miami flight. Still troubled by her agitated look at the conference's conclusion, he wanted to go over to make sure she was okay. He also, though, didn't want to appear to be trying to reopen their conversation from the night before, a dialogue she had made clear she saw as finished. He ultimately convinced himself it would be no big deal to congratulate her on how smoothly the conference had gone and walked over to where she was surveilling the gate area. *The mother hen making sure everyone is accounted for,* Percy mused as he approached her.

"Moira, I just wanted to—"

Moira, who had been looking the other direction, pivoted toward Percy, and he saw she wore the same worried expression he had seen on stage. "Percy, can't talk right now," she said abruptly. She hesitated before leaning in and lowering her voice. "Listen, something is wrong. Strange things have been going on all day, and Esteban has been very secretive whenever I ask him about why he is doing something differently than we planned. He completely took over all the arrangements for the airport, the luggage, even cancelling the bus to the airport, saying it'd be easier to have his own people handle it. I don't know exactly what is up, but warning lights are flashing in my head."

"I've felt it too," Percy chimed in, "that something is off. You know I've kind of felt that way from when you first showed up in Arcadia."

Moira gave him a sharp glance, causing Percy to add, "I mean, not that you were part of that, but the whole conference—the money, the time frame ..."

Moira's features softened. "I've been chastising myself all day for having ignored earlier warning signs. I kept rationalizing excuses when something didn't quite make sense. I think maybe ... well, probably ... because it was paying so well." She dropped her chin to her chest and waved her hand in a flustered manner, as if trying to make those thoughts disappear. Raising her head, she tried to rally. "But that doesn't matter right now. The self-recriminations can wait."

She grabbed Percy's arm and urgently whispered, "We need to keep our eyes open." Percy, who already was having a tough time with her hair brushing against him as she leaned in, just couldn't help it, a hopeful jolt of electricity shot up his arm from where her hand lay. But before he could try to cement their partnership in espionage, the boarding announcement was made for first-class passengers.

Moira straightened up, let go of his arm, and started striding purposefully toward the jetway. Looking back at Percy, she waved her boarding pass in explanation as she mouthed, "Esteban insisted." Percy sighed and looked at his pass, Seat 45E, definitely the back of the plane, probably next to the lavatories. He wondered if Esteban had insisted on that as well.

\* \* \* \* \* \*

Moira was not the only person with a worried look on their face. Mike was roaming the Bogotá airport with a mounting sense of desperation. Earlier, when Esteban had presented the special urn to Casper, Mike had excitedly texted the Operation Poetry Slam task force, alerting them to the ceremony and that "Albatross just received BIG urn." Attles had personally texted back, something he rarely did, stating he had reconfirmed that "Crenshaw, C." was on the flight itinerary for Miami, and that he was issuing an order that Crenshaw be separated upon disembarking for "individualized processing after we take care of the others." Attles had even tacked on a "Not bad, Forreo" at the end of the text, prompting an inner glow Mike felt slightly embarrassed about.

Then things went sideways. Fast. Mike had taken a seat on the van ferrying Casper and the other Miami-bound passengers to the airport and impatiently waited for Casper to board. But as the driver prepared to slide the door shut, no Casper was in sight. Mike then heard a car pulling up behind them and looked out the van's rear window. There he saw Casper and Carlos approaching a black Cadillac Escalade limousine gleaming in the late afternoon sun.

For a moment, Mike had wondered if Casper was being kidnapped, but Casper seemed quite happy to enter the back seat when Carlos opened the door, no doubt flattered he was being chauffeured to the airport while everyone else was crammed into vans.

Two men proceeded to the other side of the Escalade carrying a tall, heavily padded wooden crate. They maneuvered the crate into the back of the limousine and secured it with a mother's care. Mike could have sworn that before getting into the front passenger seat, Carlos had glanced at his van as if trying to see who was in it. The limousine then began to leave.

Mike debated trying to get out of the van before the driver slid the rear door shut, but quickly concluded that exiting would accomplish nothing other than leaving him stranded in the parking lot. Mike felt himself starting to heavily perspire. If he lost Casper at this point, Attles would wring his neck instead of the Albatross's. He calmed down a bit as the van pulled behind the Cadillac, which was still waiting to turn onto the main road, reasoning that since they both were headed to the airport, it didn't really matter if Casper arrived separately.

The van kept within easy viewing distance of the Cadillac the entire way to the airport, but just as Mike's heart rate descended out of cardiac arrest range, they came to a junction. Mike watched helplessly as the Escalade turned left toward the domestic terminal while the van continued right to the international terminal.

Panic set in again. As they pulled up to the terminal, Mike, who had sat in the back row, started pushing past his fellow passengers to get off while issuing a flurry of apologies. There was some grumbling, especially as Mike's elbows accidentally caught the back of a few heads as he scrambled forward, but he had cultivated a sufficient aura of eccentricity that he mainly provoked eye rolls and a shaking of heads. He finally got the door open and popped from the van with the urgency of a diver surfacing for air. Abandoning his luggage, he ran to a line of taxis.

Mike's Spanish was so fractured it needed a full-body cast, and at first, the cab driver thought his creative hand gestures were birds not planes. Finally, though, Mike made the driver understand he simply wanted to go to the other terminal. The driver's skeptical look changed to enthusiasm as Mike dropped a stack of money on the front seat, and off they sped. In a matter of minutes, Mike was rushing into the domestic terminal, still baffled why Casper would have been taken there.

And so it was that Mike found himself frantically wandering the cavernous passenger hall as crowds of travelers pushed past him. The background din of hundreds of conversations and convoys of luggage being wheeled and pulled made it hard to think. His features were scrunched in apprehension, his stomach forming a triple knot, when he caught the lucky break he dearly needed.

In the far left corner of the hall, he spotted a cart being pushed with a tall, wooden crate. His eyes leapt to the person propelling it forward, and Mike immediately recognized him as one of Esteban's men. The cart took a turn and disappeared down a hallway marked *Aviación Corporativa*.

Mike stopped a ticket agent returning from a break and pointing at the sign asked, "Excuse me, what is that hallway?"

Fortunately, the agent spoke English and replied, "Oh, that's for corporate jets."

In a moment of adrenaline-fueled inspiration, Mike realized Casper must be flying on the Velasquez's private plane, and began briskly walking, trying to close ground on the cart without drawing attention.

He entered the hallway just in time to observe the man pushing the cart take a sharp right into a corridor about halfway down the hall. Mike picked up his pace and spun on his heel to round the corner into the corridor where the cart had disappeared. He was three strides down the corridor when he abruptly stopped. Fifty feet away, the man was pushing the cart into a gate area where Casper and several other individuals sat chatting, one of whom wore a pilot's uniform. Through the gate's floor-to-ceiling windows overlooking the runway, he spotted a plane being fueled and readied for takeoff.

Mike quickly slipped back around the corner out of view of the gate and started madly texting. "IMPORTANT! Albatross not on flight we thought … private plane …" He craned his head around the corner to see if he could spy a tail number. The descending dusk made it difficult to see and he had to reenter the corridor and creep a few more steps toward the gate before he could make out the number. He retreated back around the corner and had just typed "Tail number HK-372" when he heard a menacing "no" that transcended all language barriers.

Mike wheeled and found himself staring into a shirt stretched taut by a cliff of a chest as sheer, massive, and intimidating as El Capitan rising into the Yosemite sky. His eyes scaled the shirt upward, button by button, and were met by a grim-faced Carlos at the summit.

Carlos immediately sprang forward and wrested the phone out of Mike's hand. As Carlos glowered at him, Mike pointed at himself saying,

"DEA," as if that would bring Carlos to heel. Carlos mockingly laughed and began brusquely shoving him, as if he were a papier-mâché doll, down the corridor and through a door one of Carlos's confederates held open. As the door slammed shut consuming Mike in total darkness, he prayed his quaking index finger had succeeded in pushing the "send" button as Carlos was snatching the phone from his hand.

The pungent smell of cleaners and disinfectants soon informed Mike that he was locked inside a broom closet. He searched the wall with his hand until he found a light switch and flicked it on. Nothing. He reached up higher on the wall until he found the light socket and discovered someone had removed the light bulb. The only thing he could make out were the words on the front of his shirt, the bright-white lettering of *Everything Hurts* just visible in the dark.

Sighing, he slowly shuffled backward until his rear end touched the back wall, slid down, and sat dejectedly on the concrete floor. Releasing a deep breath, he resigned himself to the likely prospect it was going to be a long wait before he would discover if his text had made it through.

In the corridor, a few feet down from the closet where Mike sat imprisoned amid mops, buckets, and toilet brushes, Carlos showed Esteban the screen of the confiscated phone. "Excellent," Esteban said, his voice eager as he looked at the unsent message. "Thank you, brother, you've played it perfectly from beginning to end. You may have a future in acting." Carlos's mouth hinted at an involuntary smile as Esteban continued, "Keep the phone from locking, because we're going to need to send that message in a few hours." Carlos nodded and then watched Esteban head off to the gate to wish Casper a pleasant trip aboard the Velasquez family's plane.

# CHAPTER THIRTY-FOUR

Everything was going precisely according to plan. Agents Carl Chang and Michelle Esperanza's thespian skills at feigning a panic attack—while apparently a bit overdone by Michelle, who had played Maria in a high school production of *West Side Story*—were sufficiently convincing to divert their planes to Miami. The three planes had landed within fifteen minutes of each other, and the conference attendees were now being escorted to customs, where Attles paced the room.

The agents who had been waiting at the gates reported over their radios that most of the professors, while surprised at their early reunion, suspected nothing was amiss, despite all the planes unexpectedly landing in Miami. They apparently thought the special escort to customs was simply more VIP treatment courtesy of Esteban and the conference. Only two—the conference coordinator and a Professor Percy Billings—seemed wary and asking questions, but they were still being cooperative. The agents assigned to meet Agent Forreo and the Albatross had radioed earlier that they were in position and, by this point in time, would be escorting their special guest down a different hallway to a special interrogation room.

Far from being pleased, though, Attles was becoming increasingly queasy, precisely because the operation was unfolding according to script. As a greenhorn field agent thirty years earlier, Attles's mentor had hammered into him Cardinal Rule Number One of an investigation— Something Is Terribly Wrong If Everything Is Going Exactly According to Plan. Attles's growing disquiet was interrupted by the solid-steel door to the inspection room swinging open and the Wordsworth in Bogotá contingent entering, chattering away among themselves like a group of diners whose table just came open.

The sight of Attles forcefully striding to the front of the room brought the chatter to an abrupt halt. He was not the maître d' they were expecting. He wore a midnight-black windbreaker with DEA emblazoned on the back in large, white letters, while the front sported a big, circular patch with DEA DRUG STRIKE FORCE stitched in indigo blue against an oddly happy swirl of rainbow colors.

Attles watched as the group took in the room—eye-stinging overhead fluorescent lights, two glistening stainless-steel tables at the front of the room resembling operating tables, a German shepherd sitting at his grim-faced handler's feet, and agents in every corner appareled in dark-blue military outfits with .40-caliber Glocks strapped to their waists. A luggage cart with their suitcases was next to the tables. Just behind it was a cart with the wooden crates containing the urns, and beyond it another cart with the cardboard boxes of the books destined for the college libraries. Apprehension spread across the group's countenances like a cloud's shadow moving across a field.

The unease jumped a further seismic level when Agents Esperanza and Chang entered the room wearing DEA apparel. Several of the perplexed professors turned to their neighbors and said in hushed tones, "Wait, wasn't that the passenger who needed medical attention?" Their neighbors' worried nods affirming that something was seriously amiss.

With the group now sufficiently steeped in trepidation to be properly pliant, Attles gave a hand signal, and the dog handler brought his drug-sniffing German shepherd over to the cart piled high with their bags. The dog obediently sat down with eyes fixed on the handler. "Listen," Attles began in a factual and reasoned tone, "as you very intelligent people have undoubtedly surmised, we know that at least some of you are bringing narcotics back into the country." Eyes widened, and some of the professors discreetly inched away from their companions.

"From my long experience, these events always go smoother for both you and us if there is cooperation up front. Let me be abundantly clear." His tone raised a notch in intensity, emphasizing each word that followed as if repeatedly striking a single piano key loudly and distinctly. *"We ... will ... find ... the ... drugs."* Almost all appeared in shock, a few stared at their feet, one looked about to cry. "The one and only question," he said, dialing the intensity of his voice back a level, "is whether you make it easy on yourselves."

He stared at the group expectantly. "Well, anyone?" He waited ten seconds longer, the room consumed in absolute silence other than the panting of the canine, it's tongue repeatedly moving forward and back like a bright-pink piston between two menacing rows of teeth. "Okay, then, if no one is going to step up ..." And as he turned to the dog handler, one of the professors stepped forward, sweat stains visibly pooling beneath the armpits of an ill-fitting shirt that had become partially untucked.

Attles gave an unexpectedly warm smile at the professor who Percy seemed to recall taught at a small Baptist college in Kansas. In a voice bordering on kindness, Attles said, "Thank you. You are doing this the right way, I promise." He motioned to the carts, and the professor walked over to the stack of baggage, his legs wobbling so much, Percy feared he wouldn't make it without assistance. He pointed at a generic, black suitcase toward the bottom that from the scuffs and dents must have been a longtime traveling companion. A bright-yellow ribbon was tied to the handle in an effort to make it stand out from the crowd.

An agent pulled the bag from the cart, causing the remaining dunnage to shift precariously but somehow remain atop the cart. The agent hefted the suitcase over to one of the stainless-steel tables, unsnapped the clasps with a sharp metallic sound that rang out in the oppressive silence, unfolded the suitcase, and stepped away.

As the stunned group watched, the professor sleepwalked over to the bag lying open on the table, its insides exposed beneath the harsh lights as if it was a torso about to be dissected. With sagging shoulders, the professor's hands disappeared beneath the clothes and hesitatingly began rooting below. He suddenly stopped. With downcast eyes, he pulled out an item that he clutched to his chest as if giving himself one more chance to awake from what must just be a nightmare. He then slowly straightened out his arm and unfolded his hand.

Attles stared, disbelieving, before roaring, "Do you think this is some kind of fucking joke?" causing the professor to backpedal several steps. As Attles snatched the baggie out of the professor's hand, Percy could see that it contained a half-eaten ham sandwich's worth of marijuana. Attles disdainfully threw the baggie into a trash can at the table's end.

Momentarily paralyzed, the professor stared at Attles in bewilderment, but upon realizing he wasn't going to be shackled, regained the feel of his legs and scampered to the group's rear like a hermit crab trying to outrun the incoming tide, mopping the sweat from his forehead with his shirt sleeves as he moved.

Attles resumed his authoritative pose—bushy eyebrows contracted into a scowl, hands on his hips, chest puffed out—but Percy could swear he saw a look of doubt pass across the agent's weathered features. Percy was still studying Attles's expression when, with a start, he realized Attles was gazing directly back. There was a pause as their eyes locked, and then Attles's gaze moved on to the rest of the group.

In an impatient voice, Attles addressed the group. "Okay, that's it, no more fun and games. Now we're going to get to it." It was always best to offer a little sweetness at first and try to get them to offer up the contraband on their own, but now it was time to drop the hammer. He signaled to two agents who went over to the cart containing the wooden crates of urns, and each agent proceeded to place a crate on one of the tables.

Attles walked to the table closest to him, looked at the tag on the crate, and called out, "Shangles."

One of the older men in the group, in his fifties, Percy guessed, raised his head as if being called to mount the steps to the gallows. He started to utter, "I honestly ...," but seeing Attles's glowering look, moved toward the table as if tugged by an invisible cord.

Taking his time, Attles walked over to the second table and silently read the tag hanging from the crate. Lifting his head, he barked, "Waters." Another man emerged from the cluster, several decades younger with blond hair perpetually tousled, an unkempt look Percy was pretty sure Waters

SCOTT E. SUNDBY  209

deliberately achieved by rubbing his hands through his hair to obtain a hoped-for boyish look. Shangles and Waters had been on the same conference panel, and an animosity had inexplicably arisen between them with the suddenness and ferocity of a wildfire. Given the acidic glances they exchanged as Waters walked to his urn, even the prospect of serving hard time in federal prison did not dampen their mutual dislike.

Attles returned to the first table and was about to issue an order when Agent Esperanza leaned in, a clipboard dangling in her hand, and uttered something under her breath. "What?" Attles snapped, eyebrows impatiently raised in exasperation.

"Shakespeare," she said more loudly, pointing at a sheet of paper on the clipboard. "His codename is Shakespeare."

Shangles, who had looked like a doomed man preparing to eat his final meal, perked up. "I'm Shakespeare?" He pointed at Waters and asked, "Who's he?"

Attles started to raise his hands to cut off the conversation but was too late in stopping Esperanza from responding, "Nicholas Sparks."

Shangles gave a harsh laugh. "Hah! Like the romance writer? You nailed him, all right. Total fluff, no substance. Certainly no Shakespeare."

Waters gave Shangles as threatening a stare as someone whose hair looked as if he had just exited a wind tunnel could manage, before getting off a petulant, "Shakespeare? You wish, you washed-up, old goat."

As it would turn out, Waters would have the last laugh, abandoning teaching after a denial of tenure and selling millions of books under the pseudonym B.P. Riské, including the bestselling trilogy, *Beneath the Fondue Fountain*, *The Mysteries of Caviar Cavern*, and *Atop the Strawberry Shortcake*, all featuring the debonair chef-detective Jean-Jacque Jicama.

Attles was now deeply regretting letting Esperanza convince him the Operation Poetry Slam task force should give the professors codenames. She had argued that the media would eat it up as an entertaining backstory and generate publicity for the bust, but it now seemed like a mistake. "Enough!" he shouted, slamming his palm down on the table to stop the bickering. He exhaled loudly and signaled to the agent standing next to the crated urn perched on the first table.

The agent slipped a crowbar into the crack between the top and side panels, leaned hard with his weight on the bar, and began prying the slats open with the enthusiasm of a sadistic interrogator, the resisting wood splintering, the nails screeching in protest, but finally giving up their secrets as the top panel came off. The agent pulled from the straw an urn that ignited a spontaneous group murmur. Up close, the urn was striking in a way they had not fully comprehended when the urns had been displayed at the reception on a stage thirty feet away—lithe, carefree youths painted in blues and reds pranced around the terracotta background beneath trees in full leaf, the leaves detailed in a green so verdant, they appeared to radiate light from the urn's surface.

Even Attles seemed momentarily taken aback by the urn's beauty before coming over to examine it. He carefully scanned the inside with a bright flashlight. Tapped the ceramic walls. Turned it upside down. Flipped it back upright. Shook it. As he processed each new piece of information, the accordion-like furrows on his forehead expanded and contracted as if accompanying a fast-paced tango. He then took a step back and, without warning, grabbed the crowbar from the surprised agent's hand, arced his arm upward, and swung it down hard on the urn with the force and suddenness of an executioner's axe.

Shangles uttered a reflexive "Nooo!," face aghast as the frolicking youths were reduced for eternity to a pile of shards.

Attles decisively dropped the crowbar onto the table, the raw clang of iron on steel reverberating around the prison-gray cinderblock walls. He put on a pair of latex gloves and with scrunched shoulders sifted through the flinders, picking up pieces and inspecting them beneath the bright lights like an archaeologist on a dig. Without a word, Attles stepped back and nodded at the handler who brought the German shepherd over. After a minute, with all eyes riveted on the dog as it sniffed through the debris, the canine sat back down on its haunches and the agent gave a negative shake of his head to Attles.

Attles walked over to a corner, motioning Esperanza and Chang to join him. Heads bowed together, a flurry of whispering began.

"What the hell," Attles began. "Forreo said we'd find the coke hidden in the urns."

"Would make sense that there would be some decoy urns," Chang offered. "Mike seemed pretty certain."

Attles considered the thought. "What was the name of the guy who was asking questions when they were escorted here?"

Michelle looked at her notes. "There were two—Percy Billings and Moira O'Shaughnessy."

"Which one is Billings?"

"Third from left, wearing the dark-blue shirt and wrinkled khakis."

Attles popped his head up and glanced over at the group. Bowing his head back into the huddle, he said with a tight smile, "Yeah, I wondered if that was him. S.O.B. definitely knows something. Okay, Chang, you go check on Forreo down the hall babysitting the Albatross and see if he knows anything more. Meanwhile," Attles gave a slight grin, "I'm going to have a conversation with Professor"—he looked at the list of names—"Percy Billings."

The huddle broke up, and Attles strode to the agent by the cart of urns and whispered a name. The agent searched the cart, tipping, lifting, and rearranging the crates before eventually removing one from the bottom row and carrying it to the table where the demolished urn's remains had been swept aside. The crowbar again began to do its work.

With Esperanza flanking him, Attles moved to the front of the room and called out "Billings," his voice lowered to a growl. Esperanza started to bring the clipboard with codenames forward so Attles could see it, but quickly pulled it back upon seeing the death stare Attles gave her.

In the years to come, Percy would wonder where the sense of calm had come from. That he had recognized doubt in Attles? Every bully he had ever known, from the schoolyard to faculty meetings, invariably turned out to be blustering, flexing, raging, ranting, taunting, yelling—whatever their chosen ploy to intimidate—as a way to keep others from peering behind the curtain and seeing someone they were desperately trying to hide, not just from others, but from themselves. Or maybe it was that Percy had already jumped off the high board once that day and felt emboldened?

Whatever the reason, it appeared Percy felt more in control than the figure standing in front of him, who did not like that Percy was meeting his eyes and not looking away. It was almost as if Percy had flipped on an internal autopilot of self-assuredness he hadn't known existed. He once read about how neuroscientists named the network of neurons that control one's thoughts and actions the homunculus, Latin for "little man," a term that had made Percy envision a tiny person inside the brain, drinking a mug of coffee while pulling levers, pushing pedals, monitoring meters, issuing commands. Percy would never have guessed his had a British accent, wore Savile Row tailored suits, and drank martinis shaken not stirred.

As Percy stepped forward, he heard Moira start to speak, "Listen, I'm the conference coordinator ..."

And in another move that would cause Percy to later wonder what in the world he had been thinking, he turned to Moira, smiled, shook his head as if to say, "I have this," and then—and, really, what the hell was that about—winked at her. Now, Cool Hand Luke could pull off a wink, Butch Cassidy for sure, Indiana Jones without a hitch, Han Solo could do a wink with either eye ... but Percy Billings? And as Percy stood in front of the man in the DEA windbreaker knowing he should be worried, actually, petrified, about what Esteban might have packed inside his urn, he instead found himself contemplating the meaning of a wink.

"This yours?" Attles asked. The urn had been placed on the table and appeared every bit as stunning as the one Attles had demolished. Percy's heart quickened a few beats as he saw the design. With luminescent, red hair flaming out behind him like fire out of a hot rod's exhaust pipes, Hercules was wielding his sword in full struggle with a nine-headed Hydra, each fanged head a different, vivid color as it prepared to strike. *Hercules? That can't be coincidence,* Percy thought. *Esteban must have singled this one out for me.*

The agent next to the urn called out to Attles, her voice infused with a note of enthusiastic surprise, "Sir, this one has a sealed top. It also is"—she lifted it up and down—"heavier than the others."

Giving Percy a knowing smile, Attles regained a touch of swagger as he went over to where the agent held the urn. He picked up the urn as he inspected the lid sealed with paraffin wax. "Hmm ... feels about three kilos heavy to me," he said to the agent so all could hear. "Also known as a ten-year minimum. Scrape the wax off carefully, and let's take a look." Attles turned back toward Percy. "Let me ask again. Is this yours, Professor Billings?"

Just as Percy's pulse began to race, his inner Bond retook command. *Ah, I believe this is where they open the shark tank beneath us as we dangle over it, and, I must admit, it appears Esteban may have put us in a pretty pickle. Not sure of the way out, but let's not panic quite yet.*

Percy asked Attles in a serene tone, "Might I examine it?"

"Why? Is it yours or not? Your name is on the tag."

"Apparently, though I'm sure you'll see all the tags were probably written in the same hand. The shipping of these was handled for us. I've actually never seen it up close."

"You signed a Customs Declaration form saying it was yours." As Attles ripped a piece of paper off the demolished crate, Percy recalled everyone signing a stack of papers as they left for the airport, one of Esteban's assistants explaining, "It's a mere formality to streamline the handling of the baggage."

*Not going to deny it, Percy. This pickle is getting cucumber size, but no doubt, we're going to find a way out. Have you noticed how this blustering fellow has a crease running between those rather impressive eyebrows that rivals the Mariana Trench?*

"Sir, I have the lid off," the agent called. Attles walked back over to the urn. With the eagerness of a child opening the one birthday present he'd most been waiting for, he peered in. He let out a barely audible, "What the fuck" as he reached in and pulled out a folded sheet of paper. He read it silently with Esperanza looking over his shoulder:

*Dear Percy, Thank you again for speaking at the conference. I suspect that you, like me, loved reading* Willy Wonka *growing up and the idea of the Golden Ticket. In that spirit, I thought it might be fun to include a special surprise for one of our speakers ... and you won! Inside are two copies of our favorite author, Professor Crenshaw, and his rather hefty—probably weighs several kilos!—coffee table version of A Dairymaid's Lament. You have a little bit of a ship-in-a-bottle puzzle of getting them out, but do have fun. Best wishes, Esteban*

Everyone watched as Attles and Esperanza finished reading the note, exchanged mystified looks, and proceeded over to the urn where they shone a flashlight inside. Percy's inner Bond piped up, *Well, my friend, from their expressions, whatever is happening is cheery news for us. They look like the kids who've just learned they've been cut out of the will.* And, indeed, they did.

Attles called the dog handler over, and the German shepherd sniffed in, out, and under the urn. Percy could have sworn even the dog looked disappointed as he sat down and the handler quietly said, "Negative, sir." With a murderous look in his eyes, Attles retrieved the crowbar and moved toward the urn.

The steel door flew open with such abruptness, banging loudly against the wall, that the agents reached for their weapons while everyone else jumped. Chang entered, panic etched on his face, and quickly moved to Attles. He showed Attles and Esperanza a cell phone, and Attles slammed the crowbar down on the table as he uttered a "goddammit." He looked at Chang. "Forreo's not down the hall? This is true?" Chang gave a very reluctant nod.

"Esperanza, come with me. Chang, you're in command of this"—his arm swept across the room as if holding a wished-for eraser in his hand—"of this fucking shitshow." With that, Attles and Esperanza rushed out of the room, leaving a flustered Chang at the front of the room.

"Okay, well, then," Chang began, his eyes bouncing from the floor to the group to the ceiling and back to the floor as he rocked back and forth. "We're going to go through each of these ... ahem ... items," he said, nodding over his shoulder at the carts. "It may take a while."

"I think not." A startled Chang looked at the speaker with fiery hair matching the Hercules depicted on Percy's urn. She continued, "We've been very patient. But we've already been here well over an hour, personal property has been destroyed, you have found nothing—*nada*—incriminating. And I will tell you," she squinted at the name tag on his jacket, "Agent Carl Chang, I come from a family of civil rights lawyers, and this will become a nightmare for the government if it continues."

"But, you heard my orders," Chang began in the tone of a substitute teacher watching classroom order slipping away.

"Actually, all he said is you're in charge, and listen, things clearly are not going his way. I'm telling you, in the friendliest possible way, that you don't want to hitch your wagon to"—Moira waved her hands as she searched for a description—"*whoever* that was, unless you want to bring the roof down on yourself and all the agents in this room. How you handle this from here on out can make you the subject of a very positive review from all of us," she said, turning to the group who all bobbed their heads in eager agreement, "or of a very damaging lawsuit and career-ending publicity. Think of the headline." Moira tilted her head upward as if reading a theater marquee, "Innocent Americans Subjected to Gestapo Inspection at the Border."

Percy's inner Bond piped up, *Well, damn, Percy, I can see why you're so smitten. She is dynamite. She'd be the perfect Bond girl, certainly an attractive enough chickadee.*

This comment triggered an inner response from Percy, *Whoa, now that's not okay. Maybe calling a woman a chickadee flew back in the '60s, but not today. And where, by the way, were you earlier when I was losing my cool and made a mess of things with Moira? Could have used you then.*

*Ah Percy, my dear chap, I don't do relationships. Not my forte. Think of my Bond girls' names ... Octopussy, Honey Ryder, Pussy Galore ... yes, yes, all inappropriate now, I get it, but my point is, you clearly want that whole soulmate rigmarole, and I wouldn't have the slightest idea. I'm not judging, but I've never understood the allure.*

Anyone watching Percy, and fortunately no one was, would have seen him roll his eyes and return his attention to Agent Chang.

Chang's gaze rotated around the room, checking in with each of the agents, most of whom gave a slight shrug. When his turn came, the dog handler said, "She's right. All Attles said was that you're in charge. Your call."

Chang closed his eyes, his face squeezed into the pained expression of someone whose finger had just been slammed in a door. Finally, he spoke,

"Okay, well ..." He lifted his hands, blew into them like a gambler tossing dice in hopes of a lucky seven, and then resignedly said, "You can go." He signaled to the agents who opened two large doors at the back of the room and started rolling the carts out. "You can claim your luggage in the baggage claim area."

Moira immediately started toward the doors as if a starter's pistol had sounded, the rest falling in behind her, Professor Shangles wistfully peering at the pile of his urn's remains as he went by.

Quickening his pace to catch up with Moira, Percy asked, "Family of civil rights lawyers?"

"Perhaps a slight exaggeration, but I did spend a lot of time avoiding my dissertation by binge-watching *Law and Order* reruns, and I've seen *To Kill a Mockingbird* at least three times."

Percy chuckled. "Well, you were brilliant."

Moira looked at him appreciatively. "And so were you." She stopped suddenly, almost causing a pileup of the trailing professors, and turned to him with a look of bemusement. "But what the hell was with the wink?"

She started walking quickly again, as if not wanting to give Chang a chance to change his mind, and Percy, hurrying beside her, asked, "If I were to say, 'Bond, James Bond,' would that make sense to you?"

Without slowing, Moira smiled as she glanced at him. "Well, 007, as much sense as anything did today. I still don't know what happened back there and what Esteban is up to, but I'll feel a helluva lot better once I'm seated on my flight to New York with gin and tonic in hand." She glanced at her watch while still moving at a brisk clip. "Have to double-check that my suitcase and, as strange as it sounds to say out loud, my urn are checked onto my connecting flight." Percy could see Moira shifting back into business mode. "And I'm responsible for making sure the cart with the boxes of books gets to the shipper who is delivering them to our schools, but their office is right next to baggage claim." She checked her watch again. "Even with all that, I should be able to make my connection if I hustle."

"Ah," Percy did his best to keep his voice from sounding disappointed, "so we can't get that dinner here in Miami I still owe you? I've already missed my connection."

Moira slowed slightly while looking straight into Percy's eyes. "I need to catch that flight, Percy," adding in a kind tone, "but thanks."

"Of course, of course, you're lucky you can still make yours."

Percy's stride slowed until he found himself at the rear of the trailing herd. A fellow straggler on his right piped up, his words punctuated by an occasional gasp for breath as he labored to keep up. "Nothing like slipping the executioner's noose and riding like the blazes to freedom to make one feel alive."

Percy turned to see the professor from Kansas who had obsequiously dug the bag of pot out from his suitcase. From his buoyant tone, Percy could already picture the professor, wine glass in hand, telling an epic account of his harrowing close call at the border, believing every word of his tale in which he was the lovable villain escaping the long arm of the law—a tale that would grow through the years like a well-tended plant.

Percy managed a slight smile with his eyes as he said, "They may have to call you the Kansas Kid." The professor beamed, while Percy gave a silent sigh of envy for delusions that remained unburst.

# CHAPTER THIRTY-FIVE

Michelle never would have guessed it, but a silent Attles was far more disquieting than the Old Faithful Attles reliably spewing expletives as he fulminated on everything from the weather to the time of day. She gave a sidelong glance at Attles, his hands strangling the steering wheel, eyes boring into the cars in front of him as he floored the pedal, weaving in and out down Highway 953. She would have described him as driving like a crazy person, but this was Miami.

Michelle had contacted the FAA immediately after Chang had rushed in and shown them Forreo's text message—"IMPORTANT! Albatross not on flight we thought ... private plane ... tail number HK-372"—and discovered that not only was HK-372 registered to Diego Velasquez, but it had filed a flight plan that had the jet landing at the Opa Locka Executive Airport in a half hour. She had thought that after the fiasco with the professors, Attles would have greeted this as good news since the Opa Locka airport was no more than a twenty-minute drive from Miami International at this time of night. Instead, he had gone completely quiet.

"Goddammit." A brief but welcomed eruption. Michelle looked at him expectantly. "It doesn't make fucking sense," he continued, glancing at her before returning his eyes to the road as he roared past a car missing its back fender and both taillights. "Why would Forreo's message have just come through now? The Velasquez jet was in the air a full two hours before he sent it. And where the hell is Forreo? Why isn't he answering his goddamn phone if he just sent the text."

"I'm guessing it was the first chance he had to send it without blowing the gig, and we don't know what is going on down there. Esteban or Carlos might be nearby so he can't answer without blowing his cover."

"Maybe," Attles muttered. And to Michelle's dismay, he went silent again.

Fifteen minutes later, Attles jerked the car to a halt in front of the airport's entrance. Three sleek jets gleamed beneath the halogen security lamps on the far side of the airport. From a distance, the glistening aircraft looked like a child's playthings to run around with in an outstretched arm while making "zoom" sounds. And they were playthings, in a sense ... the toys of Russian oligarchs, hedge fund moguls, and drug lords, interspersed with the occasional supermodel and Hollywood celebrity.

Moments later, a windowless, black van pulled behind them. The van's driver jumped out, boots scuffing on loose gravel as she landed. She moved quickly to the van's rear and opened the doors. Two agents dressed in black riot gear catapulted out, each armed with standard issue Glock .45s. The final two passengers then exited the van—a beagle named MJ and his handler.

Michelle had summoned backup from the Miami office as soon as they knew where they were headed. The agents now approached the car where Attles remained Sphinx-like behind the steering wheel. Michelle turned toward him. "Sir, are you ready?"

Despite the coolness of the evening, she noticed perspiration on his brow and upper lip as if he had just walked out of the tropical undergrowth surrounding the terminal building. Attles wagged his head back and forth in short bursts like he was shaking off a haymaker that left him groggy. "Yeah, nowhere to go but up that hill."

Michelle gave him a puzzled look. "What ..."

But the arrival of the agents at the car interrupted them. Attles blew out a burst of air and exited the car. "Thank you for coming, agents. It's been quite a night already."

Attles briefed the agents on the evening's events and the imminent arrival of the Albatross, a name that garnered confused looks from several agents, causing one to ask, "That's a really large bird, right?"

A question that usually would have provoked a sarcastic put-down, Attles simply responded, "Gigantic, and, according to our intel, is about to hatch one enormous egg of cocaine," causing the agents to chuckle and Attles to smile back. Michelle wished Mike and Carl were there to share her bewilderment, and although Attles regained some of his bluster as he proceeded, marked mainly by an increased sprinkling in of obscenities, he did not mention any of the doubts that had him catatonically brooding before their arrival.

Just as Attles was wrapping up the briefing, the landing lights of a jet broke through the dark, the engines deafening as the plane cruised in, the wheels emitting a high-pitched squeal as the tires met the tarmac. Attles grunted a quick, "This is it," and waved the group through a side door where Michelle had arranged for airport security to take them to the gate to meet the Velasquez jet.

Michelle, Attles, and the agents arrived at the gate and spread out in a semi-circle. Smaller than the typical departure lounge serving commercial aircraft, this was not a waiting area where passengers had to sprawl out on a coffee-stained carpet next to the lone outlet, trying to nurse one's cell phone back to life. The area was luxuriously appointed with seating clusters of supple, cream-leather chairs, perfect for sharing laughter with one's fellow sojourners before winging off to paradise.

Wearing a skirt with a hemline one latitude degree north of risqué, a beautiful, young woman employed to greet the royalty of capitalism, stood by the open jetway door. Not having been forewarned, she eyed them with alarm. A smile from Attles, intended to be reassuring, unsettled her more.

Voices echoing from the jetway caused everyone in the lounge to tense. A few seconds later, a five-foot-tall package mummified in bubble wrap appeared at the doorway on a dolly. It was pushed by two men in black suits taking turns chastising each other with "*cuidados*" and "*estupidos*" as they navigated through the doorframe.

With smiles of success, they finally popped through the jetway into the reception area, only to look around and find themselves surrounded. On their heels came a flight attendant straight off an *Esquire* cover, and behind him, rubbing his eyes, baby-blue sleep mask pushed up atop ruffled hair, a yawning Casper Crenshaw followed, one foot still in dreamland.

Hearing a brusque, "Everyone stand still, hands raised," Casper stopped and groggily looked around as if suddenly finding himself in a house of mirrors, wondering if this was one of the hallucinatory side effects his doctor had warned about when prescribing the Ambien. A harsh, "*I said*, fucking hands up" from a stocky, lantern-jawed, white-bristle-haired drill sergeant snapped Casper's eyes fully open.

"What ..."

"Quiet," the drill sergeant barked. The agents started patting down those who had exited the jet while Michelle dashed down the jetway to make sure no one else was on board. She returned with the pilot in tow, who went and stood with the other crew members. Other than Casper, no one displayed any emotion, as if being subjected to law enforcement searches was part of the Velasquez employment contract, along with full medical and dental.

A half-head shorter, Attles got within six inches of Casper and tilted his face up so that his crewcut almost brushed against Casper's chin. "Okay, Professor, you can put your hands down." Crenshaw warily lowered them, as if they might be playing a game of Simon Says, and Attles was about to bark out "hands up" again.

Attles took a half-step back and dialed down his tone. "Professor Crenshaw, I am Agent Attles of the DEA." Casper's eyes widened. "We have reason to believe you are bringing a shipment of cocaine into the country and are involved in the disappearance of a DEA agent."

"B-b-b ... but that is preposterous," Casper sputtered. "I am a world-respected literature professor who—"

"All very good. No need to give us your credentials. We know who you are," Attles replied even-handedly. "Why don't you begin by telling us where Agent Forreo is?"

"Who?"

"Agent Mike Forreo, and I'd just observe that being an accomplice to the murder of a federal DEA agent carries the death penalty."

Casper gave a wild look. "What? I have ... truly, I have no idea who that is." His desperate glance over at the jet's crew was received with stony stares. "Who is that? Give me something to work with."

"He was working undercover at your conference."

"It wasn't my conference," Casper protested.

"You do say," Attles replied, his voice saturated with sarcasm. "Are all the other professors flying back on a private jet?"

"But I'm a V.I.P. ..."

Michelle came over. "Agent Forreo was there as the poet-in-residence."

"I didn't even know there was a poet-in-residence," Casper began, his memory racing back through the past few days, madly flipping through mental mug shots when he suddenly stopped. "Wait ... was he a rather"— Casper seemed to search for a word that his inquisitors wouldn't find insulting—"unkempt fellow, dressed all in black, wore socks with sandals?"

Attles noted despondently that the befuddlement in Crenshaw's eyes could not be feigned and gave an internal "fuck."

"That's him," Michelle intervened as Attles went silent again. "Where did you last see him?"

"Well, listen, I'm not saying your ... your colleague wasn't an impressive person. I just didn't interact with him much. I mean, I guess, actually, that'd make your friend a really good undercover agent, right? Under the radar and all that? I think I remember him going out to the vans leaving for the airport, but I couldn't swear to it."

Attles, whose confidence had regained its footing upon feeling Casper bowing to his will, felt the avalanche of doubt that haunted him the entire drive over return. He had pushed all the chips in on Albatross, but it was looking more and more like a bad-beat hand. He glanced over at the urn snuggled inside its bubble-wrap carapace. He had one card left to draw. If it wasn't an ace, he was royally screwed.

Turning away so no one could see, he sucked in his breath, pivoted, and again stepped within six inches of Casper, who had started to relax after Michelle had taken over the questioning.

"Is this one of those good cop-bad cop scenarios?" Casper weakly joked looking down on the top of Attles's head, voice slightly cracking.

"No, Professor Crenshaw. Actually, this is one of your worst nightmares, not a goddamn joke." He motioned two agents over to the urn and commanded, "Unwrap that motherfucker."

Casper started to utter a "be care—" but quickly silenced himself as Attles glared at him. "Professor Crenshaw, I know you're a *scholar* of literature, but if you were, say, a mathematics *scholar,*" Attles kept pronouncing scholar in a British accent as if he were an Oxford don, "just how much cocaine do you think that urn would hold?"

"Oh, dear God." Like a fish suddenly stranded on the sand, Casper gasped for air as the possibility of what Esteban had done sank in. This was followed by a wave of nausea, causing Casper to emit a series of small burps that drew a look of intense distaste from the gate agent who remained motionless at her position next to the jetway door. "Oh God, oh God, oh God," he mumbled, his face taking on the complexion of cottage cheese.

He lifted his head toward Michelle as his possible savior. "I promise you, I didn't know, had no idea. If you need me to testi—" He caught himself mid-word as he looked over at the Velasquez jet's crew, the two black-suited men's steely eyes locked on him. "I mean, cooperate, help in any way. Oh God, oh God, oh God. This is all a terrible misunderstanding."

Attles and Michelle moved over to the urn that was now standing uncovered beneath the lounge's lights, the protective wrapping gathered at the base like a robe slipped off a lover's shoulders. In magenta lettering, beautiful calligraphy across the top of the urn declared, *La belleza es verdad, la verdad es belleza.* The naked figures painted on the urn seemed alive, exuding a sensual energy as they laughingly chased each other around the urn's circumference, heads thrown back in unbridled joy. It almost felt voyeuristic that everyone in the lounge was gazing at them. Only Casper seemed oblivious to the urn's beauty, as he continued to utter, "Oh God, oh God, oh God" with his eyes closed.

With the urn too tall to look down into, Attles ordered the two agents flanking it to put it on the ground. They eased the urn down on the carpet, and Attles got on his knees with Michelle next to him, peering in. As the flashlight's beam reflected around the cavernous inside, the good news was that Esteban had not enclosed anything inside to taunt him. The bad news was that it was completely empty and a tapping of the wall revealed that no conventional smuggling trick could explain where the cocaine was hidden.

Attles straightened back up, a bit slowly and stiffly Michelle noticed, and said to the handler, "Let's have a sniff." The handler brought the beagle over to the urn, tail wagging like a pendulum on an overwound clock, and unhooked MJ from his leash.

While waiting in the parking lot for the jet to land, the handler, with a parent's pride, had boasted to Michelle that MJ was "top dog of his drug-sniffing class." The handler had explained that while all dogs may go to heaven, all are not created equal when it comes to olfactory prowess.

Lowering his voice as if someone might get hurt feelings if overheard, he explained to Michelle, "Some dogs just can't make the cut. Not their fault, you know. Either you have it or you don't." In what she guessed was a well-rehearsed spiel from talking to junior high *Just Say No* assemblies, he continued enthusiastically, "Even with those who make the initial cut, it's like the NBA. You have a lot of players who will be forgotten in a few years, but then you have the greats. The ones who are the best, year in and year out ... the Michael Jordans"—and here he leaned down and gave the dog a treat and scratched him behind his floppy ears—"the MJs." Michelle would have wagered her pension that he carried puppy photos of MJ in his wallet.

And now, MJ's time had arrived to show why he was All-Pro. Everyone stepped back as MJ started circumnavigating the urn as it lay on its side, sniffing east to west, then south to north before, to everyone's astonishment, going inside the urn until only a wagging tail was visible, earning a few surprised "ahhs" as if MJ was performing a cute trick at a kid's birthday party.

The handler leaned toward Michelle and flirtatiously whispered, "The beauty of being a beagle" and smiled. Eventually, no ports were left for MJ to visit, and he plopped down on the carpet as if the factory shift whistle had just blown. Michelle heard the handler mutter a "damn" to himself before looking at Attles.

"Sir, MJ reports a negative." Upon hearing his name, MJ laconically lifted his head up, looked at the handler, and returned his head to his front paws.

"Stand it back up," Attles ordered. As the agents set the urn back upright, Michelle watched them observe Attles warily through side glances, leaving no doubt that his volatile reputation had been discussed in the van on the way over.

Attles paced around the urn, eyeing it as if desperate to challenge it to a duel. He finally stopped circling and took several steps away. "I see," he said softly to no one in particular. And for the first time, the thought crossed Michelle's mind that Attles looked old. Without the bluster, the eyebrows were no longer weapons of intimidation but an unkempt garden starting to claim the front porch, the creases and furrows that could project the fury of a Kansas twister when an angry scowl, only tire ruts on a dusty dirt road.

Michelle came over and gently took his elbow. "Sir, it's over. We all thought it was the Albatross. Let's go back to headquarters." To her surprise, Attles let her steer him toward the lounge's exit.

Casper, who had stopped mumbling his "oh Gods" as he watched MJ sniff the urn and perked up upon hearing that the beagle had struck out, was now attentively listening. In a voice filled with rightful indignation, Casper spoke up, "Aha! So I ... I, Professor Casper Crenshaw"—he pointed grandiosely at himself—"have been wrongly accused! You sir, made a grave mistake. I will be on the airwaves before the end of tomorrow telling my public how scandalously I was treated. Like ... like a common criminal. If I have any sway, and I assure you I do, your career is over."

Attles whirled back to face Casper, his pilot light not extinguished after all, causing Michelle to ready herself to step in between the two. "Here's the thing, Professor. You're *way* too late to my going-away party."

And before Michelle could stop him, Attles moved not toward Casper but the urn, gave it a bump with his shoulder accompanied by an "oops" while he looked directly into Casper's horrified eyes. The urn rocked slightly to the left, teetered back violently to the right, and then toppled forward as two agents dove. The crashing urn filled the room with the sound of shattering glass, shards scattering to all four corners of the lounge, the fractured figures and patterns forming a gigantic jigsaw puzzle across the floor. It had been a very bad day for frolicking youth.

Knowing it likely would be the last order he ever issued, Attles barked, "Clean this shit up" and began marching toward the exit with Michelle hurrying after.

# CHAPTER THIRTY-SIX

Sipping a Coca-Cola beneath the palm tree's shade, George "Tall Man" Campbell watched the man's wiry body gyrate up, down, and occasionally sideways as he pummeled the steel drum. A mop of white hair flopped with every movement, like a chorus line of dancers valiantly trying to keep up with a singer hepped up on meth.

George took another sip on his straw and surveyed the flip-flopped tourists arrayed around the town square, clad in their colorful shirts with prints of flowers, birds, and the occasional monkey. There weren't many in the impromptu audience, the midday tropical sun driving most visitors into the air-conditioned exile of their hotel rooms. But those who were watching wore bemused smiles, bordering on embarrassment at observing such primal joy being acted out in front of them. At a prior performance, George had even seen a mother shield her young son's eyes, as if the spectacle might catapult him straight from the sandbox into puberty.

True, the other members of the Steel Band Serenaders grumbled about having to let the eccentric Yank join their rehearsals once a week. And they could be downright petulant when he'd jam with them for a few songs on Friday nights at The Debauchery Factory, the nightclub at the singles' resort where intoxicated mainlanders used plastic shark teeth to pay for drinks with names like One Night Stand, Sex a' Peel, Horny Tequila Dog, and for those alone at the end of the evening, Nightshade.

George was the first to admit his fellow Serenaders' grousing had merit. He had never known anyone to be so naturally bereft of rhythm as the man everyone called "the Brons," whose eight-beat bore no relation to any counting system ever devised by humankind. The Brons was living proof that while marching to the beat of one's own drummer might be a virtue in some situations, it was not a trait to be celebrated when it came to playing in a band.

When the Brons would play with the Serenaders, the band would become like the entertainer who spun plates atop sticks, getting more and more spinning until one plate would begin to wobble, then another, another, and another, and soon, all the plates wobbled on disaster's brink as the entertainer maniacally dashed from stick to stick, trying to keep each whirling. The Brons' lack of rhythm was the plate that first started wobbling when he would join the Serenaders on stage. Within half a minute, all the band members were precariously wobbling, desperately trying to recapture the lost beat before it all came crashing down. But as George reminded his mates when they'd start griping upon seeing the Brons walk up the dirt path to the studio where they practiced, the Yank's generous monthly cash contributions paid for their rehearsal space and kept them awash in ganga and Red Stripe.

Plus, and George didn't voice it out loud to his bandmates, he liked the guy. It didn't take a genius to surmise that the Brons—no last name ever mentioned—was running from his past, but that hardly distinguished him from most expats on the island. No, it was that George had never seen playing music, if you called what the Brons did music, transform someone so completely. Taciturn bordering on gruff without mallets in his hands, the Brons lit up with childish delight once he started pounding away.

George drained the last of the Coca-Cola with a final, long pull on the straw. He placed the bottle gently on the little café's table and patted the envelope in his pocket with the Yank's latest contribution to the Serenaders' coffers. He waited for a brief break in the pounding, caught the drummer's eye, gave him a thumbs-up, received a manic grin in return, and strolled off.

\* \* \* \* \* \*

SCOTT E. SUNDBY 229

The end was as swift as it was expected. True to his word, the Albatross had been on every news program within a day and became the poster-child du jour for victims of law enforcement overreaching.

The DEA made no effort to defend Attles. Called before the DEA high command, he was told that quietly retiring was, by far, his wisest course of action. The press release announcing he was stepping down spoke of his desire to spend more time with his family.

On his last day, he walked down the hallway with a box under one arm containing the few personal items he kept in his office. He wished the DEA handled dismissals like the old Westerns when a soldier was drummed out of the corps. At least then the soldier could look everyone in the eye as he marched out of the fort to the steady beat of a drum. Instead, Attles had to watch his ex-colleagues scurry into their offices as they spotted him coming, denying him the satisfaction of showing them he was unbent.

Attles found some comfort in the fact that not long after his dismissal, the Albatross had created his own controversy. Casper had enraged the literary, academic, racial justice, and ornithological communities all at once by announcing that the book he was writing was going to be called, *I Know Why the Caged Albatross Sings*. Worse for Casper, Fortuna had grown bored with him, and the sound inside his head of a ball rolling around a roulette wheel kept him awake most nights. Weeks later, Fortuna was still nowhere to be seen, and a sleep-deprived Casper was still on the talk-show circuit issuing abject public apologies, blaming his tone deafness on PTSD after "being manhandled by poetry-hating thugs."

But whatever. By the time Casper was uttering his public *mea culpas*, Attles had stopped paying attention. To the few people who bothered to ask him what he was going to do after leaving the DEA, he would enigmatically reply that he was "going in search of the Messiah." Suspecting that Attles was suffering a psychotic break—especially since he delivered this pronouncement while uncharacteristically grinning—the answer, as he had hoped, shut down all further inquiry. But, in fact, it was true.

Although Attles had harbored suspicions of how he had been played by Esteban, he hadn't been certain until he'd heard Forreo's recounting at the formal debriefing that followed every major investigation. Mike told his inquisitors about the last-minute switch of terminals, how Carlos had snatched his phone as he tried to send the text alerting the Operation Poetry Slam task force, and how he had finally been freed by a janitor several hours later—a janitor who seemed surprisingly unsurprised to open the cleaning closet and find Mike squatting in the dark amid the mops and brooms.

Attles had done his best to sit there stoically as Mike told his story, even though his internal monologue was saying, "Well, holy goddamn eureka." Once Attles knew that the text message that sent them scrambling off in search of the Albatross had to have been sent by Carlos or Esteban and not Mike, he had his answer.

He had no one to blame but himself for forgetting the lesson he had drilled into every newly minted agent. Before the City cleaned up Times Square and cutesy cupcake shops replaced the adult movie theaters, he would take his rookie recruits down to the Square for a field trip. They'd weave in and out of the grifters and gropers wearing grimy Spider-Man, Elmo, and Cookie Monster costumes until he spotted his destination—an upturned milk crate where a man wearing a dark-purple pork pie hat and calling himself "Porky" was showing a group of tourists three cards. He'd ask one of them to keep an eye on the queen as the "winning lady," and then place the three cards atop the crate. If they correctly picked which was the queen, and they always miraculously did in the beginning, they'd win a couple dollars. As the wager grew in proportion to the mark's burgeoning overconfidence, however, they were out fifty bucks before they knew it.

Over the years, he'd observed a number of three-card monte dealers, but Porky had a street-earned doctorate in psychology that set him apart as the Sigmund Freud of con men. He was the master of using misdirection so that the marks didn't even realize they'd been fleeced as they walked away. And yet, Attles had ignored the most fundamental lesson that observing Porky taught—never get fooled into thinking you know the winning card. The only way to succeed is to kick the milk crate over and grab all the cards.

For two weeks after the debriefing, Attles checked his computer multiple times a day. Finally, the entry appeared. The next morning, he threw a briefcase into the back seat of a rental car and headed toward the New Jersey Turnpike. From there, he hopped onto the interstate, set cruise control to avoid any chance of a speeding ticket that might show where he had driven, crossed the Pennsylvania border, and rehearsed the plan again in his mind.

He arrived mid-afternoon at a campus enjoying an early summer breather from the bustle of students. A chorus of cicadas singing from trees in full leaf filled the air as he walked. Two groundskeepers on ladders were taking down a banner hanging above the student union's entrance congratulating the college's new graduates. Attles called up to them for directions and a few minutes later was ascending the steps to a modern, red brick building with Messiah College Library spelled out in silver metallic letters next to a welcoming glass entryway.

Peering through the windows, he could see that the main reading room was deserted except for a lone librarian behind the front desk. Attles took a deep breath, pushed open the doors, and walked up to the desk, glancing about as if uncertain how to proceed.

"Can I help you?" The question from the young man in a white-and-blue-checkered shirt came with the chipper tone of someone starved for human interaction.

"Um ... yes, I'm here trying to help out my daughter." With an air of pride, Attles continued, "She teaches here but is away on sabbatical, and I was hoping I could pick up some books she needs."

"Of course! Who is your daughter and what does she need?" The librarian eagerly swiveled his chair to the monitor in front of him, fingers hovering over the keyboard, ready to spring into action.

"Professor Angela Lawson-Ogobwe. She teaches poetry in the English department."

The librarian unthinkingly turned his attention back to Attles, puzzlement etched across his face, and started to ask, "Did you say Angela..." before noticing the look of resigned hurt that Attles had studiously practiced in the mirror for the past two weeks.

"I'm the Lawson part," Attles volunteered in a weary voice, as if he had been through this a thousand times and would no doubt go through it ten thousand more.

"Oh my, no, that wasn't what ... certainly didn't mean ... I just wanted to make sure I heard you, what you said, correctly." The librarian's words came crashing out like a ten-car pileup on the freeway. "Your daughter is wonderful, and we are so lucky to have her here," he continued, trying to settle himself. But despite his protestations, Attles knew the librarian was frantically trying to figure out how much trouble he might be in for unconsciously assuming that the white man standing in front of him could not be Professor Lawson-Ogobwe's father.

His voice all benevolence, Attles's face took on a conciliatory expression. "Listen, people make the mistake all the time, please don't worry. But might I get those books? Do you need some identification?"

With a strained laugh, the librarian uttered, "Of course not," and buzzed open the turnstile to the reading room, gesturing for Attles to enter. "*Mi casa es tu casa*," he offered, followed by another forced laugh. "What can I help you find?"

Attles told him, and the librarian perked up slightly with the comfort of returning to familiar terrain. "Oh, how fortunate. They just got delivered the other day and logged into new acquisitions."

"That's what Angela told me ... that she had been checking her computer daily and saw them pop up yesterday. It's why she asked me to drive on down." Resuming a tone of familial pride, Attles added, "You know, she was one of the presenters at the conference."

"I did not! Well, how wonderful is that! I'll be right back!" and the librarian hopped off toward the stacks, happy to be making amends.

Ten minutes later, Attles was holding two large, leather-bound volumes. Each volume had *The Official Proceedings of the Wordsworth in Bogotá Conference, Volumes I & II* pressed into its cover in gold print. He ran his calloused fingertips over the lettering admiringly, and then carefully lowered the volumes into a briefcase capable of holding enough clothes for an around-the-world voyage.

"What do I need to do to check these out?"

"Not a thing," the librarian beamed. "I've already checked them out to your daughter's faculty account." He lowered his voice to a tone of conspiratorial confidentiality, "You know, the faculty never return them when they're due because we're not allowed to fine them."

Attles shook his head sympathetically over the rampant lawlessness. "Well, listen, you have made all of this easier than I could ever have hoped. Thank you a thousand times over."

"Oh my, not at all." The librarian waved his hand as if dismissing any thought that there had been trouble, adding, "It was my sincere pleasure." He waited until the doors shut behind Attles before letting his lips push out a loud sigh of relief and plopping down in his chair. With arms plaintively outstretched, he asked the empty reading room, "When did being a librarian become so perilous?"

\* \* \* \* \* \*

After a final flourish that left his arms feeling the good ache of having pushed the limit, the Brons began packing up the drum, his sweat-drenched T-shirt hanging loose. He glanced inside the upturned pork pie hat he set out for tips. Two shiny Canadian dimes, an arcade token, and a stick of chewing gum stared up at him. At least this time, the gum was still in its wrapper. But no worries. He put the hat out simply because that seemed what a proper busker would do, not because he depended on the tips.

As he snapped the drum case shut, he surreptitiously scanned the departing crowd, wondering if he'd ever be free of the need to do so. About a month after his visit to the Messiah College Library, the campus newspaper, *The Daily Pulse*, reported that Professor Lawson-Ogobwe had returned from her sabbatical to discover her office vandalized and her home burglarized. The article revealed that the crimes remained unsolved by the local police, although a disgruntled former student was a "person of interest." When he read the story, he knew the hunt by Esteban was on.

He felt some security in knowing that only two people could connect him to the missing books. He was counting on the librarian keeping his mouth shut from embarrassment. As to the second, no one but Attles knew of his visit to a chemist who Attles had repeatedly tried but failed to send to the federal penitentiary. Not only was the chemist—a former pharmaceutical research scientist—a master of covering his tracks so that Attles could never find his secret lab, but he had earned the nickname of "The Alchemist" through an uncanny ability to disguise cocaine as innocuous substances. The Alchemist's surprise at opening the door and finding his nemesis standing on his front stoop, even recoiling a step upon seeing Attles, was nothing compared to the shock when he examined the volumes Attles pulled out of the briefcase.

His eyes eerily enlarged by the magnifying glass's lens, the Alchemist had kept shaking his head in awe as he examined the tomes under a variety of special lamps, carefully dripping different solvents from an array of eye droppers onto the pages, muttering words like "magnificent" and "astounding."

Although it took Attles hours to convince the chemist he was not being set up as part of a sting operation, they eventually formed a partnership. The Alchemist not only would convert the pages that had been soaked in liquid cocaine back into a marketable powder form, but he would also handle the bulk sale. In return, they would split the proceeds fifty-fifty. Given the voluminous size of the conference's proceedings, a verbosity Esteban had encouraged through his generous stipends to the professors and minimum page mandates, Attles and the Alchemist would each walk away with a little over two million, a nice little supplement to his government pension.

Once Attles's humiliation had healed, helped considerably by the poultice of an overflowing Cayman bank account, he was able to step back and fully acknowledge Esteban's virtuosity. Attles' laptop had continued to ping every time *The Official Proceedings of the Wordsworth in Bogotá Conference, Volumes I & II* appeared in the college library of one of the conference participants, followed shortly afterward by their disappearance with a "missing" or "unretrievable" entry in the online catalog. Esteban's men apparently simply paid midnight visits to the libraries through a door left ajar or an unlocked window rather than going through the charade of checking them out. By his rough calculation, once Esteban collected all the volumes and converted them back into cocaine, minus, of course, the two volumes Attles had gotten to first, one was talking a haul of about forty million.

And the scheme was clever—he still couldn't quite bring himself to say brilliant—as the task force had fallen hard for the decoys of the urns and the Albatross. Porky couldn't have done better. Attles still had a nagging suspicion that someone at the Miami airport must have alerted Esteban and Carlos when to send Forreo's text. The timing was perfect, causing them to dash off to Opa Locka just as they were likely to turn their attention to the luggage cart of books once it became evident the urns were empty. He had ruled out Forreo, Chang, and Esperanza, and, in fact, had been careful to make sure all the blame was heaped on him for the failed mission so their careers would be unharmed. But who?

Perhaps nobody. The timing could have just been Esteban's lucky guess that became Attles's bad luck. Or, then again, in the end could one really call it bad luck?

The Brons smiled to himself, something he was startled to realize he was doing with some frequency, along with swearing a lot less. He took a draught of his post-concert beer, the bar's dark coolness a welcomed shelter from the mid-afternoon broil. He instinctively looked over as the tavern door pushed open. The brilliant sunlight transformed the entering patron into a silhouette, and, for a second, he was reminded of a painting on his grandmother's wall of a soul ascending to heaven against a backdrop of blinding, golden light. This person, though, was neither angel nor assassin ... just a tourist in search of a Mai Tai.

He slid off the barstool, his laceless sneakers sticking to a floor that eons of spilled beer had turned into a barroom version of the La Brea Tar Pits. He stretched, letting the pleasant fatigue from the drumming fully seep into his bones, and headed toward the door, every step emitting a satisfying squeak. A siesta would be fuc— just perfect.

# CHAPTER THIRTY-SEVEN

*"Mierda!"* The flashlight beam took one final scan of the living room, revealing cushions torn open, emptied drawers, bookcases with their contents spilled on the floor.

"I know. We're screwed," the other man replied in Spanish, also wielding a flashlight. "Esteban was pissed as hell when we came up empty at that other college. Another one is really going to send him over the edge." He looked around the wasteland that the house had become. "But they're not here––I'm sure of that. Don't envy you telling him."

"Me? I told him last time. Your turn." Still bickering, they stepped onto the front porch of the house at 41 Raven Lane. A quarter moon cast just enough light they could turn off their flashlights. One of the men kicked a porch swing out of frustration, sending it careening wildly back and forth, squeaking loudly on its chains.

The other man uttered a vehement, "Quiet, asshole," which triggered an equally strong, "Yeah, right, like someone can hear us in the middle of goddamn nowhere. Let's get out of here."

The men got into the car, the passenger slamming his door, the driver easing his shut, and they bounced down the driveway with the headlights off. They drove past a For Sale sign in the front yard barely visible in the moon's glow and could just make out the shape of a giant oak tree off to the right. Perhaps if their lights had been on, or the moon had been a little brighter, they would have looked more closely and wondered.

The grand old oak was a storied tree—a tree that knew how to keep secrets of first kisses and eternal vows of love, whose massive trunk provided comforting support for a body sobbing when those vows were broken. But it had never witnessed a secret like this one before. A man with a shovel digging a deep hole, lowering a package wrapped in heavy plastic, replacing the dirt with a circle of fresh potting soil around the trunk, planting a colorful skirt of azaleas and rhododendrons, and, finally, placing a garden gnome at the trunk's base holding a sign saying "Bless this Garden." The gnome was going to take some getting used to.

# CHAPTER THIRTY-EIGHT

"I'm sorry, Esteban, I don't know where Percy is these days." She paused, still absorbing the news. "To be honest, I didn't even know he had left his position. We haven't talked since the conference."

Hearing the undertone of regret in Moira's voice, Esteban knew she was telling the truth. He was surprised how happy that made him, to be certain someone was not lying to him.

"Oh, of course, Moira. I just have some final travel reimbursements I was trying to get to him, and they came back from Arcadia as undeliverable. But don't worry about it. I'll follow up with his department, and I'm sure they can help me get them to him." The line went awkwardly silent before Esteban spoke again, "But tell me, how are you?"

The next five minutes was a painful exchange of updates, both acutely aware a friendship they had once wrapped themselves in like a favorite comforter had unraveled. She was not surprised to learn Esteban was taking a break from grad school to help with the family business or that he wasn't sure when he'd return to the States.

Moira, in return, filled him in on the slow slog of her dissertation writing, comparing it to pulling teeth with a rusty pliers, one molar at a time without Novocain. But while the 'old Esteban' would have filled the air with sympathetic laughter and a lilting "*Dios mio*" his distracted, "I'm sure you'll finish it" and "it will be great" made her feel like a patient whose therapist was clearly impatient to get home and pour a tumbler of Scotch.

She desperately wanted to ask how he could have used her and Percy the way he had, placing them in the bull's-eye of some rabid DEA agent who Esteban apparently had it in for. But she didn't. Not because Esteban had sent her a check afterward for five thousand dollars with a note attached saying, "I'm so sorry to hear about the trouble at the airport. I hope this helps pay for some therapy," the note signed with a smiley face. She had not smiled, and the check sat in her desk drawer uncashed. No, she didn't ask because she knew he'd have to lie, and it seemed not just pointless, but wrong to knowingly bring more deception into the world.

After Esteban clicked off, Moira turned her gaze to the corkboard above her desk. While it was true she had not talked to Percy since the conference, she had heard from him. Next to her treasured baseball card was pinned a postcard she had received a few weeks after the conference. Looking down at her was one of Monet's famous *Water Lily* impressionist paintings. On the back, Percy had scribbled a quick message (in reality, he had rewritten it several times and had purchased five of the same postcard from the college bookstore, knowing he'd botch at least a few).

*My dear M, As I hope the painting on the front makes clear, your words made a lasting impression ... and, yes, that deserves an audible groan. Mrs. Monet concurs with you that my impressionist viewing skills leave plenty of room for improvement, but, for what it's worth, she also thinks reason for hope exists. Anyway, hoping you haven't applied to law school quite yet, even if you'd make an amazing barrister. P.S. I'm writing this in a booth at The Fifth Chance Saloon, although Reggie has a remorseful air as he moves around the bar that makes me think the sign outside may soon be upped to an even half dozen. Yours, P*

When the card had tumbled out of her overstuffed mailbox and landed picture-side up, Moira had smiled upon instantly surmising the sender's identity. Her smile had widened after she picked it up, leaned against the wall, and read the message. Her immediate thought was to go that afternoon to the gift shop at the Metropolitan Museum of Modern Art to look for a message-in-a-bottle to send back, knowing a return package or note would soon follow, and the pendulum of easy banter, teasing, and shared thoughts would resume its pleasant swing. But without ever making a conscious decision to abandon the plan, she had not followed through. Eventually, it just seemed too late.

# CHAPTER THIRTY-NINE

Moira found a parking spot a few blocks away and staked out her destination. The squat, light-gray concrete building—actually, gray was too charming a description as it was more the hue of moldy bread—made Stalinist architecture appear as cozy as a Cotswolds cottage by comparison. The metal-framed windows resembling gun slits were rusted from decades of steeping in the salt air. The glass panes apparently had last been washed during the Eisenhower administration. On the plus side, the structure appeared impregnable to a category-five hurricane and the zombie apocalypse likely to follow.

With a psychopath's merciless glee, the Miami summer mugged Moira as soon as she stepped out of the car, the humidity and heat making each breath a conscious effort. The cooling sea breezes of her April visit were long gone, replaced with the stifling air of a sweat lodge.

By the time she walked the two blocks to the building, her bangs were plastered to her forehead and tributaries of perspiration trickled down her back and sides. The blast of air conditioning she hoped would rescue her when she pulled open the building's front door turned out to be no more than a sneeze, the cooling system wheezing its last gasps. The warm moisture of the lobby's interior was perfect for orchid growing.

She pushed her bangs to the side and scanned the directory. White plastic letters on a black letterboard spelled out the office building's tenants and their office number. A few listings had a letter hanging akilter, while others were missing a letter altogether. She guessed that the House of C-ats

Direct Order Company did not, in fact, have a warehouse full of yowling felines. She found the listing for Project Headlights, Office 622.

Moira crossed the lobby and pushed the elevator button. She pushed again. Once more. Nothing. Sighing, she eyed the staircase with lemon-yellow paint peeling off its walls, revealing a surplus World War II coat of army-tank green underneath. Resigned to the reality that no deodorant was up to the task that lie ahead, she began climbing.

She did her best to not think too hard on what certain odors might be or to touch the banister snaking along the stairwell. She caught her breath as she reached the sixth floor landing and began walking down the deserted hallway. The wooden office doors with frosted windows made her feel like she was in a black-and-white noir film where the down-on-his-luck private eye waited for the client's knock that would change his fortunes. From the offices' deserted looks, the knock never came.

Moira spotted the door to Office 622 up ahead. A piece of paper was taped next to it, *Project Headlights* handprinted with a magic marker in bright-blue letters. The door was cracked open, and over a stack of papers she could see a head bent with a cowlick sticking up like a rooster's comb. Despite impending heatstroke, she grinned upon spying a pair of wooden drumsticks mounted on the wall, crossed like oars above a fireplace in a captain's quarters.

He didn't look up in response to the light rap on the door, but called out "come in" as he finished reading the page in front of him. When he did look up, his jaw moved for a few seconds without words coming out. Finally, his vocal cords found traction. "I must say, your dedication in delivering pizzas anywhere is truly unsurpassed."

Moira nodded. "Well, I tried to deliver it to your office in Arcadia first, but they gave me this address and told me you'd left to seek your fortune." Making a show of looking around the office, she added, "And clearly, you found it." Percy laughed and gestured to a chair, a bulky wooden relic salvaged from a street curb as it waited for the next trash pickup.

"I'd offer to turn this on you"—he pointed at a small desk fan whirring on a table and blowing directly on him, his hair doing a light fandango in the fan's breeze—"but I'm afraid you'll be offended, thinking I'm trying to turn you into one of those Vogue models with their hair blowing back."

"Oh dear God, please, please offend away! It's so damn hot." Percy turned the fan so it was blowing on her. She closed her eyes, lethargically tilted her head back, flushed cheeks matching her hair, and let the waves of air ripple over her. After a half minute, during which Percy tried to figure out if he should feel guilty for thinking she really did look the part of a cover shoot, Moira sat back up, slightly revived.

"Tell me—" they both began at the same time. Percy immediately followed with a call of "Jinx," adding, "and if I remember the laws of the playground jungle correctly, that means I get to decide who goes first." He paused for a second. "So tell me, what brings you here, other than a desire to lose water weight?"

"Well, I have an aunt in Fort Lauderdale (this was true) I've been meaning to visit (this was vaguely true), so when Esteban called a few days ago telling me you were no longer at Arcadia"—was it her imagination or did Percy's eyes widen in concern at the news Esteban had called her—"I thought it'd be a good chance to kill two birds with one stone." Watching Percy's eyes reflexively go to the phone on his desk, she interjected, "I thought of calling, but I don't trust Esteban, and it seemed like news better delivered in person."

Percy nodded pensively. "Did Esteban say why he was trying to track me down?"

"Something about getting you some reimbursements."

Percy nodded again, kneading the back of his right hand with the fingers of his left. "And how long ago did you say he called?"

"Let's see, I guess it'd have been five, no, four days ago." Percy again looked distracted, like he was calculating the odds of a wager. She asked, "Everything okay?"

"Um ... yes, I'm sure it is." He turned his attention back to her. "But you!" he exclaimed, clapping his hands lightly as if that would make any other thoughts scatter. "How is that dissertation writing going?"

She described the feeling of having her teeth extracted one by one without anesthesia and liked that he noticeably winced at the image even as he laughed and said, "I trust your grad school health insurance covers dental implants as an education-related medical condition?"

"Unfortunately, I fear I'm going to have to wait until I'm making the big bucks as an adjunct."

Percy's expression was both bemused and sympathetic before asking, "Seriously, though, do you mind if I ask what part you're writing at the moment? Sometimes the last thing I want to do is talk about what I'm working on because it seems hopeless and will just depress me more, but I did really like your project last we talked."

She picked a paper clip up off the desk and began unbending it. "You're right. Most times, I'd rather talk about *anything* else." She hesitated before continuing. "But I'm actually at a bit of a logjam and wouldn't mind having a sounding board." And she began explaining the section she was working on.

As they brainstormed, she felt, for the first time in months, the excitement of the ideas that first drew her to grad school. After a half hour of free-associating about how to bring together several themes she'd been struggling with, Percy leaned forward on his elbows and said, "You know, Moira, you're really onto something with your thesis, as painful as writing it might be." After a brief pause, he added, "I just hope you finish before you have to gum all your meals. Mashed potatoes and applesauce become monotonous."

Moira smiled and twirled the paper clip she had unconsciously bent and unbent so many times it had become a miniature Rodin. She placed it down on the desk as her features took on a more serious cast. "Okay, my turn to do the interrogating. What in God's name are you up to?" Her voice vied between a tone of curiosity and incredulity.

Percy's face beamed, and his hands became animated as he spoke. "I know it seems a bit crazy, but I've started this non-profit, *Project Headlights*. As you can see"—his arms swept around the dingy office—"I've got the 'non' part of non-profit nailed down tight." He liked how she listened with interest, the corners of her mouth flirting with a smile.

"And listen, I know I've already bemoaned way too loudly to you"—she gave a brief shake of her head no—"that I was trapped in a cul-de-sac, that I needed to do something where I felt I was seizing the moment rather than the moment seizing me." Percy stood up and turned toward the window as he continued speaking, his wispy frame outlined against the sky. "And what I realized was that I still wanted to share my love of books with others, but I wanted to share it with those who would be reading not because it was on a syllabus, but because it brings them joy—or relief—as a way to deal with the world."

He turned back to face her. "You'll find this hard to believe," he said, his face taking on a look of wry sarcasm, "but growing up, I didn't quite fit in." His look became intensely earnest as he continued, "And it probably wouldn't be an overstatement to say books saved me by giving me hope that a world, or really worlds, were out there where I could be happy. But at some point, I let the fact I was good at literature ... acing exams, clever literary critiques, all the academic bells and whistles ... become the reason I was reading instead of what drew me in the first place."

Sitting back down, his voice got softer. "I actually resigned my position at Arcadia while still in Bogotá. Just knew I had to get out, even though I wasn't sure what came next."

Moira interrupted, "Not that it's all about me, but I hope our ... our disagreement at the conference didn't cause you to act rashly."

Percy looked down at the desktop, mindlessly picked up the paper clip sculpture Moira had placed there and began twisting and turning it. "Not really. Let's just say our"—he smiled as he lifted his gaze to meet her eyes— "our disagreement may have given me a needed push. In any case, I wasn't sure what I was going to do until I started reading the news about the immigration crisis." A rare touch of anger infused his next words, "People are dying at sea on homemade rafts or crossing the desert, and those who make it here are thrown into detention camps, including families, young kids. Can you imagine? People seeking hope tossed into a place where all hope is banished? I couldn't stop thinking about the kids. When I was their age, I was feeling sorry for myself because I wasn't chosen for kickball, and here they were, in another country, being treated like criminals for seeking a better life."

246 WORDSWORTH IN BOGOTÁ

Although Moira was listening keenly, she also couldn't help thinking she rather liked the fiery Percy.

"So, I know this sounds on some level like a parody ... here are people behind barbwire fences with armed guards in miserable living conditions, some on cots in tents ... and what do I want to bring them? Books." He shook his head back and forth, acknowledging the absurdity.

The passion in his voice became infused with cracks of doubt as he went on, "I mean, believe me, I know the real heroes are the immigration lawyers, the activists fighting for more humane treatment. I can't help but hope, though, that if I can get a book to those kids, it might make at least one child's day a little better. Maybe a kid on a cot can escape her hell for a few minutes if she travels the train to Hogwarts? Or find hope in a companion like Anne of Green Gables? Or go to sleep with a belief in their ability to save the world after listening to a chapter of *A Wrinkle in Time* or *The Golden Compass*?"

Moira reached across the desk and put her hand on his arm. "Percy, it's a worthy windmill. I'd tilt at it too."

Percy became reanimated, his hands making small karate chops as he spoke. "I'm also trying to get permission to bring in volunteers to read, because you know, many of the kids can't read, or only barely. And then, of course, there's the challenge of language. I'm trying to get books in Spanish, Creole, and Portuguese to start with. Plus, I need to figure out the optimal reading level to reach the most kids."

He stopped, realizing he was running through his daily checklist out loud. "Sorry, more moving parts than you might think." He hesitated for a moment. "And then there is the biggest moving part of all—the money. Luckily, my parents haven't sold my grandparents' old house yet, so I can squat there for a while. But as you can gather from my surroundings, I'm not rocking the fundraising." He paused again as if contemplating what to say next. "I actually almost had to fold up shop until ... an anonymous donor materialized ... it isn't ideal, and I'm hoping once I get a footing ..."

"Percy, did you go to a loan shark?" Moira asked, laughing at the thought.

Percy forced a smile in reply, "Well, if so, I'm hoping my medical covers broken kneecaps because not sure I could repay it."

Surprised by his seriousness, Moira didn't ask further about the anonymous donor. "Well, might I suggest a change of name for your next fundraising appeal. Project Headlights? I thought you had gone into the auto parts business when I first saw it."

This time, Percy responded with a chuckle. "Ah, okay, good to know. I rather like the name. Comes from a quote I've always loved about writing—that trying to write is like 'driving at night in the fog. You can only see as far as your headlights, but you can make the whole trip that way.' It's actually wonderful life advice generally, don't you think? And I thought how each book is a headlight for the reader. Helps get you a little farther down the foggy road. But your point is a good one. If people think I'm trying to peddle oil filters and brake pads, I've definitely outwitted myself."

"So I like the headlights idea, but maybe package it with something like, I don't know, Libraries without Walls? A philanthropist might be less likely to toss away that fundraising letter than one saying only 'Project Headlights,' unless, of course, they're restoring a '65 Mustang at the time."

"Libraries without Walls? Damn, Moira, that's a really good name. I have a director of marketing position open ... pays incredibly well."

He suddenly looked exhausted. He wiped some beads of sweat from his forehead with a Pollo Tropical napkin left over from a lunchtime foray to the local fast food restaurant. "So," Percy suggested, "I think we should head out for an ice-cold cerveza to celebrate the new name."

Moira made a face at the thought of falling back into the clutches of the heat and humidity.

Percy grinned at her expression. "Oh, but here's what you don't know. Come four"—he looked at his watch—"so in just a little over fifteen minutes, like clockwork, we'll get what we call the cocktail-hour thunderstorm. It lasts a half hour or so, and then the sun will reappear and the rain will have cooled it down from suffocating to sweltering, and then to light perspiring, which down here we call winter. You still play hopscotch with any patch of shade as you walk, but you don't feel like you're going to pass out on the sidewalk. By the way, before you report us to the

Temperance League for starting our cocktail hour at four, keep in mind it is Thor who chose that hour, not us. We had no choice."

"Thor? Are you switching religions on me? Shouldn't it be Zeus?"

"I've become nondenominational."

"Ah, I see," Moira said, shaking her head in mock exasperation, "you're hard to keep up with."

*Thor felt his foot being shaken and groggily looked down before angrily uttering, "Can't you see I'm in the middle of a nap, you chubby pain in the ass? What the hell are you doing in Asgard, anyway. Shouldn't you be over on Mount Olympus?"*

*"Oh, I'm soooo sorry, you big galoot, but you've overslept again. You're supposed to be raining down thunderbolts at this very moment. Someone's love is riding on it."*

*"I'm sure a little longer won't matter." Thor's face took on a faraway look. "I was in the middle of a dream." He glared at Cupid. "And can't you just shoot one of your flaming arrows?"*

*"They don't flame. Oh never mind. Listen, one of my long-term projects is finally doing things right, but you need to do your fecking job to help him make it work. And don't forget, you big oaf, when Sif wouldn't give you the time of day, you came crawling to me and promised"—Cupid's voice took on a supplicant's tone—"Oh, Cupid, if only you'll make her love me, I'll be forever grateful."'*

*Thor sighed, stretched for a lightning bolt, the rustling of his garments blocking the sun's rays. "Okay, okay. I'll let you play that guilt card you've been holding in that tiny toga of yours for a good millennia, but this makes us even. Understood, you curly-haired gnat?"*

Glancing through the narrow window, Moira could see that the sky was indeed darkening quickly, the afternoon taking on an ominous, midnight cast. The first distant peal of thunder filtered in through the window. Moira's voice became serious, "Let me ask before Thor begins in earnest. This new project of yours"—she tilted her head up at the pair of crossed drumsticks on the wall—"you feel like you're playing the drums?" The thunderclaps grew closer. Powerful enough that Moira could feel the vibrations.

Percy intertwined his fingers and propped his chin atop the steeple of his hands. "I've thought a lot about that." The first drops of rain pelted the window as he unclasped his hands and leaned back. "And you play a role in it." Moira's eyebrows arched inquisitively.

"So every Saturday morning, I walk by this ball field in my neighborhood, and there's a group of older men out there playing softball. I mean, I'm guessing some are in their eighties, definitely a lot in their seventies.

"And at first I found them—and I hope this doesn't sound ageist, though I'm sure it does—fascinating to watch. They take it pretty seriously, wear full uniforms, have team names, the whole shebang. But when they'd hit the ball and run or move to field the ball, it's in this herky-jerky slow motion, like they're marionettes and each body part is attached to its own string. Sometimes one of them looks so fragile as their arms and legs flail around all akimbo, you think the puppet master in the sky is about to yank them right up off the field.

"But here's the thing." Percy looked slightly embarrassed as he pulled up the memory. "Although I always stopped and watched for a few minutes on my Saturday morning walks, I'd never really looked at their faces. And then I remembered your story about the comedian who you took a class from." Percy's tone became mischievous. "I think it was a graduate-level class in driving safely?" Becoming solemn again, he continued, "And you said you came to realize the comedian loved teaching the class, even though you first assumed he must hate it. And so I looked at the faces of these men, and even though their bodies were anything but spry as they ran, the expression they wore was of a sprinter winning the gold as he breaks the finish tape. In their minds, they were absolutely flying."

The storm outside had begun to calm, the thunder becoming distant as the front moved on to a cocktail party farther west, strands of sun breaking through the straggling clouds.

"*And?*" Moira asked after a few seconds of silence.

"Oh, there's supposed to be a moral to my story?" He grinned. "Well, like those eighty-year-old sandlot players, I need to relish my current feeling of contentment, even if it might just be for the moment. So, yes, I feel like I've had the courage to get up on the stage when the chance came. Might everything change?"—his expression darkened—"Certainly, I have some potential problems I need to solve." He looked at Moira before continuing with an air of resolution, "But I'm taking it step by step, or perhaps I should say page by page. Now, let's hopscotch over to where we can grab a cocktail and maybe even dinner while you can still chew."

Percy moved toward the door, flipping off the light switch as Moira rose from the chair. She turned as they walked through the doorway. "By the way, I was hoping we could take in an impressionist art exhibit while I'm in town."

The hallway of deserted offices soaked up Percy's delighted laughter like a parched garden welcoming a springtime shower.

# CHAPTER FORTY

Percy flutter-kicked the sheets off. He hadn't felt this good in ages. Dinner had been marvelous. The wild-caught grouper had been cooked and seasoned to perfection, the fingerling potatoes in a smoked paprika and cayenne pepper sauce sumptuous, the Malbec's bouquet exquisite. That, at least, had been what he envisioned, but being Friday night in Miami, all the places he thought might impress Moira were booked solid.

Just as his spirits sagged, she had spotted a restaurant on a side street in Little Havana. The café had only five tables, their Formica tops covered with white-paper tablecloths. Laughter spilling out of the kitchen created a delightful ambience. They had devoured tapas, drunk sangria, and talked ... and talked ... and talked. Even a McDonald's would have seemed like a Michelin star restaurant. Such is blossoming love.

He thought about asking her to spend the night, and maybe he didn't because, secretly, he still feared rejection. But he convinced himself that when he said "good night," it was because he had pressing business to take care of now that Moira was back in his life.

Percy had always been a savant when it came to puzzles and detecting hidden patterns. A high school aptitude test even suggested he would be an excellent CIA analyst because of his talent for separating the wheat from the chaff when processing large amounts of material. For several days after receiving the aptitude results, he had daydreamed of postings in Barcelona and Prague and Budapest, ferreting out enemy moles. Then he learned an analyst was stuck in the Langley headquarters, the only "mole" part being a windowless office in the basement. He had instead turned his puzzle-solving abilities to dominating Scrabble games.

Upon returning to Arcadia after the conference, Percy used this aptitude to mull over all of the events, the curious and uncurious, as he packed moving boxes and sifted through the detritus known as his office. Then, like the crossword answer suddenly revealing itself after a number of dead ends, he didn't need any more clues. He knew. It had to be the volumes that were to arrive at the Arcadia College library any day.

He hadn't figured out all the details, but Esteban's rush to publish the proceedings, his insistence on a minimum number of pages, the use of Moira as the enforcer ... all had seemed strange from the start. Then came the events at the airport. Esteban clearly wanted that strange DEA agent to go running off in frustration before the search could move beyond the urns to the books that Esteban had arranged to be delivered to the college libraries. Once he added it all up, Percy was wagering the books held the answer. Unsure what to do with the knowledge, he asked one of his students who worked in the library to notify him when the volumes arrived for cataloguing. The student had called a few days later.

Percy once read about psychological experiments showing humans don't really have free will, that they act unconsciously and rationalize their reasons for it afterward. And while he wasn't exactly in a fugue state after walking out of the library with the two heavy volumes under his arm, he also could not have explained his intentions. Revenge on Esteban for using him and Moira as pawns? The adrenaline rush of walking to the precipice's edge and looking down? His inner 007 challenging the Fates to a duel at ten paces without consulting him?

He honestly did not know. He was, however, aware enough to know that he should avoid having the conference proceedings checked out under his name, and had switched the circulation cards so it appeared he was crossing the quad to his office with two volumes of the Oxford Literature Criticism series.

After taking the volumes back to his house, Percy at first thought he must have been wrong. He had expected to open the books and find them hollowed out, but a close inspection revealed no place drugs could be hidden. He laughed at himself and concluded his James Bond fantasies had gotten out of hand, even felt a wave of relief he had been mistaken.

But then, his fingertip, moist with the condensation of his water glass, touched one of the printed words, causing it to blur. He ran his fingertip over the words on a number of pages, the ink running on all of them. Carefully rubbing the pages between his fingers revealed a texture he had never felt before. These were books Esteban counted on not raising suspicion if someone quickly perused them on their arrival and would then be catalogued, shelved, and forgotten.

After his discovery, he spent the day staring at the two volumes like an impulse buy one began to deeply regret. And by the time dusk arrived, he knew he had to return them to the library. Not only was there the little matter of taking property belonging to a Colombian drug cartel, but the reality sank in he had no idea what to do with them, as valuable as they might be. Placing a classified ad on Craig's List, "Chemical expert in processing Schedule One narcotics needed. Complete discretion a must," seemed unwise. Ultimately, he decided he'd settle for the satisfaction of having figured out Esteban's scheme and smuggle them back into the stacks the next morning with no one the wiser.

Then his student from the library called. The conference organizers had telephoned "to double-check that the conference proceedings had arrived," and to the librarian's great dismay, it was discovered they were missing. The student explained that he had luckily remembered Professor Billings asking about them earlier. Did he have any idea where they might be? Lucky indeed. Percy hoped he kept the panic out of his voice as he expressed great surprise and dismay at the news the volumes were missing, explaining he hadn't had a chance to see them yet.

The student had chirped back, "No worries, Professor Billings. I'll let the person who called know you have no idea where they are either. He, a Mr. Velasquez, I believe, had hoped you might know after I told him you had requested them." Percy silently cursed the competence of work-study students, and then abruptly ended the call with a quick, "Thanks, Adam, my dinner is burning on the stove. Need to run."

After he calmed down, his first inclination had been to try and get the volumes back into the library that night after it closed. But the library would be locked up, and he couldn't rule out that Esteban's henchmen had it staked out ... or that the police would stop someone lurking around the library late at night ... or that security cameras might record him, and he'd have to explain why he was breaking into the library at 3 a.m.

Unable to come up with a good option, and worried Esteban's confederates might show up any minute, he buried the books beneath the oak tree that night. He planted the garden around the tree the next morning after a quick run to a nursery, returning with the flowers and guardian gnome.

The following nights, he slept only a few hours. He bolted upright in bed whenever the night breeze rustled the branches. A passing car caused his heart to pound until he heard it continue on. He was grateful when, a few days later, he had finished hastily packing, listed his house for sale, and could throw his suitcases in the trunk and head to Miami.

It was barely a month after arriving in Miami that the Arcadia sheriff called to report the break-in at his house, and a week later when the doorbell rang. As he inched the door open he immediately recognized the woman as the Oracle, the translator from the conference. Only this time, she was as haunting as a stone effigy, wordlessly handing him an envelope. She turned and left before he could open it:

*Dear Percy, This will sound odd, but the conference volumes shipped to the Arcadia College Library are missing. Who would have guessed we'd be so popular people would want to steal them??? The library thought you might be able to help find them. I very much hope so. I am certain you understand why knowing the volumes are safe means a great deal to me.*

*After a little checking, by the way, I discovered you have a fledgling new venture in Miami. Congratulations. I know, though, that such ventures are expensive to start up. You'll be thrilled, therefore, to learn that our newly created Velasquez Foundation for the Future of Literature just donated to your project. You will find the funds have been directly deposited into your personal account as a "thank you in advance" for helping find the volumes. When you've located them, call Cristo at C&S Auto Salvage Yard down on the Miami River, and he'll arrange the pickup. Yours fondly, Esteban*

A deposit of $9,995 was already in his bank account when he checked that afternoon. An amount Percy recognized snuck under the ten-thousand-dollar amount that would have triggered a money laundering report from the bank to the Feds, but also would be impossible to explain if the DEA got an anonymous tip to look into Percy's finances. He had not asked for the money and hated that it gave Esteban a card to play against him, but there it was.

In the end, since he didn't know how to return the money to Esteban and couldn't very well go to the authorities given that the proverbial body was literally buried in his front yard, he rationalized he might as well use it to help keep the floundering Project Headlights afloat a little longer. But what to do next?

Before Moira's arrival, Percy had been inclined to continue acting innocent. He'd offer to try and track down the volumes, but then claim failure despite knowing he wouldn't be believed. Returning the volumes would give away the one thing—the belief Percy was the key to getting them back—that might keep Esteban at bay. And who was to say Esteban wouldn't be bent on revenge if he returned them?

But Moira's news changed everything. It had been almost two weeks since the Oracle had shown up at Percy's doorstep, and yet Esteban had contacted Moira to ask about Percy's whereabouts only a few days ago, *after* he already knew Percy was in Miami. Why would Esteban do that? It must have been to send a message.

At first, he worried the message was a vague threat that something might happen to Moira if he didn't cooperate. But as much as Esteban's personality had changed from what Moira told him, it seemed impossible to imagine him harming her. No, Percy concluded, approaching Moira, knowing she would then reach out to Percy, had to be Esteban's way of reassuring Percy he would be safe if he returned the volumes. Now, if anything happened to him, Moira would know Esteban had been looking for him and could go to the authorities. Esteban had wisely turned Moira into Percy's insurance policy. The smitten Percy couldn't help adding as an afterthought, *and what a perfect insurance policy she is.*

Percy took out a piece of paper and drew a map of his front yard in Arcadia that resembled the drawing of a treasure map in a children's picture book. It didn't need to be elaborate since the gnome sat directly over the buried treasure. He placed the map inside an envelope and called Cristo at C&S Salvage, who said someone would be over promptly.

Less than an hour later, the doorbell rang and the Oracle was once more standing on his front stoop. This time, she was smiling as she took the envelope containing the map from Percy's outstretched hand. In her mesmerizing voice, she simply said, "Esteban thanks you."

He closed the door and glanced at his watch. Three o'clock. Only two hours until Moira returned from her aunt's house. He gave a delighted chuckle at the thought she'd be pulling up in his driveway. He poured himself a glass of wine and looked out the window at a blue sky with Ionic columns of summer clouds towering upward.

He walked to the bookcase where several shelves were filled with books from half-unpacked boxes scattered around the floor. He put down the wine glass and from the top shelf pulled down a hardcover copy of *Ulysses*. Almost eight hundred pages long, it felt as heavy as the unused barbells sitting at the bottom of his bed.

*Ulysses* was one of his dark secrets—he had never finished it. In fact, never made it more than a quarter of the way through before setting it aside. For an English literature professor, this was the equivalent of a French chef not liking butter.

But the unfinished book still served a critical purpose—the hiding of an even bigger secret. He opened it to page 597 and looked at three pages meticulously inserted so that no one would ever know they were not part of Leopold Bloom's day of wandering Dublin. Three pages he had surgically removed with a razor blade from Volume Two of *The Official Proceedings of the Wordsworth in Bogotá Conference* just before burying them. Three pages because, as Percy's inner 007 had whispered in his ear, *"Sometimes, one just never knows."*

# ABOUT THE AUTHOR

*Photo Credit: Adam F. Scales, Invisible Lens Photography, Philadelphia*

Scott E. Sundby lives in South Florida and works in the criminal law area, a fruitful combination for someone in search of interesting stories. Always on the lookout for new experiences, he has taught law at ten different universities in seven countries. He has published a non-fiction book, *A Life and Death Decision: A Jury Weighs the Death Penalty*, and a children's picture book, *Cut Down to Size at High Noon*. *Wordsworth in Bogotá* is his debut novel.

When not teaching law or writing, he prides himself on having mastered the art form of making hard boiled eggs, a skill he thought was greatly undervalued until he saw them on a NYC restaurant menu for $13. It is now Plan B for his retirement.

# DEDICATION AND ACKNOWLEDGMENTS

Writing this book has provided a wonderful escape from the daily world. Along the way, I imposed on friends and family to provide feedback and let me know what was working, and, more importantly, what was not. I would like to give a warm 'thank you' to Bob and Selma Bernard and to Sloan White for taking the time to read a draft. My sister-in-law, Barb Sundby, went above and beyond familial duty in providing feedback, as did my children, Kelsey, Christopher, and Taylor. My wife, Katie, was my alpha and omega, reading and critiquing each chapter as it was written, dispensing wise advice as the storyline developed, and providing unflagging support and encouragement while searching for a publisher.

And, finally, a heartfelt thank you to copy editor and proofreader extraordinaire, Joyce Mochrie, owner of *One Last Look*. Joyce gave me peace of mind by catching everything from typos to misspellings to punctuation snafus.

At various points, I reference the works of others. Some are identified in the text, but I would like to give recognition to those who are not. The country and western song line, *It was bad enough you left me, but you had to tell me why*, comes courtesy of my wonderful guitar teacher Diana Schofield, who recalled it as a song title her sister, Debbie Madsen, and songwriting partner, Bill Idland, came up with, although the song was never written.

The reference to the humorous pieces about Miami's crime wave of the 1990s was to columns written by Dave Barry, then a *Miami Herald* journalist, now a national treasure.

The line, *Jesus loves me but He can't stand you*, is the title of a song by the Austin Lounge Lizards that is both hilarious and insightful.

The song Carl remembers his dad playing on the stereo, "Hellhound on My Trail," is an old blues song by the incomparable Robert Johnson.

The line, *We are all asleep until we fall in love*, is from *War and Peace* by an obscure Russian novelist named Leo Tolstoy.

The lines about *writing is like driving at night in the fog* that give rise to Percy's Project Headlights are by E.L. Doctorow in *Writers at Work: The Paris Review Interviews*.

Finally, Scharlotte Holdman, who Moira interns for one summer, was a very real person and one of the most remarkable people I have ever met. Bringing her into the story hopefully provides a small bit of recognition to someone who deserves to be celebrated and honored.

# NOTE FROM SCOTT E. SUNDBY

Word-of-mouth is crucial for any author to succeed. If you enjoyed *Wordsworth in Bogotá*, please leave a review online—anywhere you are able. Even if it's just a sentence or two. It would make all the difference and would be very much appreciated.

Thanks!
Scott E. Sundby
www.scottsundby.com

We hope you enjoyed reading this title from:

Subscribe to our mailing list – *The Rosevine* – and receive **FREE** books, daily deals, and stay current with news about upcoming releases and our hottest authors.
Scan the QR code below to sign up.

Already a subscriber? Please accept a sincere thank you for being a fan of Black Rose Writing authors.

View other Black Rose Writing titles at
and use promo code
**PRINT** to receive a **20% discount** when purchasing.